# BATTLING BOY

# BATTLING BOY

## PAUL POPE

**COLOR BY
HILARY SYCAMORE**

First Second
**NEW YORK**

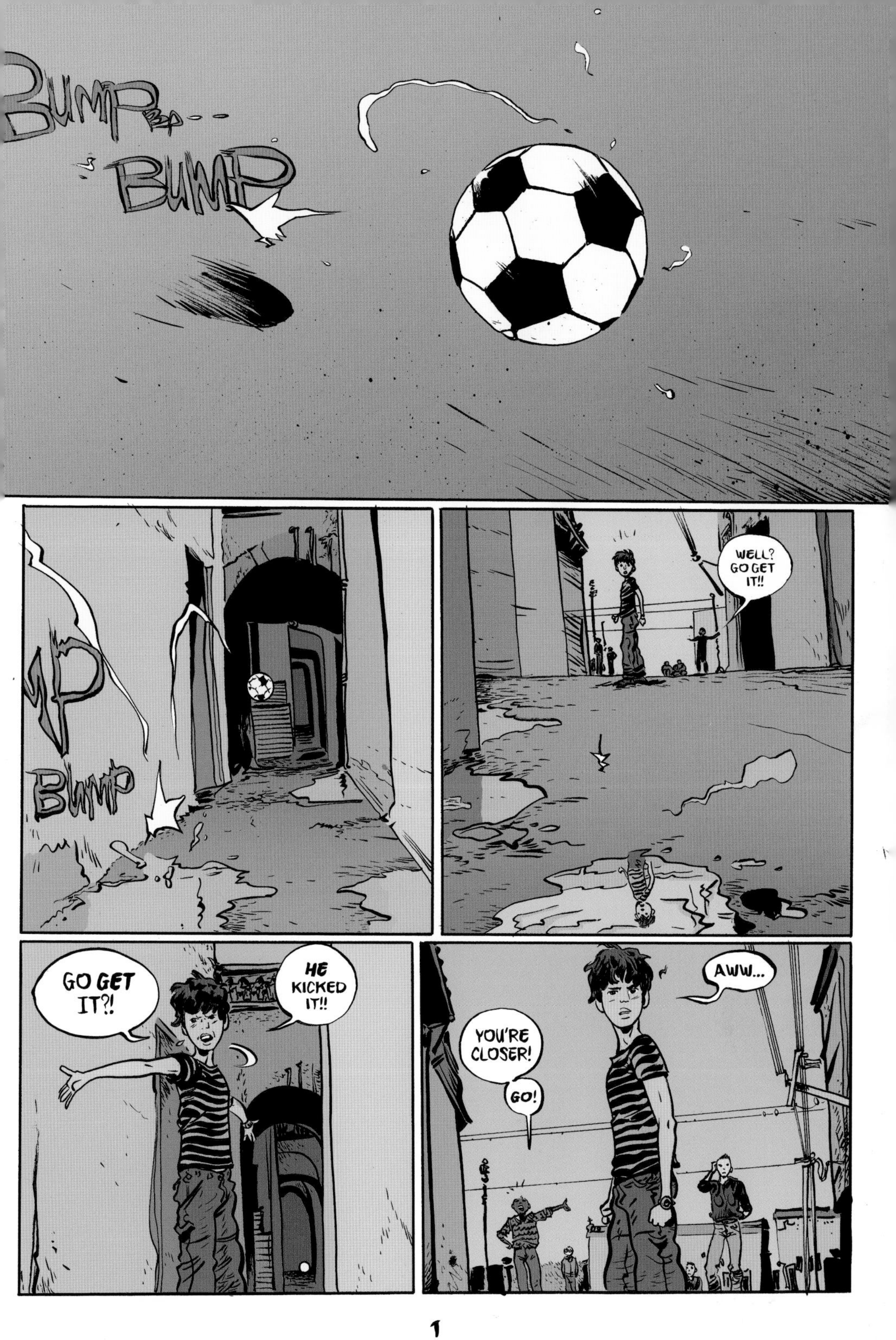
BUMP
BUMP
MP
BUMP
WELL? GO GET IT!!
GO GET IT?!
HE KICKED IT!!
AWW...
YOU'RE CLOSER!
GO!

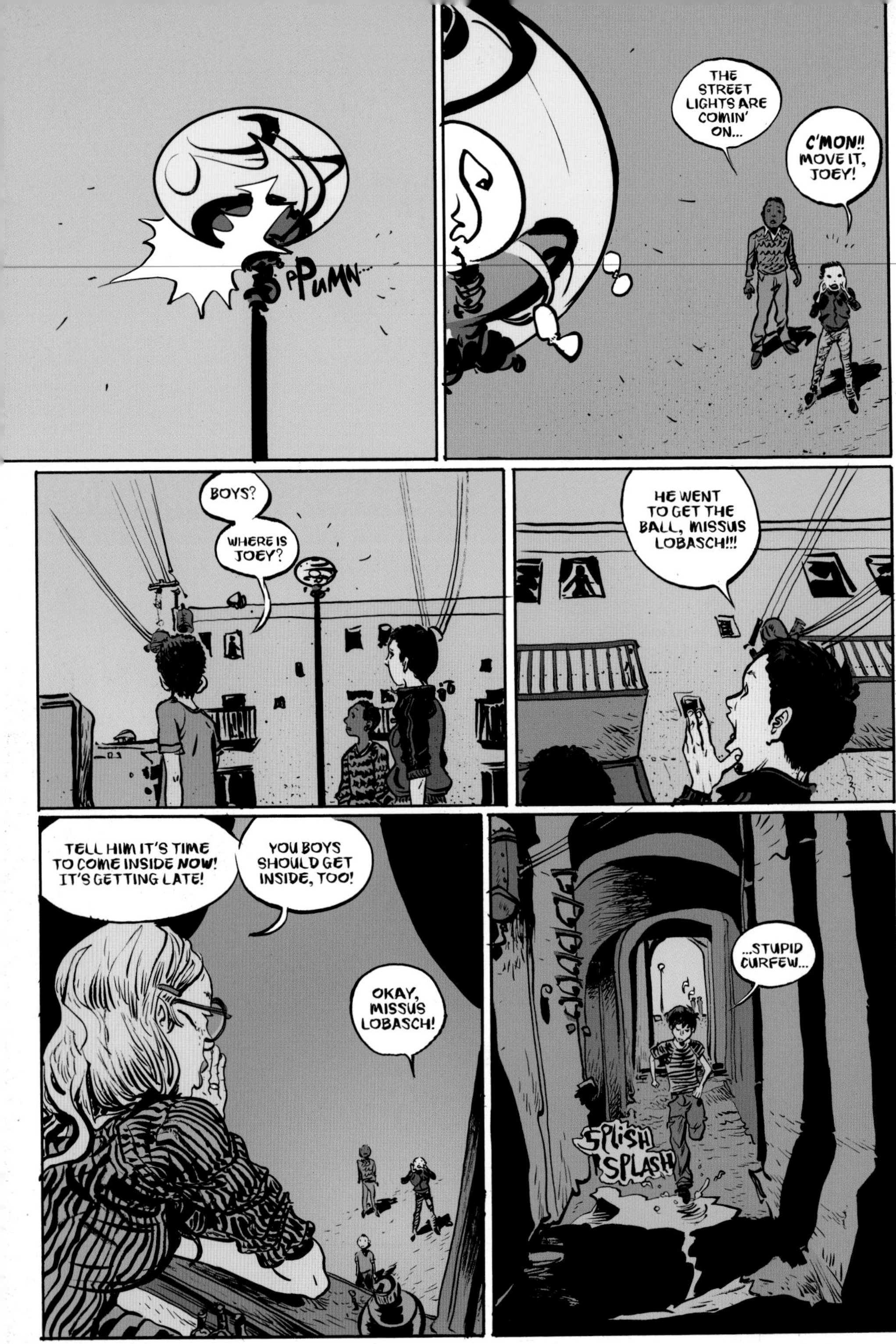

PPUMN...
THE STREET LIGHTS ARE COMIN' ON...
C'MON!! MOVE IT, JOEY!
BOYS?
WHERE IS JOEY?
HE WENT TO GET THE BALL, MISSUS LOBASCH!!!
TELL HIM IT'S TIME TO COME INSIDE NOW! IT'S GETTING LATE!
YOU BOYS SHOULD GET INSIDE, TOO!
OKAY, MISSUS LOBASCH!
...STUPID CURFEW...
SPLISH SPLASH

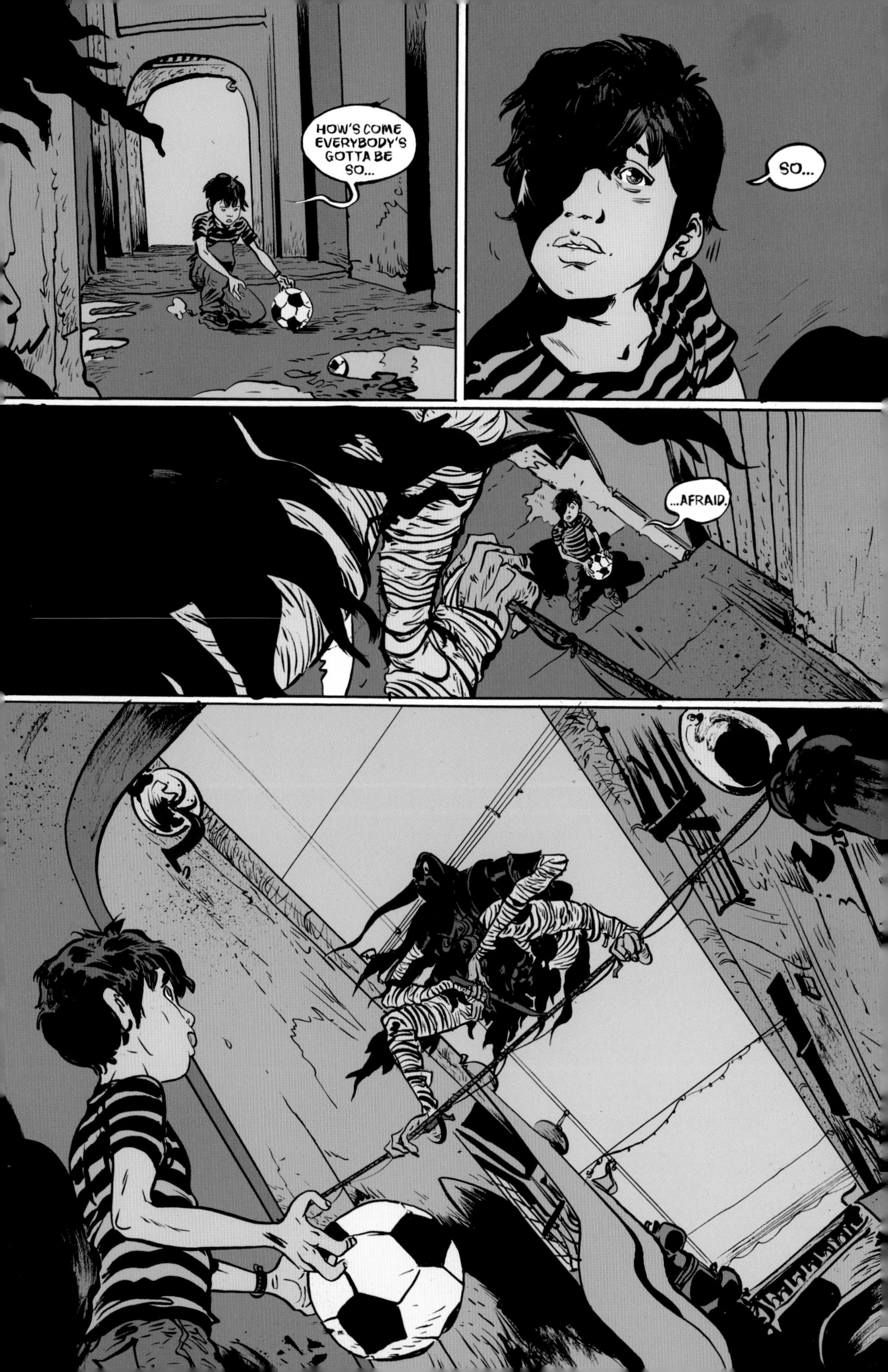
HOW'S COME EVERYBODY'S GOTTA BE SO...
SO...
...AFRAID.

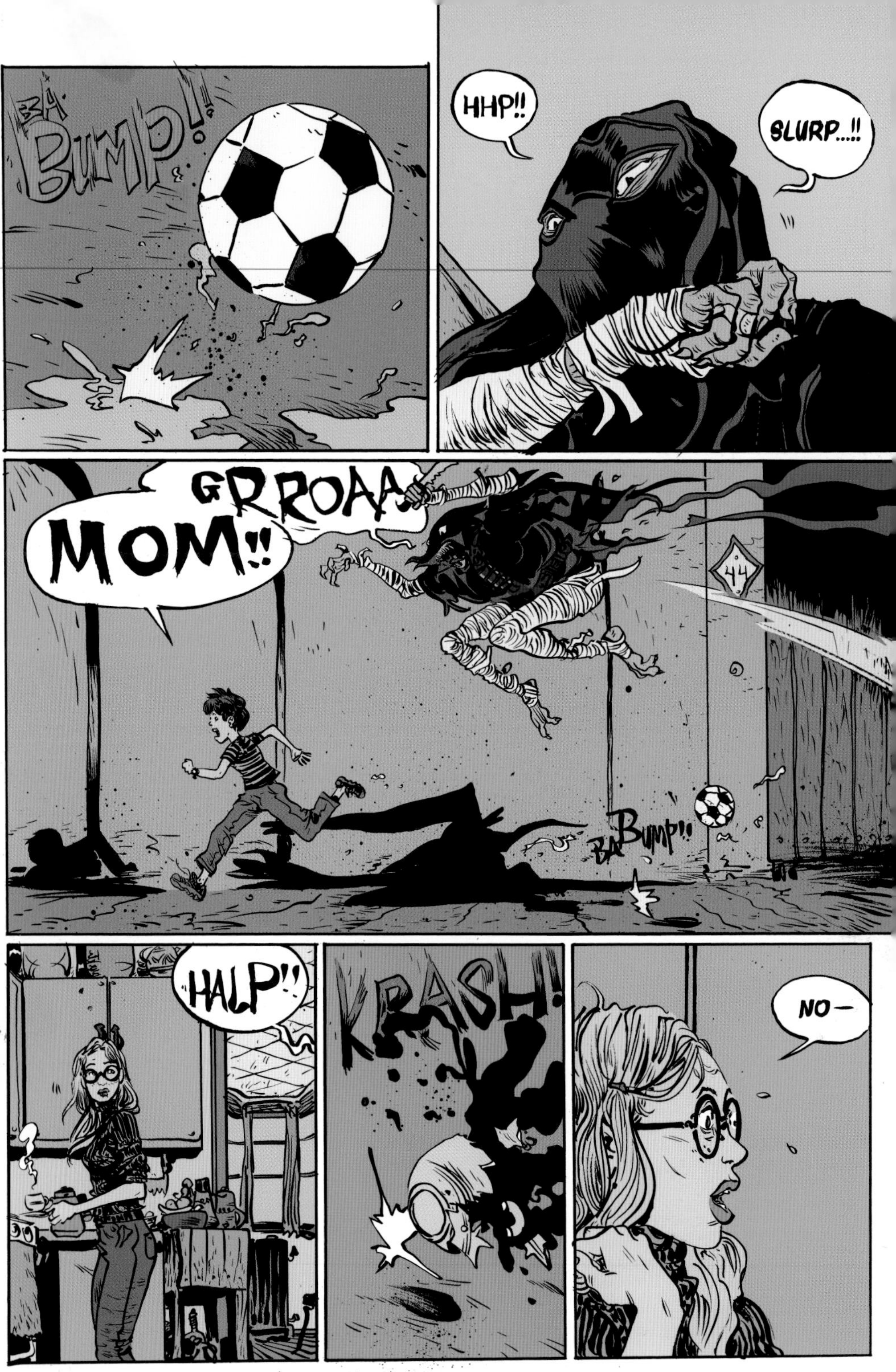
BA-BUMP!!
HHP!!
SLURP...!!
GRROAA
MOM!!
BA BUMP!!
HALP!!
KRASH!
NO—

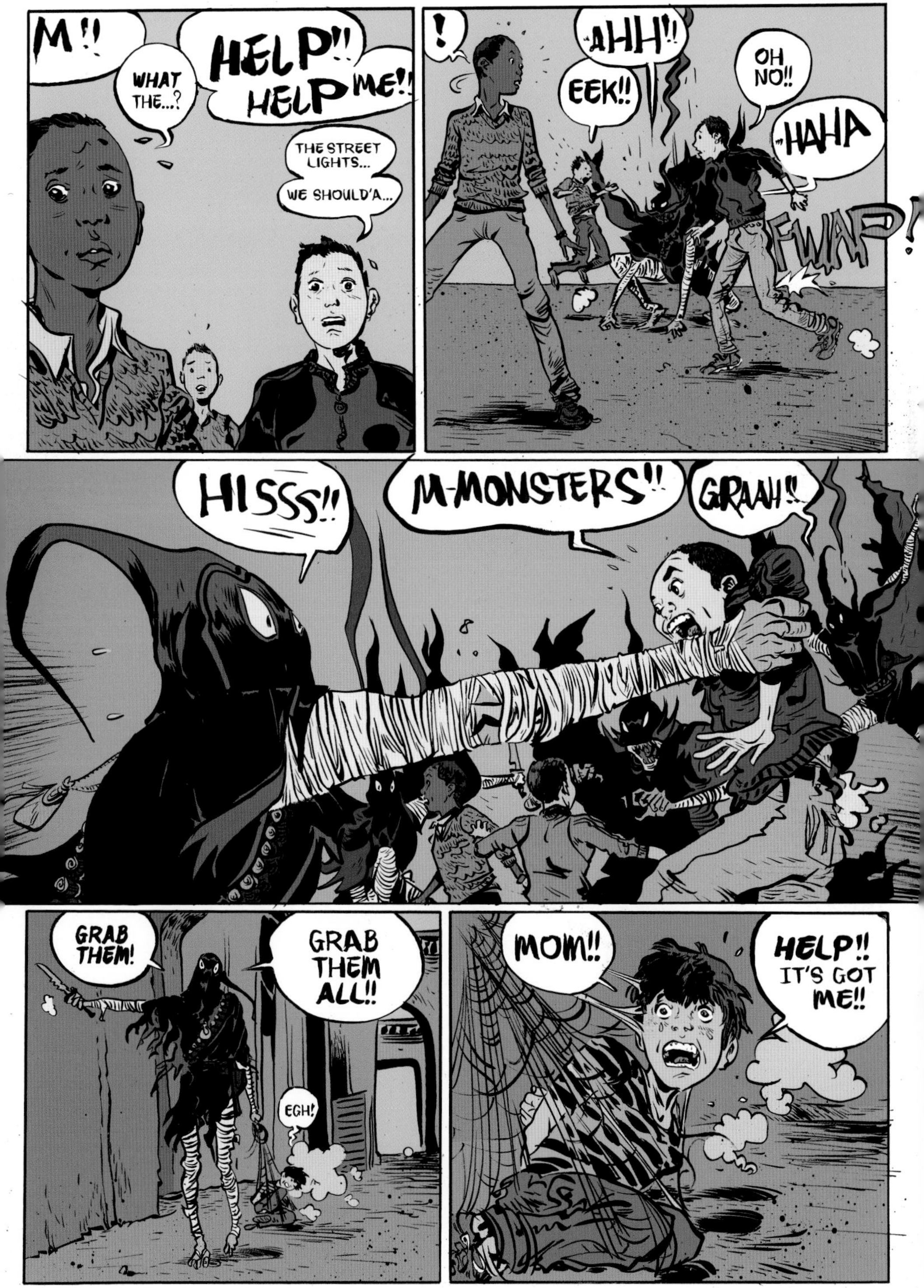
M!!
WHAT THE...?
HELP!! HELP ME!!
THE STREET LIGHTS...
WE SHOULD'A...
!
AHH!!
EEK!!
OH NO!!
HAHA
FWAP!
HISSS!!
M-MONSTERS!!
GRAAH!!
GRAB THEM!
GRAB THEM ALL!!
EGH!
MOM!!
HELP!! IT'S GOT ME!!

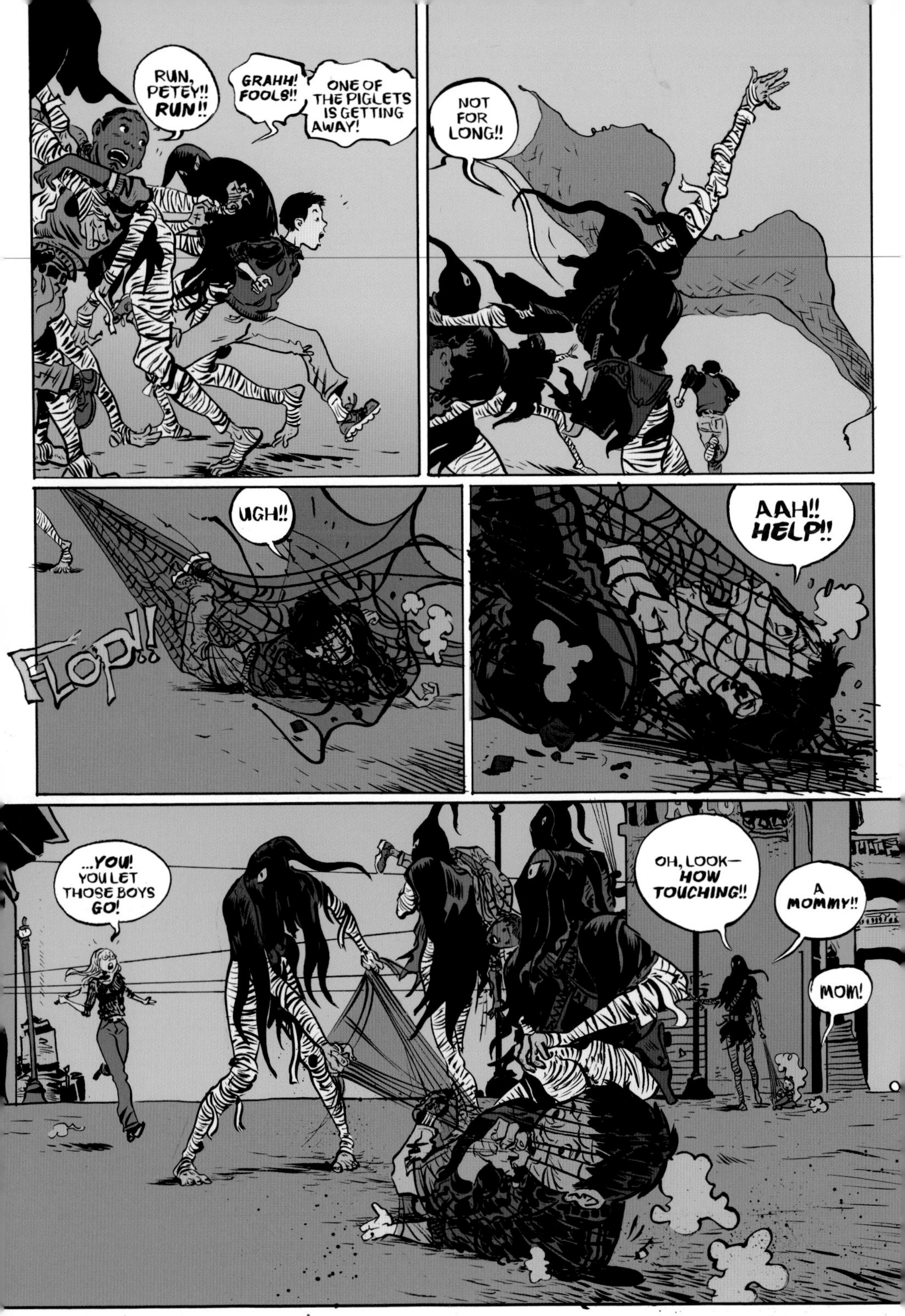
RUN, PETEY!! RUN!!
GRAHH! FOOLS!!
ONE OF THE PIGLETS IS GETTING AWAY!
NOT FOR LONG!!
UGH!!
FLOP!!
AAH!! HELP!!
...YOU! YOU LET THOSE BOYS GO!
OH, LOOK— HOW TOUCHING!!
A MOMMY!!
MOM!

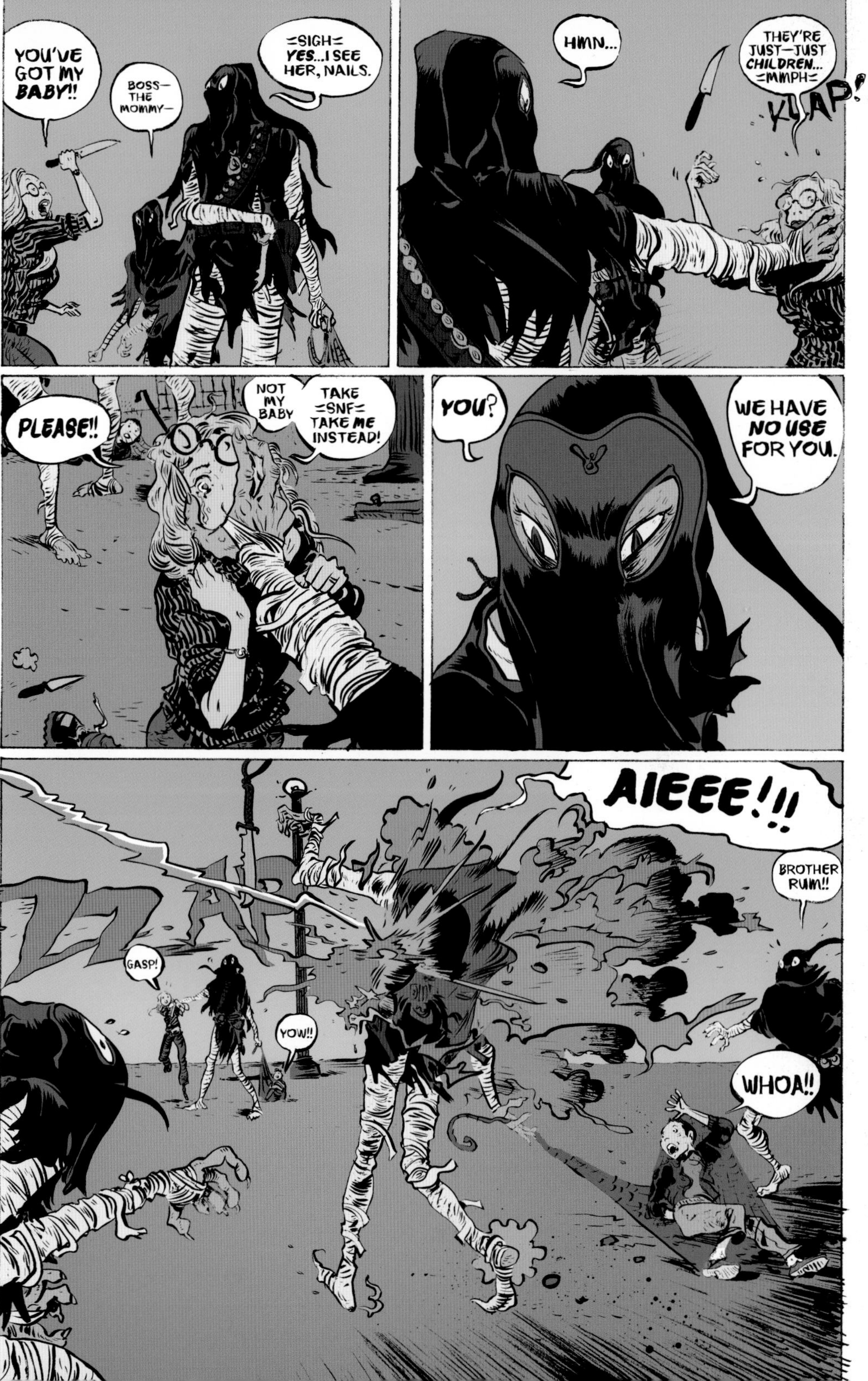
YOU'VE GOT MY BABY!!
BOSS— THE MOMMY—
=SIGH= YES...I SEE HER, NAILS.
HMN...
THEY'RE JUST—JUST CHILDREN... =MMPH
KLAP!!
PLEASE!!
NOT MY BABY
TAKE =SNF= TAKE ME INSTEAD!
YOU?
WE HAVE NO USE FOR YOU.
AIEEE!!!
BROTHER RUM!!
GASP!
YOW!!
WHOA!!

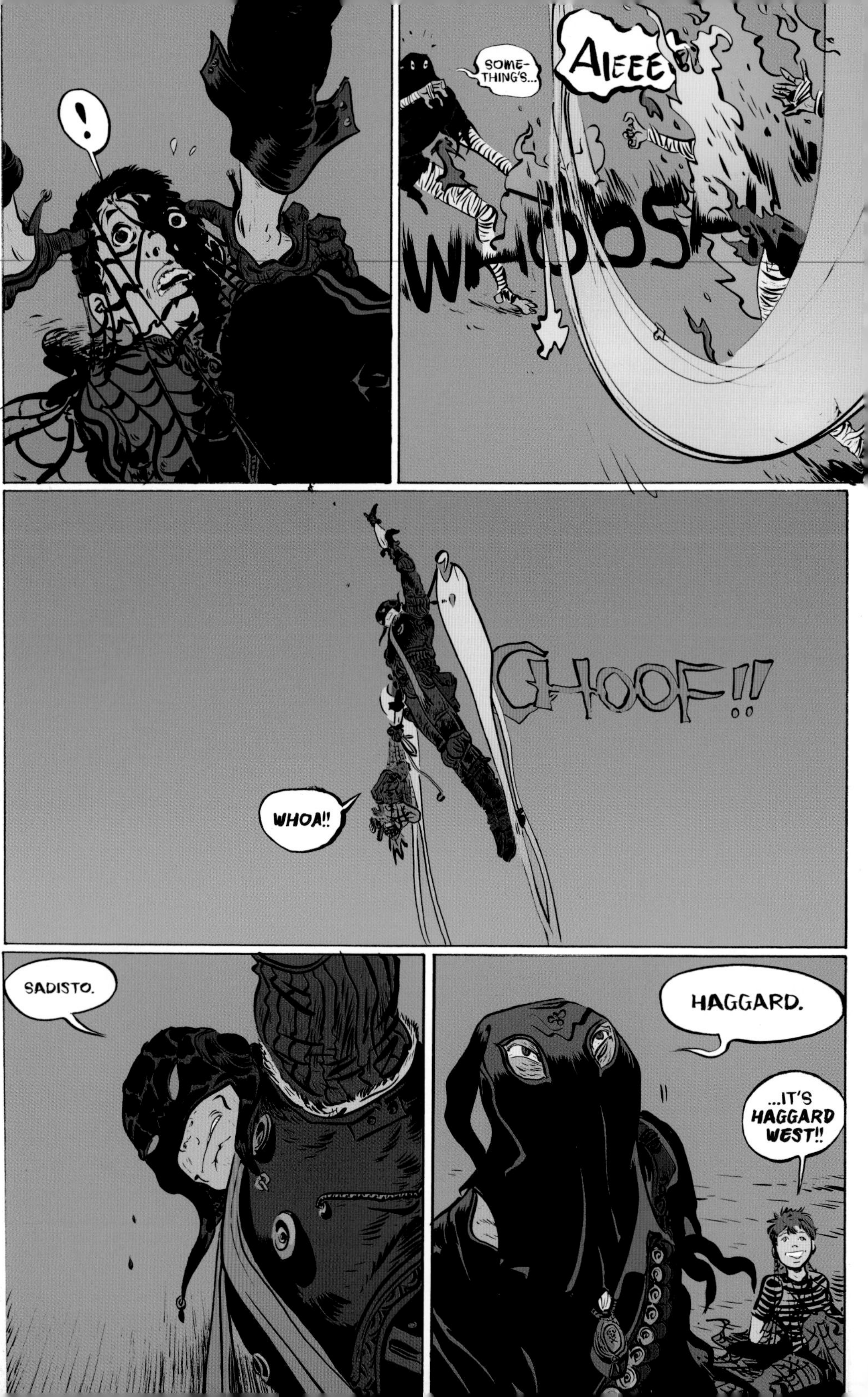

!
SOME-THING'S...
AIEEE
WHOOSH
CHOOF!!
WHOA!!
SADISTO.
HAGGARD.
...IT'S HAGGARD WEST!!

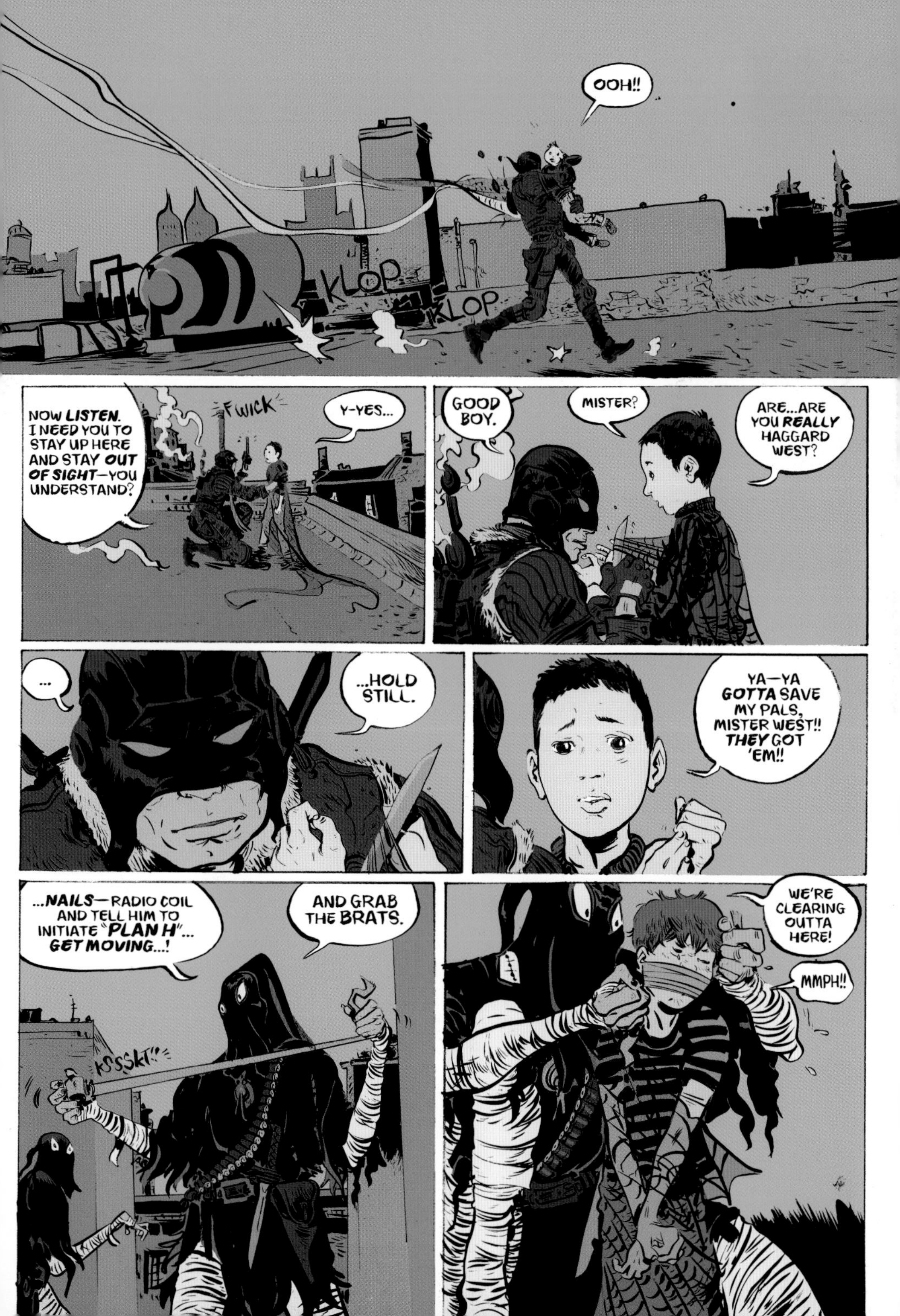
OOH!!
KLOP
KLOP
NOW LISTEN. I NEED YOU TO STAY UP HERE AND STAY OUT OF SIGHT—YOU UNDERSTAND?
FWICK
Y-YES...
GOOD BOY.
MISTER?
ARE...ARE YOU REALLY HAGGARD WEST?
...
...HOLD STILL.
YA—YA GOTTA SAVE MY PALS, MISTER WEST!! THEY GOT 'EM!!
...NAILS—RADIO COIL AND TELL HIM TO INITIATE "PLAN H"... GET MOVING...!
AND GRAB THE BRATS.
KSSSKT!!
WE'RE CLEARING OUTTA HERE!
MMPH!!

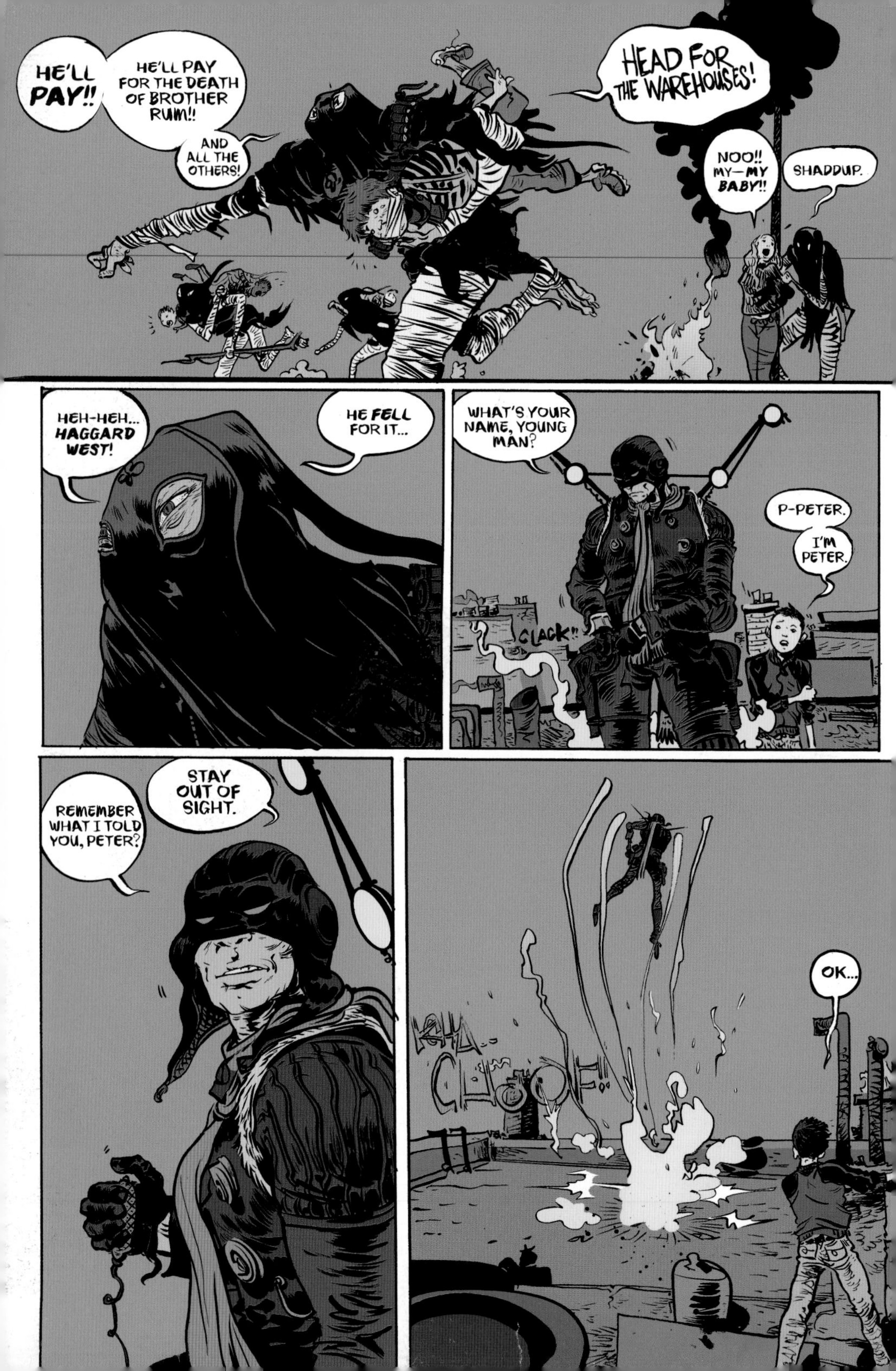
HE'LL PAY!!
HE'LL PAY FOR THE DEATH OF BROTHER RUM!!
AND ALL THE OTHERS!
HEAD FOR THE WAREHOUSES!
NOO!! MY—MY BABY!!
SHADDUP.
HEH-HEH... HAGGARD WEST!
HE FELL FOR IT...
WHAT'S YOUR NAME, YOUNG MAN?
P-PETER.
I'M PETER.
CLACK!!
REMEMBER WHAT I TOLD YOU, PETER?
STAY OUT OF SIGHT.
KSHA--
CLOOOF!!
OK...

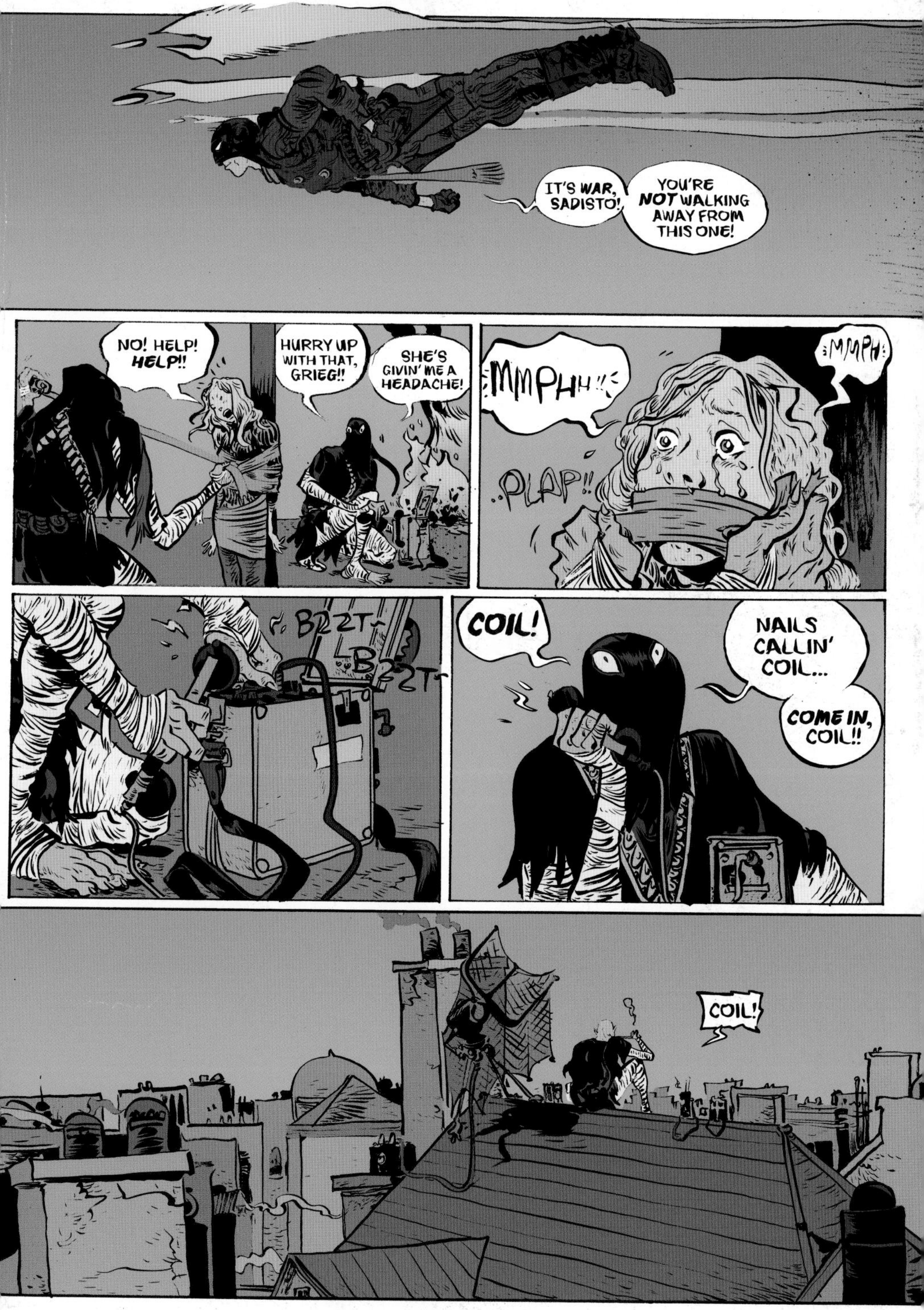
IT'S WAR, SADISTO!
YOU'RE NOT WALKING AWAY FROM THIS ONE!
NO! HELP! HELP!!
HURRY UP WITH THAT, GRIEG!!
SHE'S GIVIN' ME A HEADACHE!
MMPHH!!
PLAP!!
MMPH
BZZT-
BZZT-
COIL!
NAILS CALLIN' COIL...
COME IN, COIL!!
COIL!

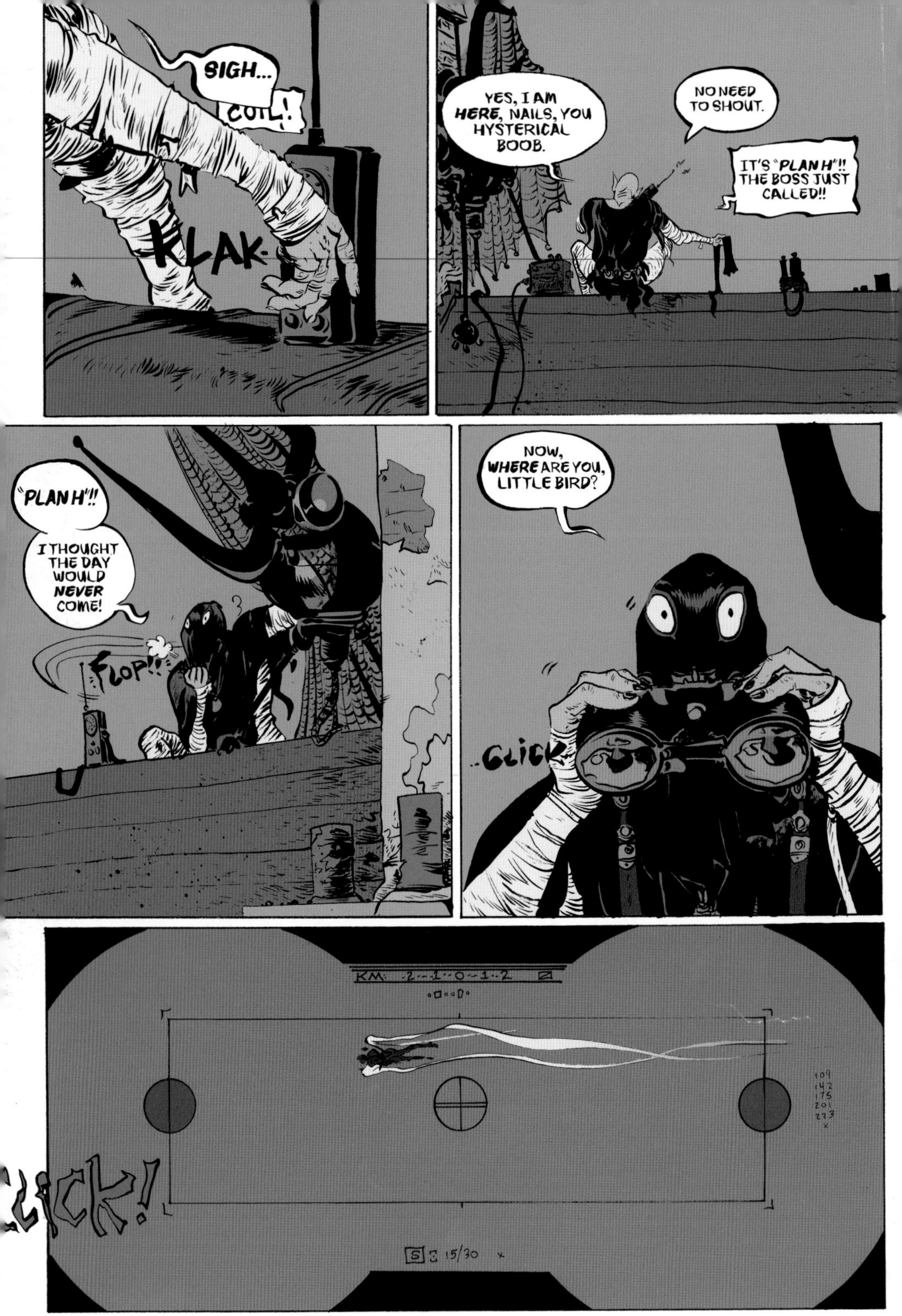
SIGH...
COIL!
KLAK
YES, I AM HERE, NAILS, YOU HYSTERICAL BOOB.
NO NEED TO SHOUT.
IT'S "PLAN H"!! THE BOSS JUST CALLED!!
"PLAN H"!!
I THOUGHT THE DAY WOULD NEVER COME!
FLOP!!
NOW, WHERE ARE YOU, LITTLE BIRD?
CLICK
KM: 2 1 0 1 2
109
142
175
201
223
S 15/30
CLICK!

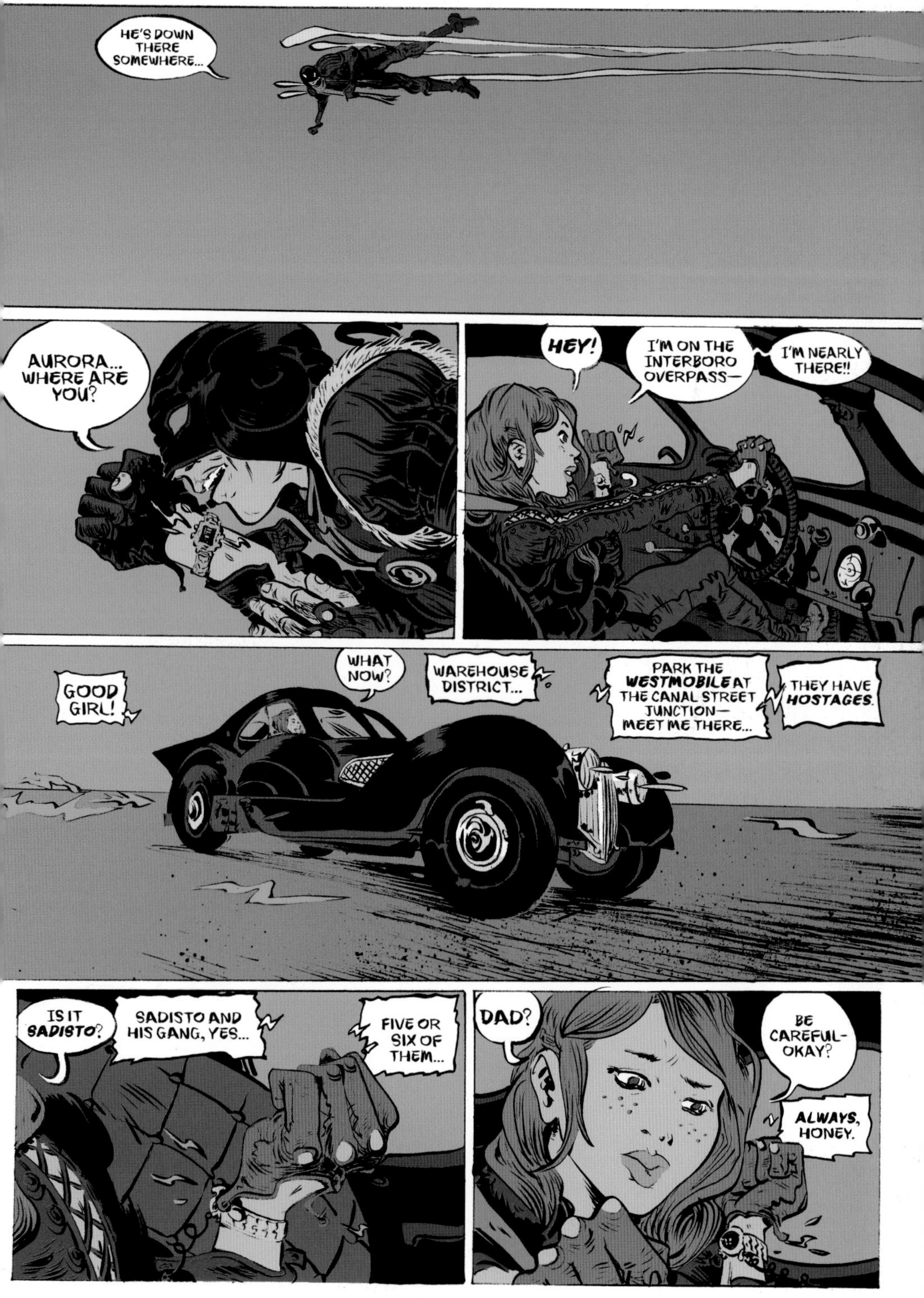
HE'S DOWN THERE SOMEWHERE...
AURORA... WHERE ARE YOU?
HEY!
I'M ON THE INTERBORO OVERPASS—
I'M NEARLY THERE!!
GOOD GIRL!
WHAT NOW?
WAREHOUSE DISTRICT...
PARK THE WESTMOBILE AT THE CANAL STREET JUNCTION— MEET ME THERE...
THEY HAVE HOSTAGES.
IS IT SADISTO?
SADISTO AND HIS GANG, YES...
FIVE OR SIX OF THEM...
DAD?
BE CAREFUL- OKAY?
ALWAYS, HONEY.

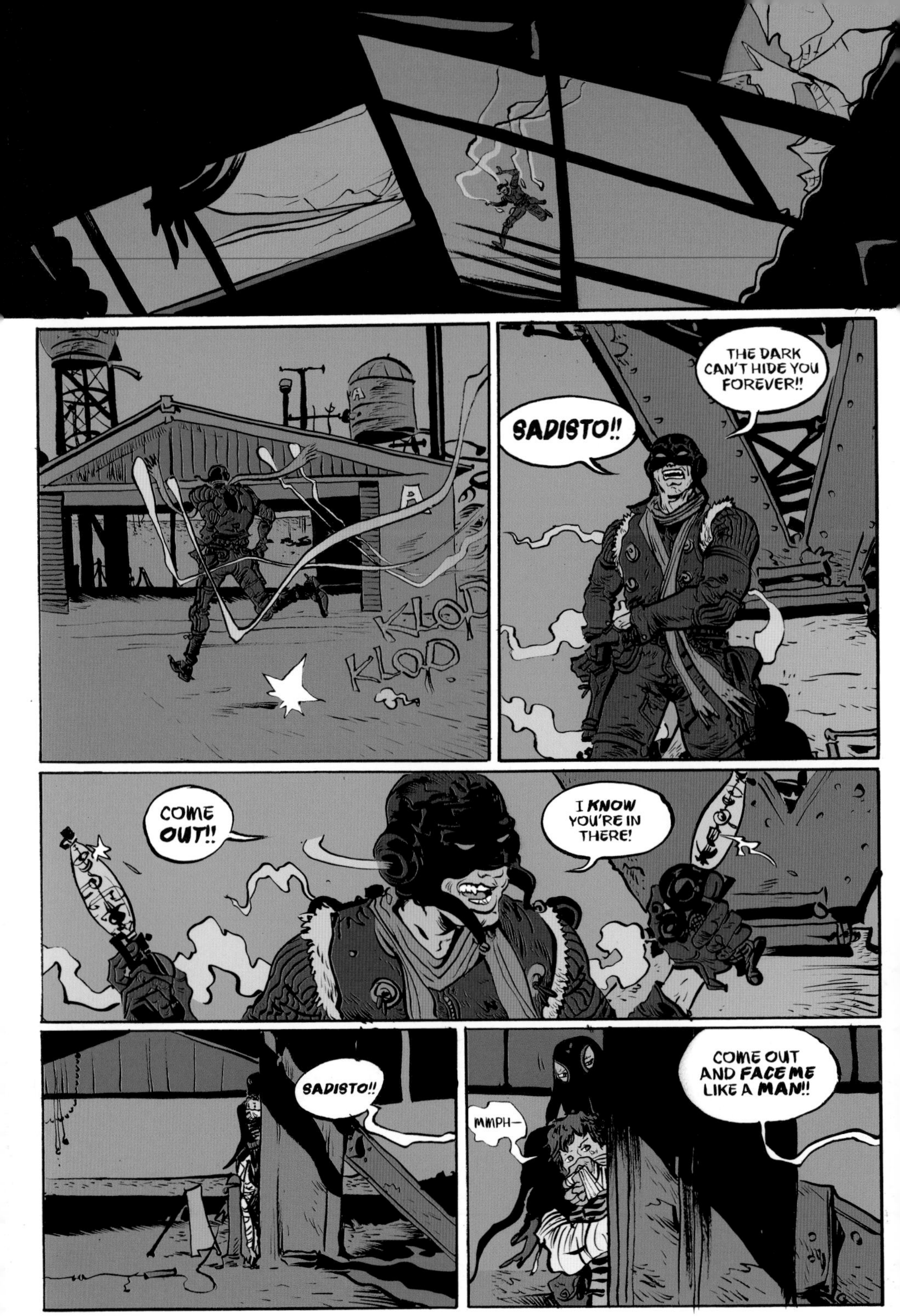
KLOP
KLOP
SADISTO!!
THE DARK CAN'T HIDE YOU FOREVER!!
COME OUT!!
I KNOW YOU'RE IN THERE!
SADISTO!!
MMPH—
COME OUT AND FACE ME LIKE A MAN!!

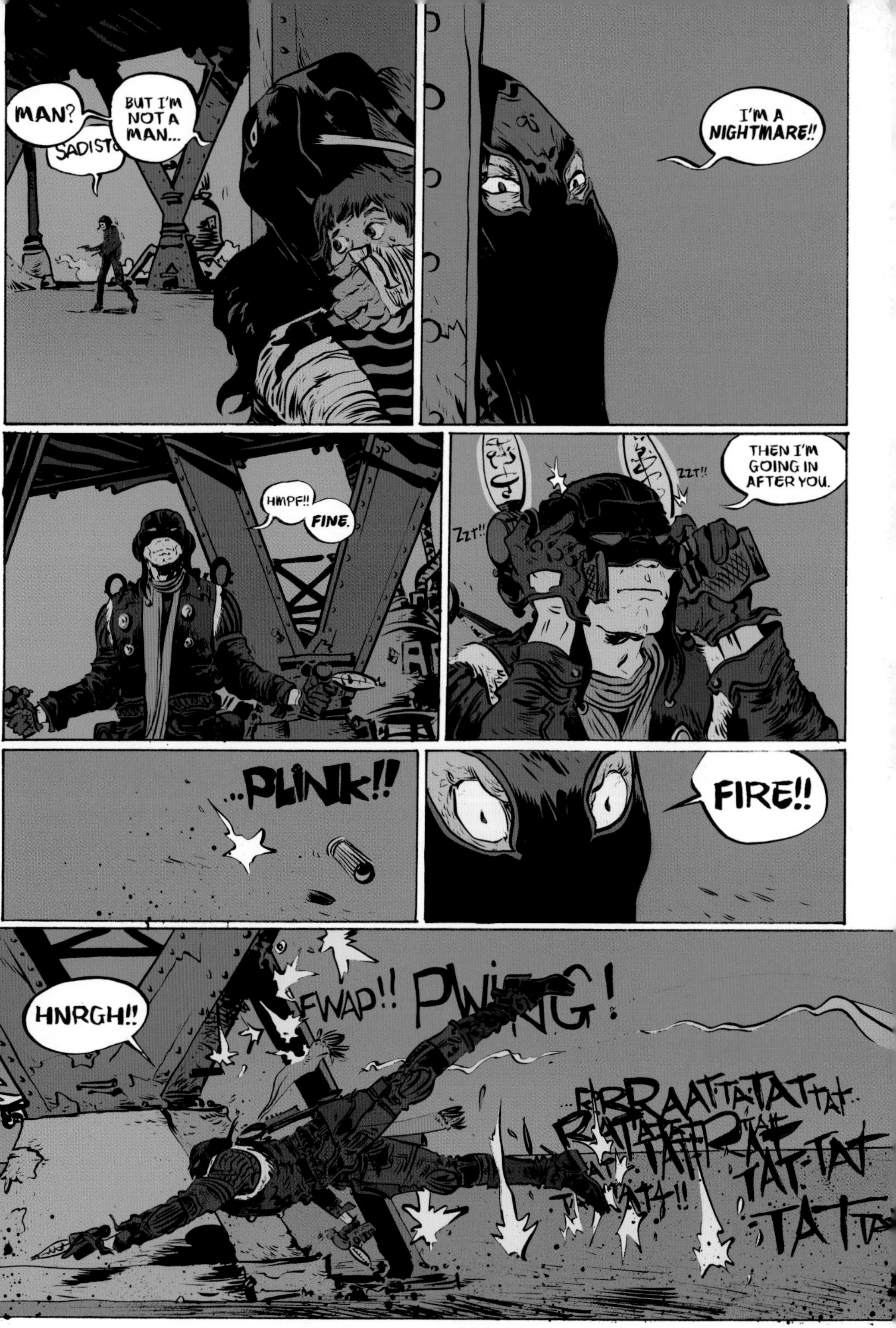
MAN?
SADISTO
BUT I'M NOT A MAN...
I'M A NIGHTMARE!!
HMPF!! FINE.
THEN I'M GOING IN AFTER YOU.
ZZT!!
ZZT!!
...PLINK!!
FIRE!!
HNRGH!!
FWAP!!
PWING!
TAT-TAT
TAT

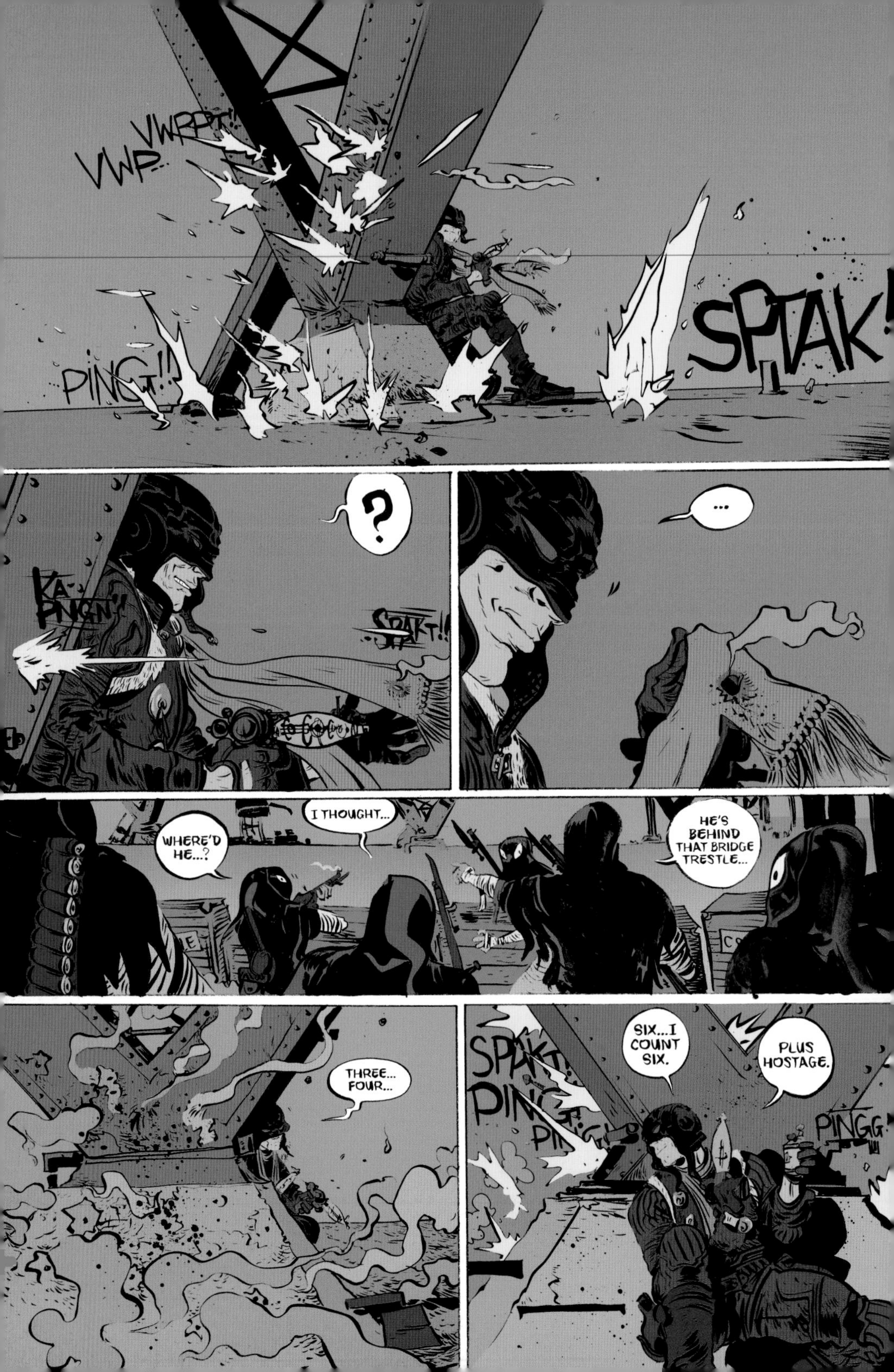
VWRPT!!
VWP...
PING!!
SPTAK!
?
KA-PINGN!!
SPAKT!!
...
I THOUGHT...
WHERE'D HE...?
HE'S BEHIND THAT BRIDGE TRESTLE...
THREE... FOUR...
SIX...I COUNT SIX.
PLUS HOSTAGE.
SPAKT!
PING!
PING!
PINGG!!

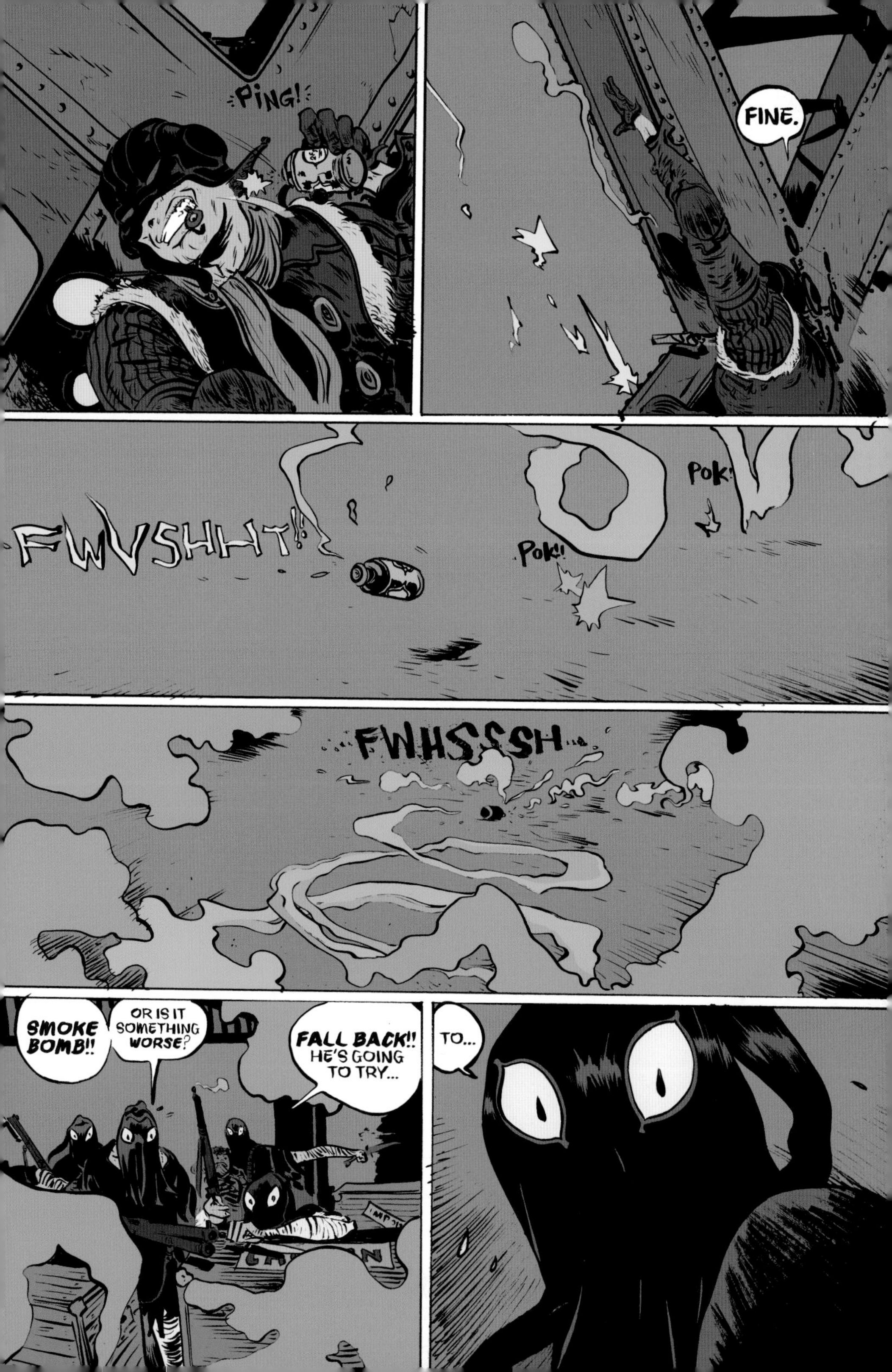
PING!
FINE.
FWVSHHT!!
POK!
POK!!
FWHSSSH
SMOKE BOMB!!
OR IS IT SOMETHING WORSE?
FALL BACK!! HE'S GOING TO TRY...
TO...

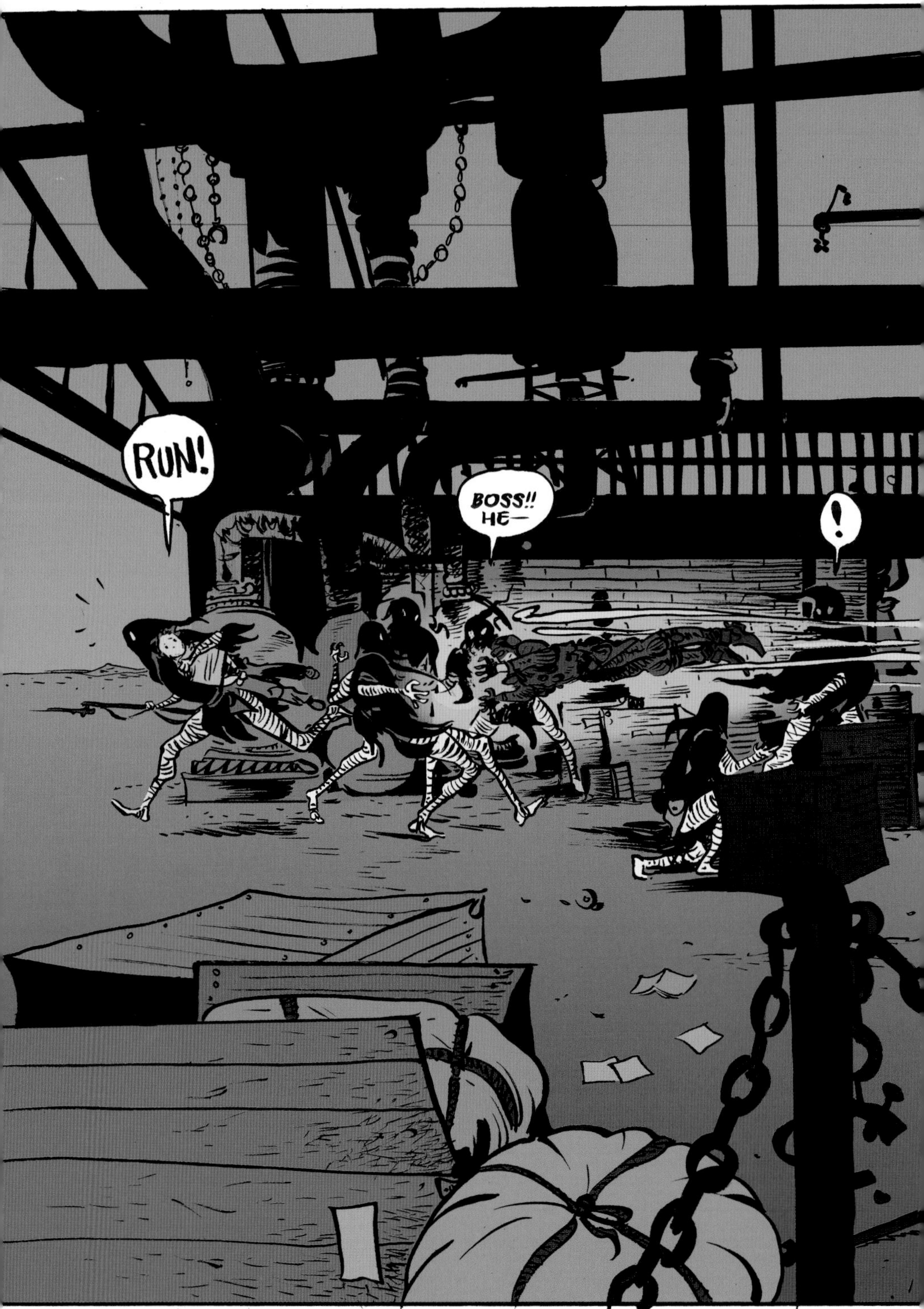
RUN!
BOSS!! HE—
!

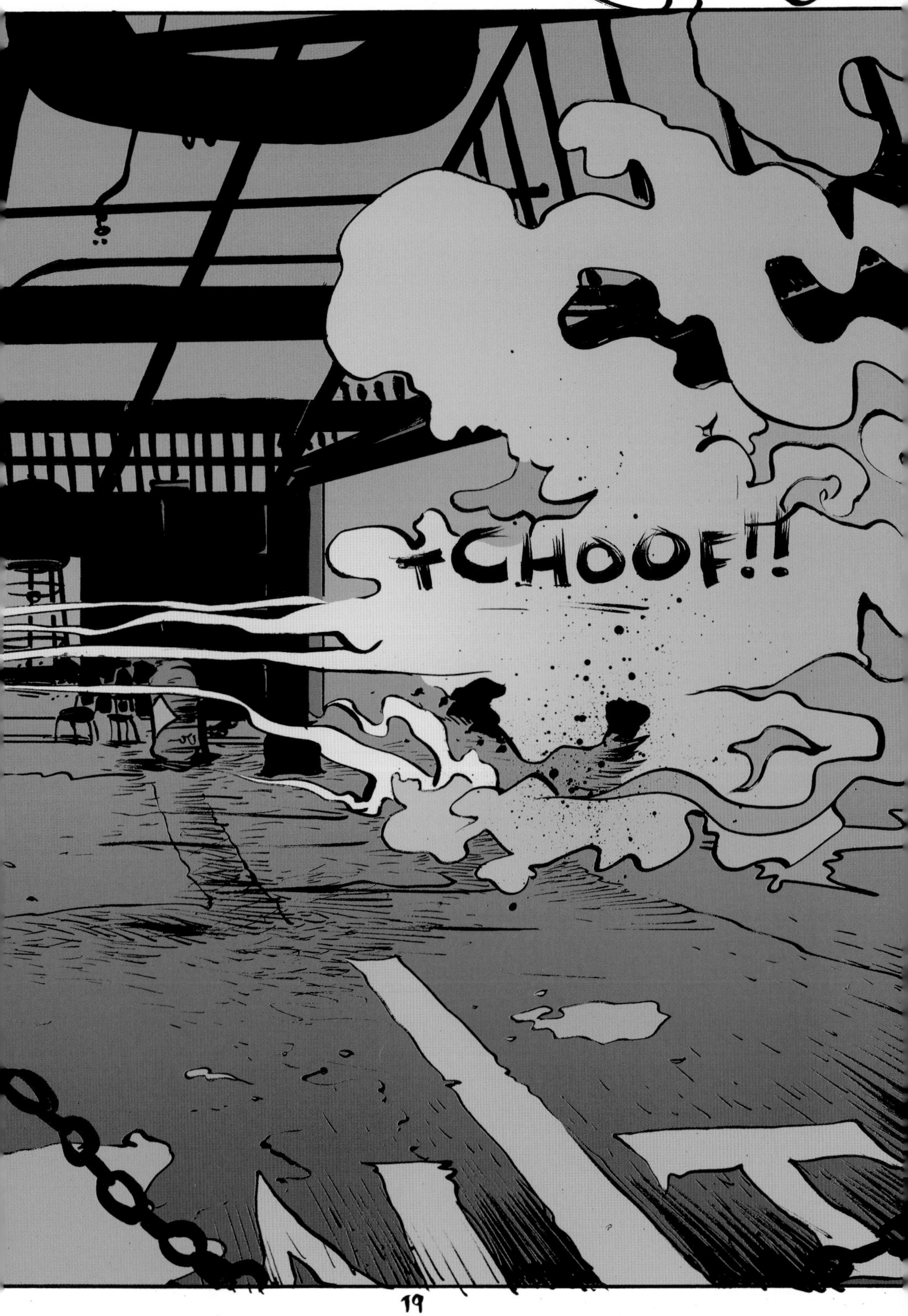
TCHOOF!!

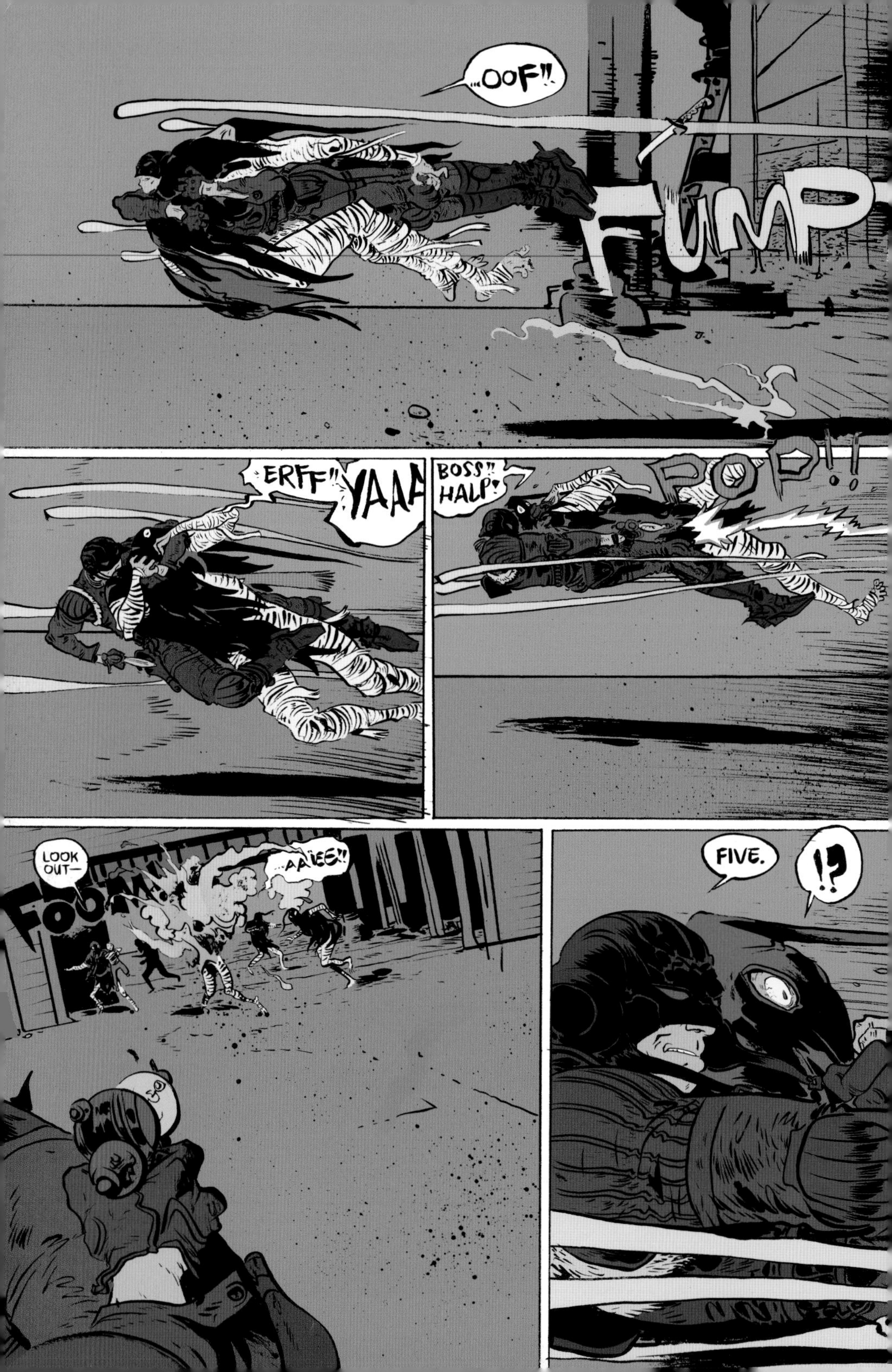
...OOF!!
FUMP
ERFF!!
YAAA
BOSS!! HALP!
POP!!
LOOK OUT—
FOOM
...AAIEE!!
FIVE.
!?

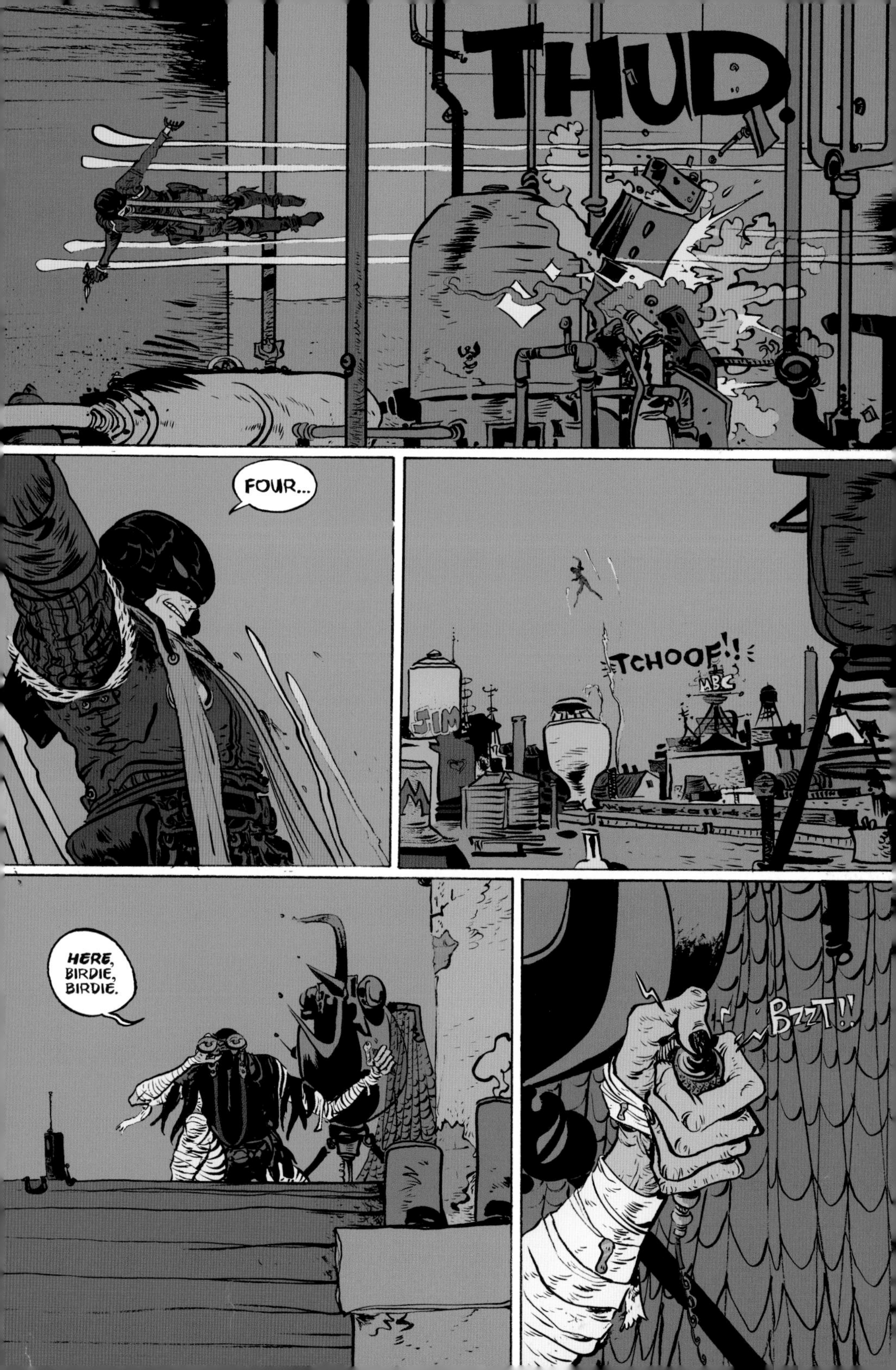
THUD
FOUR...
TCHOOF!!
JIM
MBC
HERE, BIRDIE, BIRDIE.
BZZT!!

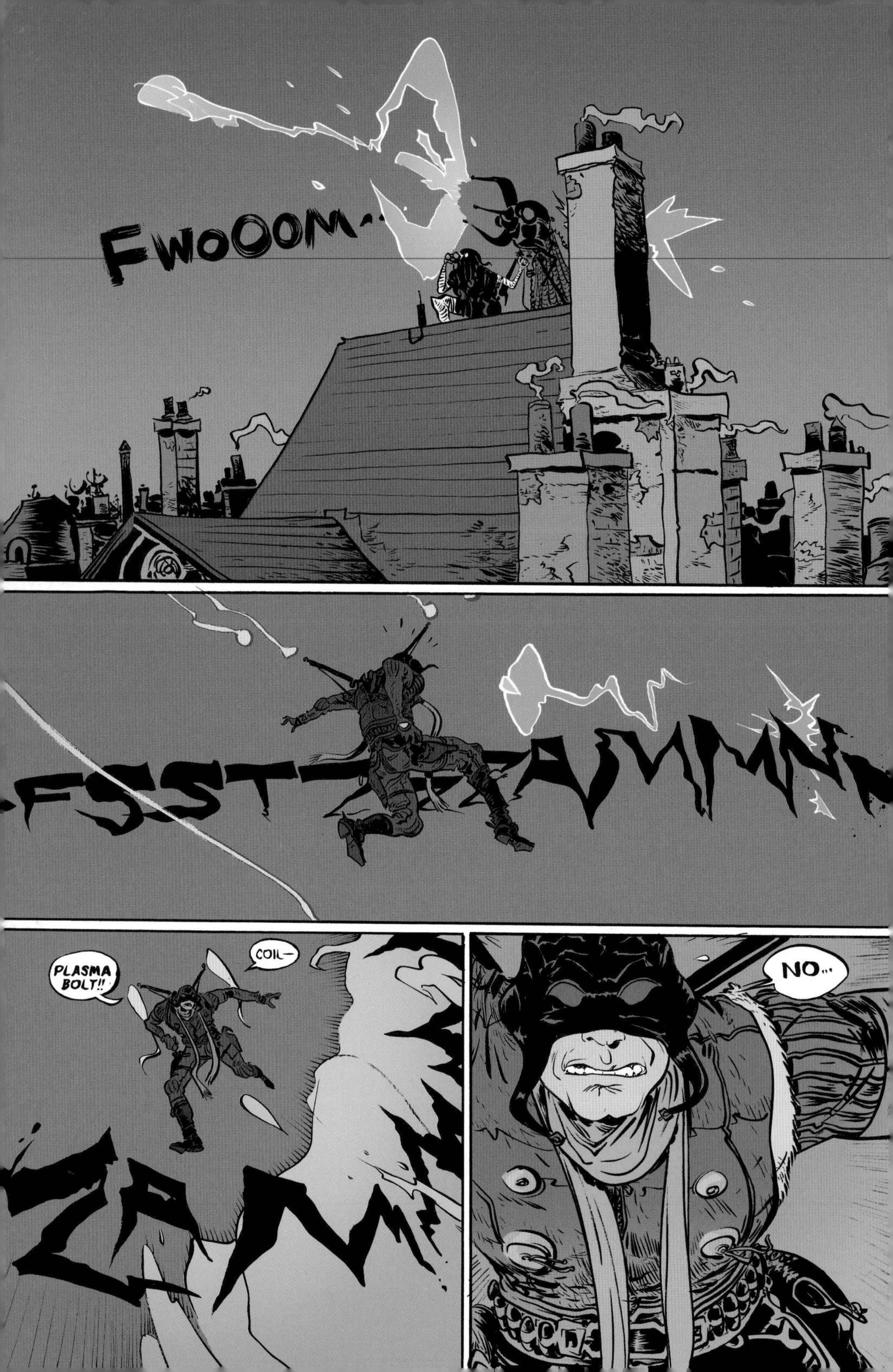
FWOOOM...
PLASMA BOLT!!
COIL—
NO...

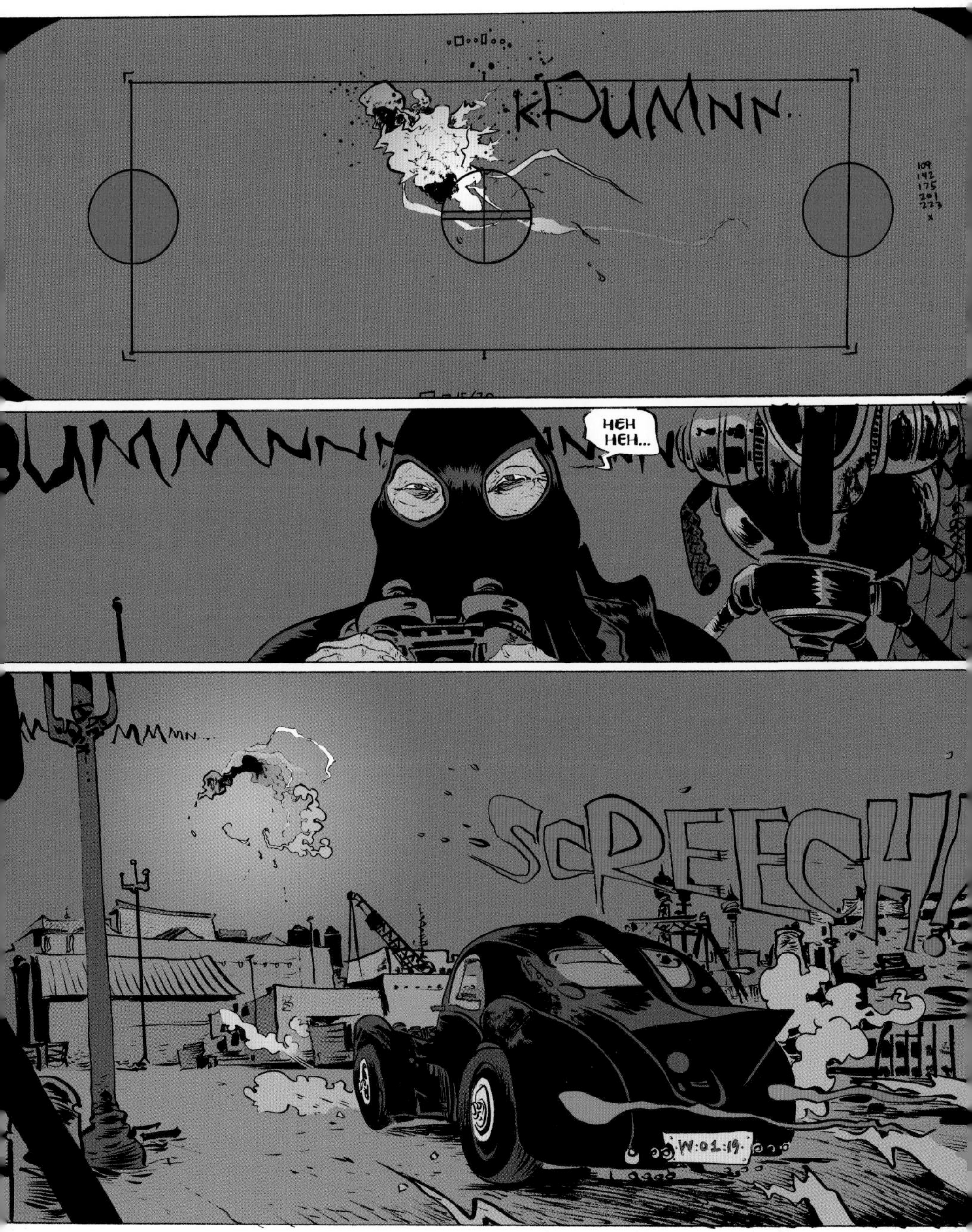
KRUMMNN
109
142
175
201
223
x
BUMMMNNN
HEH HEH...
MMMN...
SCREECH!
W·01·19

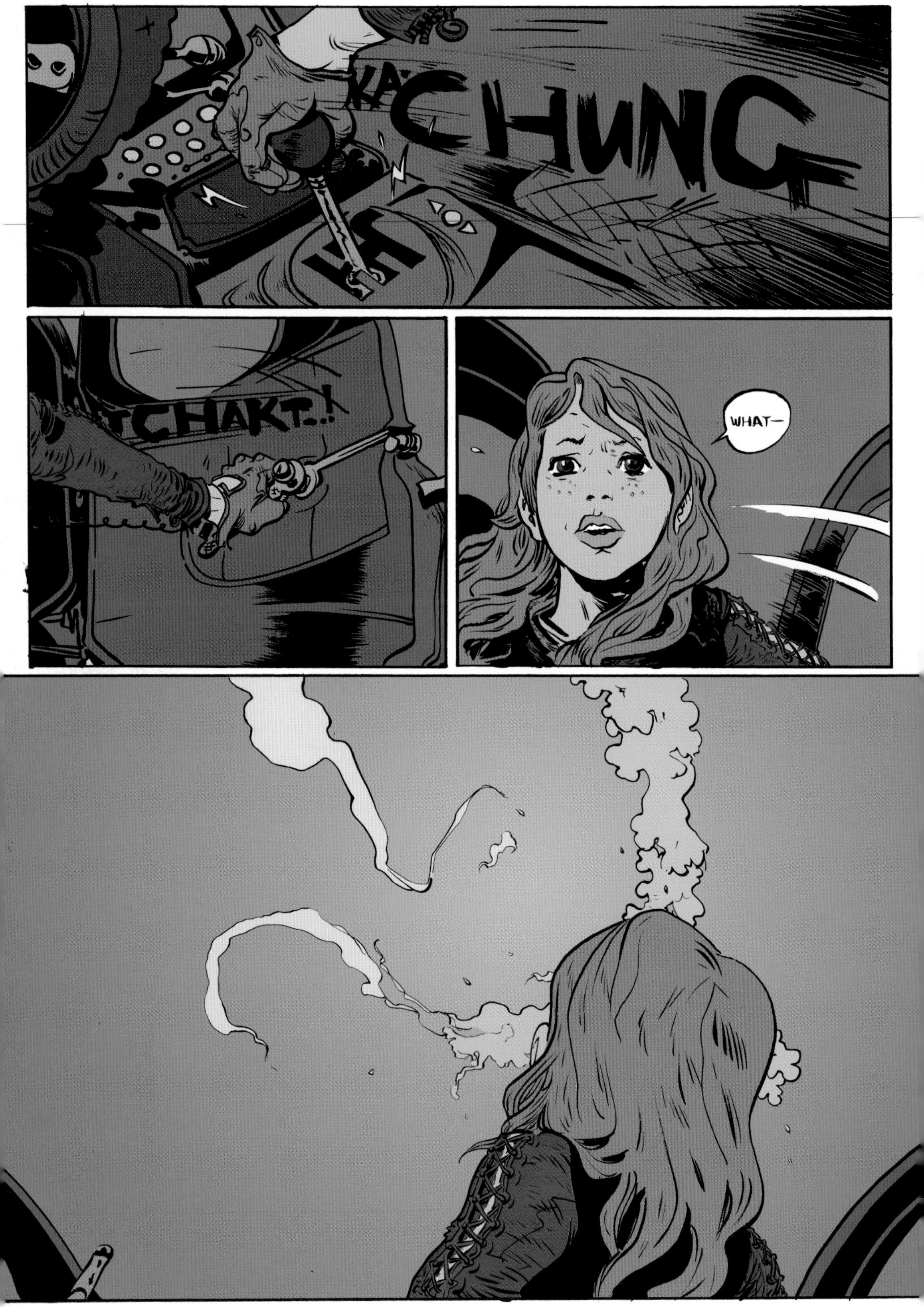
KA-CHUNG
TCHAKT..!
WHAT—

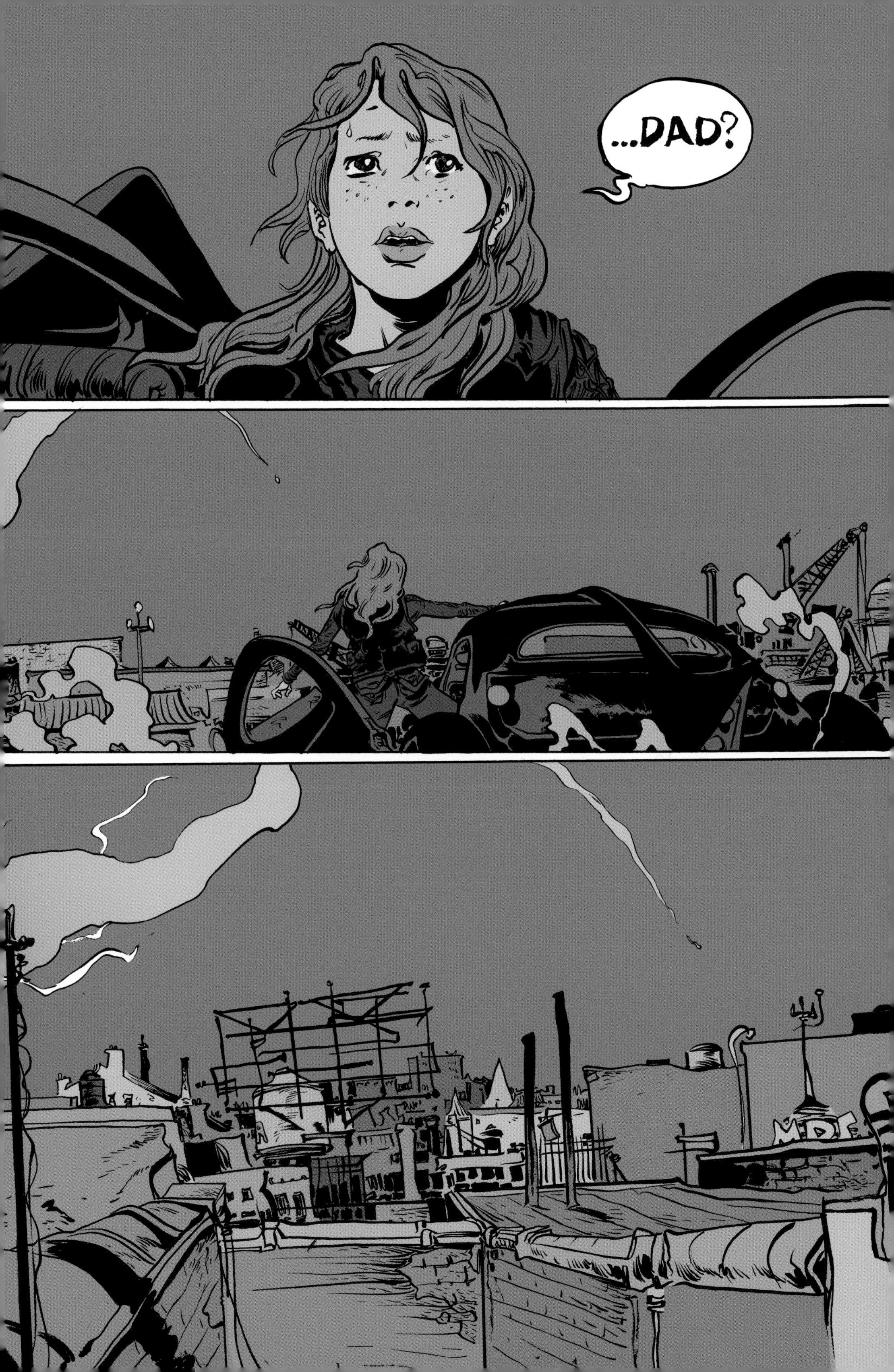
...DAD?

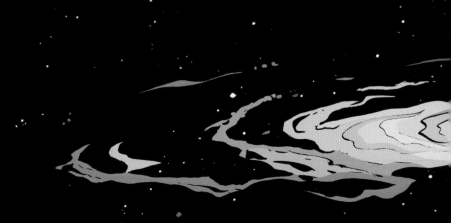

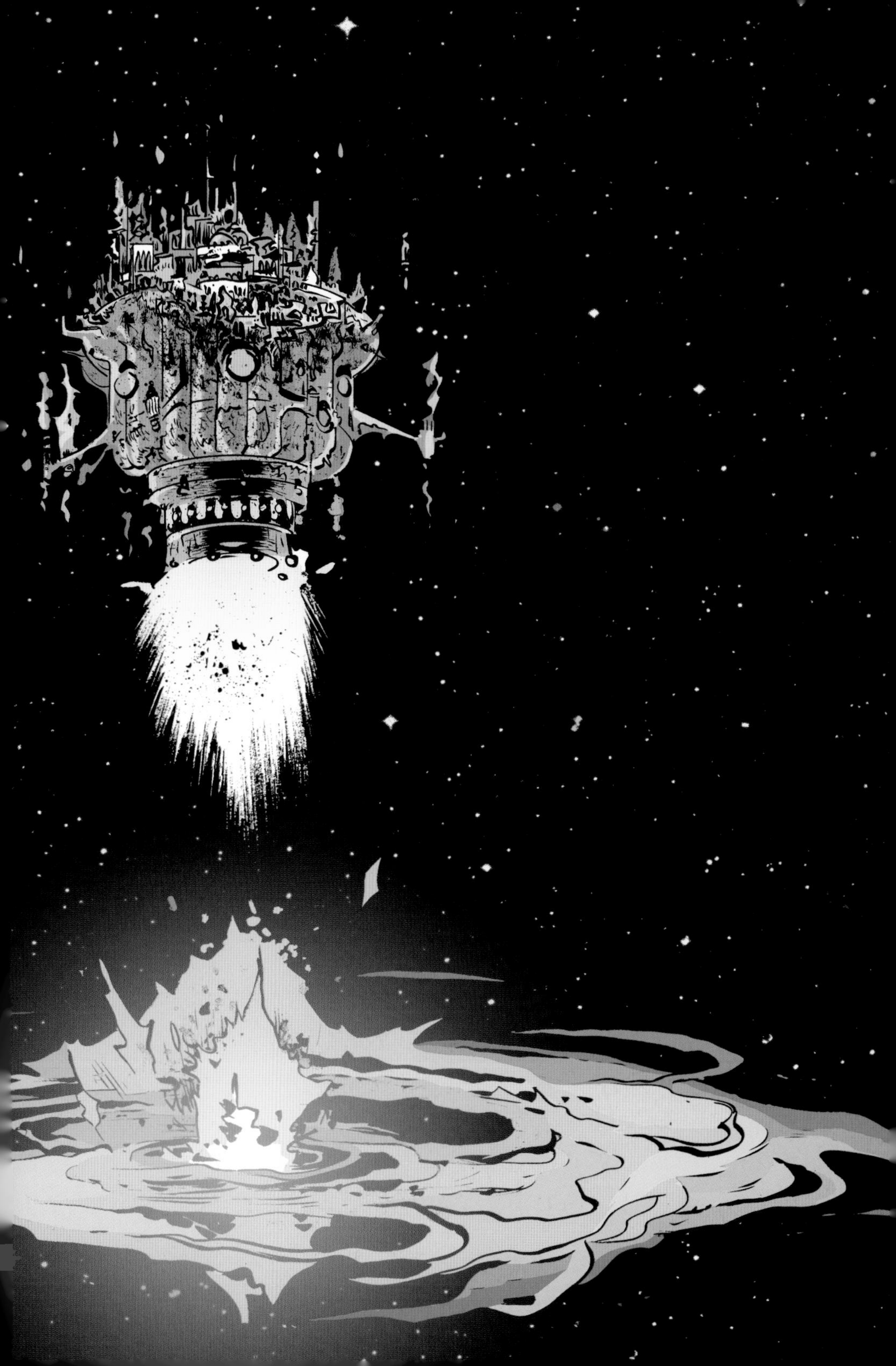

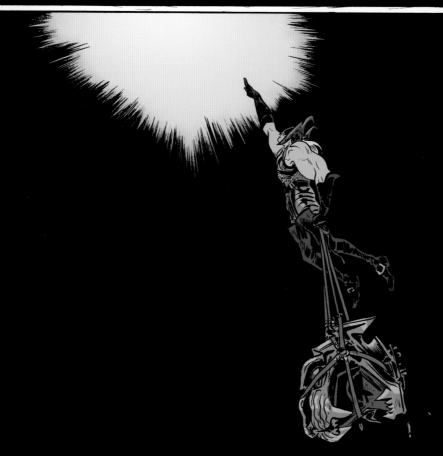

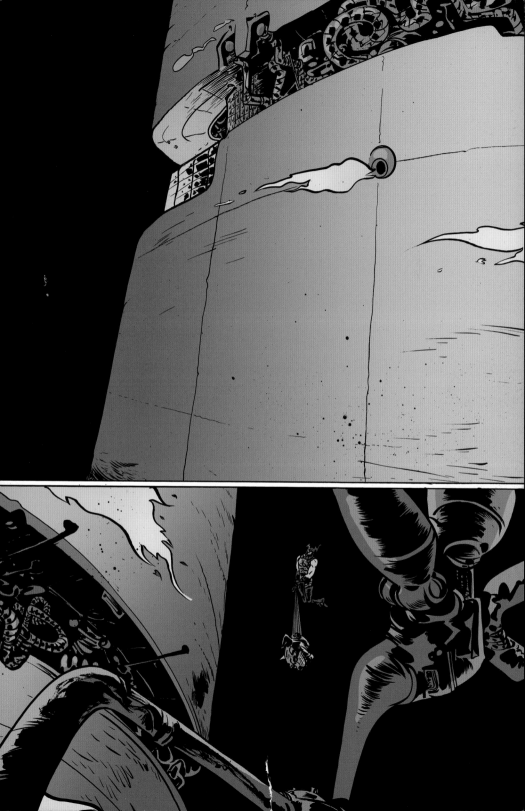

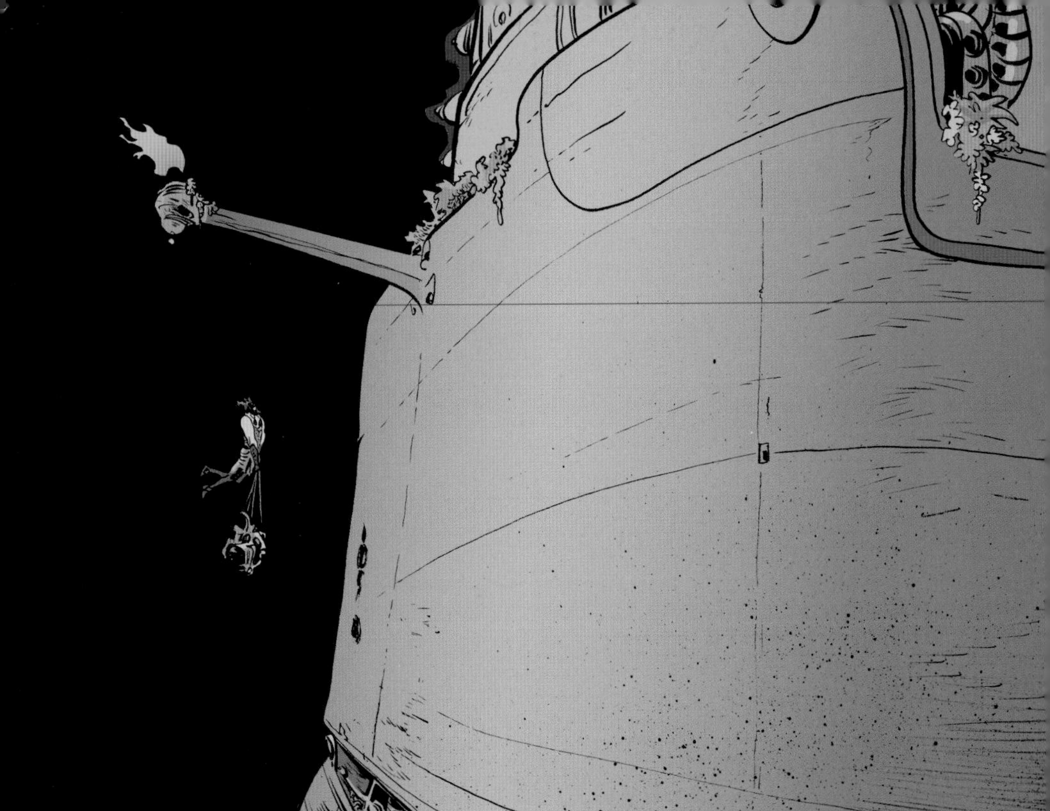

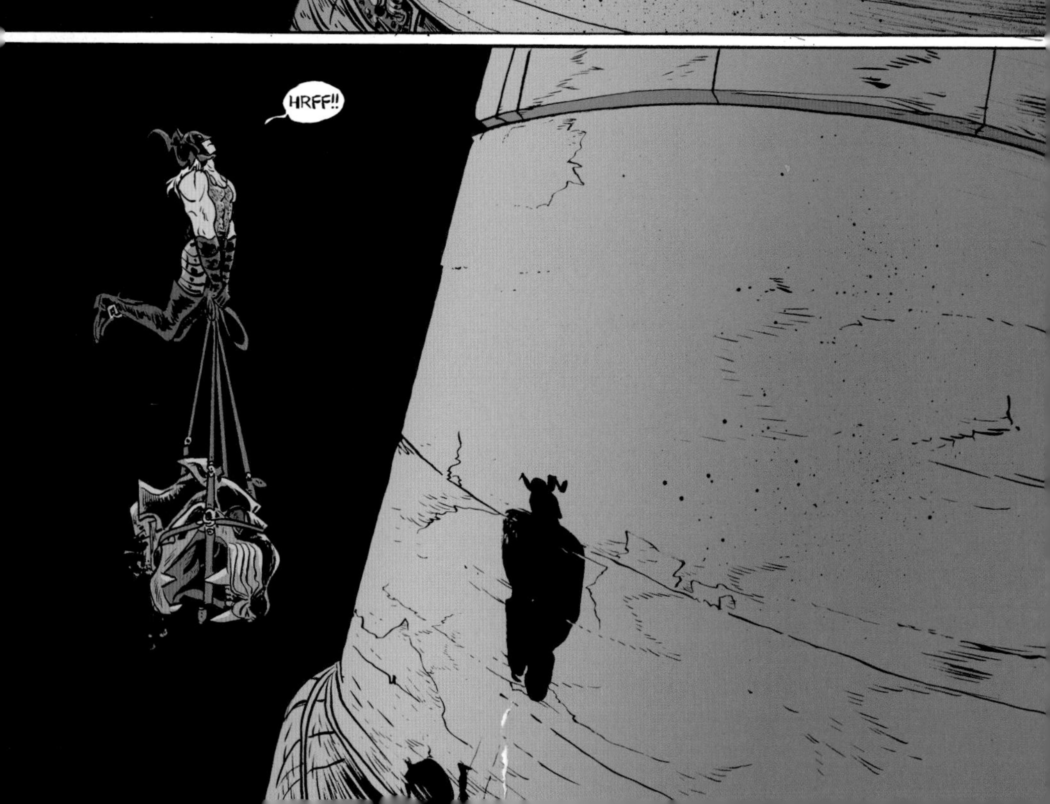
HRFF!!

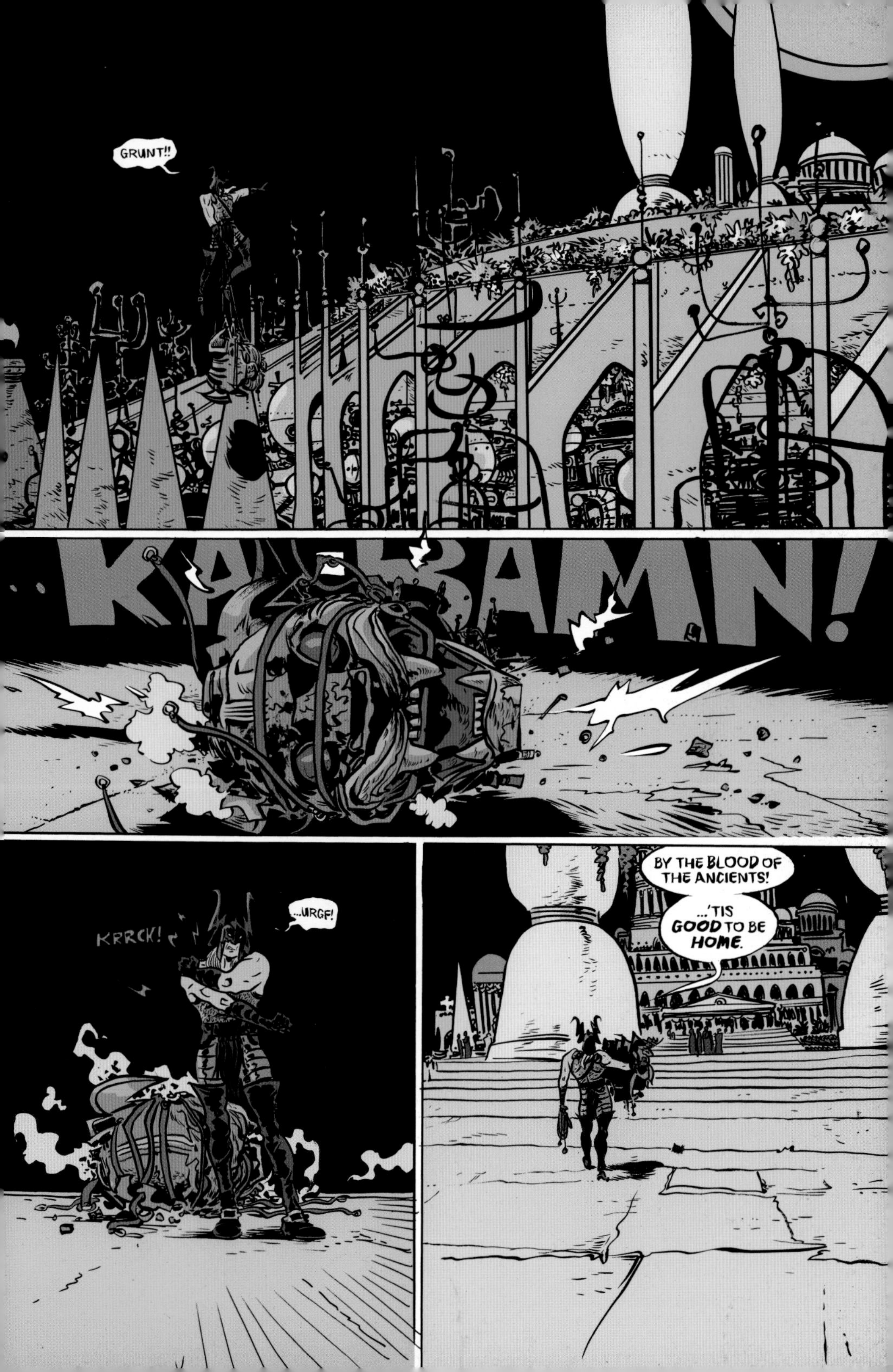
GRUNT!!
...KABLAMN!
KRRCK!
...URGF!
BY THE BLOOD OF THE ANCIENTS!
...'TIS GOOD TO BE HOME.

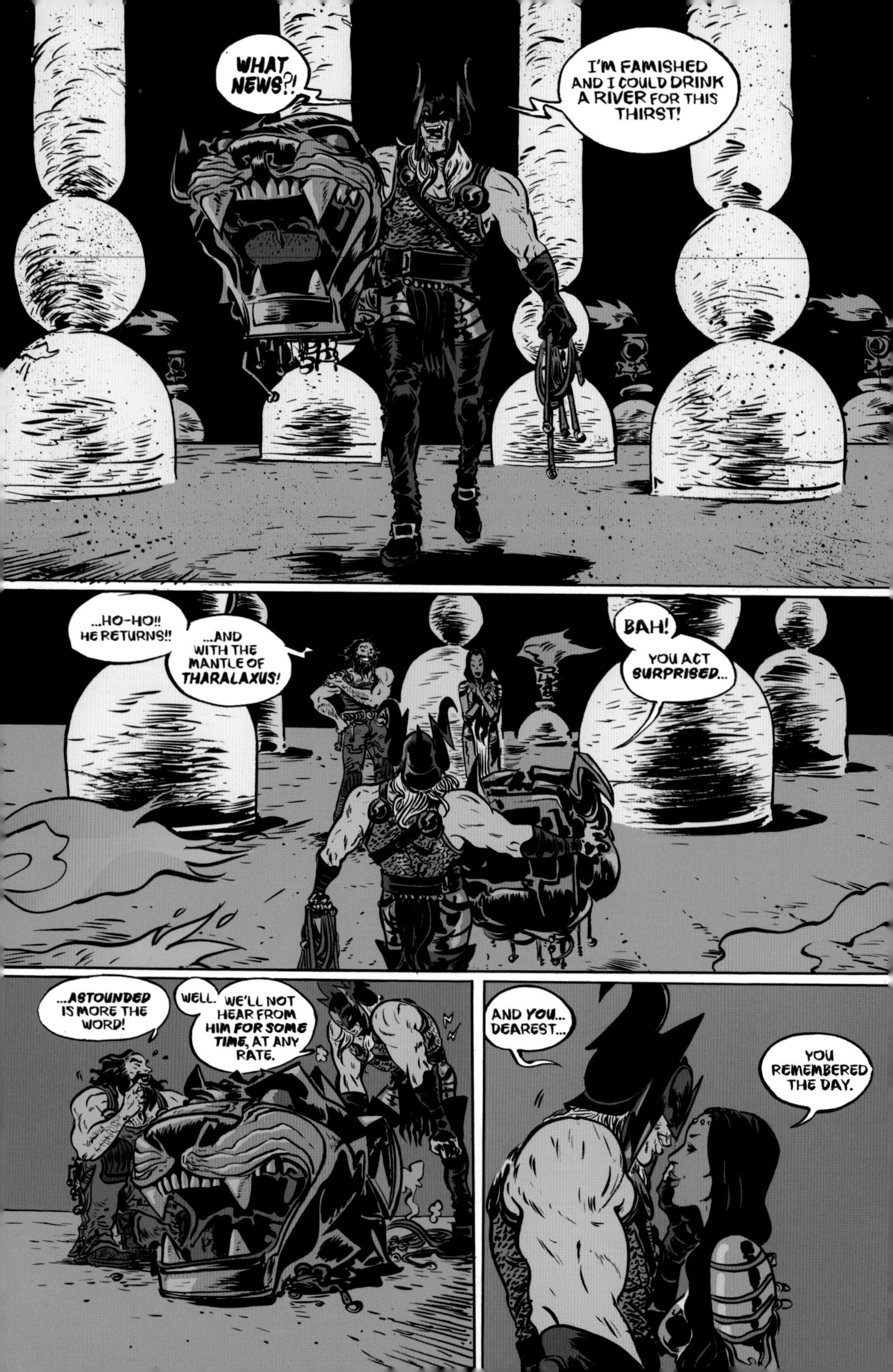
WHAT NEWS?!
I'M FAMISHED AND I COULD DRINK A RIVER FOR THIS THIRST!
...HO-HO!! HE RETURNS!!
...AND WITH THE MANTLE OF THARALAXUS!
BAH!
YOU ACT SURPRISED...
...ASTOUNDED IS MORE THE WORD!
WELL. WE'LL NOT HEAR FROM HIM FOR SOME TIME, AT ANY RATE.
AND YOU... DEAREST...
YOU REMEMBERED THE DAY.

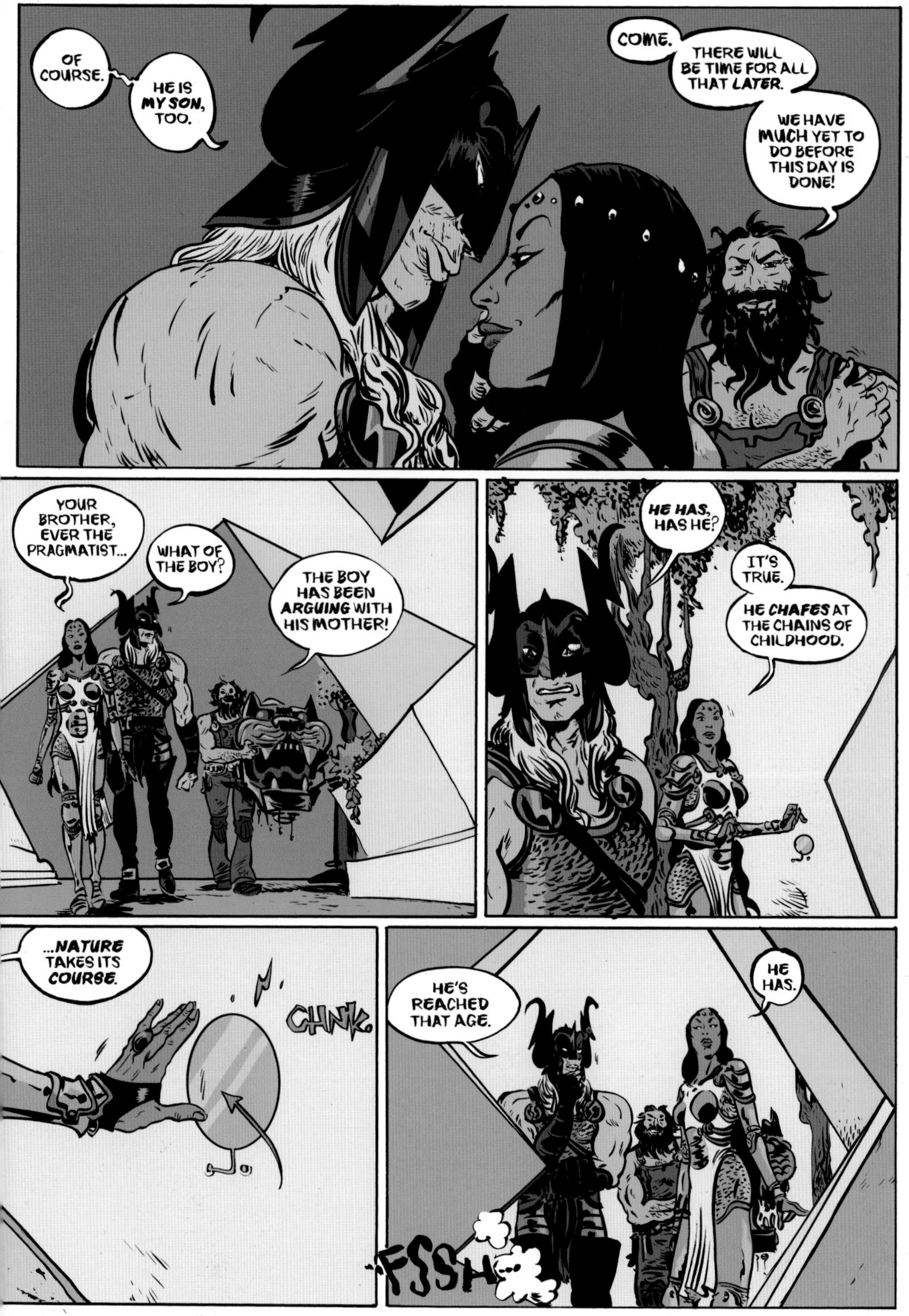
OF COURSE.
HE IS MY SON, TOO.
COME.
THERE WILL BE TIME FOR ALL THAT LATER.
WE HAVE MUCH YET TO DO BEFORE THIS DAY IS DONE!
YOUR BROTHER, EVER THE PRAGMATIST...
WHAT OF THE BOY?
THE BOY HAS BEEN ARGUING WITH HIS MOTHER!
HE HAS, HAS HE?
IT'S TRUE.
HE CHAFES AT THE CHAINS OF CHILDHOOD.
...NATURE TAKES ITS COURSE.
CHNK.
HE'S REACHED THAT AGE.
HE HAS.
FSSH

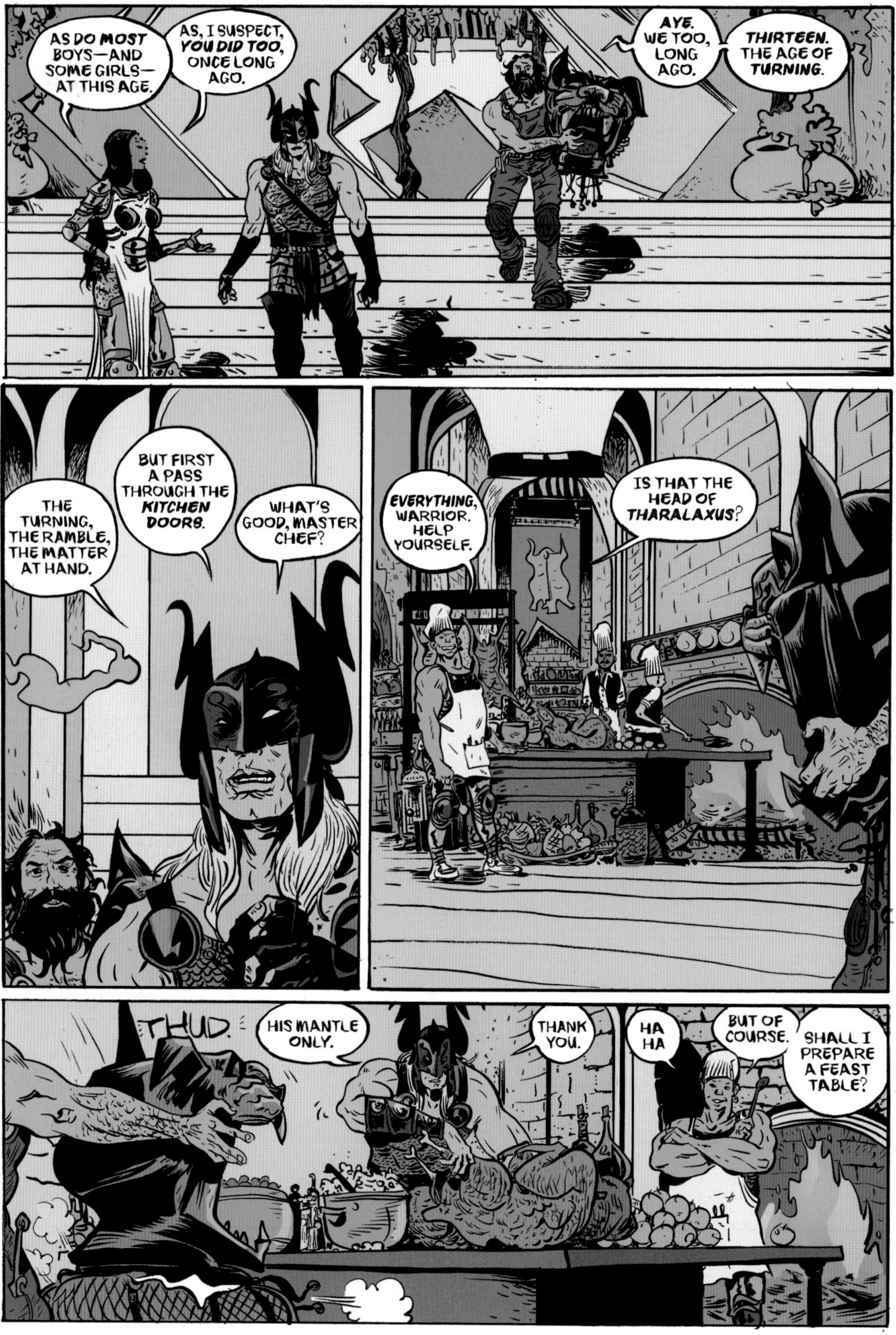
AS DO MOST BOYS—AND SOME GIRLS—AT THIS AGE.
AS, I SUSPECT, YOU DID TOO, ONCE LONG AGO.
AYE. WE TOO, LONG AGO.
THIRTEEN. THE AGE OF TURNING.
THE TURNING, THE RAMBLE, THE MATTER AT HAND.
BUT FIRST A PASS THROUGH THE KITCHEN DOORS.
WHAT'S GOOD, MASTER CHEF?
EVERYTHING, WARRIOR. HELP YOURSELF.
IS THAT THE HEAD OF THARALAXUS?
THUD.
HIS MANTLE ONLY.
THANK YOU.
HA HA
BUT OF COURSE.
SHALL I PREPARE A FEAST TABLE?

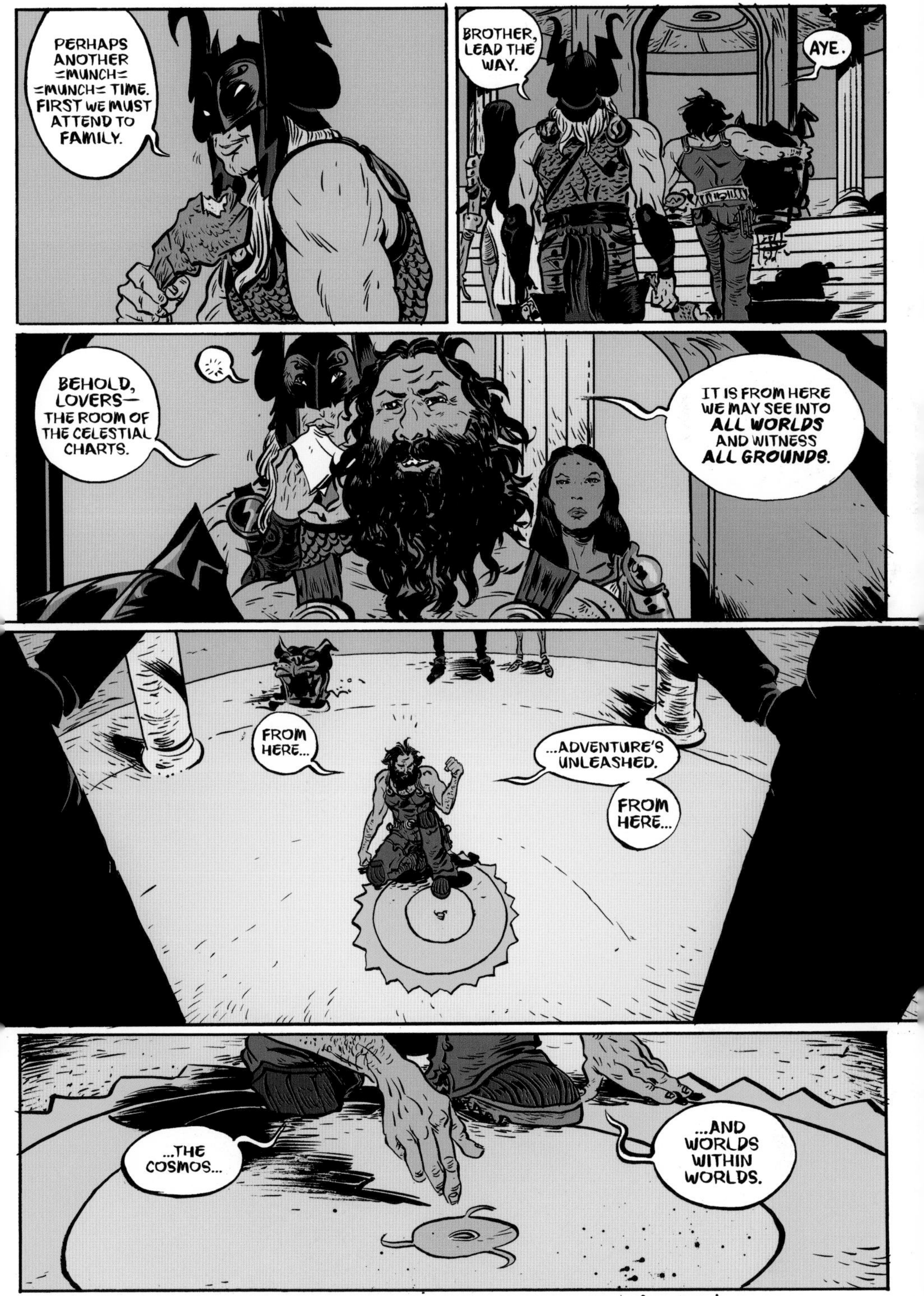
PERHAPS ANOTHER =MUNCH= =MUNCH= TIME. FIRST WE MUST ATTEND TO FAMILY.
BROTHER, LEAD THE WAY.
AYE.
BEHOLD, LOVERS— THE ROOM OF THE CELESTIAL CHARTS.
IT IS FROM HERE WE MAY SEE INTO ALL WORLDS AND WITNESS ALL GROUNDS.
FROM HERE...
...ADVENTURE'S UNLEASHED.
FROM HERE...
...THE COSMOS...
...AND WORLDS WITHIN WORLDS.

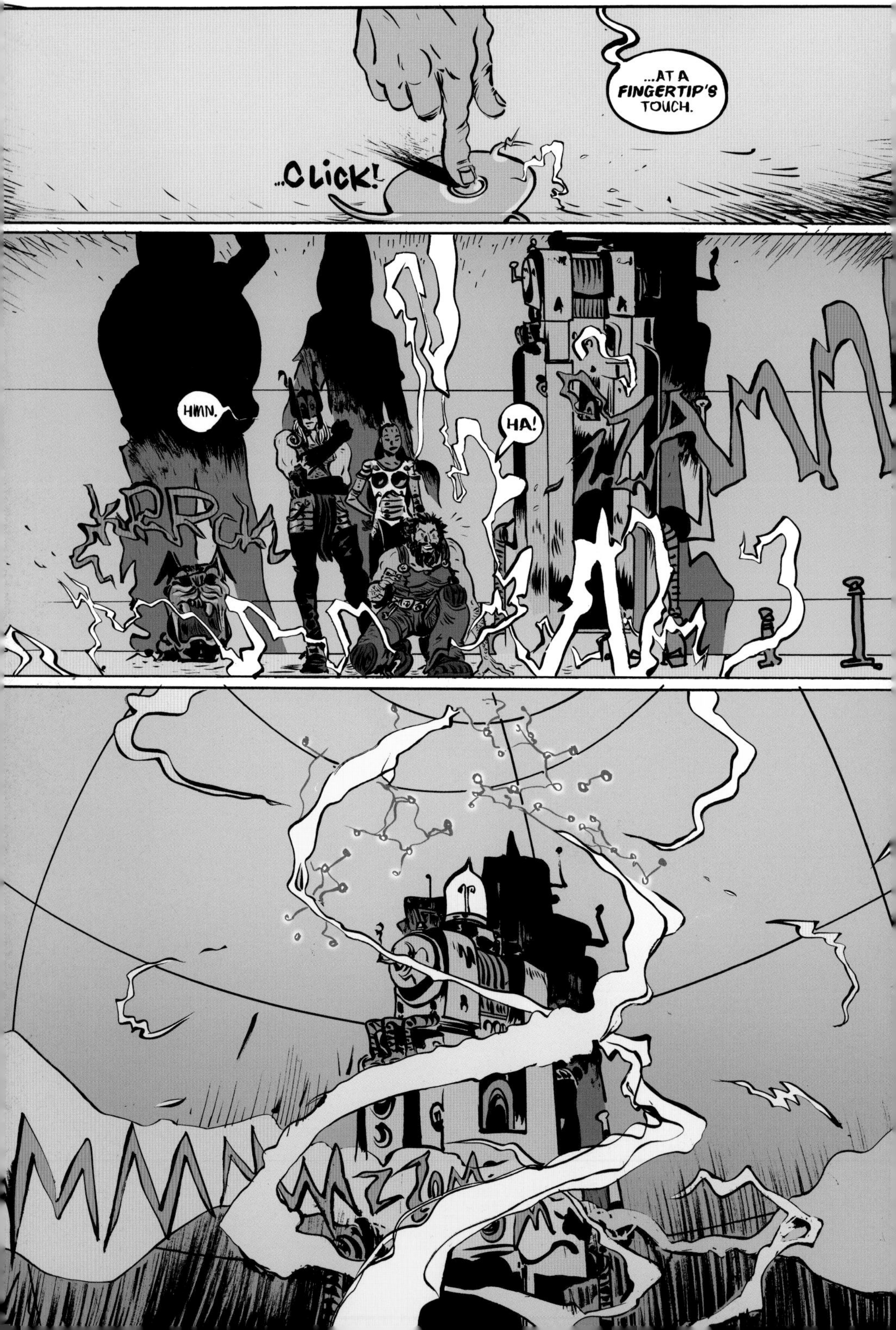
...AT A FINGERTIP'S TOUCH.
..CLICK!
HMN.
HA!
KRRCK
VRAMM
MMMM
VAZZOOM

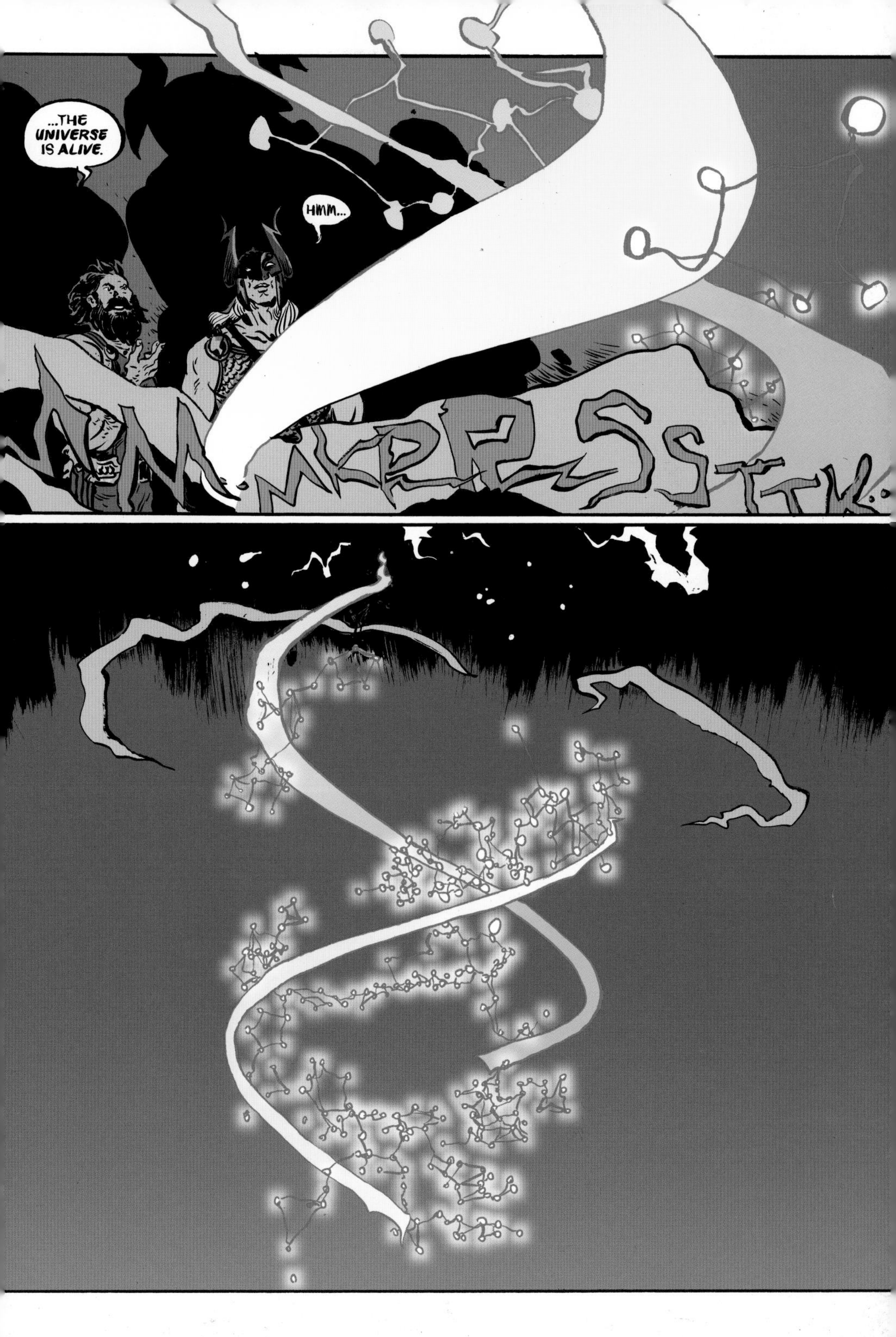
...THE UNIVERSE IS ALIVE.
HMM...

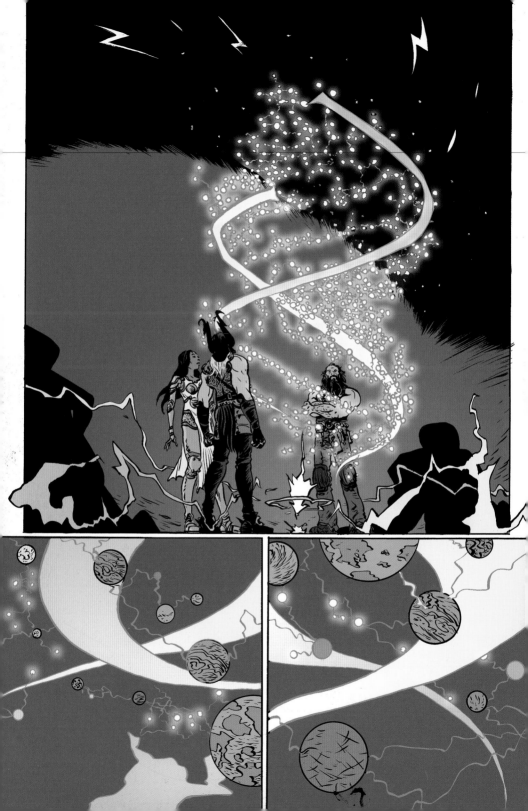

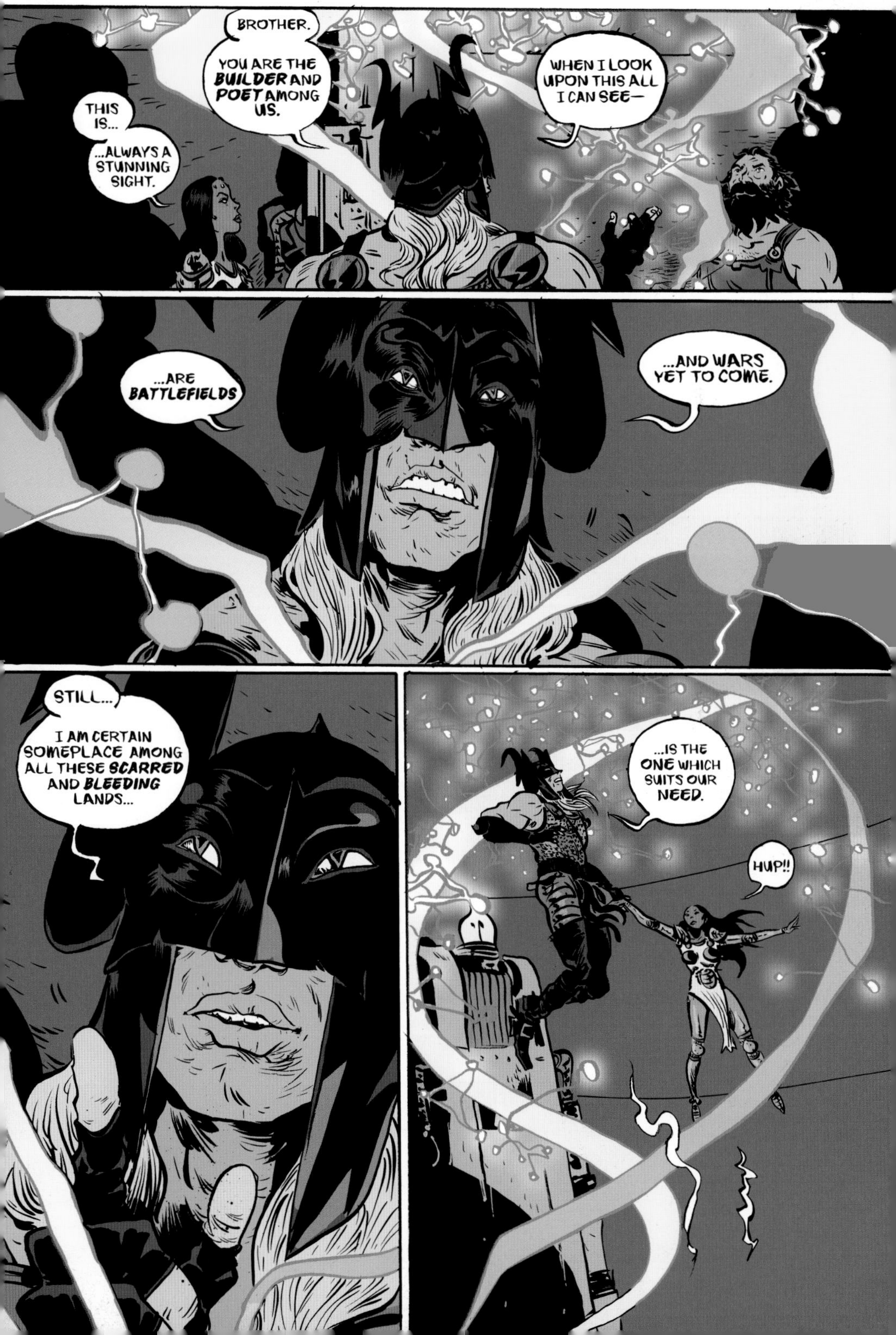
THIS IS... ...ALWAYS A STUNNING SIGHT.
BROTHER.
YOU ARE THE BUILDER AND POET AMONG US.
WHEN I LOOK UPON THIS ALL I CAN SEE—
...ARE BATTLEFIELDS
...AND WARS YET TO COME.
STILL...
I AM CERTAIN SOMEPLACE AMONG ALL THESE SCARRED AND BLEEDING LANDS...
...IS THE ONE WHICH SUITS OUR NEED.
HUP!!

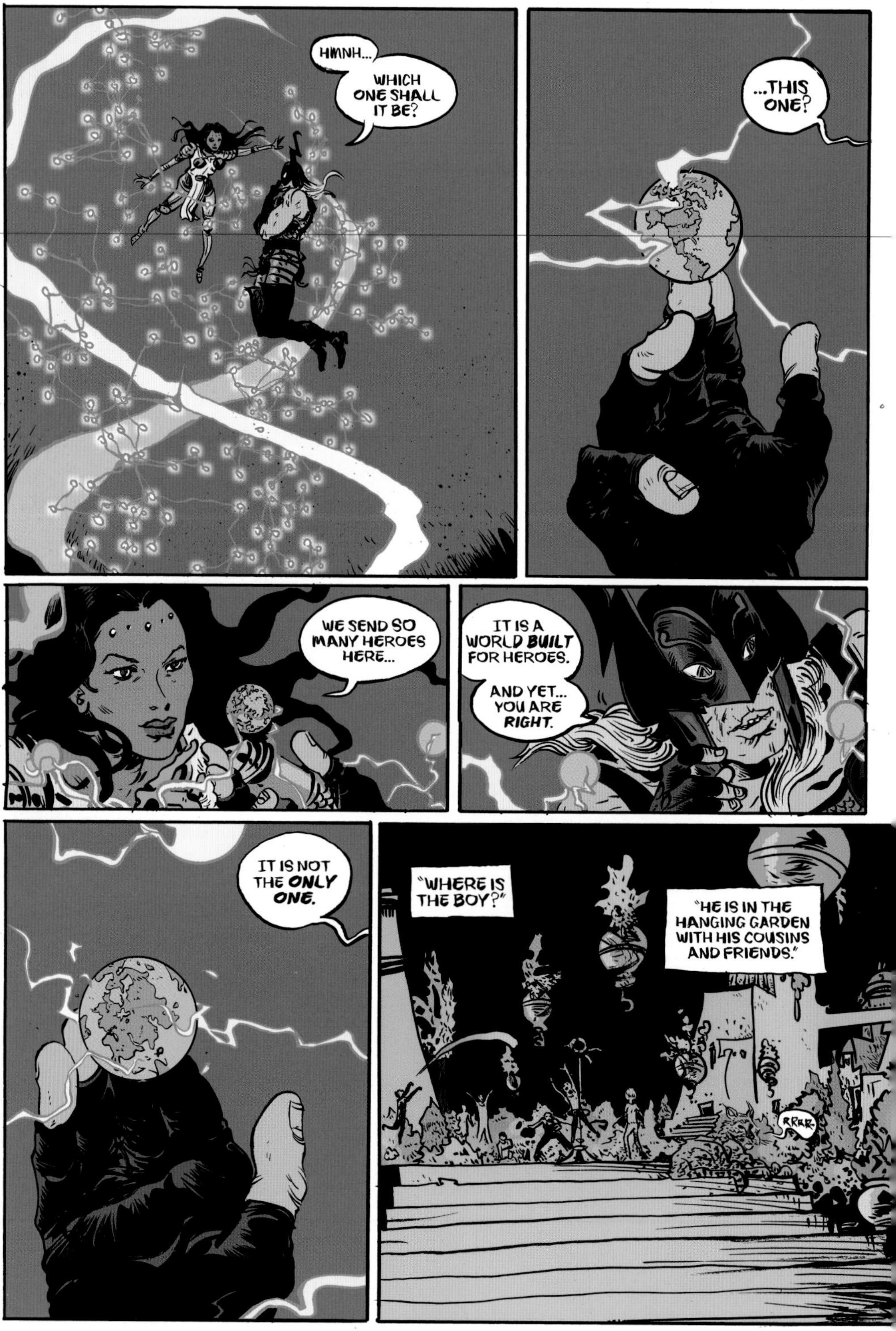
HMNH...
WHICH ONE SHALL IT BE?
...THIS ONE?
WE SEND SO MANY HEROES HERE...
IT IS A WORLD BUILT FOR HEROES.
AND YET... YOU ARE RIGHT.
IT IS NOT THE ONLY ONE.
"WHERE IS THE BOY?"
"HE IS IN THE HANGING GARDEN WITH HIS COUSINS AND FRIENDS."
RRRR-

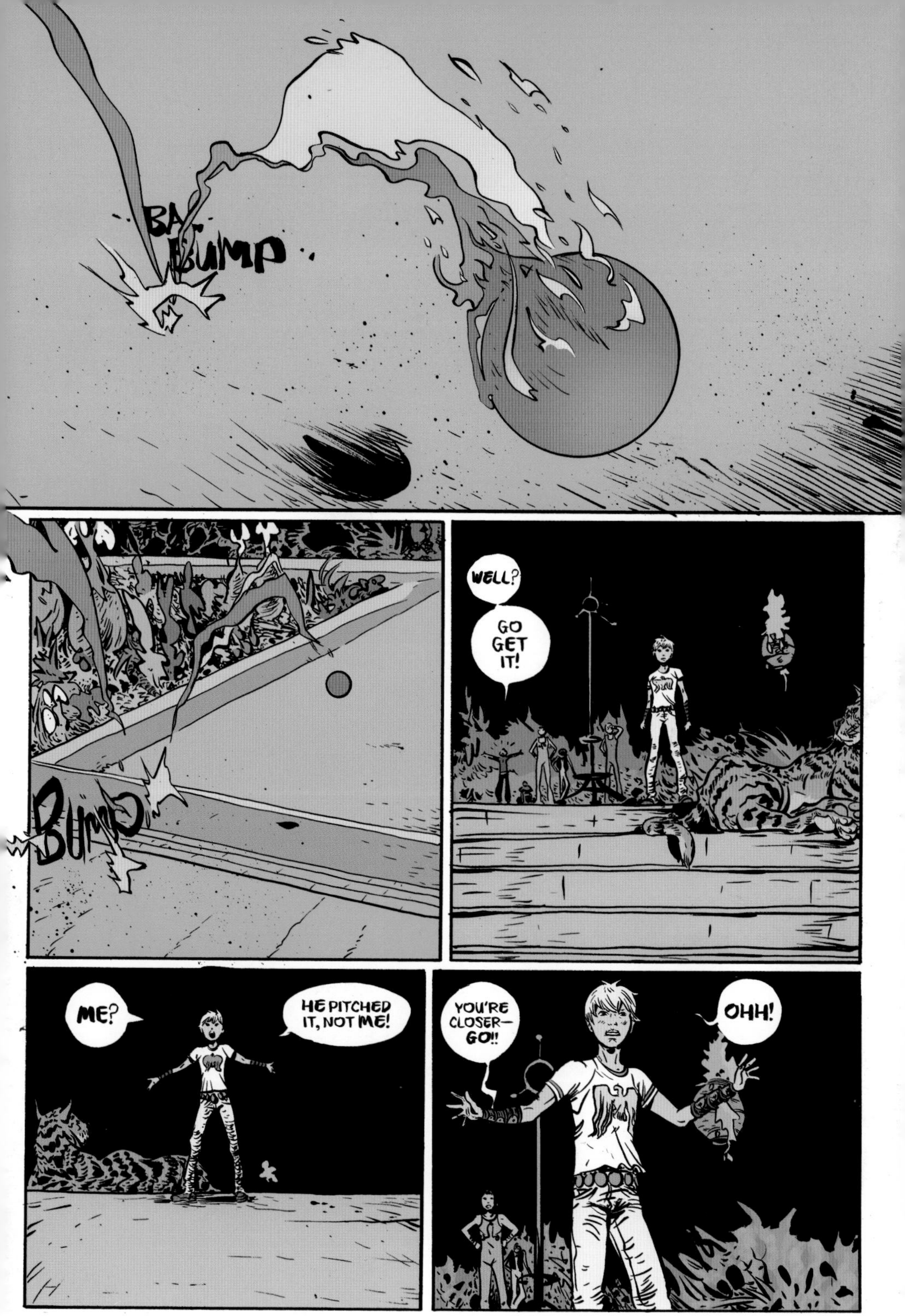
BA-BUMP
BUMP
WELL?
GO GET IT!
ME?
HE PITCHED IT, NOT ME!
YOU'RE CLOSER— GO!!
OHH!

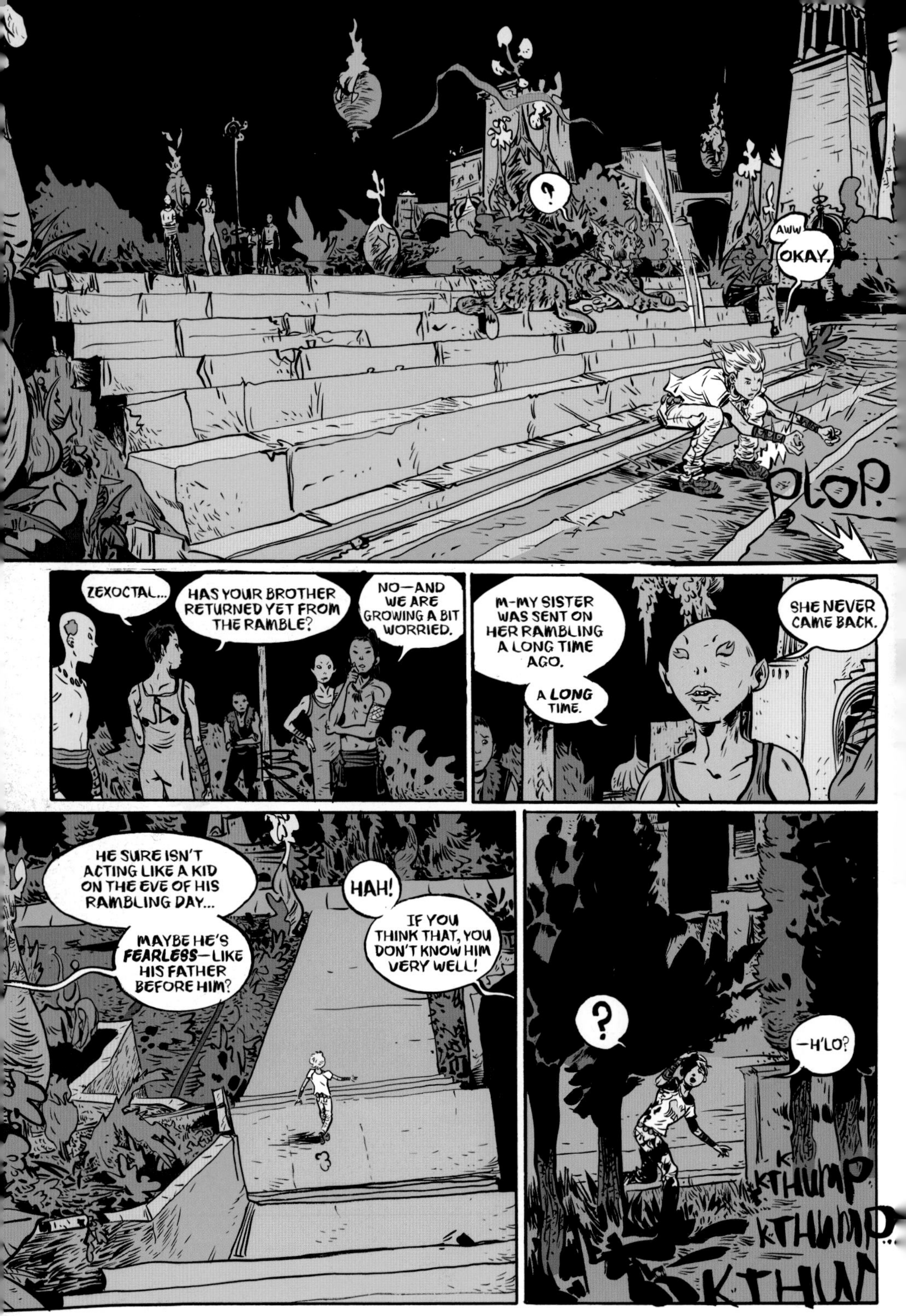
?
AWW
OKAY.
PLOP.
ZEXOCTAL...
HAS YOUR BROTHER RETURNED YET FROM THE RAMBLE?
NO—AND WE ARE GROWING A BIT WORRIED.
M-MY SISTER WAS SENT ON HER RAMBLING A LONG TIME AGO.
A LONG TIME.
SHE NEVER CAME BACK.
HE SURE ISN'T ACTING LIKE A KID ON THE EVE OF HIS RAMBLING DAY...
MAYBE HE'S FEARLESS—LIKE HIS FATHER BEFORE HIM?
HAH!
IF YOU THINK THAT, YOU DON'T KNOW HIM VERY WELL!
?
—H'LO?
KTHUMP
KTHUMP...
KTHU

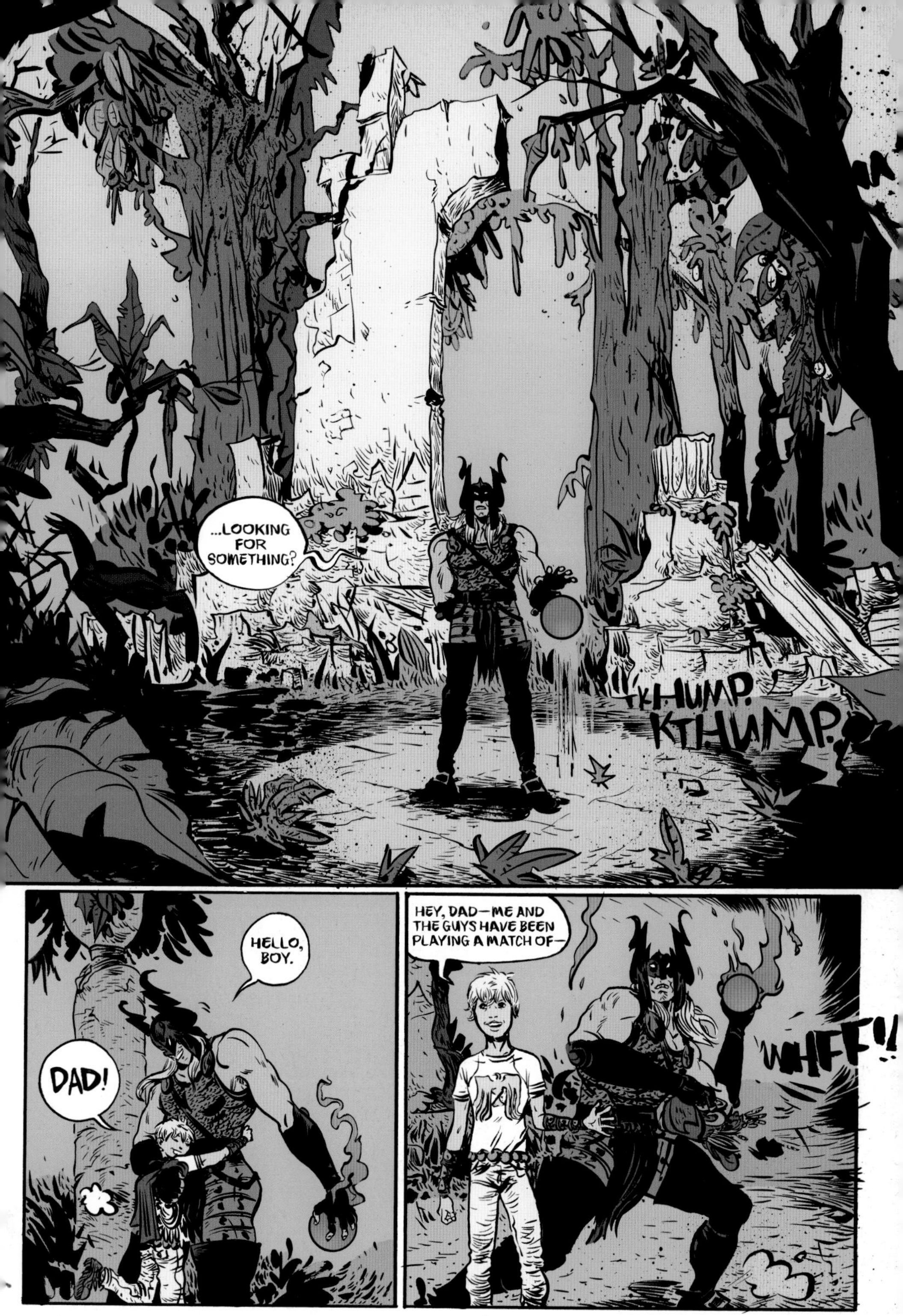
...LOOKING FOR SOMETHING?
THUMP. KTHUMP.
HELLO, BOY.
DAD!
HEY, DAD—ME AND THE GUYS HAVE BEEN PLAYING A MATCH OF—
WHFF!!

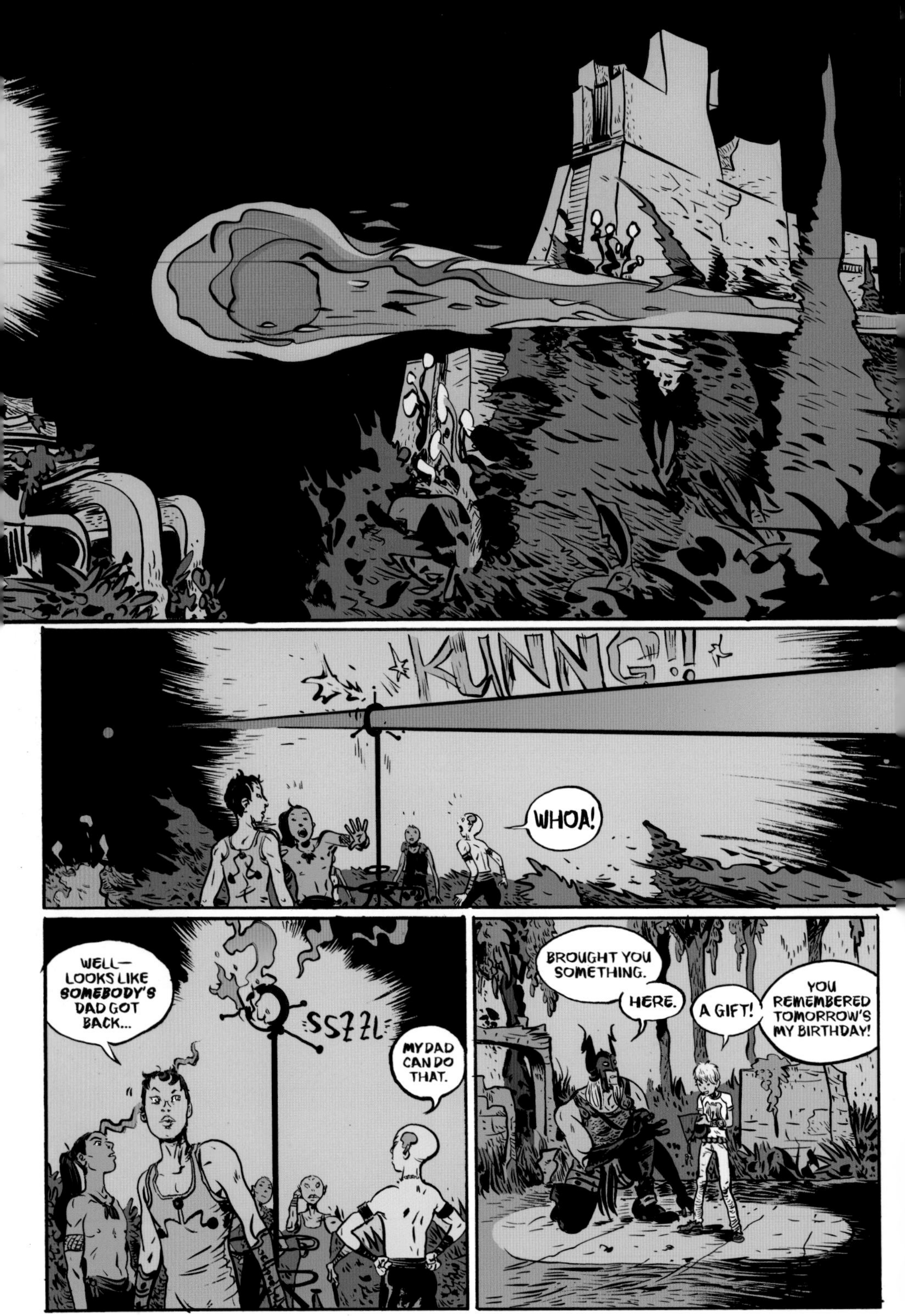
KUNNG!!
WHOA!
WELL— LOOKS LIKE SOMEBODY'S DAD GOT BACK...
SSZZL
MY DAD CAN DO THAT.
BROUGHT YOU SOMETHING.
HERE.
A GIFT!
YOU REMEMBERED TOMORROW'S MY BIRTHDAY!

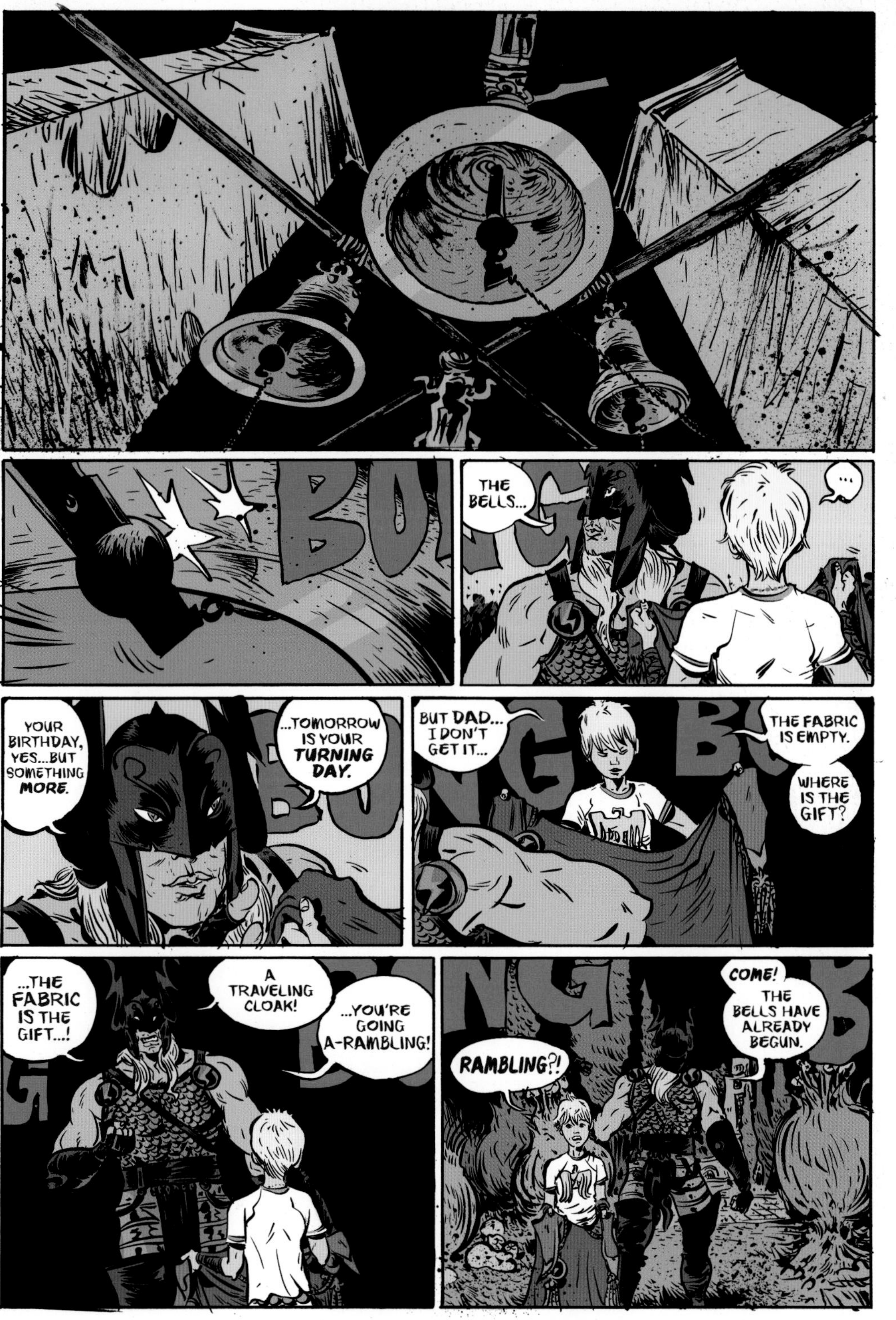

BONG
THE BELLS...
...
YOUR BIRTHDAY, YES...BUT SOMETHING MORE.
...TOMORROW IS YOUR TURNING DAY.
BUT DAD... I DON'T GET IT...
THE FABRIC IS EMPTY.
WHERE IS THE GIFT?
...THE FABRIC IS THE GIFT...!
A TRAVELING CLOAK!
...YOU'RE GOING A-RAMBLING!
RAMBLING?!
COME!
THE BELLS HAVE ALREADY BEGUN.

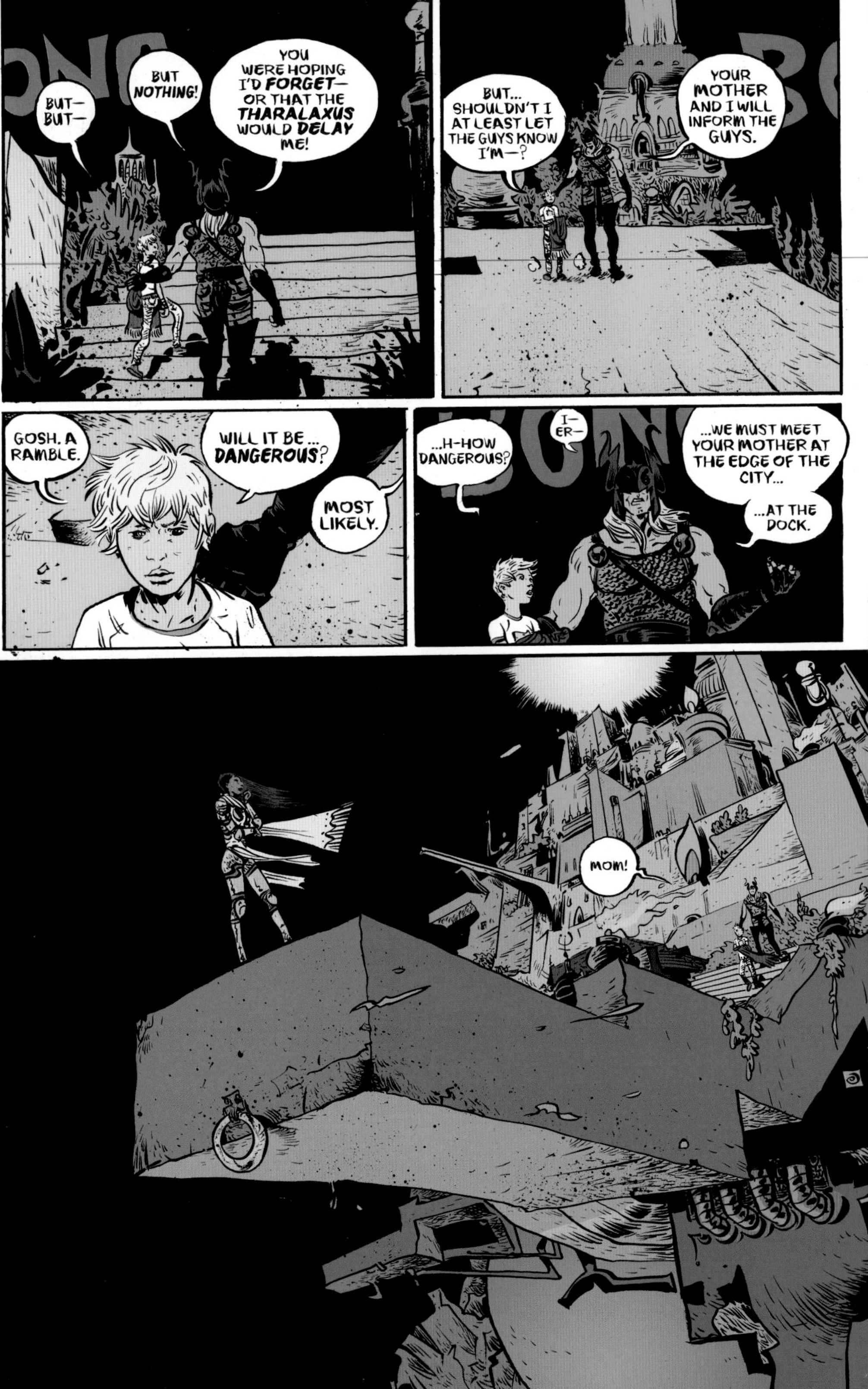
BONG
BUT—
BUT—
BUT
NOTHING!
YOU
WERE HOPING
I'D FORGET—
OR THAT THE
THARALAXUS
WOULD DELAY
ME!
BO
BUT...
SHOULDN'T I
AT LEAST LET
THE GUYS KNOW
I'M—?
YOUR
MOTHER
AND I WILL
INFORM THE
GUYS.
GOSH. A
RAMBLE.
WILL IT BE...
DANGEROUS?
MOST
LIKELY.
BONG
...H-HOW
DANGEROUS?
I—
ER—
...WE MUST MEET
YOUR MOTHER AT
THE EDGE OF THE
CITY...
...AT THE
DOCK.
MOM!

MOM, I...

YES, I KNOW, SON.

LISTEN TO YOUR FATHER.

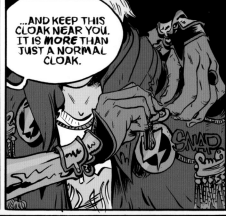

...AND KEEP THIS CLOAK NEAR YOU. IT IS *MORE* THAN JUST A NORMAL CLOAK.

OH, MY SON. MY BOY...

AW, MOM...

AND NOW, BOY...

BEFORE THE BELLS STRIKE THIRTEEN.

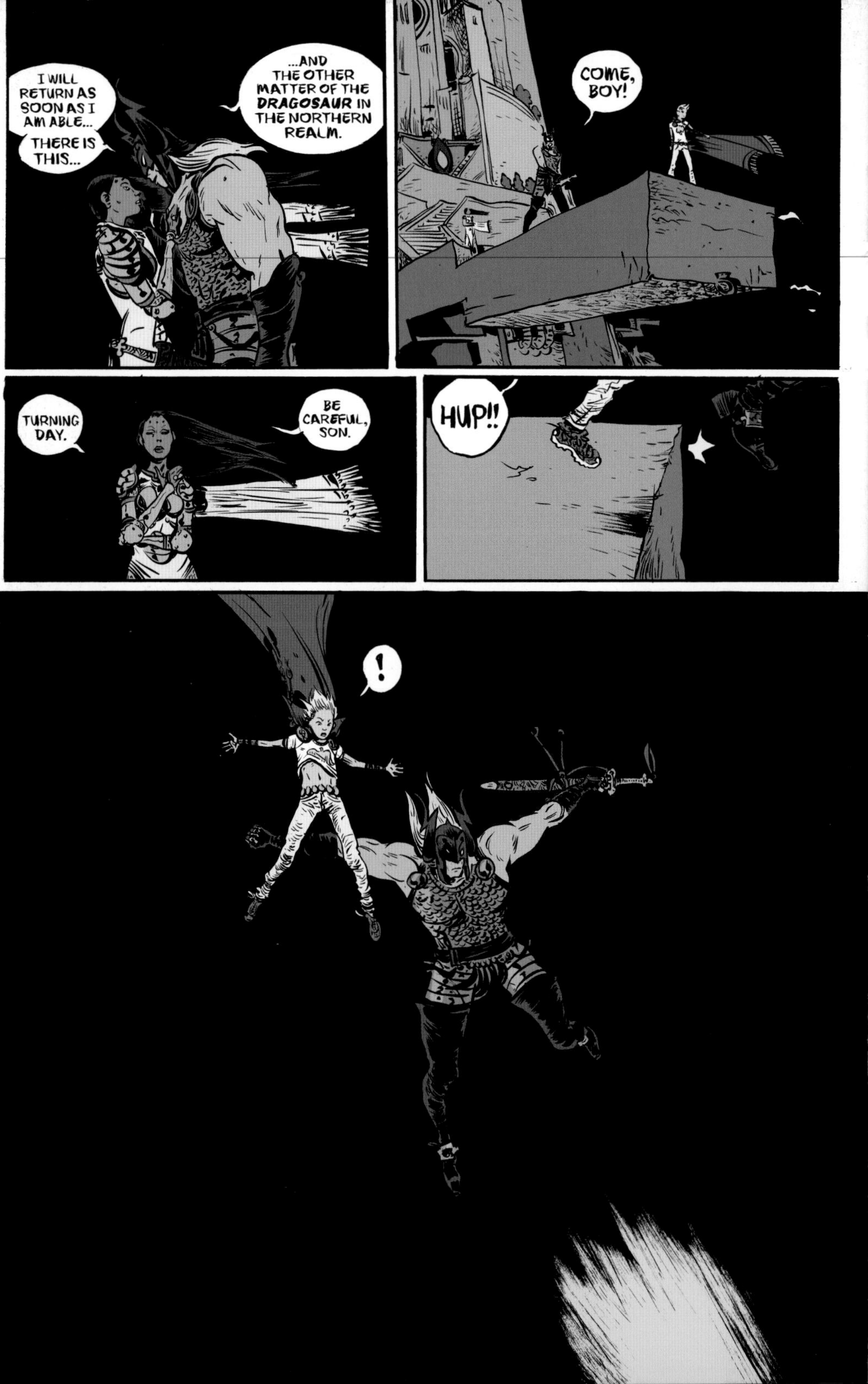
I WILL RETURN AS SOON AS I AM ABLE...
THERE IS THIS...
...AND THE OTHER MATTER OF THE DRAGOSAUR IN THE NORTHERN REALM.
COME, BOY!
TURNING DAY.
BE CAREFUL, SON.
HUP!!
!

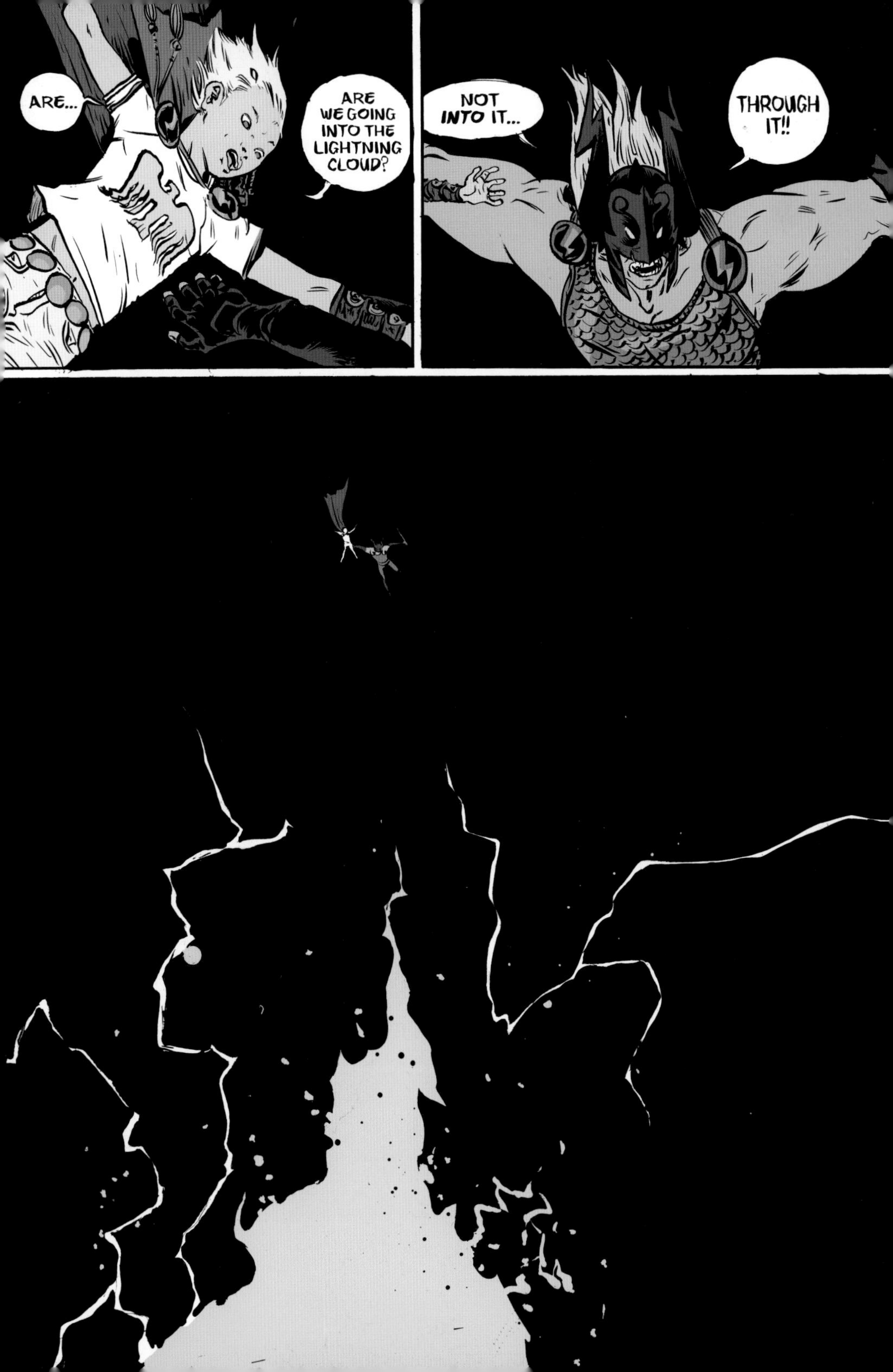
ARE...
ARE WE GOING INTO THE LIGHTNING CLOUD?
NOT INTO IT...
THROUGH IT!!

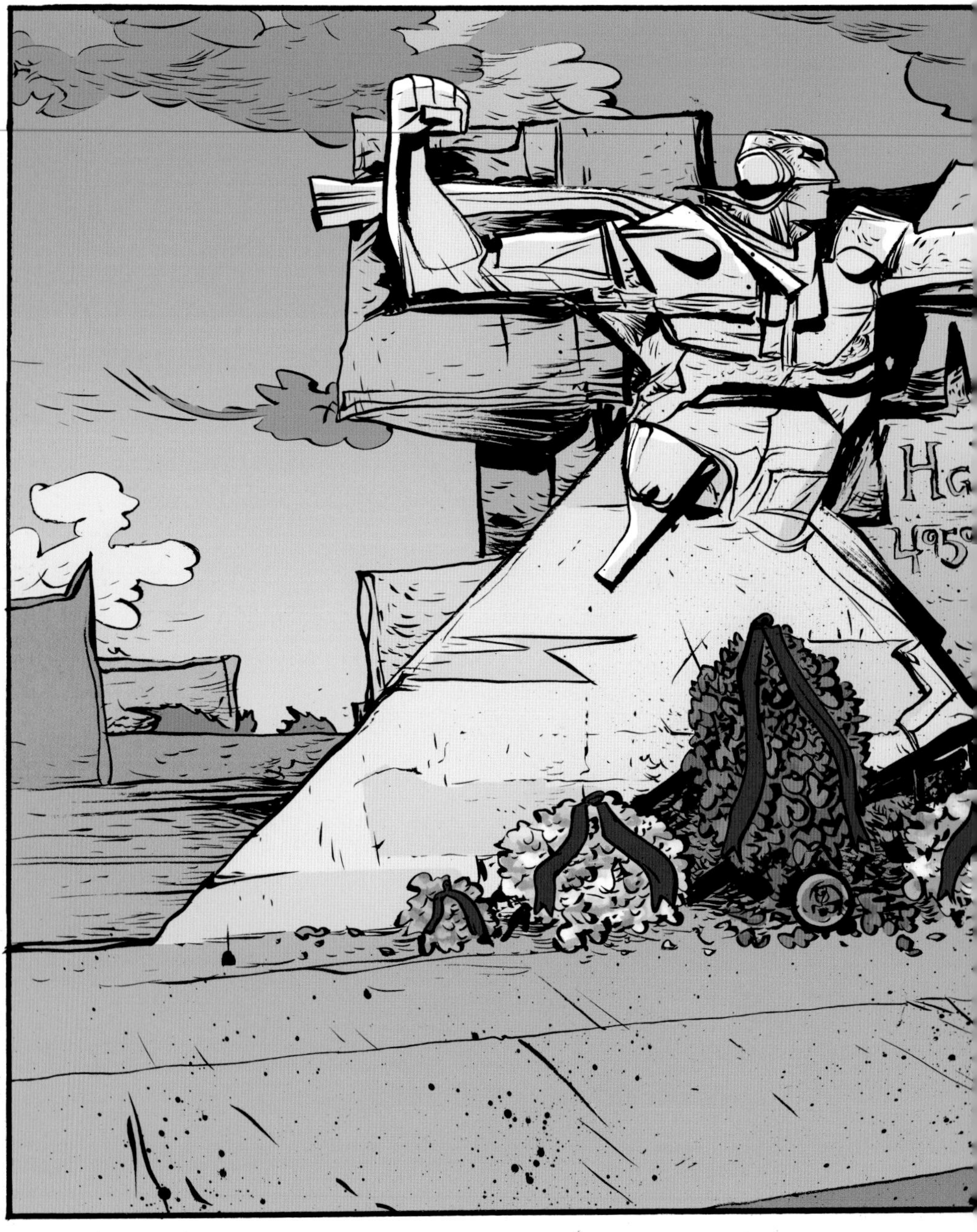

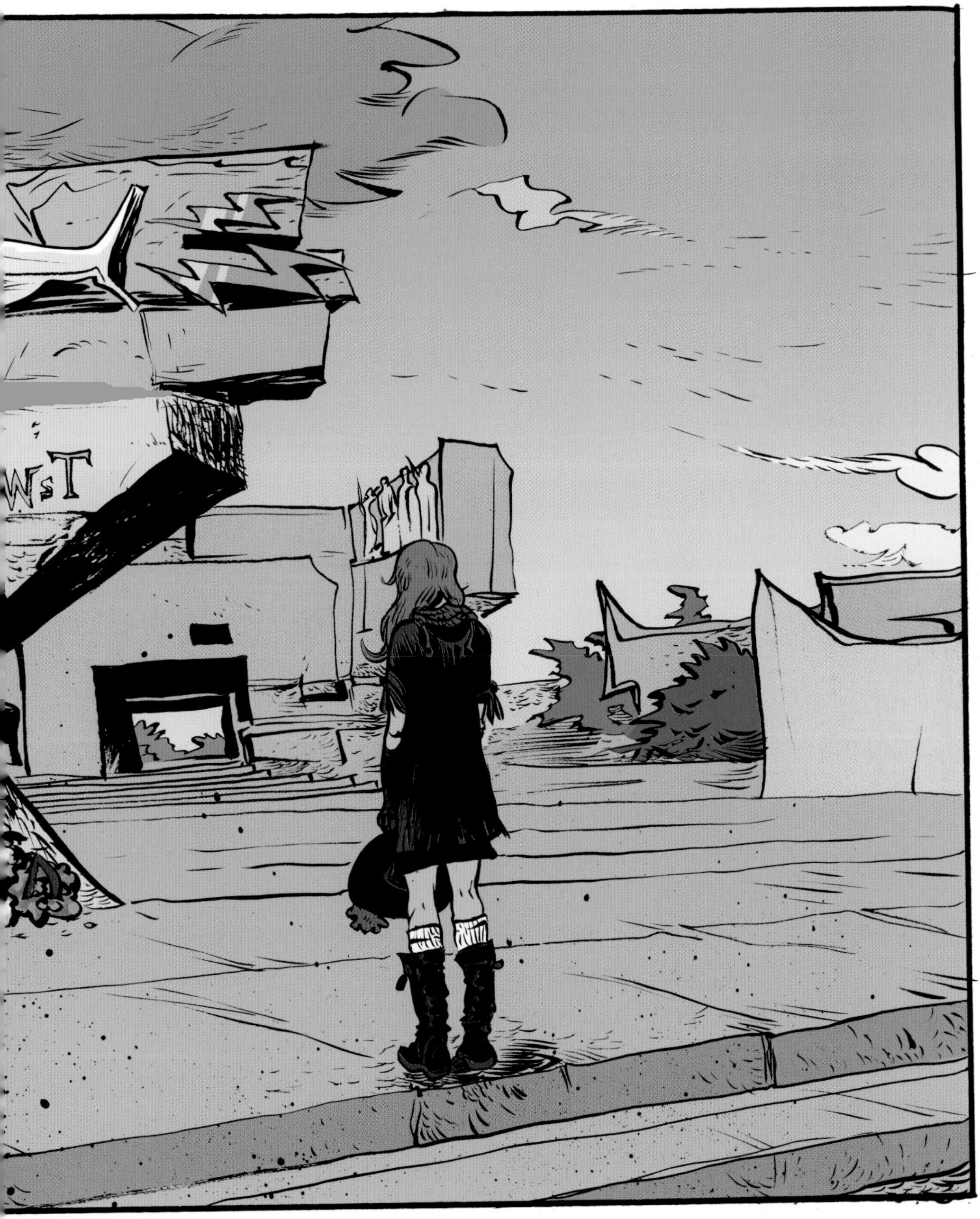
WsT

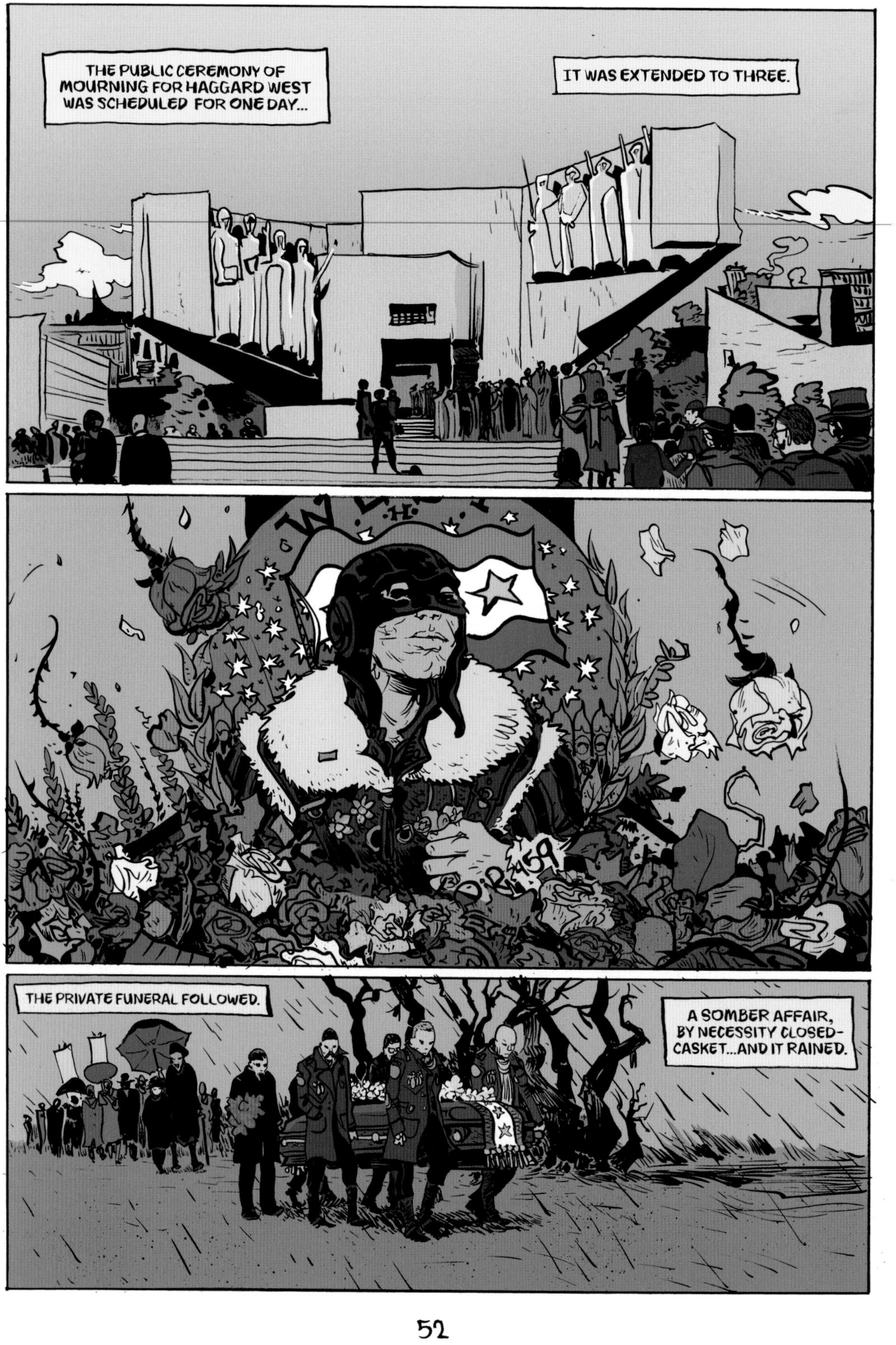
THE PUBLIC CEREMONY OF MOURNING FOR HAGGARD WEST WAS SCHEDULED FOR ONE DAY...
IT WAS EXTENDED TO THREE.
THE PRIVATE FUNERAL FOLLOWED.
A SOMBER AFFAIR, BY NECESSITY CLOSED-CASKET...AND IT RAINED.

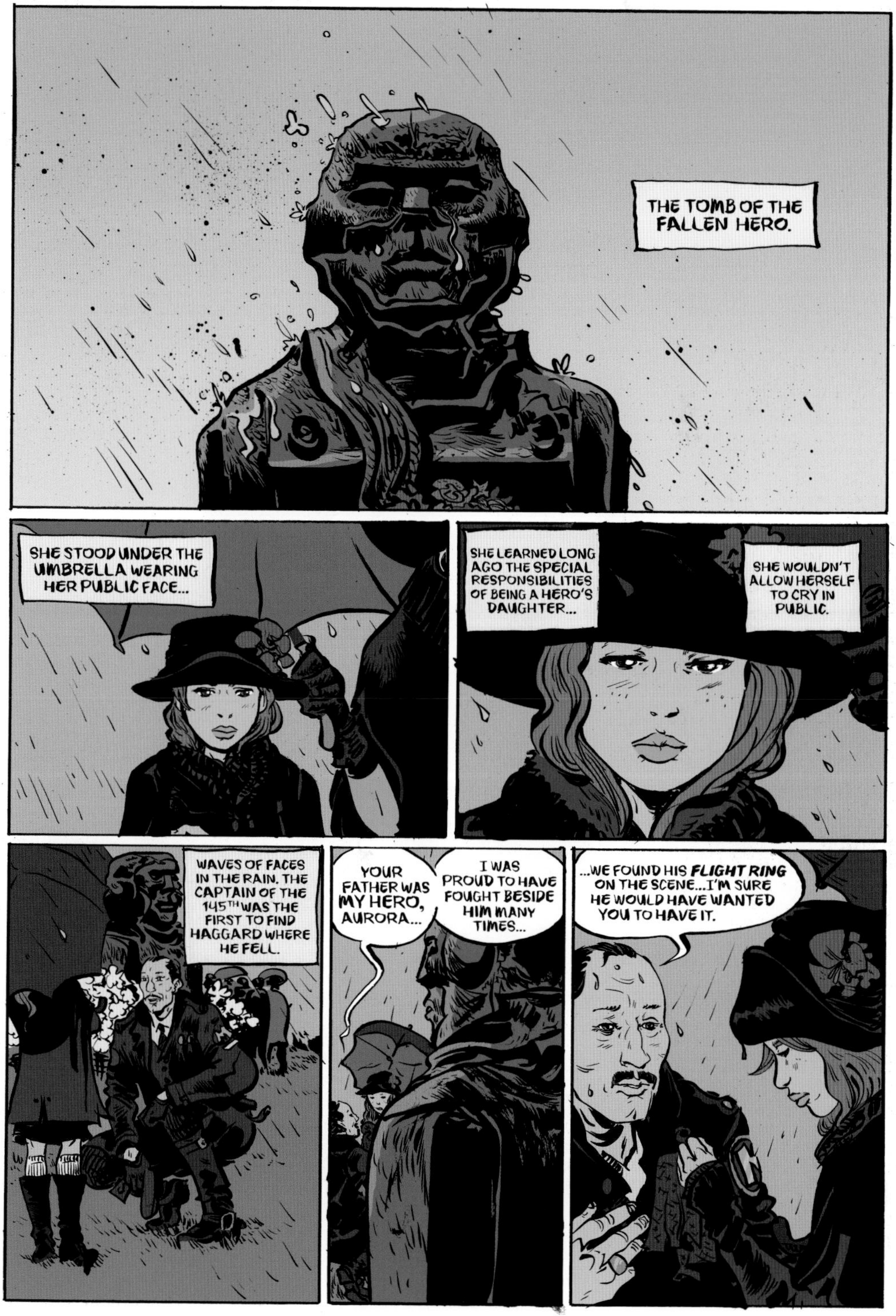
THE TOMB OF THE FALLEN HERO.
SHE STOOD UNDER THE UMBRELLA WEARING HER PUBLIC FACE...
SHE LEARNED LONG AGO THE SPECIAL RESPONSIBILITIES OF BEING A HERO'S DAUGHTER...
SHE WOULDN'T ALLOW HERSELF TO CRY IN PUBLIC.
WAVES OF FACES IN THE RAIN. THE CAPTAIN OF THE 145TH WAS THE FIRST TO FIND HAGGARD WHERE HE FELL.
YOUR FATHER WAS MY HERO, AURORA...
I WAS PROUD TO HAVE FOUGHT BESIDE HIM MANY TIMES...
...WE FOUND HIS FLIGHT RING ON THE SCENE...I'M SURE HE WOULD HAVE WANTED YOU TO HAVE IT.

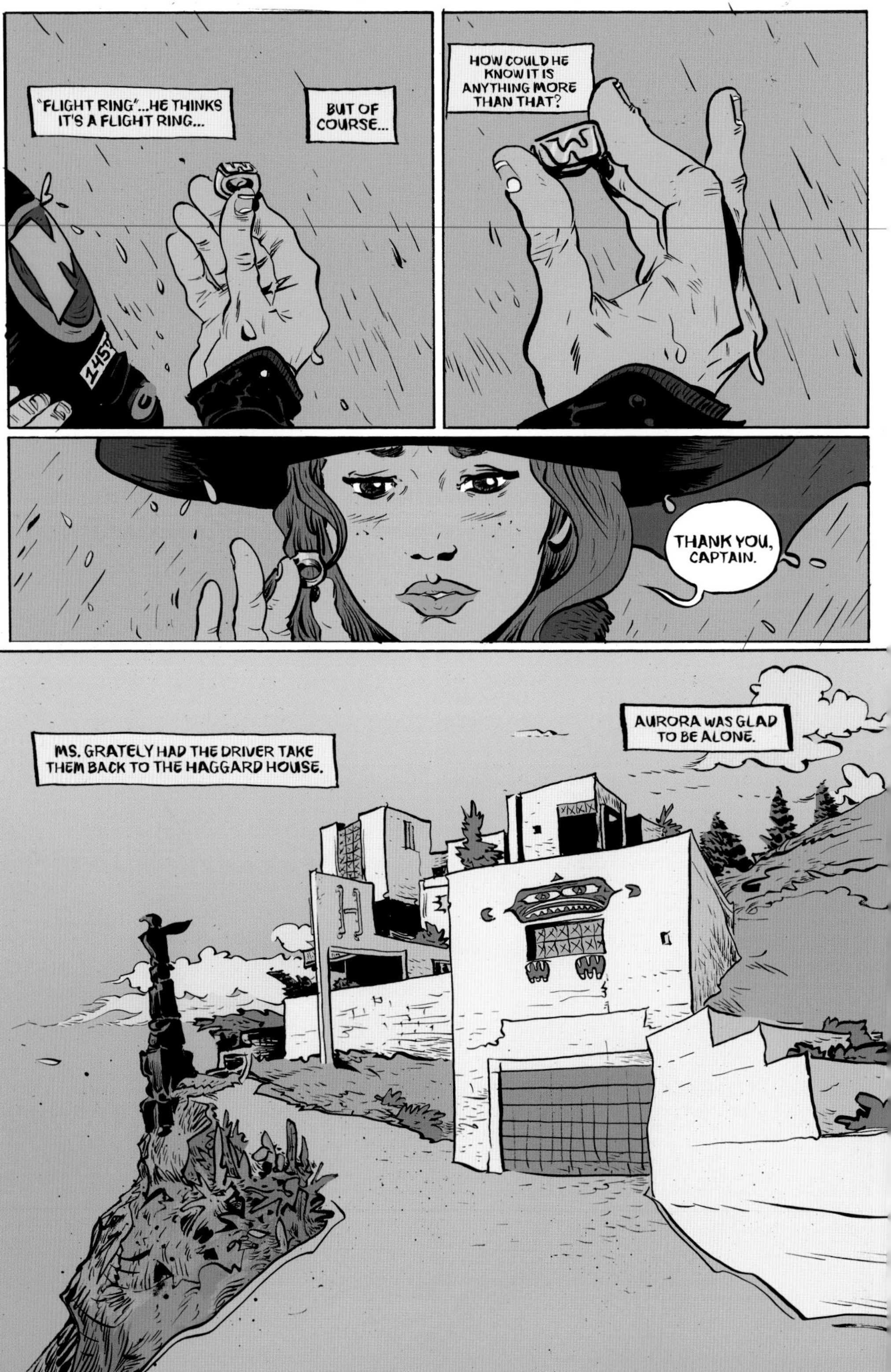
"FLIGHT RING"...HE THINKS IT'S A FLIGHT RING...
BUT OF COURSE...
HOW COULD HE KNOW IT IS ANYTHING MORE THAN THAT?
THANK YOU, CAPTAIN.
MS. GRATELY HAD THE DRIVER TAKE THEM BACK TO THE HAGGARD HOUSE.
AURORA WAS GLAD TO BE ALONE.

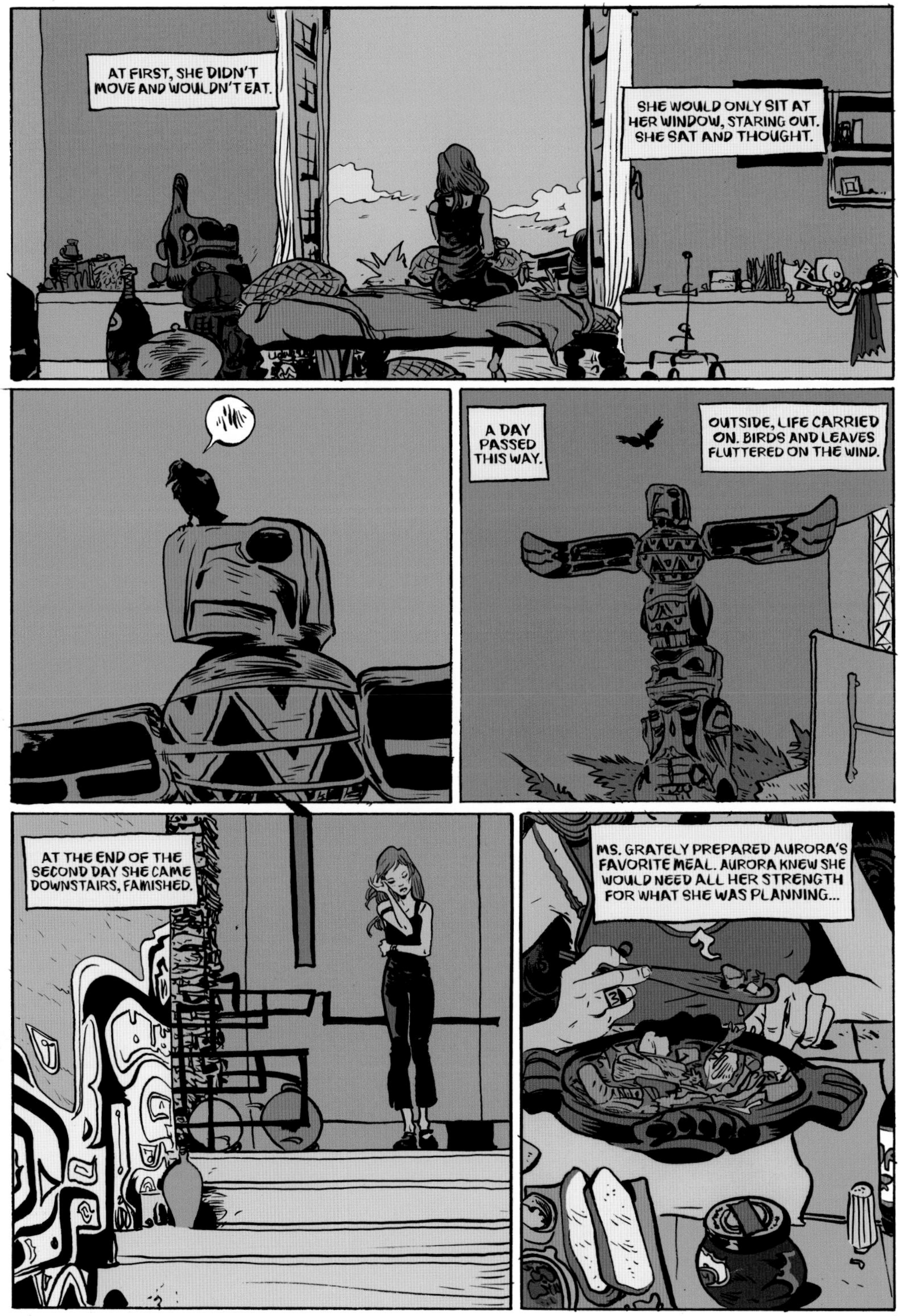

AT FIRST, SHE DIDN'T MOVE AND WOULDN'T EAT.
SHE WOULD ONLY SIT AT HER WINDOW, STARING OUT. SHE SAT AND THOUGHT.
A DAY PASSED THIS WAY.
OUTSIDE, LIFE CARRIED ON. BIRDS AND LEAVES FLUTTERED ON THE WIND.
AT THE END OF THE SECOND DAY SHE CAME DOWNSTAIRS, FAMISHED.
MS. GRATELY PREPARED AURORA'S FAVORITE MEAL. AURORA KNEW SHE WOULD NEED ALL HER STRENGTH FOR WHAT SHE WAS PLANNING...

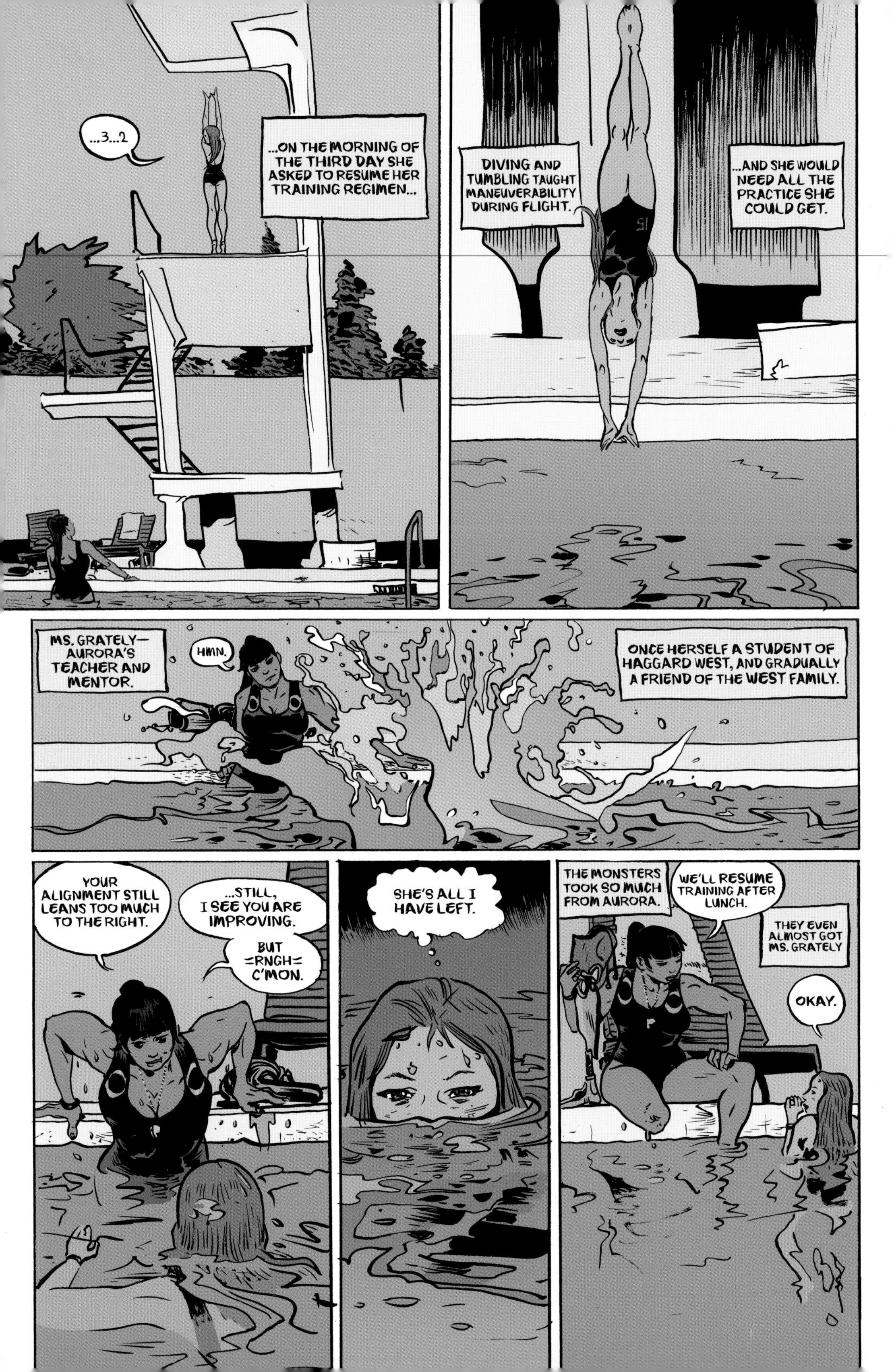
...3...2
...ON THE MORNING OF THE THIRD DAY SHE ASKED TO RESUME HER TRAINING REGIMEN...
DIVING AND TUMBLING TAUGHT MANEUVERABILITY DURING FLIGHT.
...AND SHE WOULD NEED ALL THE PRACTICE SHE COULD GET.
MS. GRATELY—AURORA'S TEACHER AND MENTOR.
HMN.
ONCE HERSELF A STUDENT OF HAGGARD WEST, AND GRADUALLY A FRIEND OF THE WEST FAMILY.
YOUR ALIGNMENT STILL LEANS TOO MUCH TO THE RIGHT.
...STILL, I SEE YOU ARE IMPROVING.
BUT =RNGH= C'MON.
SHE'S ALL I HAVE LEFT.
THE MONSTERS TOOK SO MUCH FROM AURORA.
WE'LL RESUME TRAINING AFTER LUNCH.
THEY EVEN ALMOST GOT MS. GRATELY
OKAY.

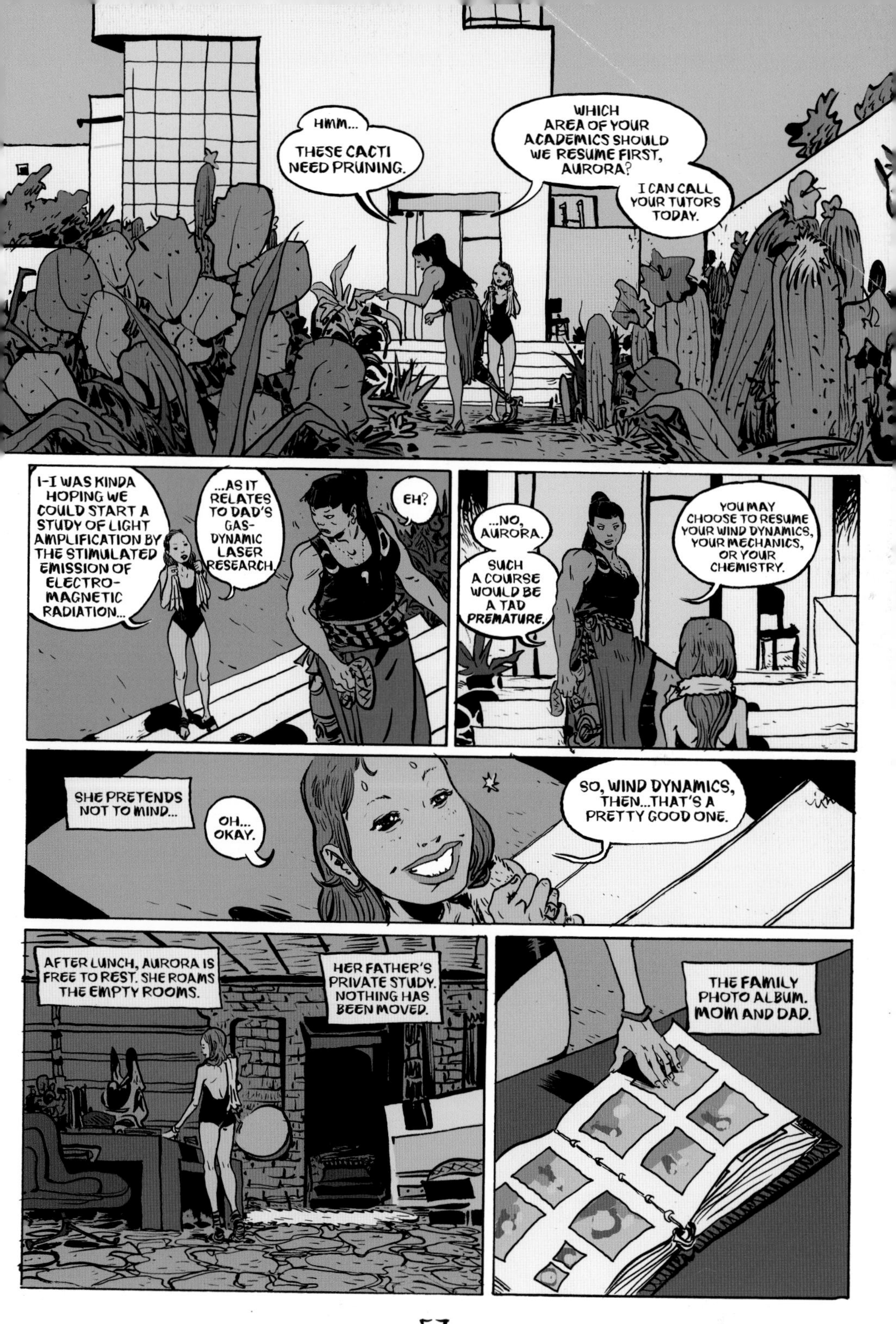
HMM... THESE CACTI NEED PRUNING.
WHICH AREA OF YOUR ACADEMICS SHOULD WE RESUME FIRST, AURORA?
I CAN CALL YOUR TUTORS TODAY.
I-I WAS KINDA HOPING WE COULD START A STUDY OF LIGHT AMPLIFICATION BY THE STIMULATED EMISSION OF ELECTRO-MAGNETIC RADIATION...
...AS IT RELATES TO DAD'S GAS-DYNAMIC LASER RESEARCH.
EH?
...NO, AURORA.
SUCH A COURSE WOULD BE A TAD PREMATURE.
YOU MAY CHOOSE TO RESUME YOUR WIND DYNAMICS, YOUR MECHANICS, OR YOUR CHEMISTRY.
SHE PRETENDS NOT TO MIND...
OH... OKAY.
SO, WIND DYNAMICS, THEN...THAT'S A PRETTY GOOD ONE.
AFTER LUNCH, AURORA IS FREE TO REST. SHE ROAMS THE EMPTY ROOMS.
HER FATHER'S PRIVATE STUDY. NOTHING HAS BEEN MOVED.
THE FAMILY PHOTO ALBUM. MOM AND DAD.

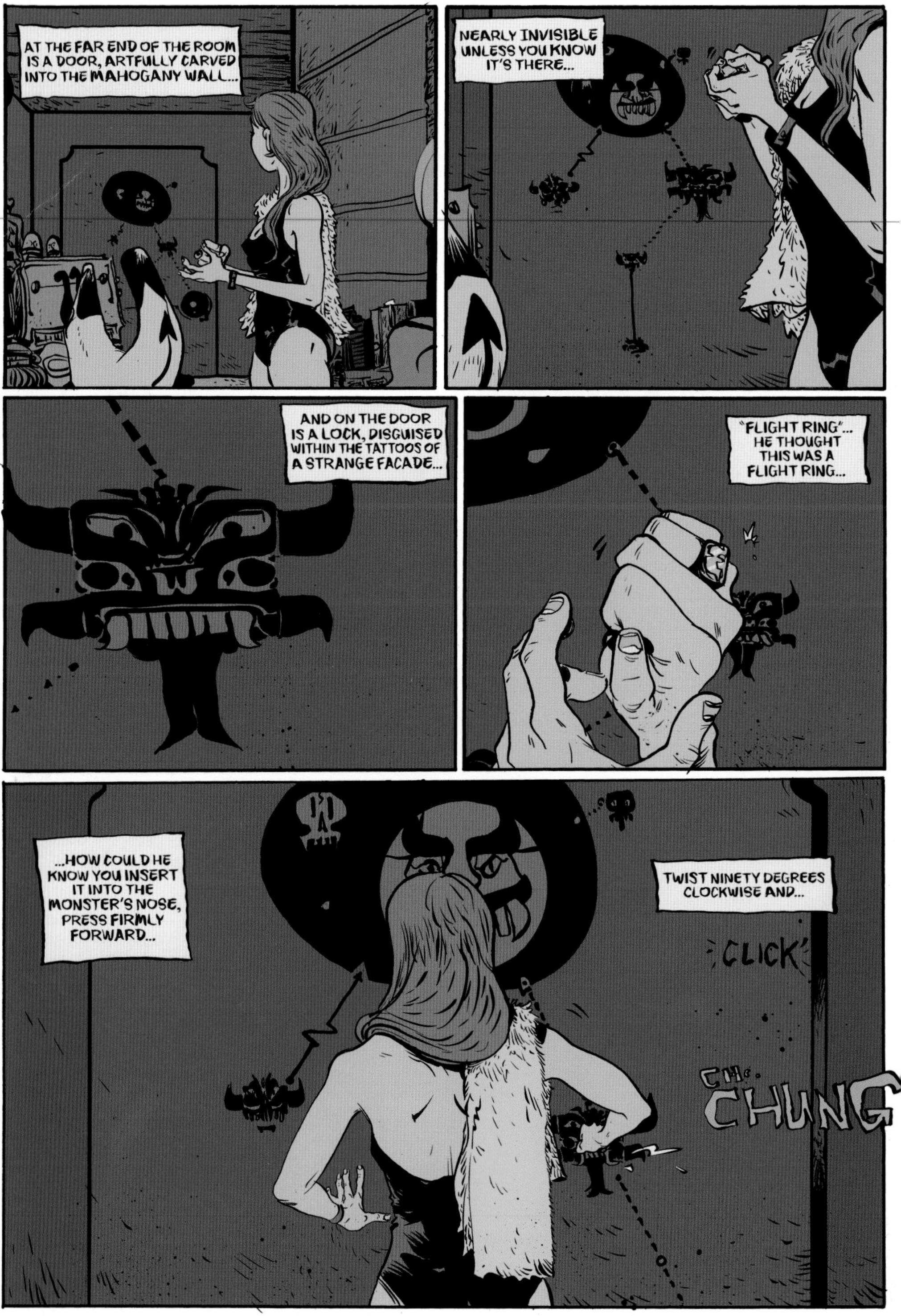
AT THE FAR END OF THE ROOM IS A DOOR, ARTFULLY CARVED INTO THE MAHOGANY WALL...
NEARLY INVISIBLE UNLESS YOU KNOW IT'S THERE...
AND ON THE DOOR IS A LOCK, DISGUISED WITHIN THE TATTOOS OF A STRANGE FACADE...
"FLIGHT RING"... HE THOUGHT THIS WAS A FLIGHT RING...
...HOW COULD HE KNOW YOU INSERT IT INTO THE MONSTER'S NOSE, PRESS FIRMLY FORWARD...
TWIST NINETY DEGREES CLOCKWISE AND...
CLICK
CH CHUNG

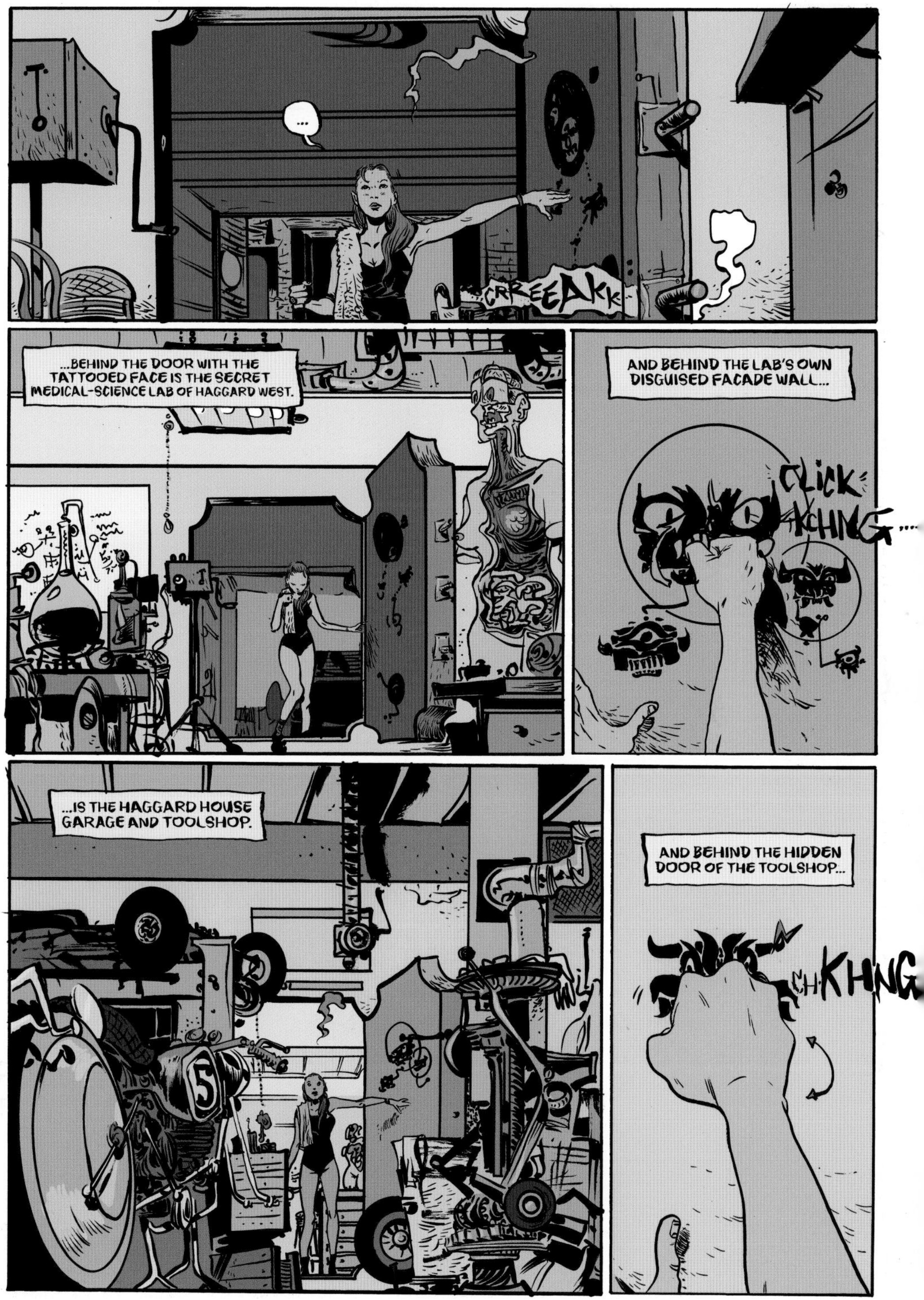
...
CRREEAKK
...BEHIND THE DOOR WITH THE TATTOOED FACE IS THE SECRET MEDICAL-SCIENCE LAB OF HAGGARD WEST.
AND BEHIND THE LAB'S OWN DISGUISED FACADE WALL...
CLICK
KCHNG...
...IS THE HAGGARD HOUSE GARAGE AND TOOLSHOP.
AND BEHIND THE HIDDEN DOOR OF THE TOOLSHOP...
CH-KHNG

THE WEAPONS ROOM.

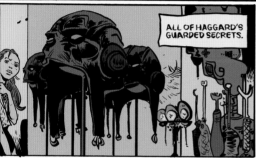

ALL OF HAGGARD'S GUARDED SECRETS.

HIS EXPERIMENTS AND FINDINGS.

AND IN THE CORNER OF THE ARSENAL AN ORNATE LOCKED WOODEN BOX:

ONLY TWO PEOPLE HAVE EVER KNOWN THE COMBINATION TO THE BOX'S MAGNOLOCK...

1 2 3 4 5

BLEEP BLOOPT! BLP!

1 2 3 4 5

...NOW, IT'S ONLY ONE.

KTCHACHK!

TCHKF!!

1 2 3 4 5

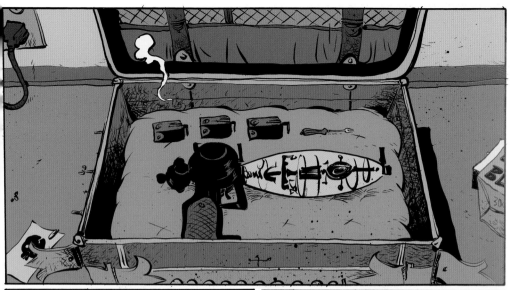

HAGGARD'S BLASTER— THREE SHOTS PER MINUTE. WHEN FULLY-CHARGED... LETHAL.

HE ALWAYS HINTED HE HAD OTHER SECRETS FOR HER WHEN SHE WAS OLDER...

:POK!

...BUT WHAT THOSE MIGHT BE SHE'LL NEVER KNOW.

KA-CHACK!!

...AND IT WAS THERE, IN THAT ROOM, ON THE AFTERNOON OF THE THIRD DAY...

...AURORA KNEW WHAT SHE WOULD DO.

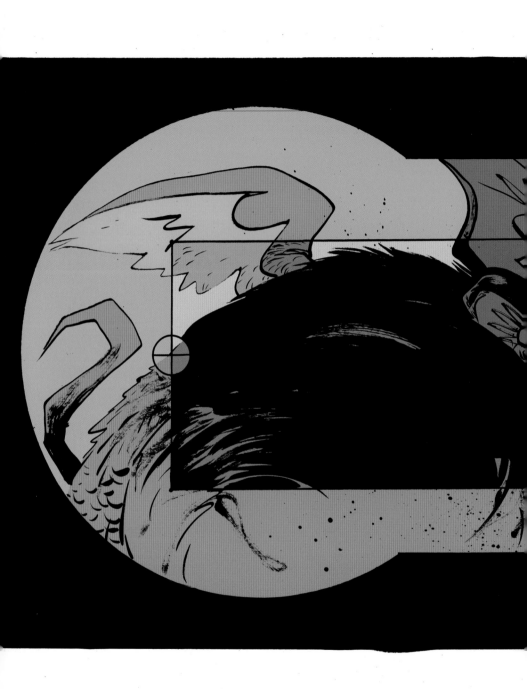

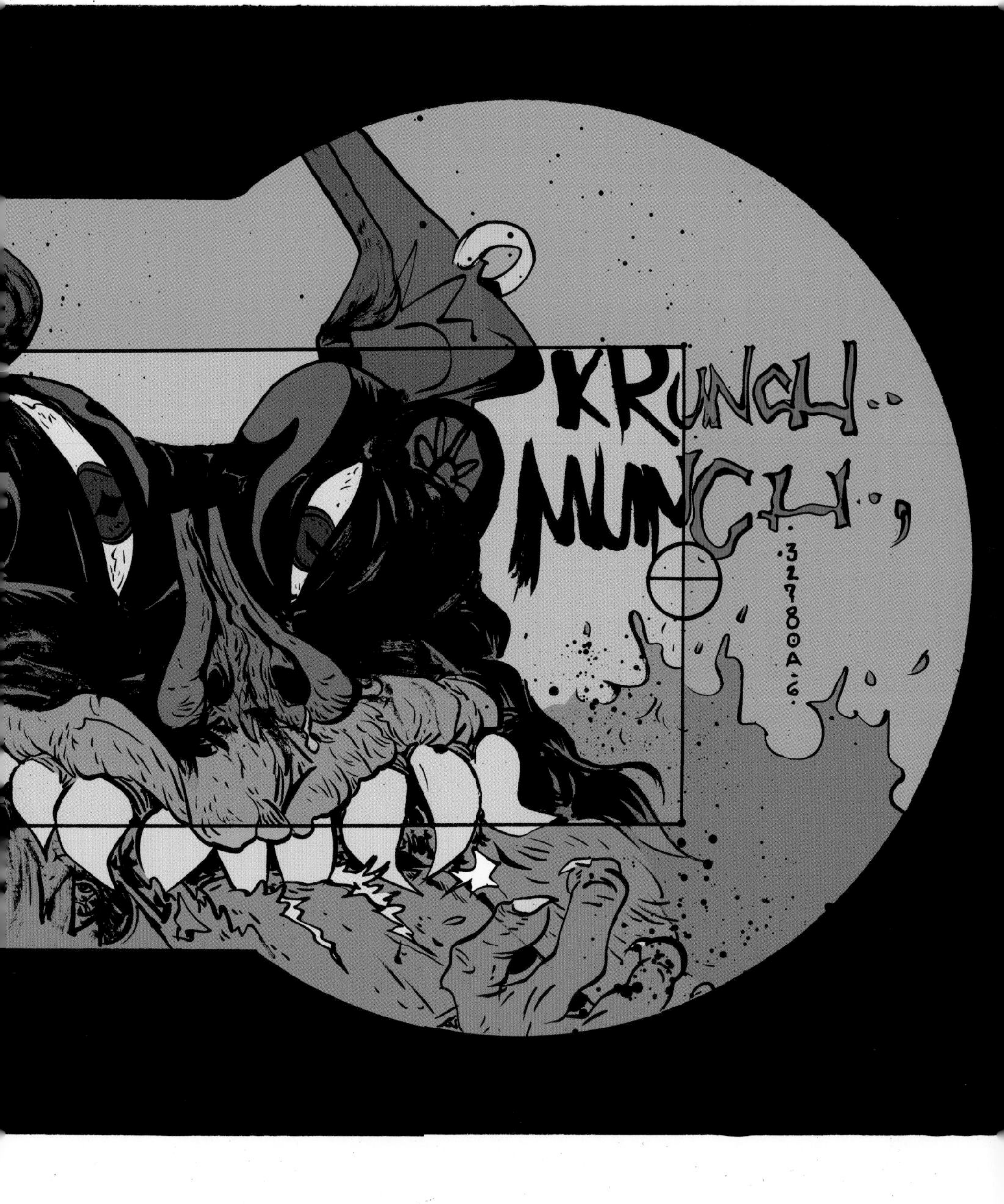
KRUNCH
MUNCH
3278OA6

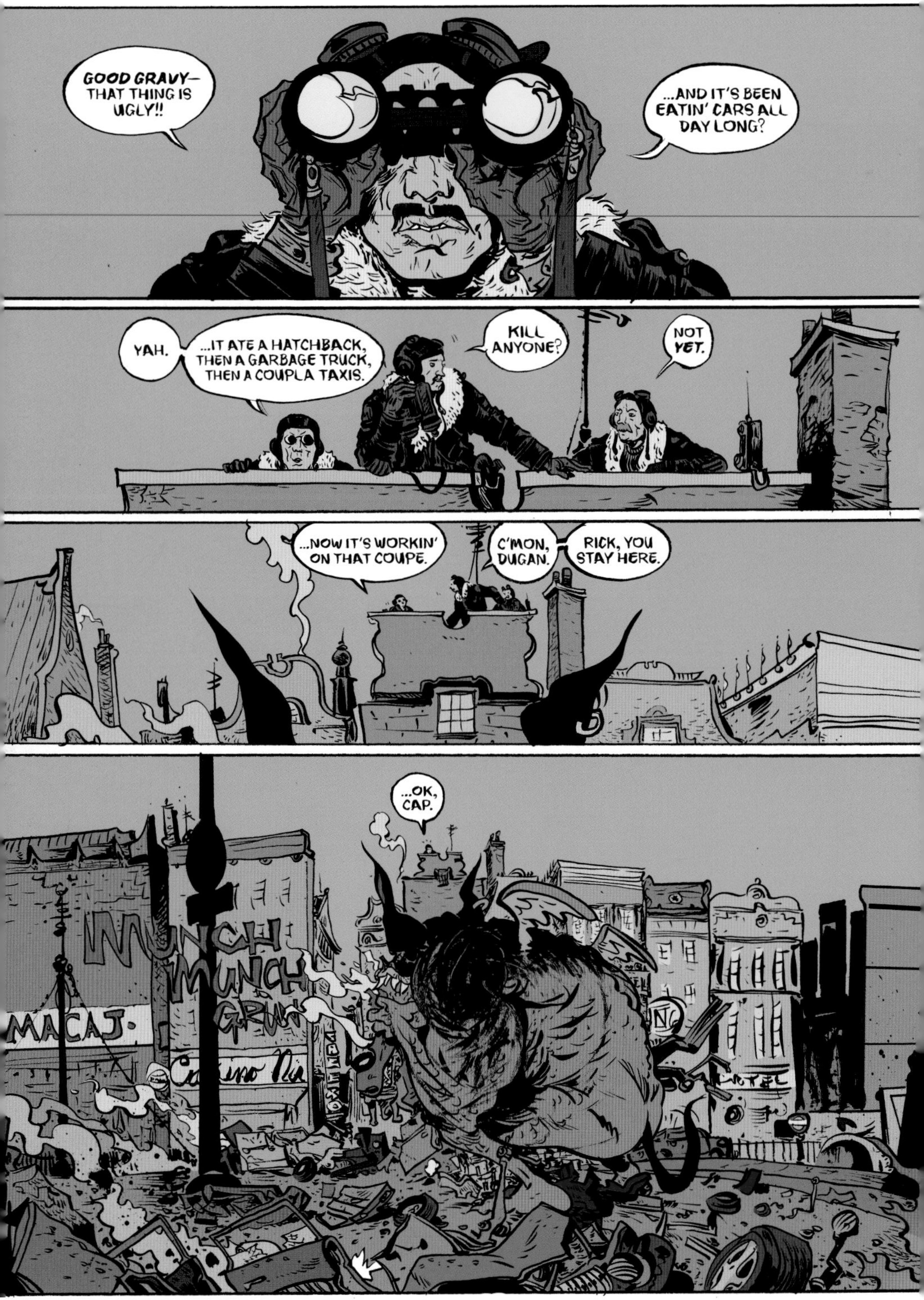
GOOD GRAVY—THAT THING IS UGLY!!
...AND IT'S BEEN EATIN' CARS ALL DAY LONG?
YAH.
...IT ATE A HATCHBACK, THEN A GARBAGE TRUCK, THEN A COUPLA TAXIS.
KILL ANYONE?
NOT YET.
...NOW IT'S WORKIN' ON THAT COUPE.
C'MON, DUGAN.
RICK, YOU STAY HERE.
...OK, CAP.
MUNCH
MUNCH
MACAJ

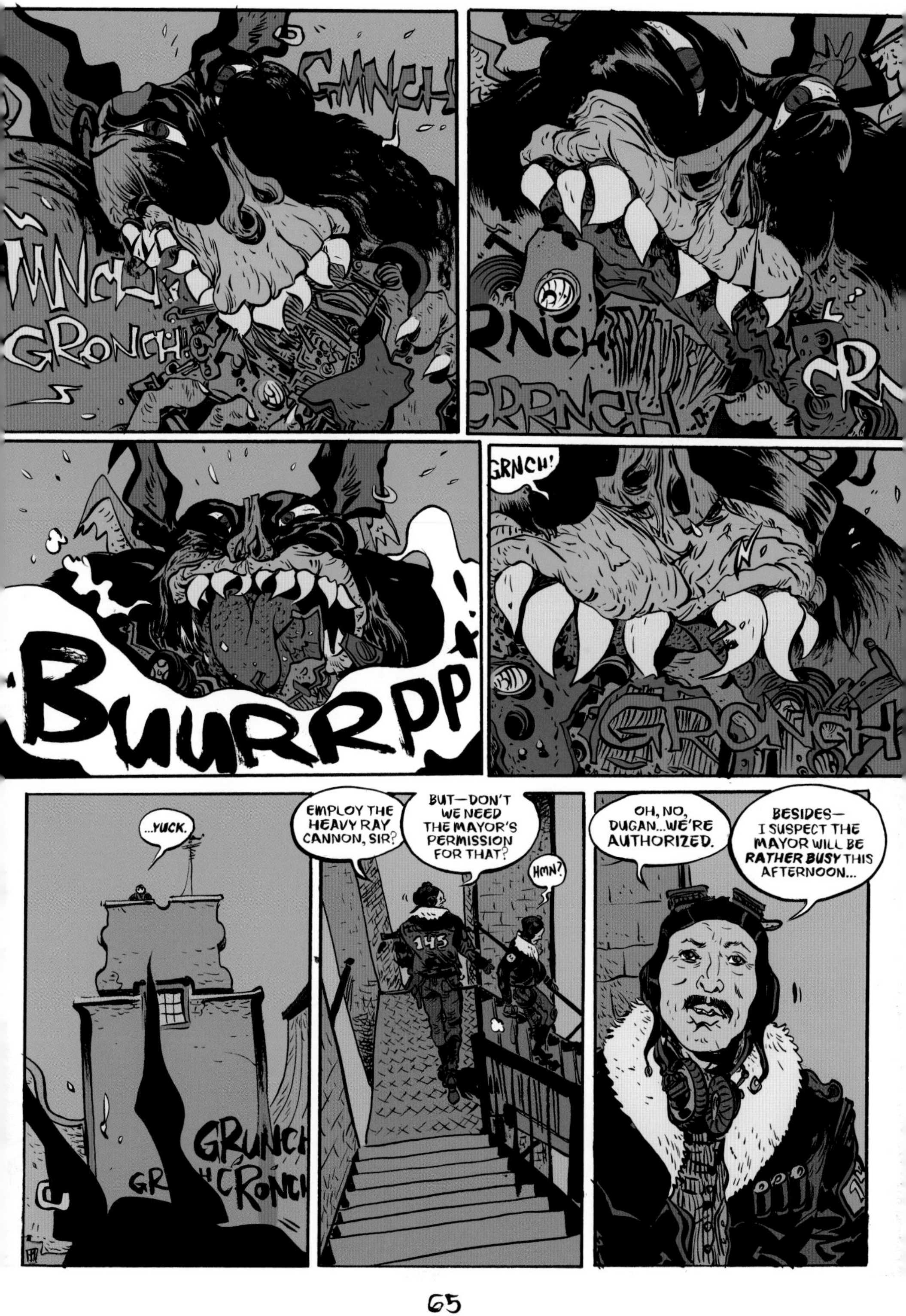
GMNCH
MNCH!
GRONCH!
RNCH
CRRNCH
CRN
BUURRPP
GRNCH!
GRONCH
...YUCK.
GRUNCH
GR
CRONCH
EMPLOY THE HEAVY RAY CANNON, SIR?
BUT—DON'T WE NEED THE MAYOR'S PERMISSION FOR THAT?
HMN?
OH, NO, DUGAN...WE'RE AUTHORIZED.
BESIDES— I SUSPECT THE MAYOR WILL BE RATHER BUSY THIS AFTERNOON...

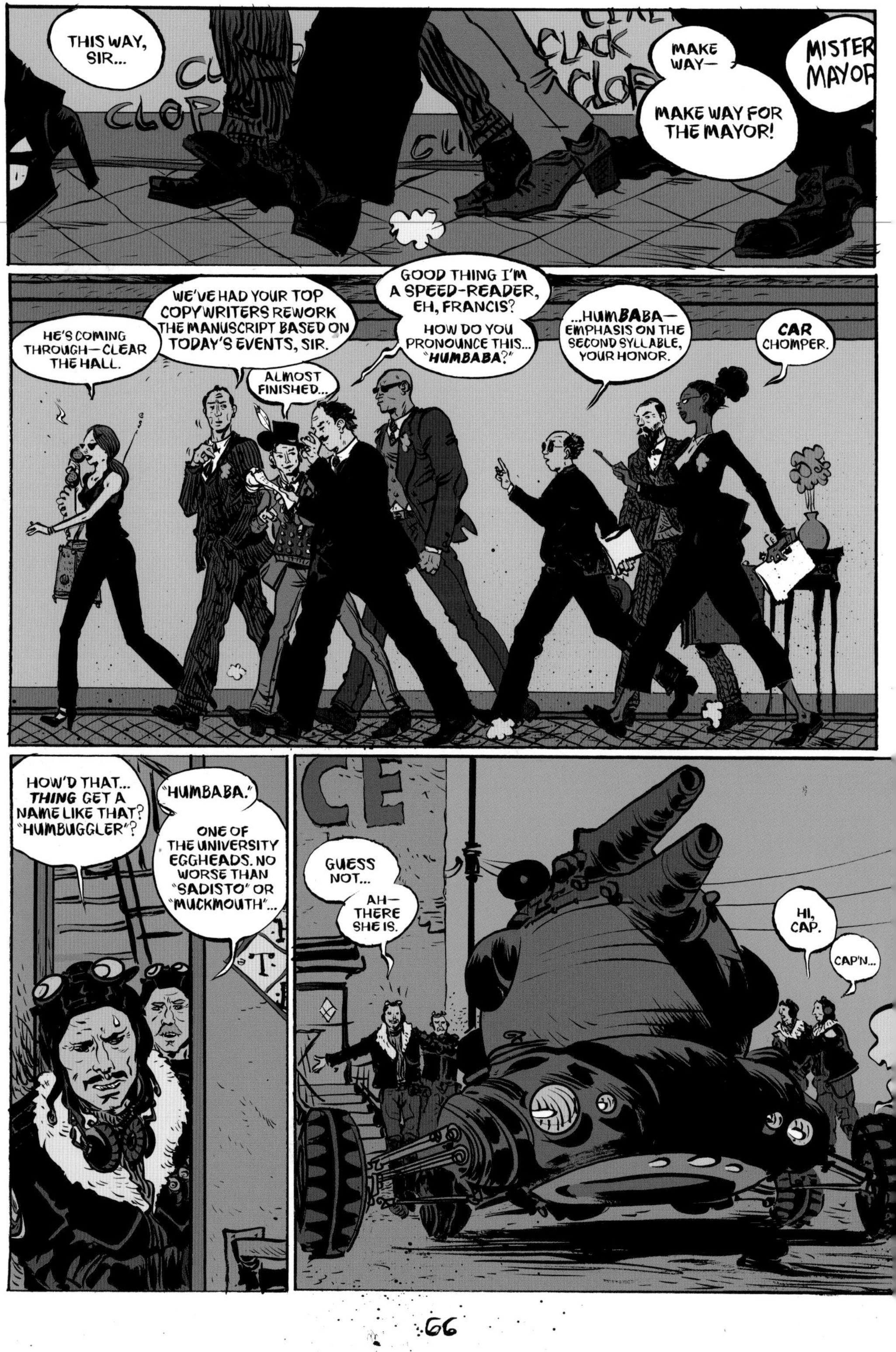

THIS WAY, SIR...
CLOP
CLACK
CLOP
MAKE WAY—
MAKE WAY FOR THE MAYOR!
MISTER MAYOR
HE'S COMING THROUGH—CLEAR THE HALL.
WE'VE HAD YOUR TOP COPYWRITERS REWORK THE MANUSCRIPT BASED ON TODAY'S EVENTS, SIR.
ALMOST FINISHED...
GOOD THING I'M A SPEED-READER, EH, FRANCIS?
HOW DO YOU PRONOUNCE THIS... "HUMBABA?"
...HUMBABA— EMPHASIS ON THE SECOND SYLLABLE, YOUR HONOR.
CAR CHOMPER.
HOW'D THAT... THING GET A NAME LIKE THAT? "HUMBUGGLER"?
"HUMBABA."
ONE OF THE UNIVERSITY EGGHEADS. NO WORSE THAN "SADISTO" OR "MUCKMOUTH"...
GUESS NOT...
AH— THERE SHE IS.
HI, CAP.
CAP'N...

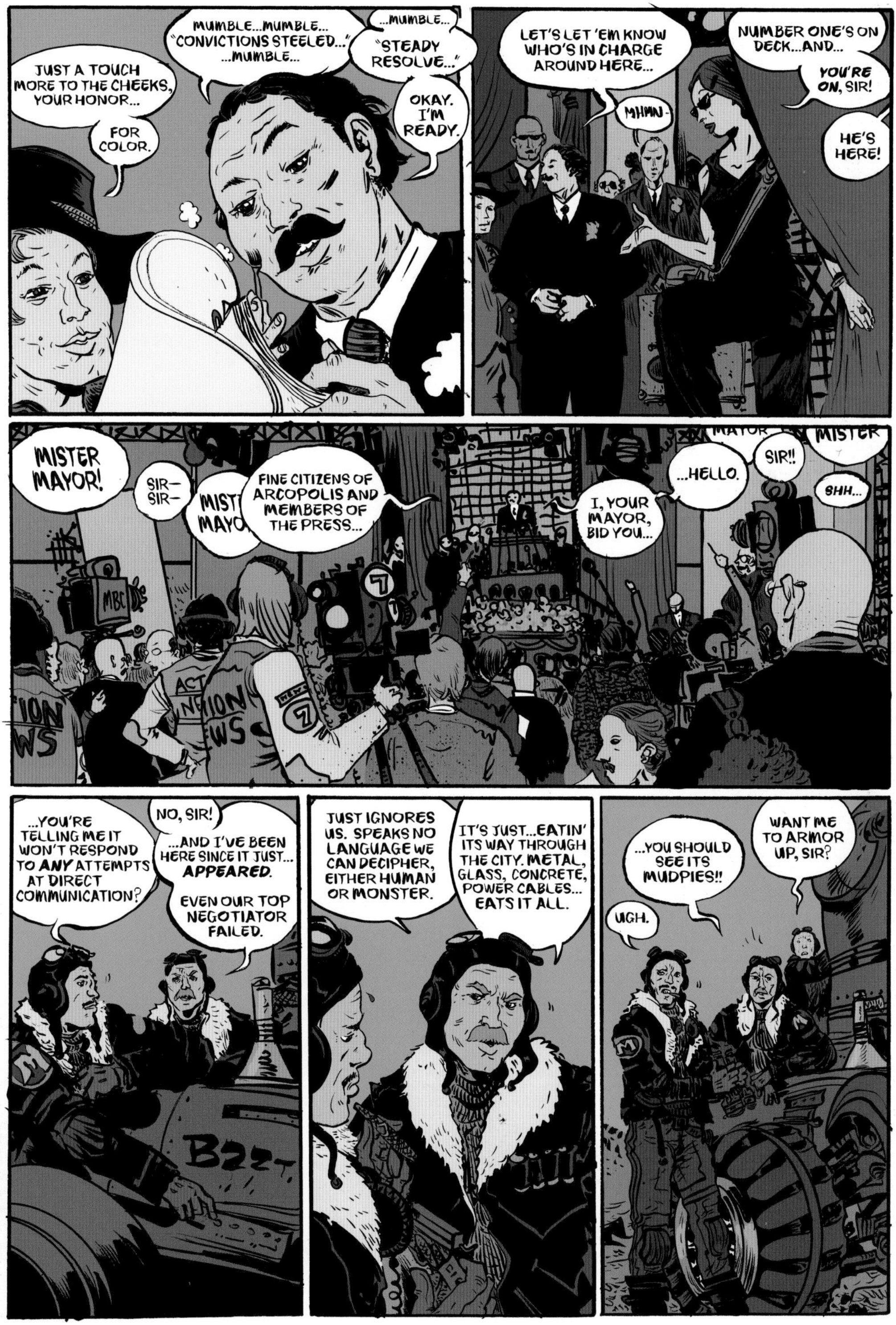
JUST A TOUCH MORE TO THE CHEEKS, YOUR HONOR...
FOR COLOR.
MUMBLE...MUMBLE... "CONVICTIONS STEELED..." ...MUMBLE...
...MUMBLE...
"STEADY RESOLVE..."
OKAY. I'M READY.
LET'S LET 'EM KNOW WHO'S IN CHARGE AROUND HERE...
MHMN-
NUMBER ONE'S ON DECK...AND...
YOU'RE ON, SIR!
HE'S HERE!
MISTER MAYOR!
SIR- SIR-
FINE CITIZENS OF ARCOPOLIS AND MEMBERS OF THE PRESS...
I, YOUR MAYOR, BID YOU...
...HELLO.
SIR!!
MISTER
SHH...
...YOU'RE TELLING ME IT WON'T RESPOND TO ANY ATTEMPTS AT DIRECT COMMUNICATION?
NO, SIR!
...AND I'VE BEEN HERE SINCE IT JUST... APPEARED.
EVEN OUR TOP NEGOTIATOR FAILED.
BZZ-
JUST IGNORES US. SPEAKS NO LANGUAGE WE CAN DECIPHER, EITHER HUMAN OR MONSTER.
IT'S JUST...EATIN' ITS WAY THROUGH THE CITY. METAL, GLASS, CONCRETE, POWER CABLES... EATS IT ALL.
...YOU SHOULD SEE ITS MUDPIES!!
UGH.
WANT ME TO ARMOR UP, SIR?

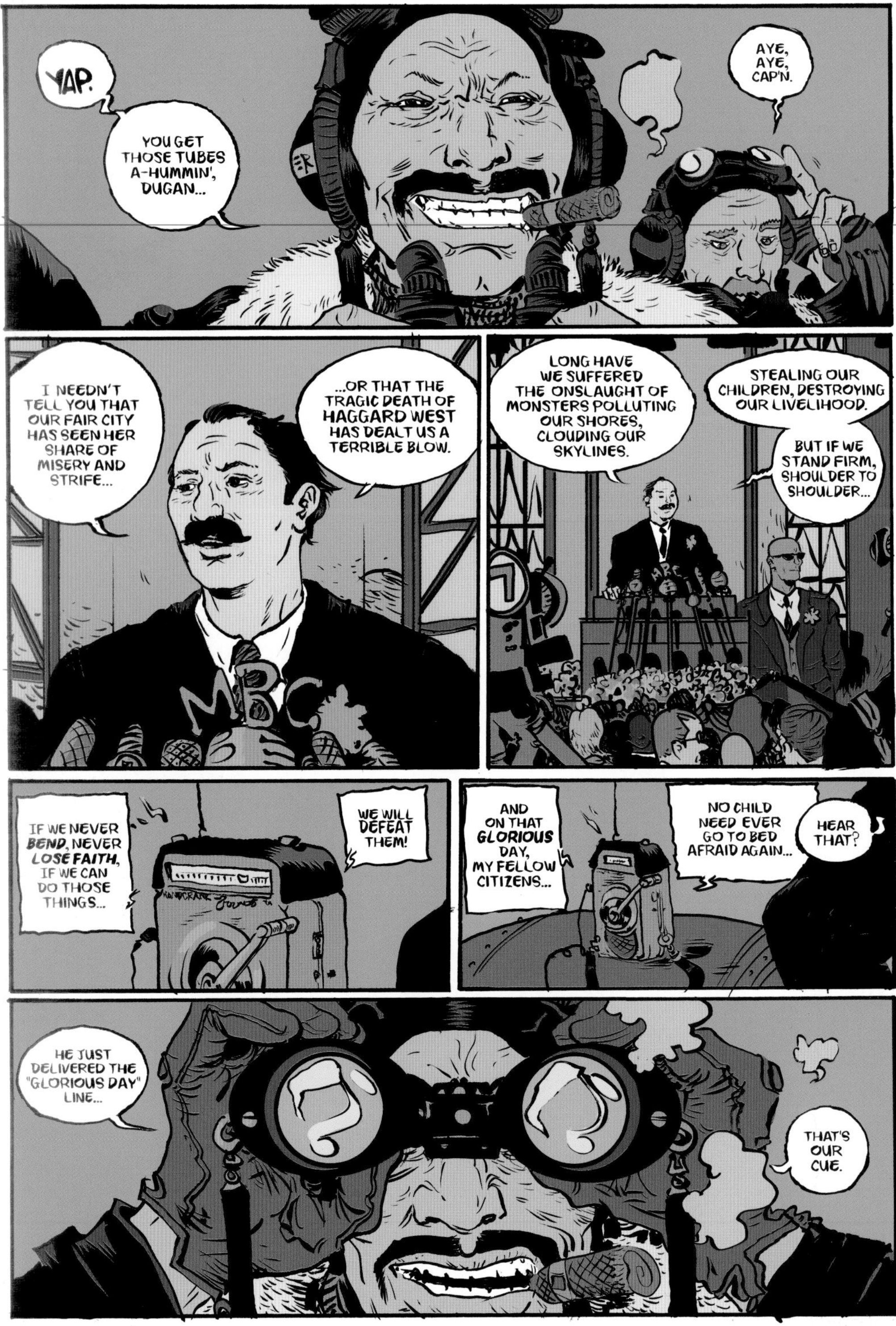
YAP.
YOU GET THOSE TUBES A-HUMMIN', DUGAN...
AYE, AYE, CAP'N.
I NEEDN'T TELL YOU THAT OUR FAIR CITY HAS SEEN HER SHARE OF MISERY AND STRIFE...
...OR THAT THE TRAGIC DEATH OF HAGGARD WEST HAS DEALT US A TERRIBLE BLOW.
LONG HAVE WE SUFFERED THE ONSLAUGHT OF MONSTERS POLLUTING OUR SHORES, CLOUDING OUR SKYLINES.
STEALING OUR CHILDREN, DESTROYING OUR LIVELIHOOD.
BUT IF WE STAND FIRM, SHOULDER TO SHOULDER...
IF WE NEVER BEND, NEVER LOSE FAITH, IF WE CAN DO THOSE THINGS...
WE WILL DEFEAT THEM!
AND ON THAT GLORIOUS DAY, MY FELLOW CITIZENS...
NO CHILD NEED EVER GO TO BED AFRAID AGAIN...
HEAR THAT?
HE JUST DELIVERED THE "GLORIOUS DAY" LINE...
THAT'S OUR CUE.

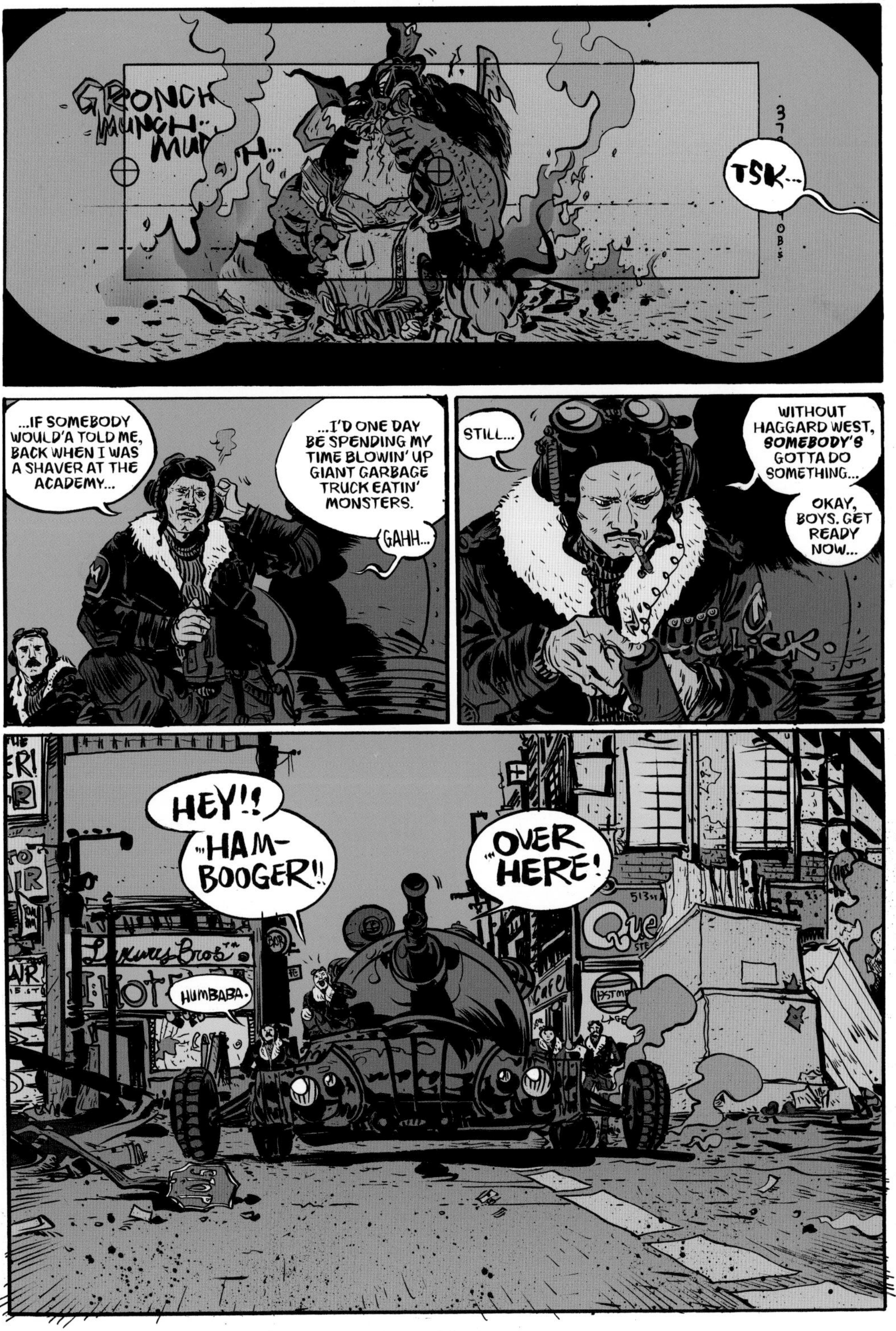
GRONCH
MUNCH...
MUNCH...
TSK...
...IF SOMEBODY WOULD'A TOLD ME, BACK WHEN I WAS A SHAVER AT THE ACADEMY...
...I'D ONE DAY BE SPENDING MY TIME BLOWIN' UP GIANT GARBAGE TRUCK EATIN' MONSTERS.
GAHH...
STILL...
WITHOUT HAGGARD WEST, SOMEBODY'S GOTTA DO SOMETHING...
OKAY, BOYS. GET READY NOW...
CLICK
HEY!!
HAM-BOOGER!!
OVER HERE!
HUMBABA.

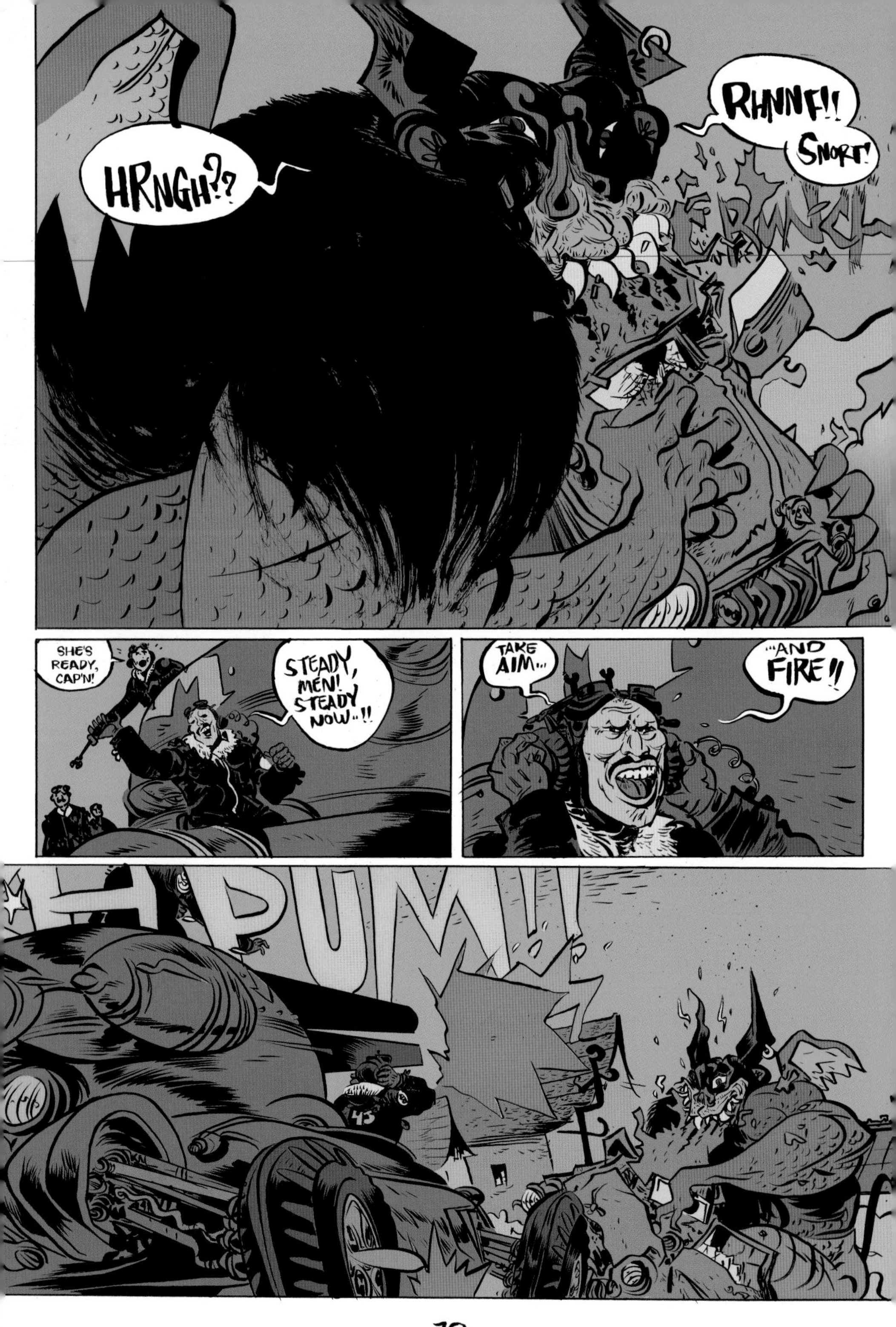
RHNNF!!
SNORT!
HRNGH!?
SHE'S READY, CAP'N!
STEADY, MEN! STEADY NOW..!!
TAKE AIM...
...AND FIRE!!
PUM!!

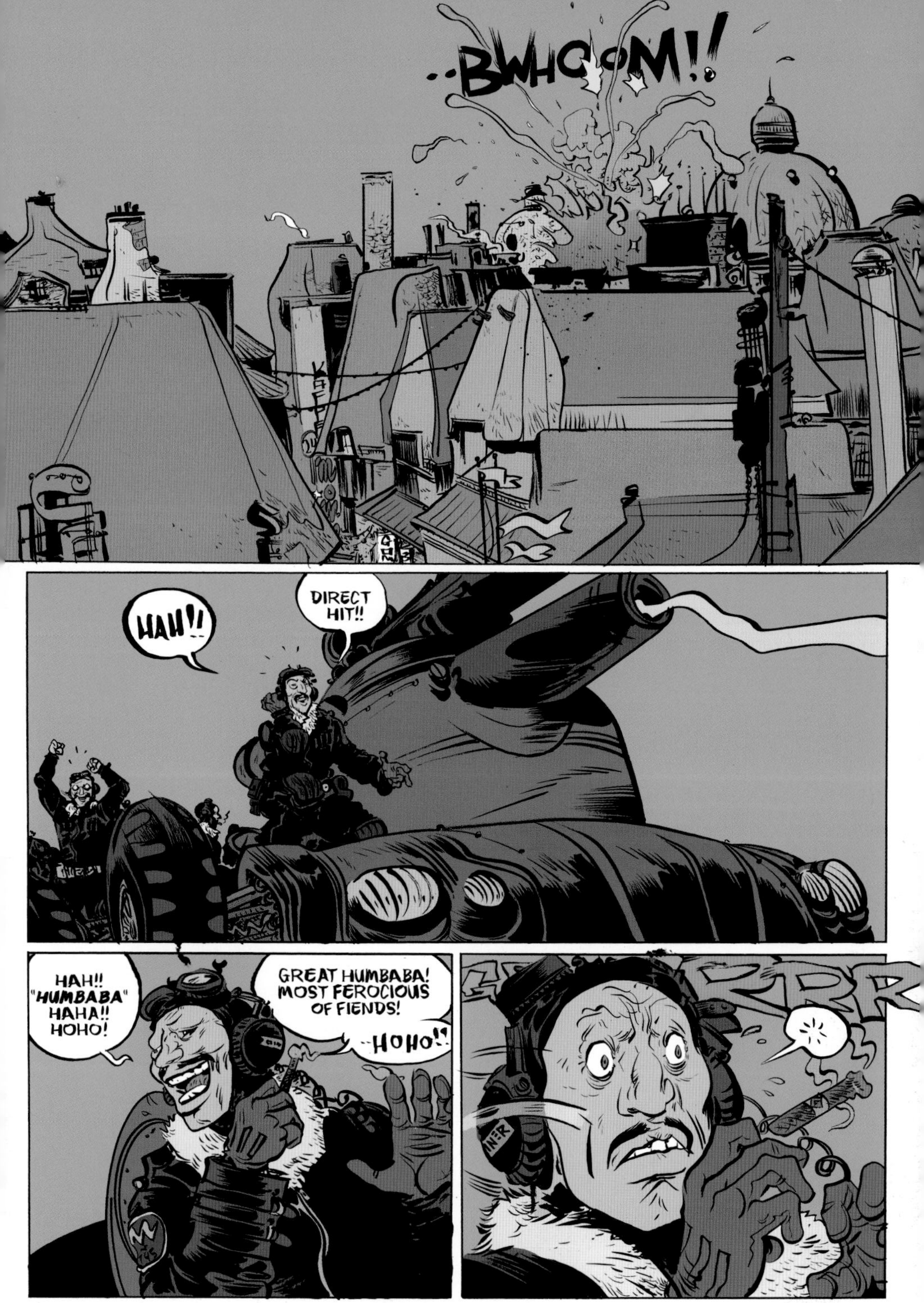
BWHOOM!!
HAH!!
DIRECT HIT!!
HAH!! "HUMBABA" HAHA!! HOHO!
GREAT HUMBABA! MOST FEROCIOUS OF FIENDS!
HOHO!!

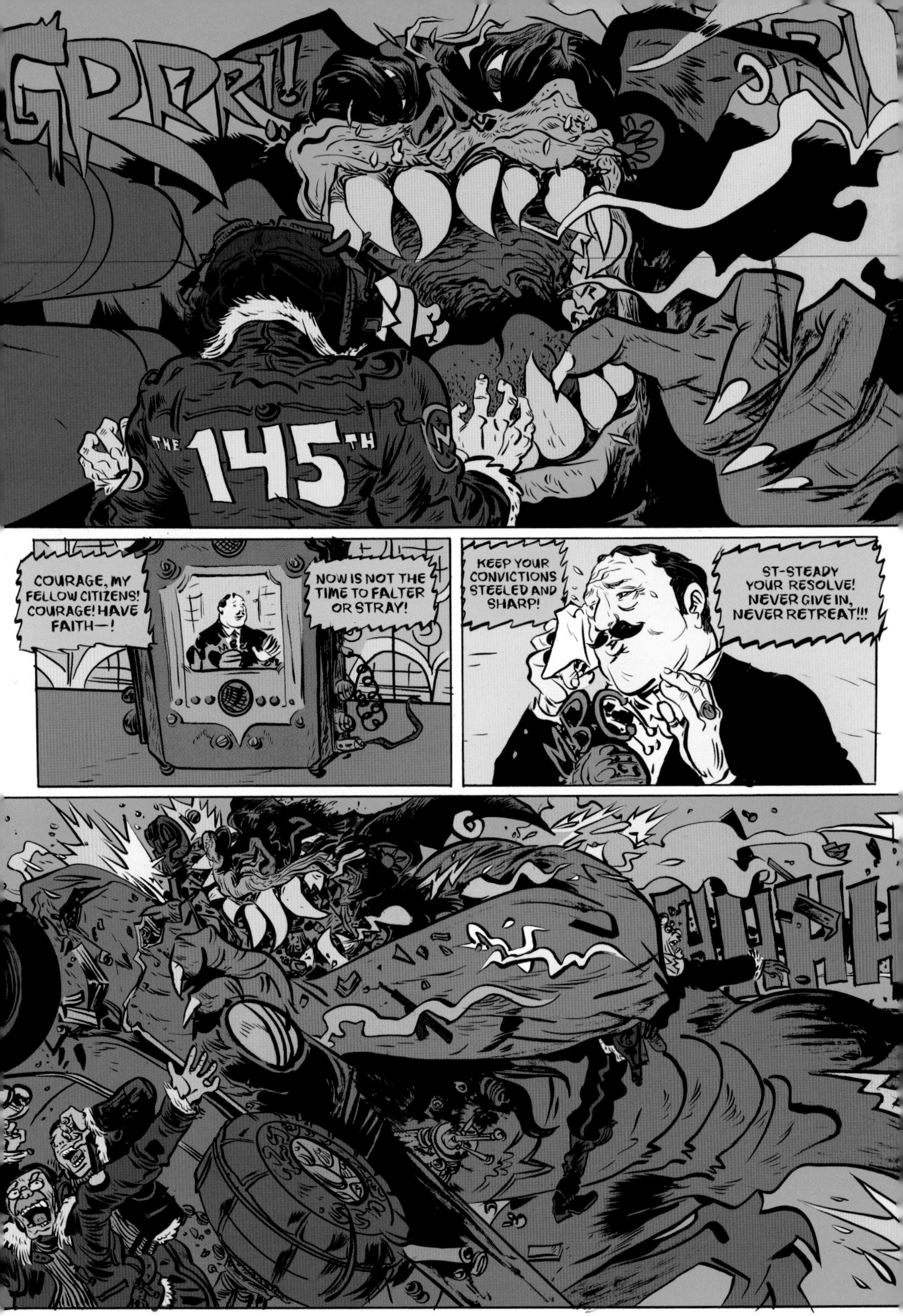
THE 145TH
COURAGE, MY FELLOW CITIZENS! COURAGE! HAVE FAITH—!
NOW IS NOT THE TIME TO FALTER OR STRAY!
KEEP YOUR CONVICTIONS STEELED AND SHARP!
ST-STEADY YOUR RESOLVE! NEVER GIVE IN, NEVER RETREAT!!!

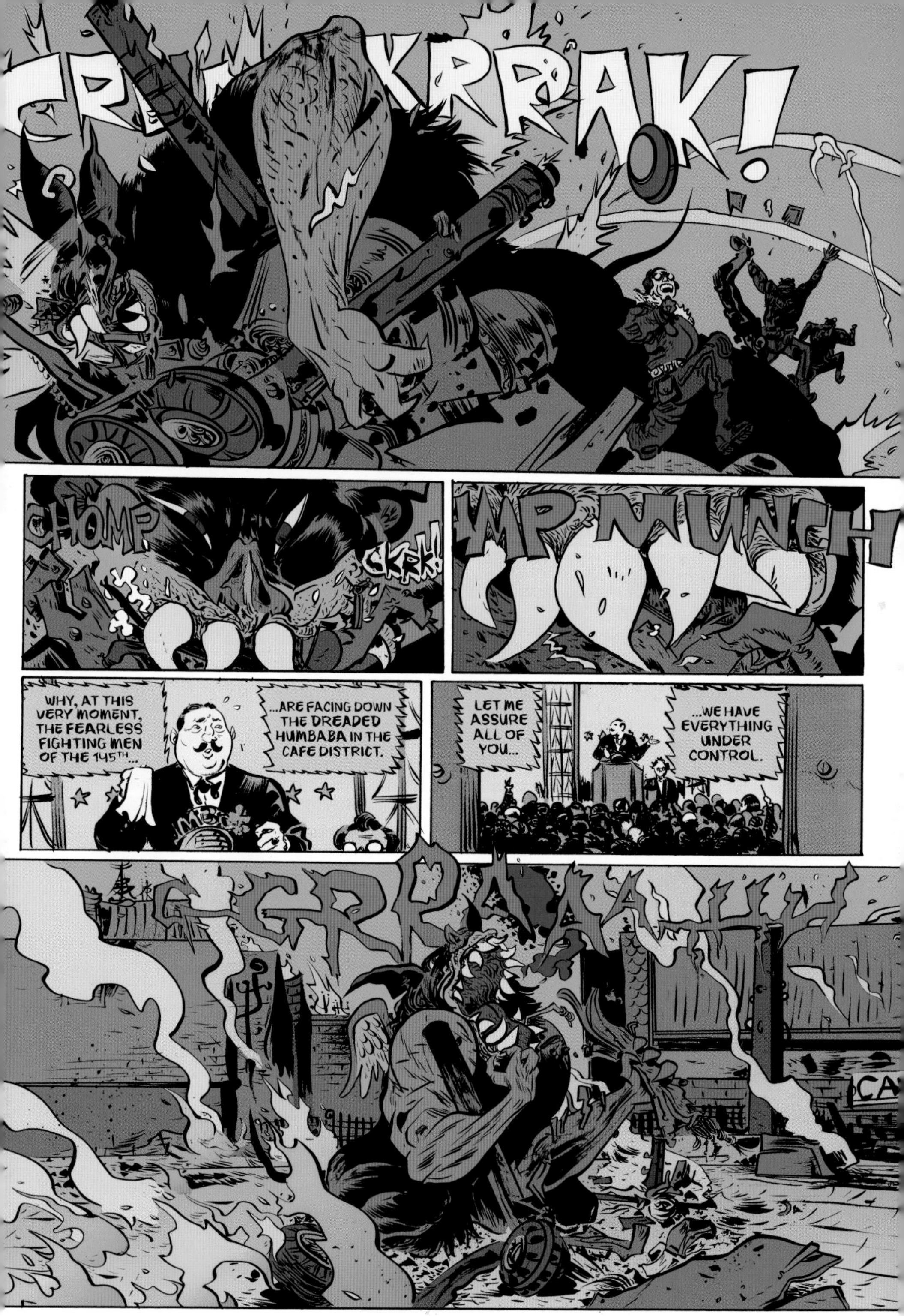
KRRAK!
CHOMP
CKRK!
MP MUNCH
WHY, AT THIS VERY MOMENT, THE FEARLESS FIGHTING MEN OF THE 145TH...
...ARE FACING DOWN THE DREADED HUMBABA IN THE CAFE DISTRICT.
LET ME ASSURE ALL OF YOU...
...WE HAVE EVERYTHING UNDER CONTROL.
GRRAAHH

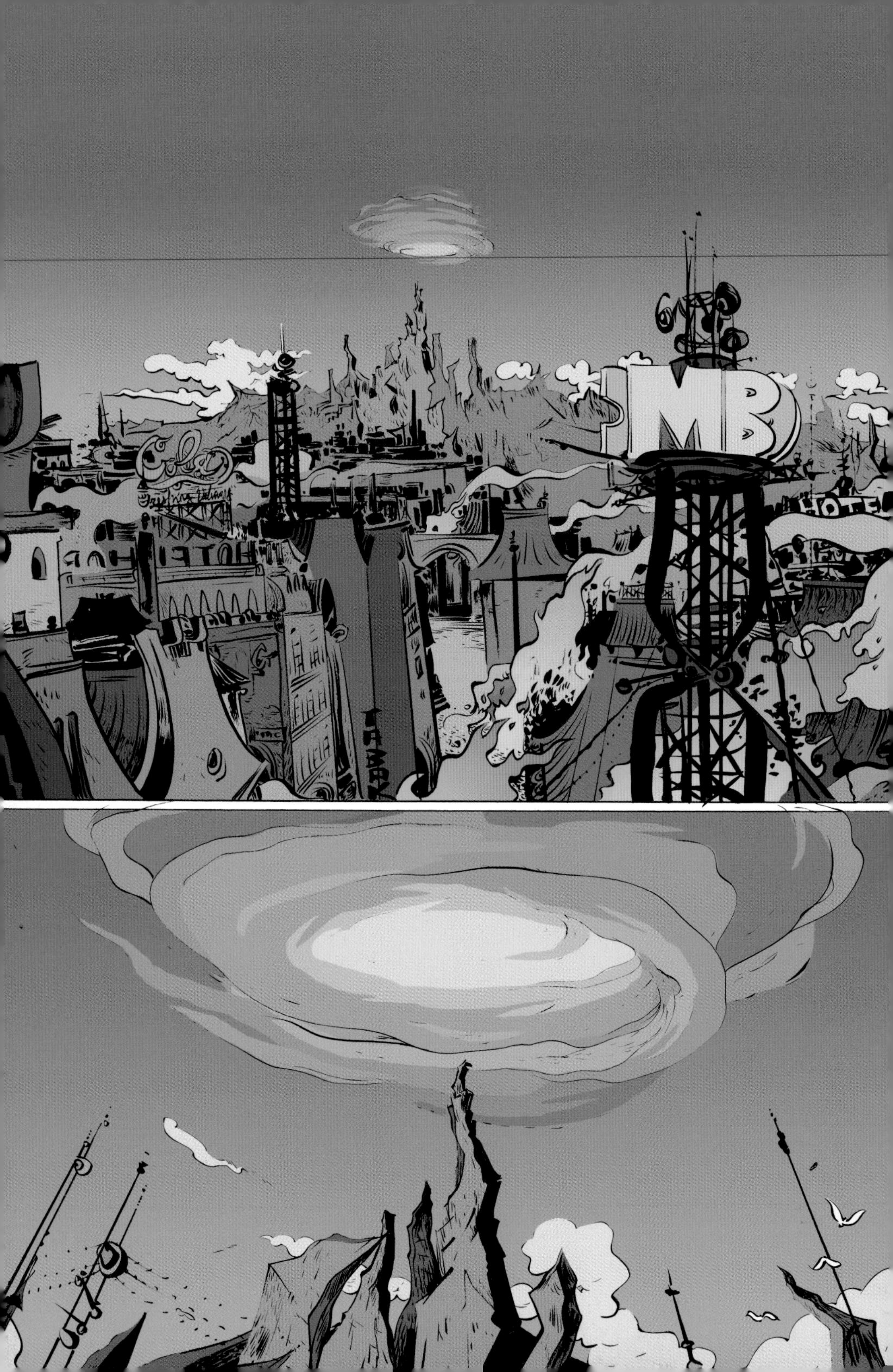
MB
HOTE

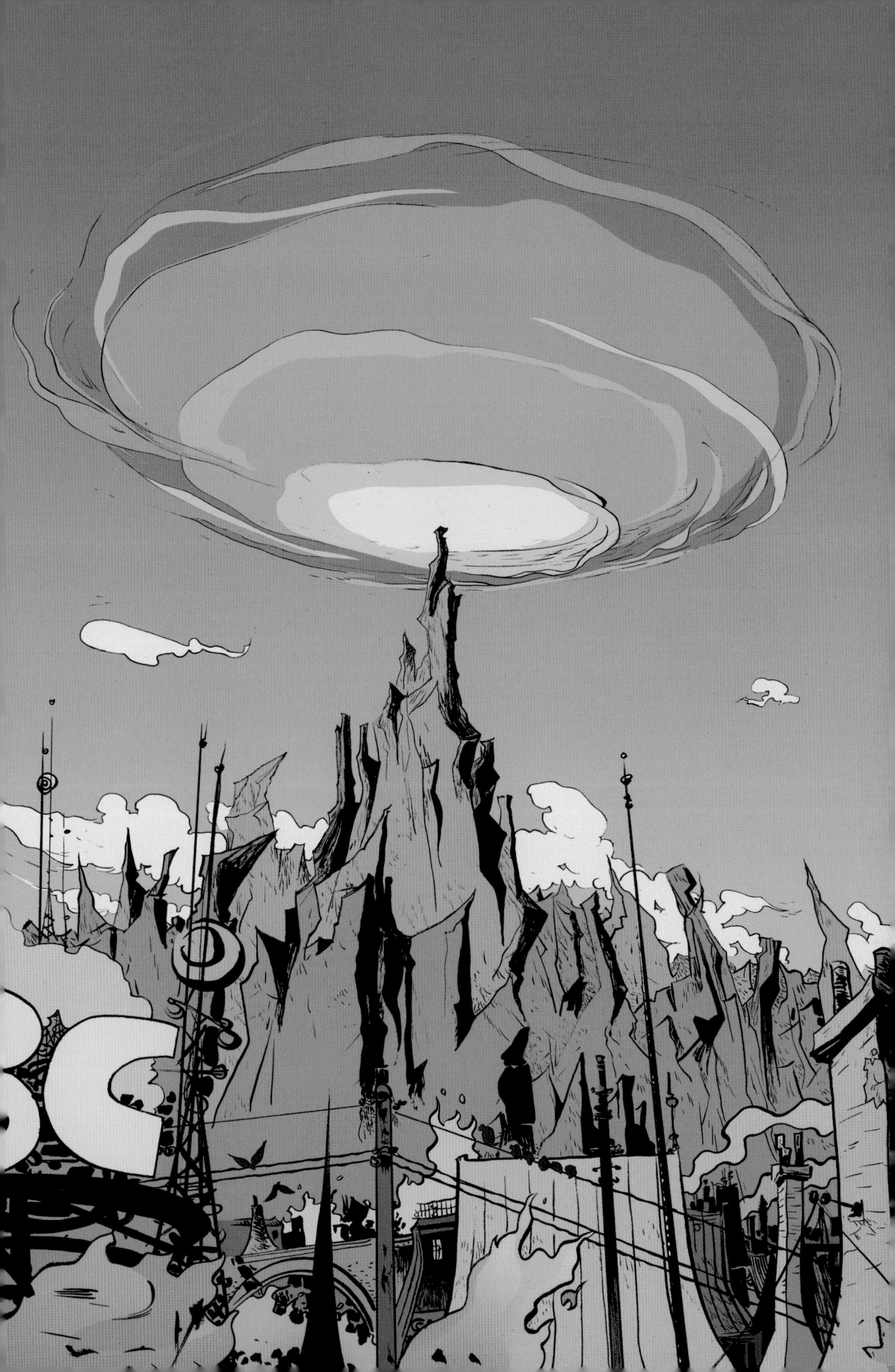

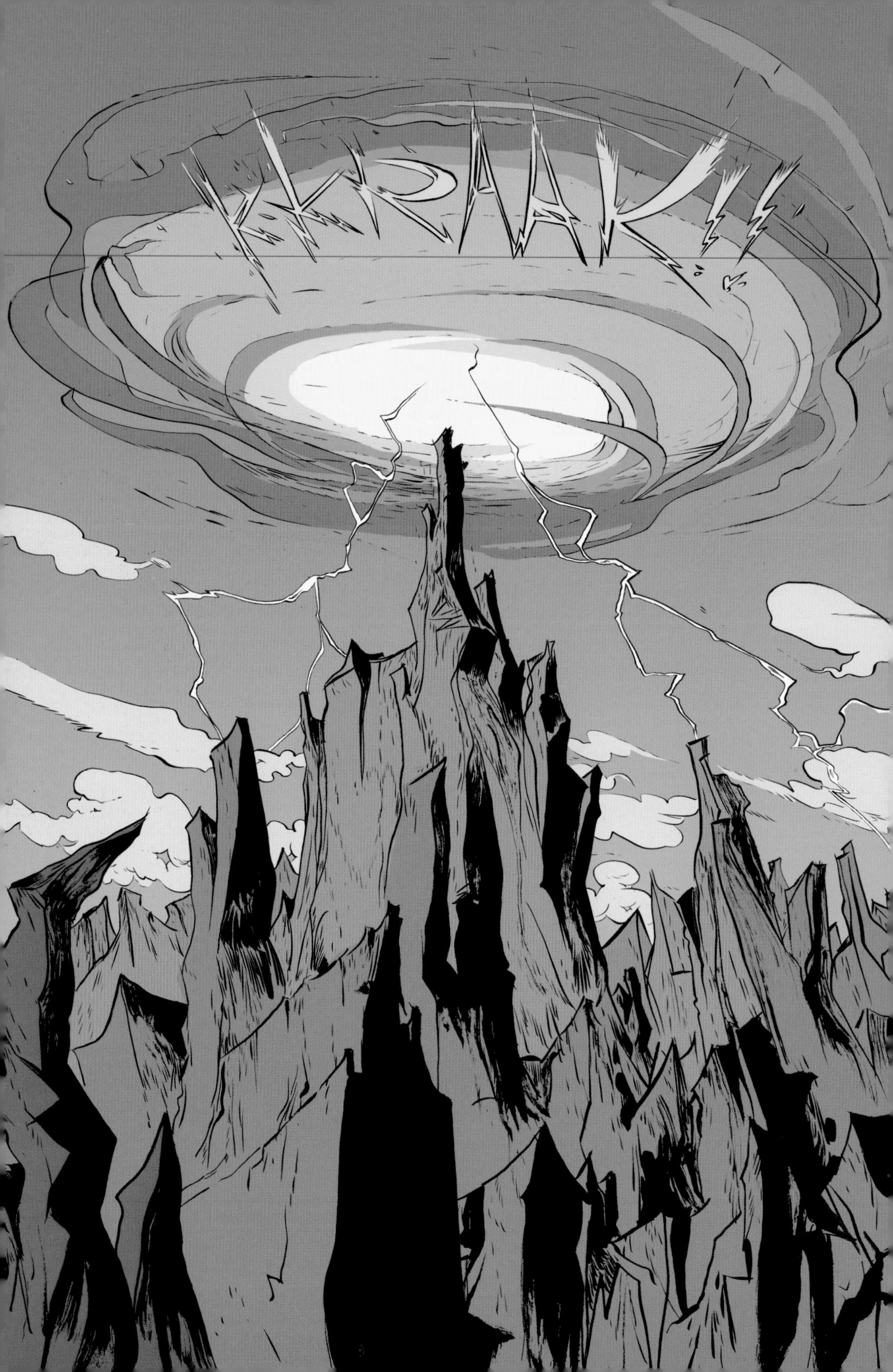
KKRAAK!!

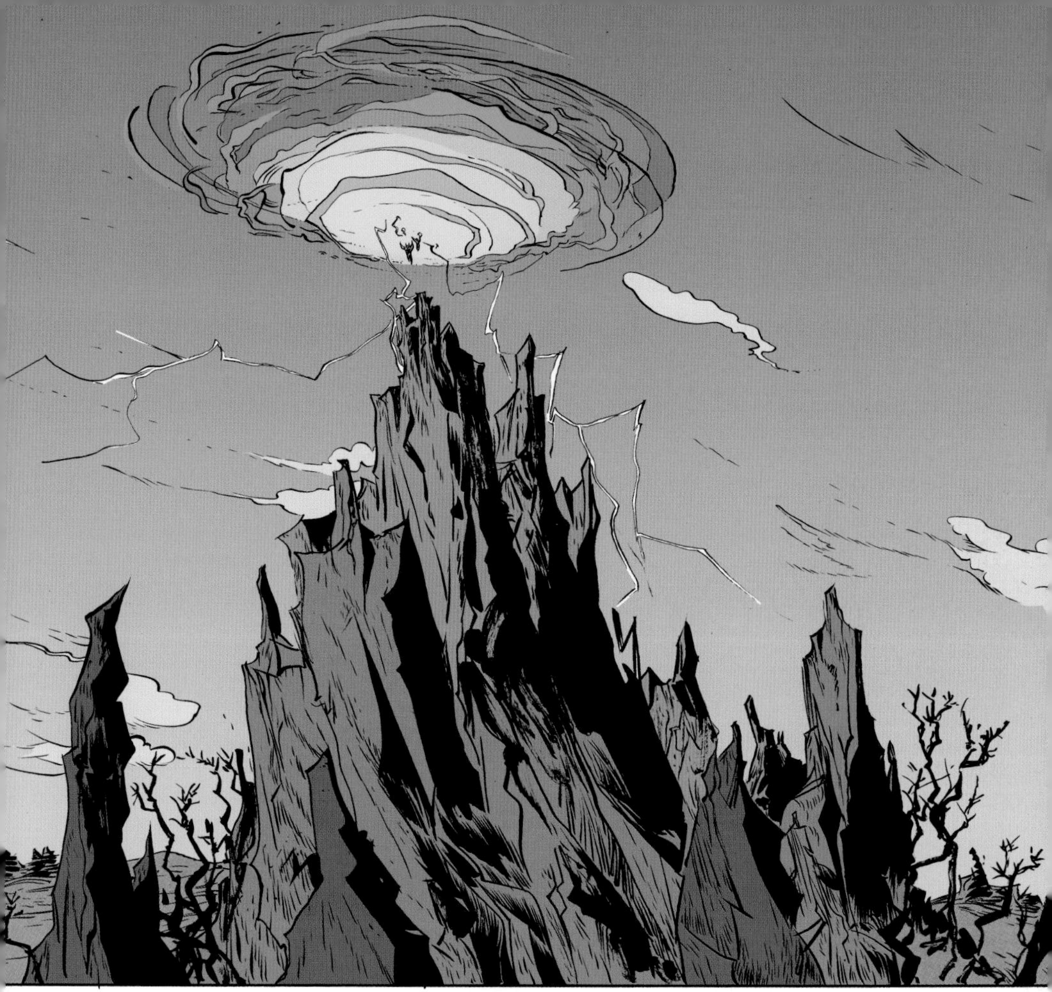
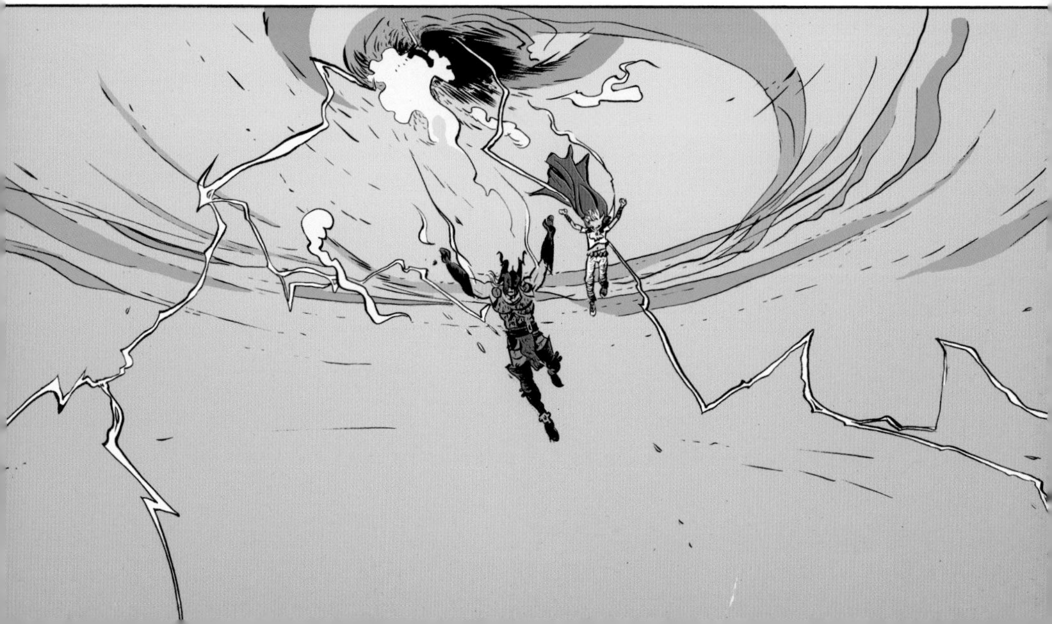

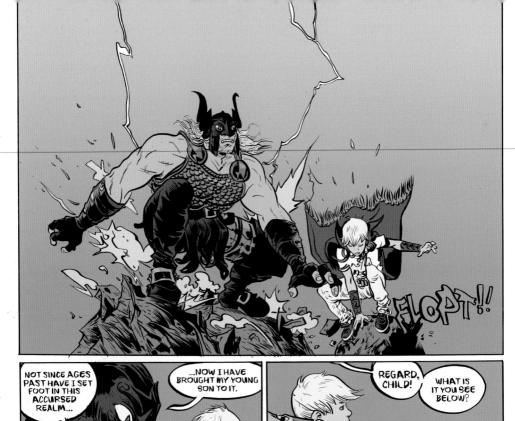

FLOPT!!

NOT SINCE AGES PAST HAVE I SET FOOT IN THIS ACCURSED REALM...

...NOW I HAVE BROUGHT MY YOUNG SON TO IT.

REGARD, CHILD!

WHAT IS IT YOU SEE BELOW?

...!

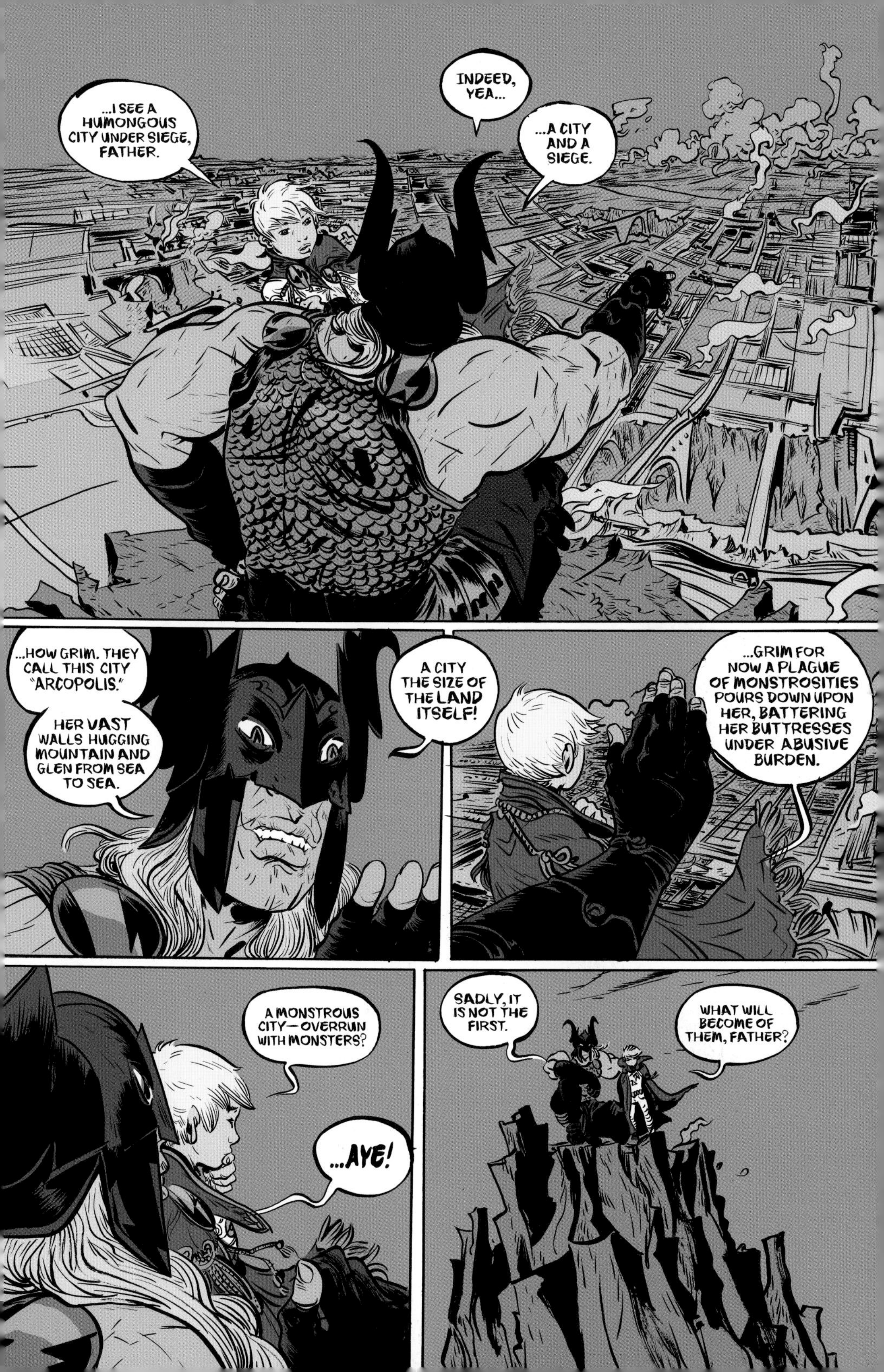
...I SEE A HUMONGOUS CITY UNDER SIEGE, FATHER.
INDEED, YEA...
...A CITY AND A SIEGE.
...HOW GRIM. THEY CALL THIS CITY "ARCOPOLIS."
HER VAST WALLS HUGGING MOUNTAIN AND GLEN FROM SEA TO SEA.
A CITY THE SIZE OF THE LAND ITSELF!
...GRIM FOR NOW A PLAGUE OF MONSTROSITIES POURS DOWN UPON HER, BATTERING HER BUTTRESSES UNDER ABUSIVE BURDEN.
A MONSTROUS CITY—OVERRUN WITH MONSTERS?
...AYE!
SADLY, IT IS NOT THE FIRST.
WHAT WILL BECOME OF THEM, FATHER?

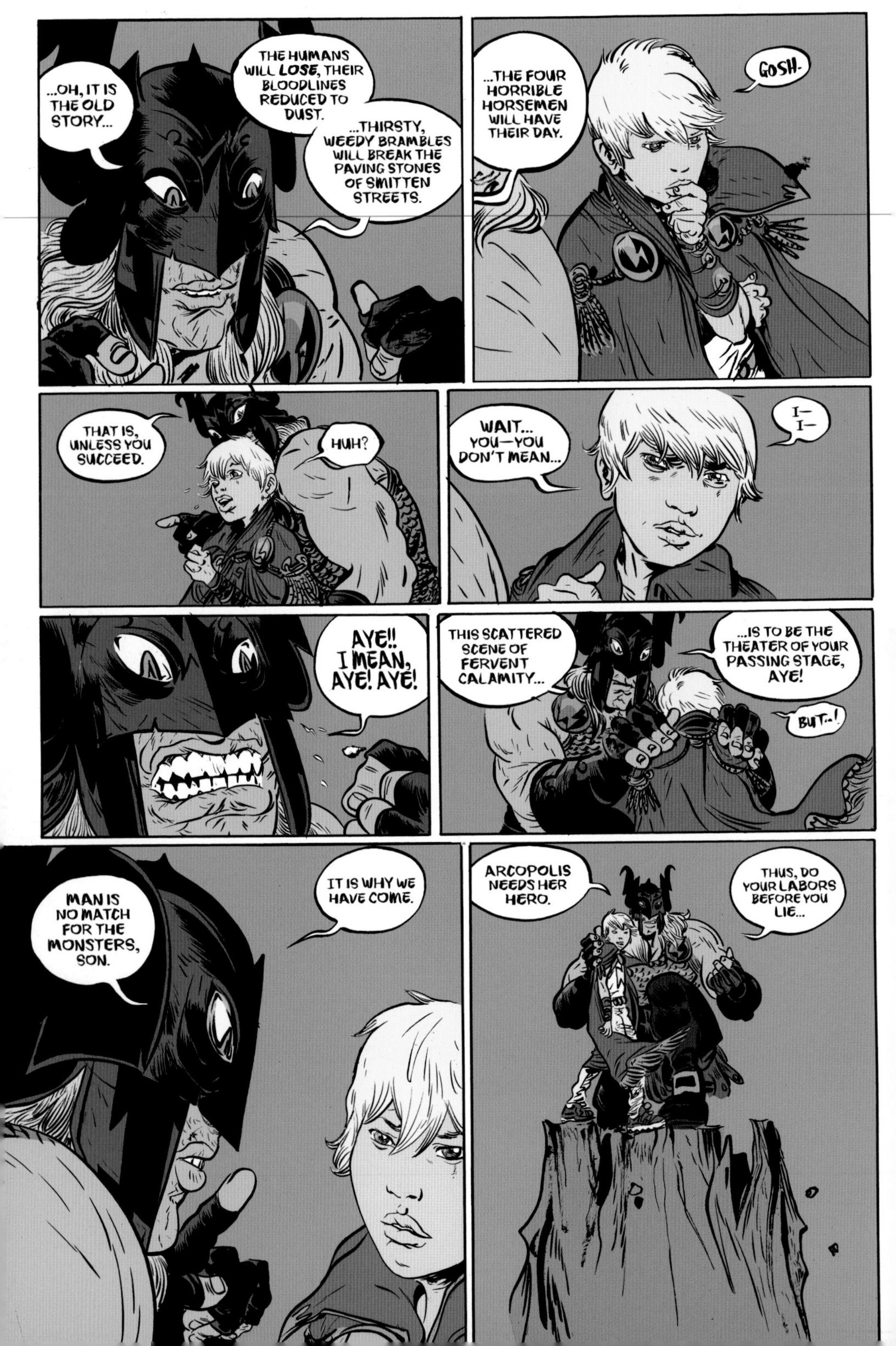
...OH, IT IS THE OLD STORY...
THE HUMANS WILL LOSE, THEIR BLOODLINES REDUCED TO DUST.
...THIRSTY, WEEDY BRAMBLES WILL BREAK THE PAVING STONES OF SMITTEN STREETS.
...THE FOUR HORRIBLE HORSEMEN WILL HAVE THEIR DAY.
GOSH.
THAT IS, UNLESS YOU SUCCEED.
HUH?
WAIT... YOU—YOU DON'T MEAN...
I— I—
AYE!! I MEAN, AYE! AYE!
THIS SCATTERED SCENE OF FERVENT CALAMITY...
...IS TO BE THE THEATER OF YOUR PASSING STAGE, AYE!
BUT..!
MAN IS NO MATCH FOR THE MONSTERS, SON.
IT IS WHY WE HAVE COME.
ARCOPOLIS NEEDS HER HERO.
THUS, DO YOUR LABORS BEFORE YOU LIE...

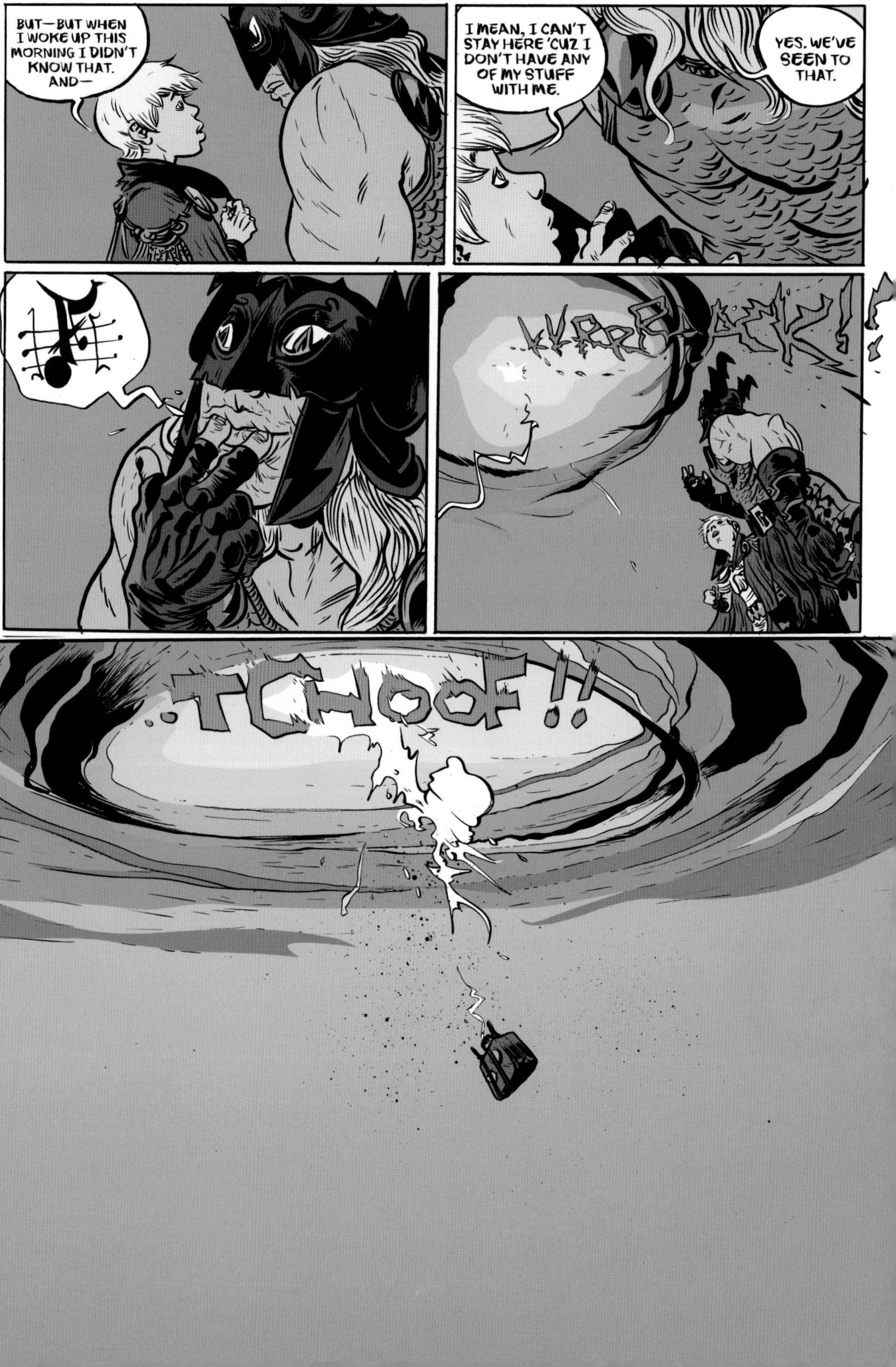
BUT—BUT WHEN I WOKE UP THIS MORNING I DIDN'T KNOW THAT. AND—
I MEAN, I CAN'T STAY HERE 'CUZ I DON'T HAVE ANY OF MY STUFF WITH ME.
YES. WE'VE SEEN TO THAT.
TCHOOF!!

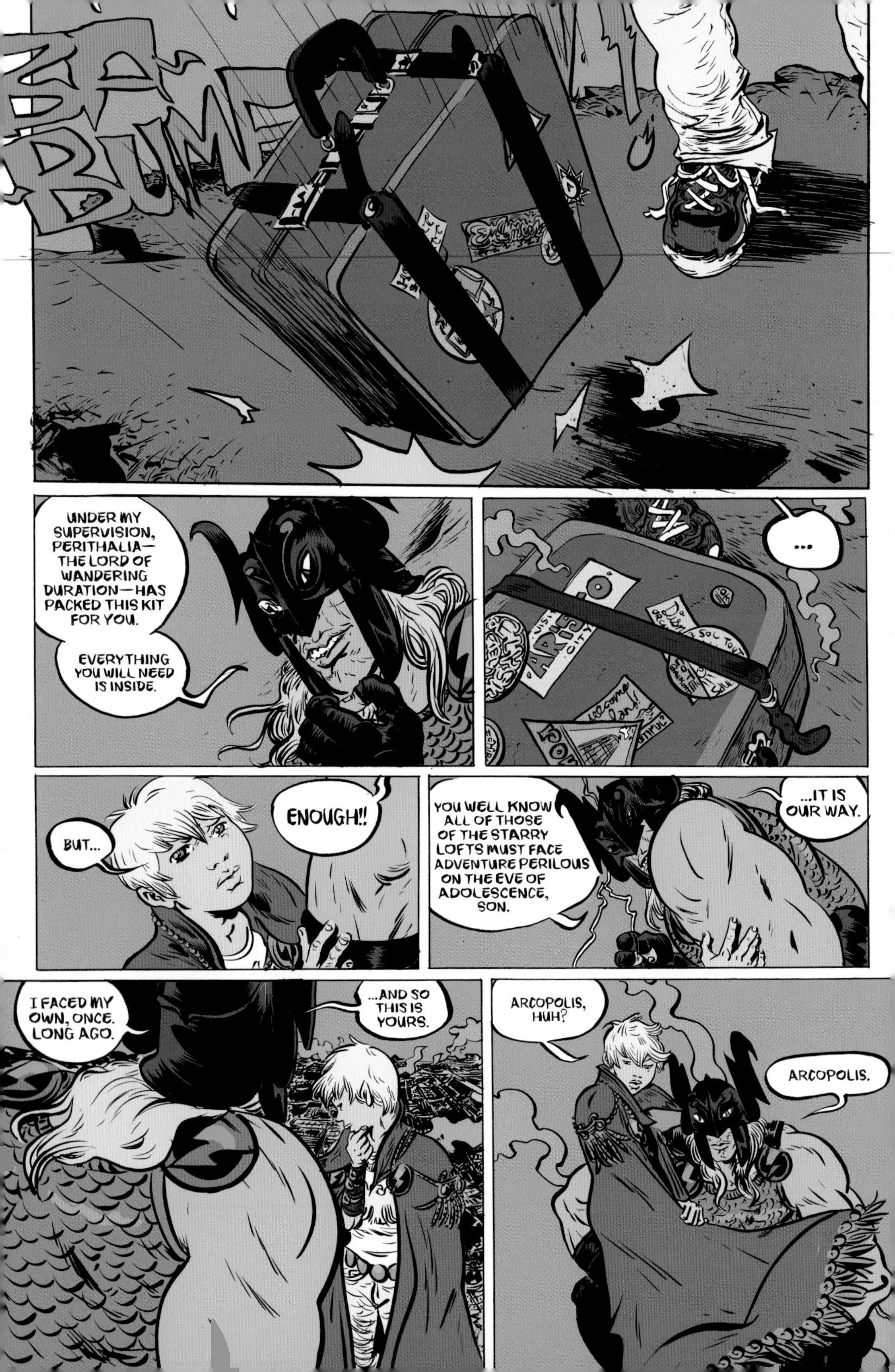
BUMF
UNDER MY SUPERVISION, PERITHALIA—THE LORD OF WANDERING DURATION—HAS PACKED THIS KIT FOR YOU.
EVERYTHING YOU WILL NEED IS INSIDE.
...
BUT...
ENOUGH!!
YOU WELL KNOW ALL OF THOSE OF THE STARRY LOFTS MUST FACE ADVENTURE PERILOUS ON THE EVE OF ADOLESCENCE, SON.
...IT IS OUR WAY.
I FACED MY OWN, ONCE. LONG AGO.
...AND SO THIS IS YOURS.
ARCOPOLIS, HUH?
ARCOPOLIS.

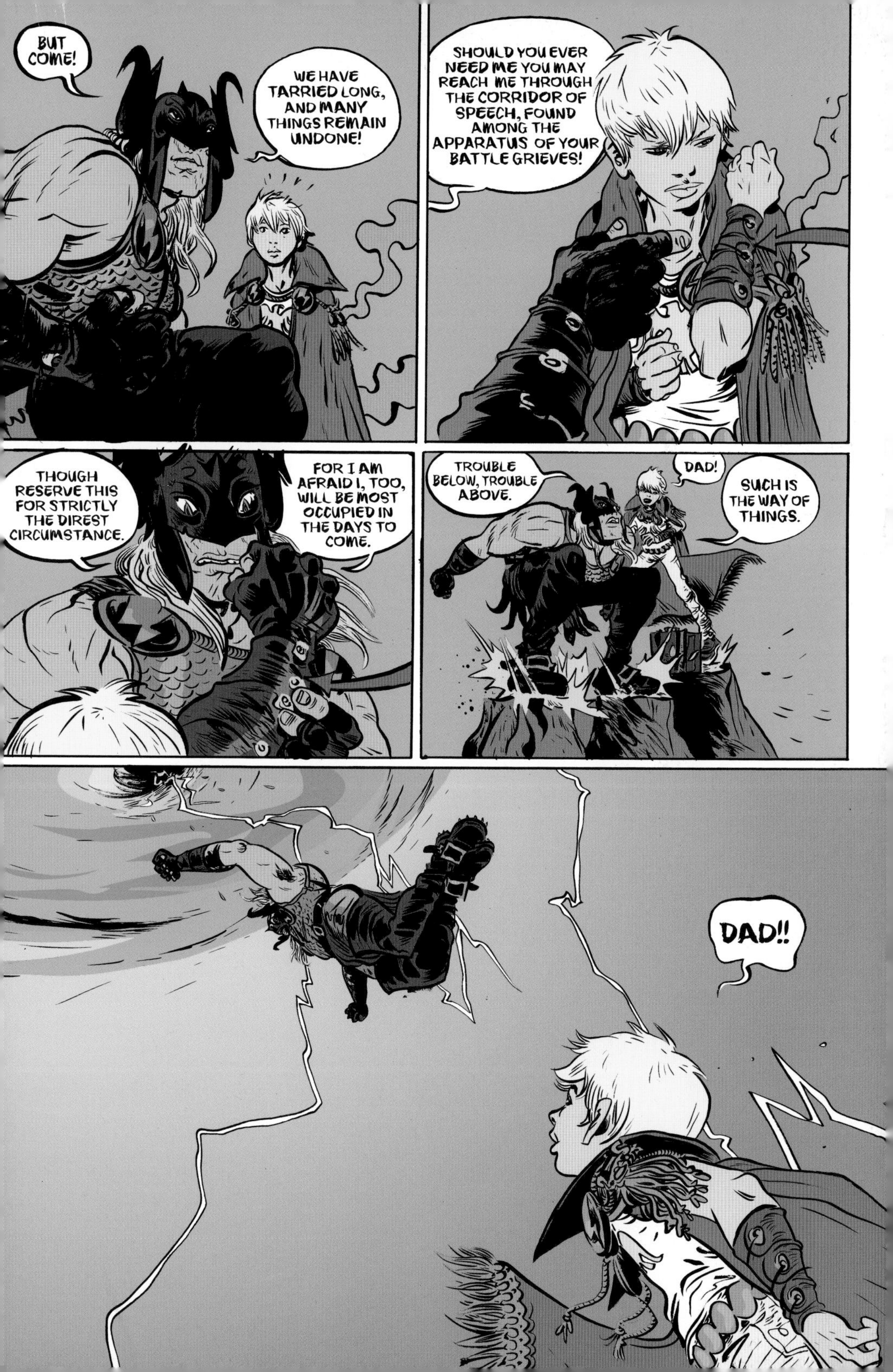
BUT COME!
WE HAVE TARRIED LONG, AND MANY THINGS REMAIN UNDONE!
SHOULD YOU EVER NEED ME YOU MAY REACH ME THROUGH THE CORRIDOR OF SPEECH, FOUND AMONG THE APPARATUS OF YOUR BATTLE GRIEVES!
THOUGH RESERVE THIS FOR STRICTLY THE DIREST CIRCUMSTANCE.
FOR I AM AFRAID I, TOO, WILL BE MOST OCCUPIED IN THE DAYS TO COME.
TROUBLE BELOW, TROUBLE ABOVE.
DAD!
SUCH IS THE WAY OF THINGS.
DAD!!

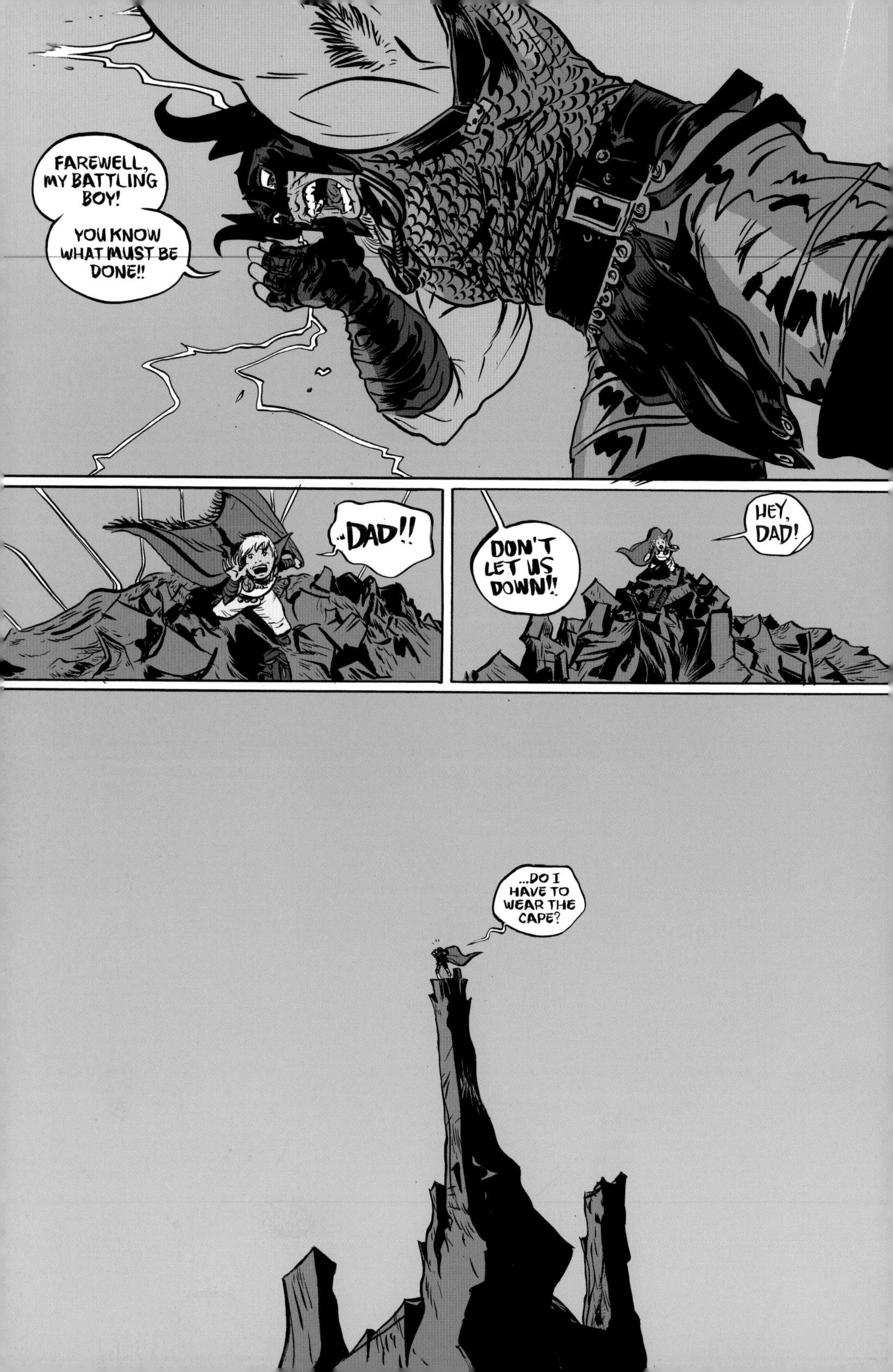
FAREWELL, MY BATTLING BOY!
YOU KNOW WHAT MUST BE DONE!!
...DAD!!
HEY, DAD!
DON'T LET US DOWN!!
...DO I HAVE TO WEAR THE CAPE?

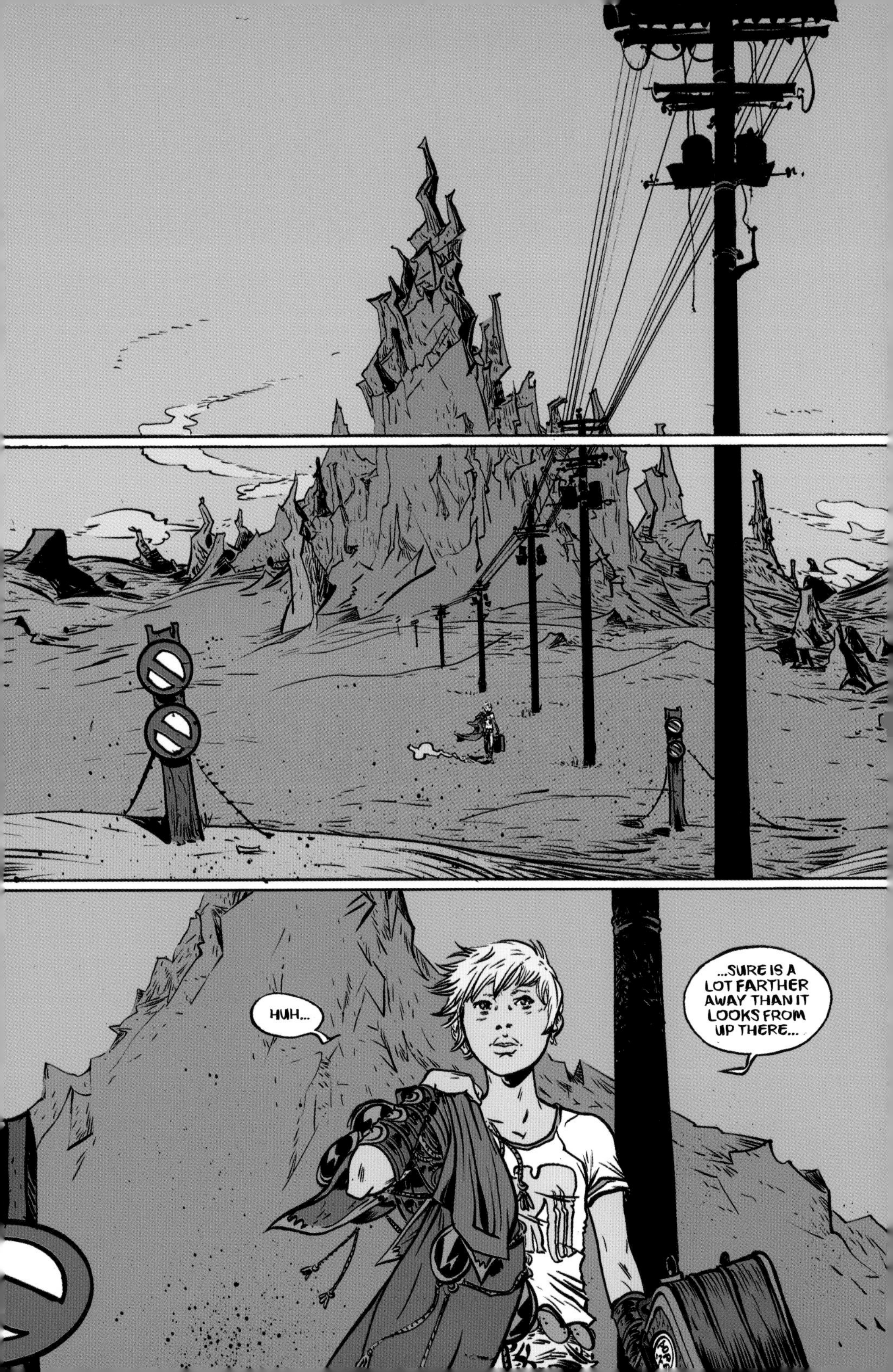
HUH...
...SURE IS A LOT FARTHER AWAY THAN IT LOOKS FROM UP THERE...

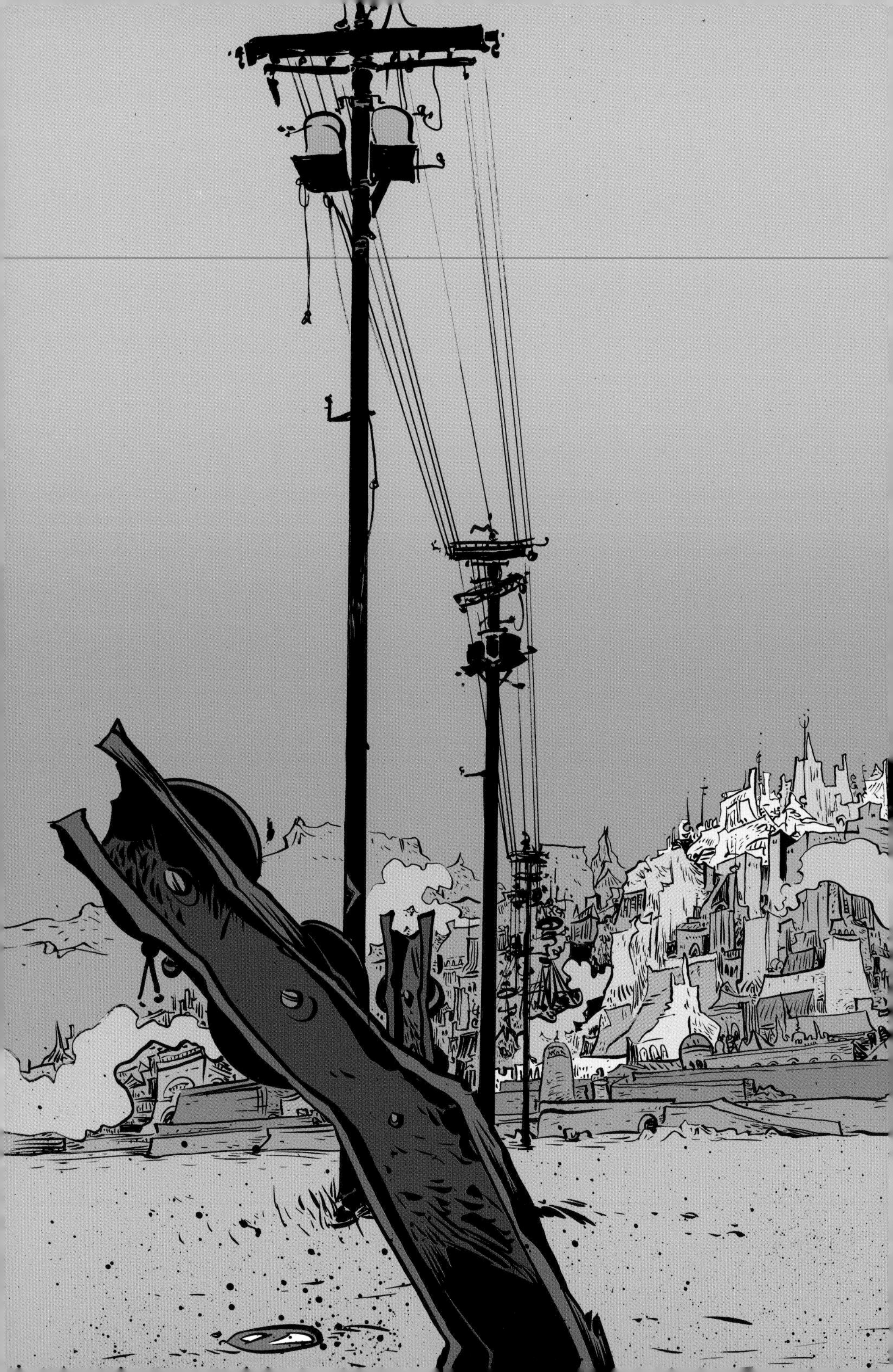

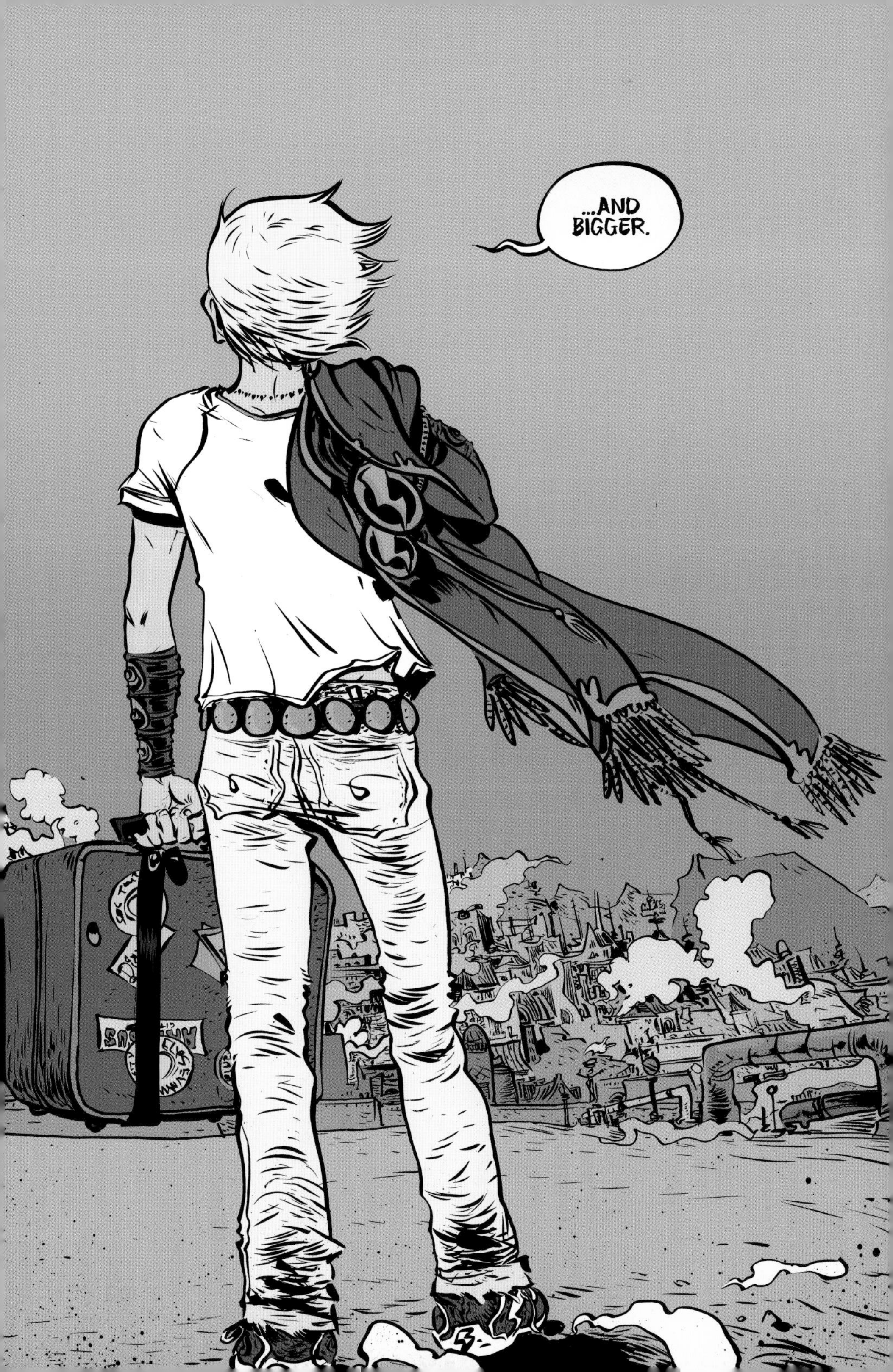
...AND BIGGER.

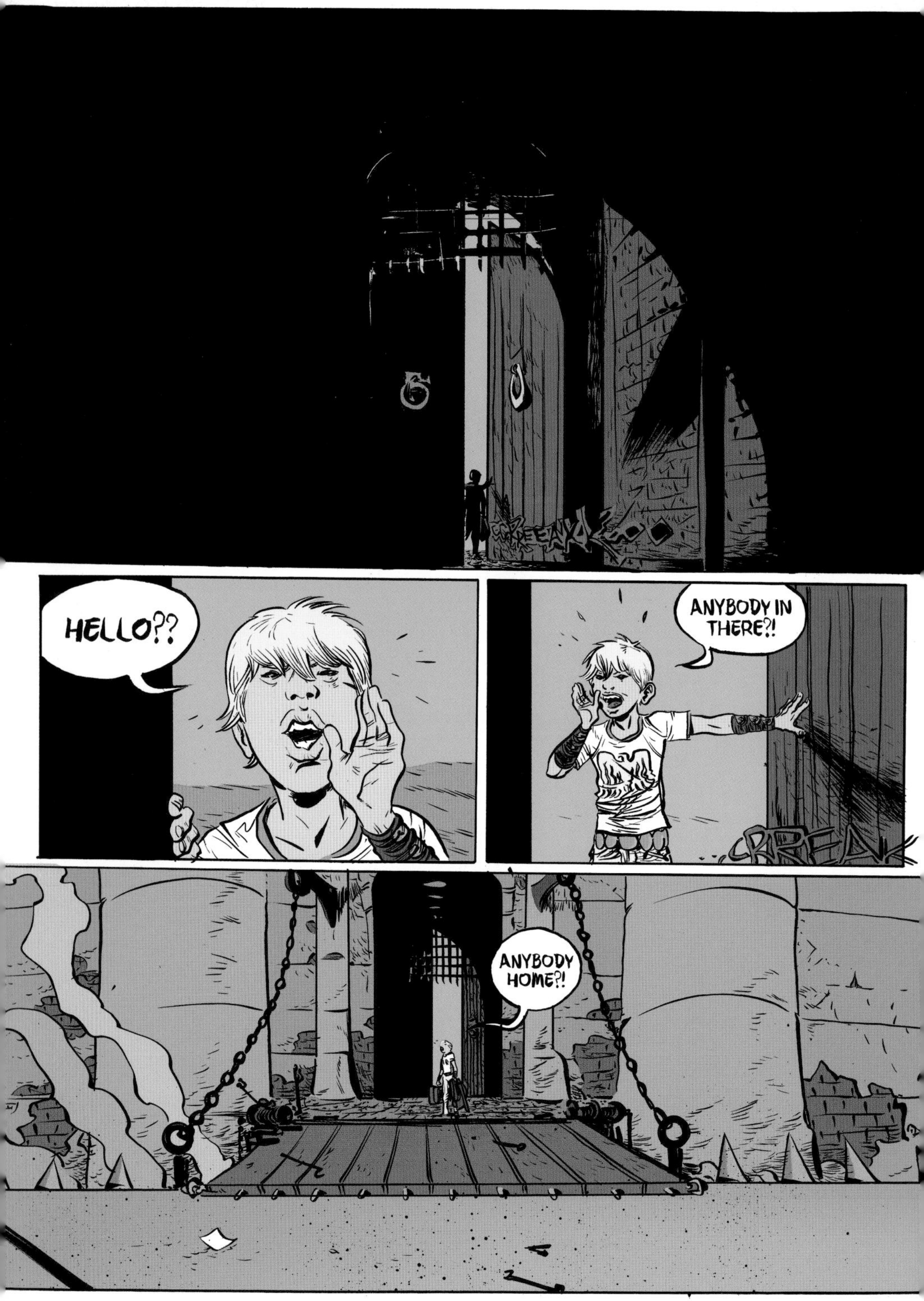
CCRREEAK
HELLO??
ANYBODY IN THERE?!
CRREAK
ANYBODY HOME?!

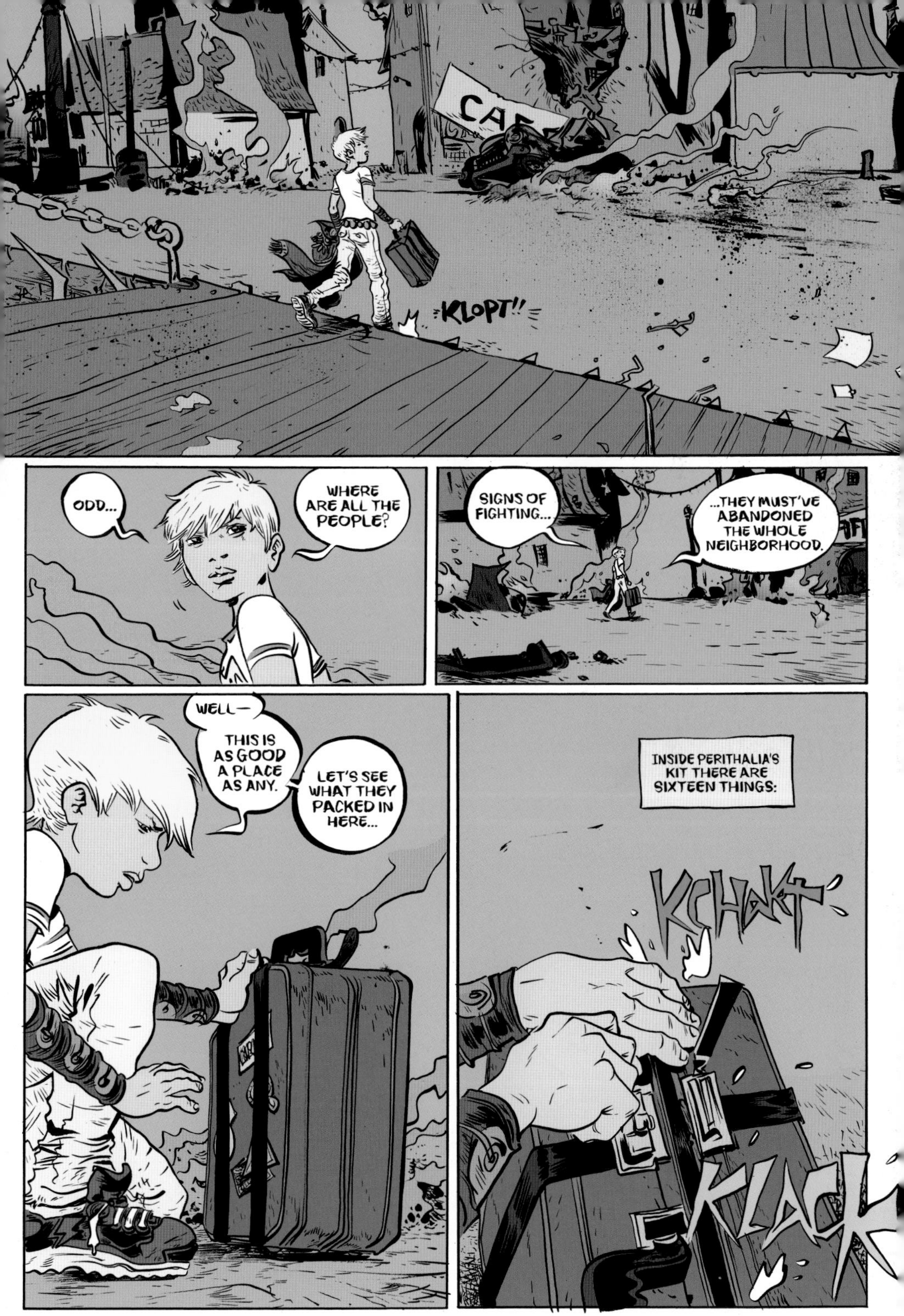
CAF
KLOPT!!
ODD...
WHERE ARE ALL THE PEOPLE?
SIGNS OF FIGHTING...
...THEY MUST'VE ABANDONED THE WHOLE NEIGHBORHOOD.
WELL—
THIS IS AS GOOD A PLACE AS ANY.
LET'S SEE WHAT THEY PACKED IN HERE...
INSIDE PERITHALIA'S KIT THERE ARE SIXTEEN THINGS:
KCHAKT
KLACK

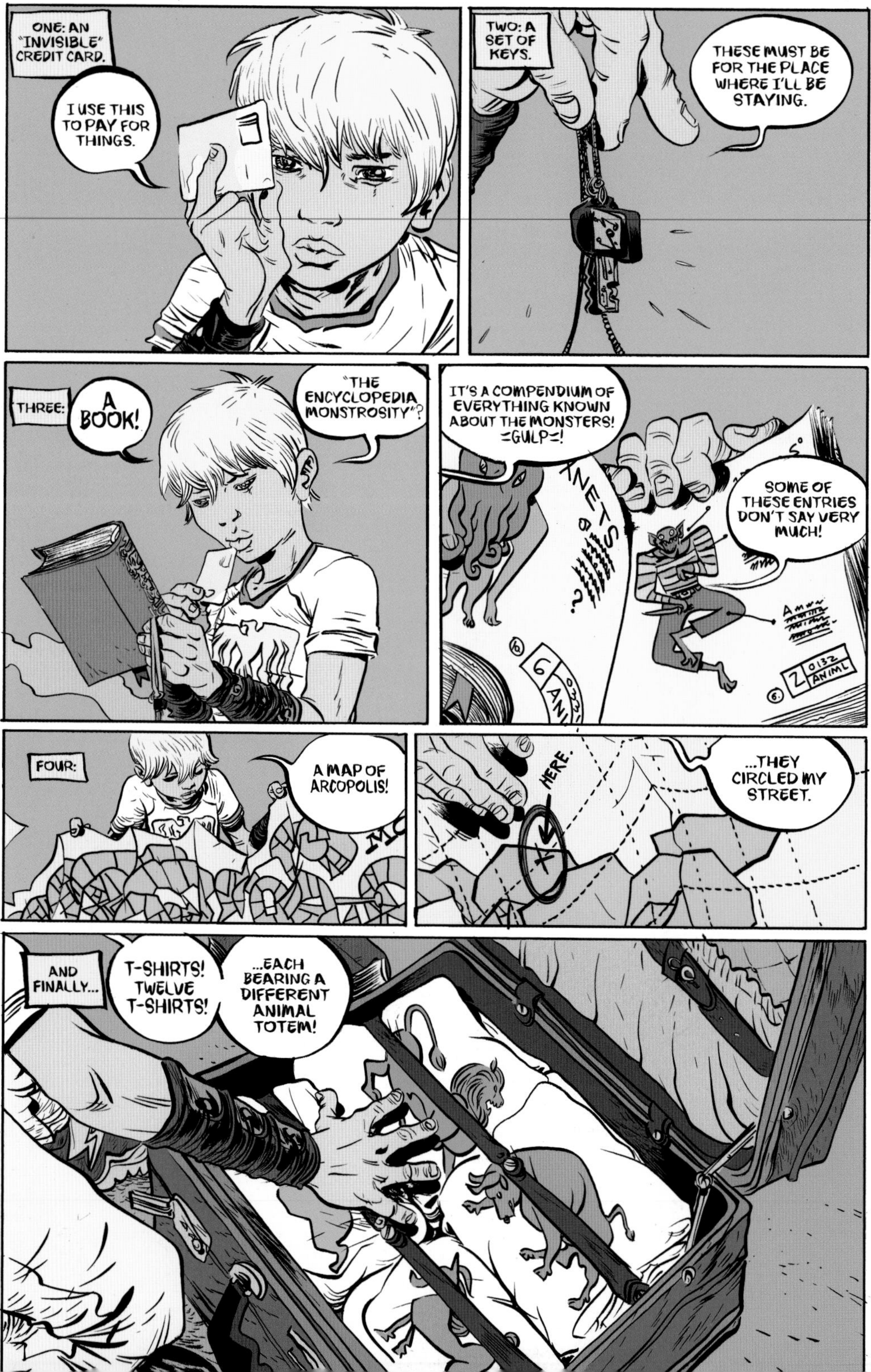
ONE: AN "INVISIBLE" CREDIT CARD.
I USE THIS TO PAY FOR THINGS.
TWO: A SET OF KEYS.
THESE MUST BE FOR THE PLACE WHERE I'LL BE STAYING.
THREE:
A BOOK!
"THE ENCYCLOPEDIA MONSTROSITY"?
IT'S A COMPENDIUM OF EVERYTHING KNOWN ABOUT THE MONSTERS! =GULP=!
SOME OF THESE ENTRIES DON'T SAY VERY MUCH!
FOUR:
A MAP OF ARCOPOLIS!
HERE.
...THEY CIRCLED MY STREET.
AND FINALLY...
T-SHIRTS! TWELVE T-SHIRTS!
...EACH BEARING A DIFFERENT ANIMAL TOTEM!

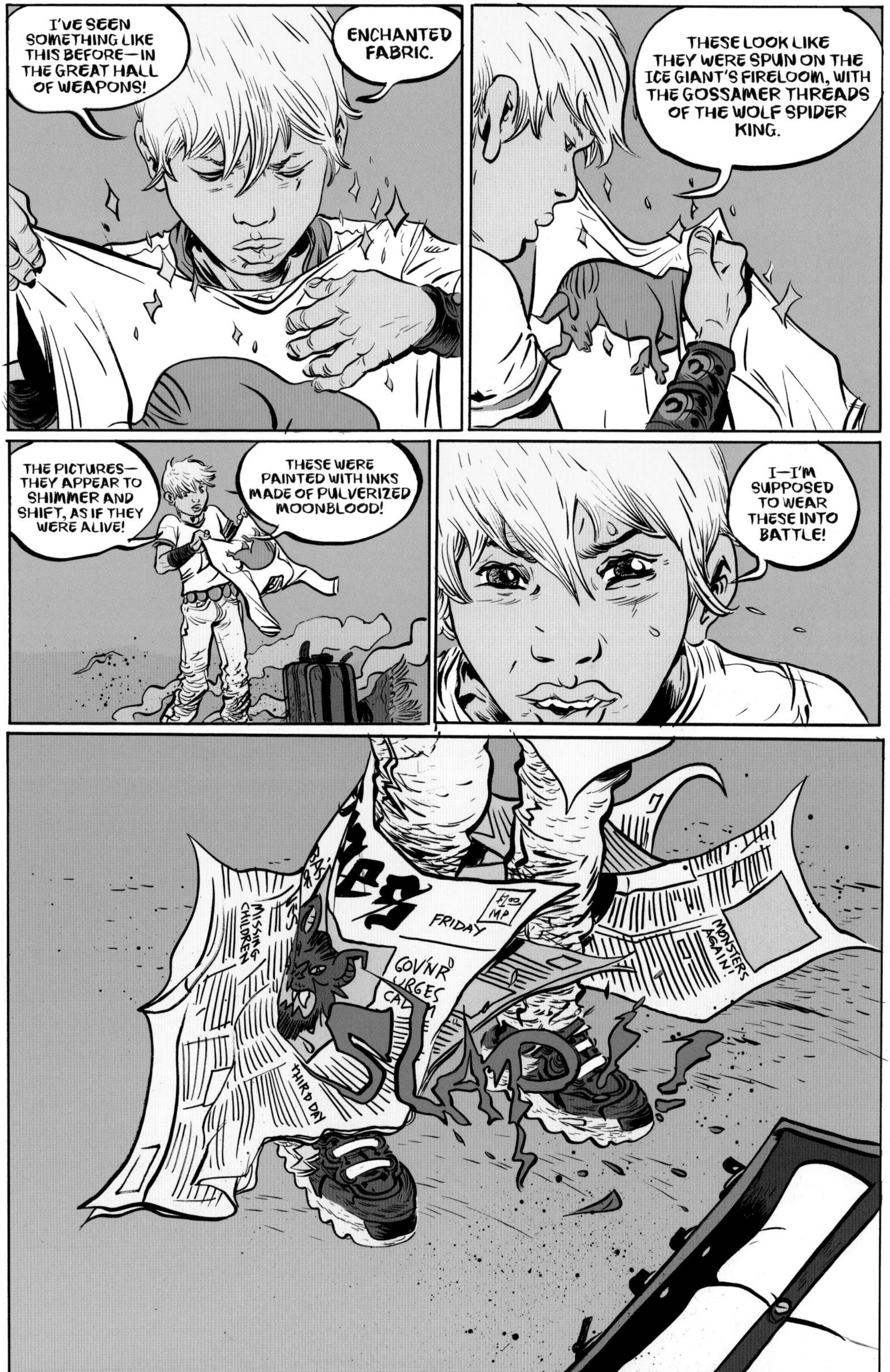
I'VE SEEN SOMETHING LIKE THIS BEFORE—IN THE GREAT HALL OF WEAPONS!
ENCHANTED FABRIC.
THESE LOOK LIKE THEY WERE SPUN ON THE ICE GIANT'S FIRELOOM, WITH THE GOSSAMER THREADS OF THE WOLF SPIDER KING.
THE PICTURES—THEY APPEAR TO SHIMMER AND SHIFT, AS IF THEY WERE ALIVE!
THESE WERE PAINTED WITH INKS MADE OF PULVERIZED MOONBLOOD!
I—I'M SUPPOSED TO WEAR THESE INTO BATTLE!
MISSING CHILDREN
FRIDAY
GOV'NR URGES CALM
MONSTERS AGAIN!
THIRD DAY

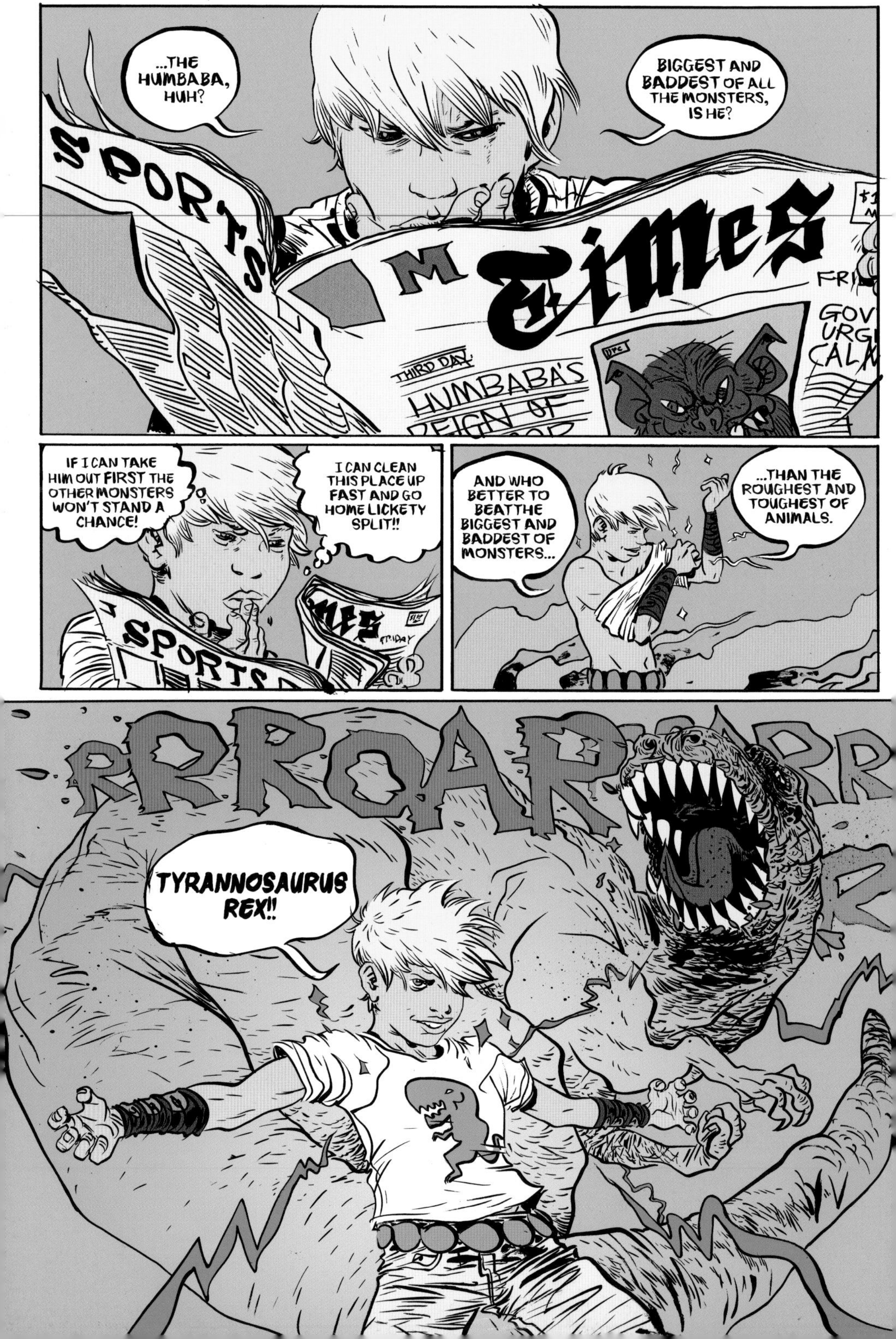
...THE HUMBABA, HUH?
BIGGEST AND BADDEST OF ALL THE MONSTERS, IS HE?
SPORTS
M Times
FRI
GOV URG CALM
THIRD DAY: HUMBABA'S REIGN OF
IF I CAN TAKE HIM OUT FIRST THE OTHER MONSTERS WON'T STAND A CHANCE!
I CAN CLEAN THIS PLACE UP FAST AND GO HOME LICKETY SPLIT!!
SPORTS
FRIDAY
AND WHO BETTER TO BEAT THE BIGGEST AND BADDEST OF MONSTERS...
...THAN THE ROUGHEST AND TOUGHEST OF ANIMALS.
RRRROAR
TYRANNOSAURUS REX!!

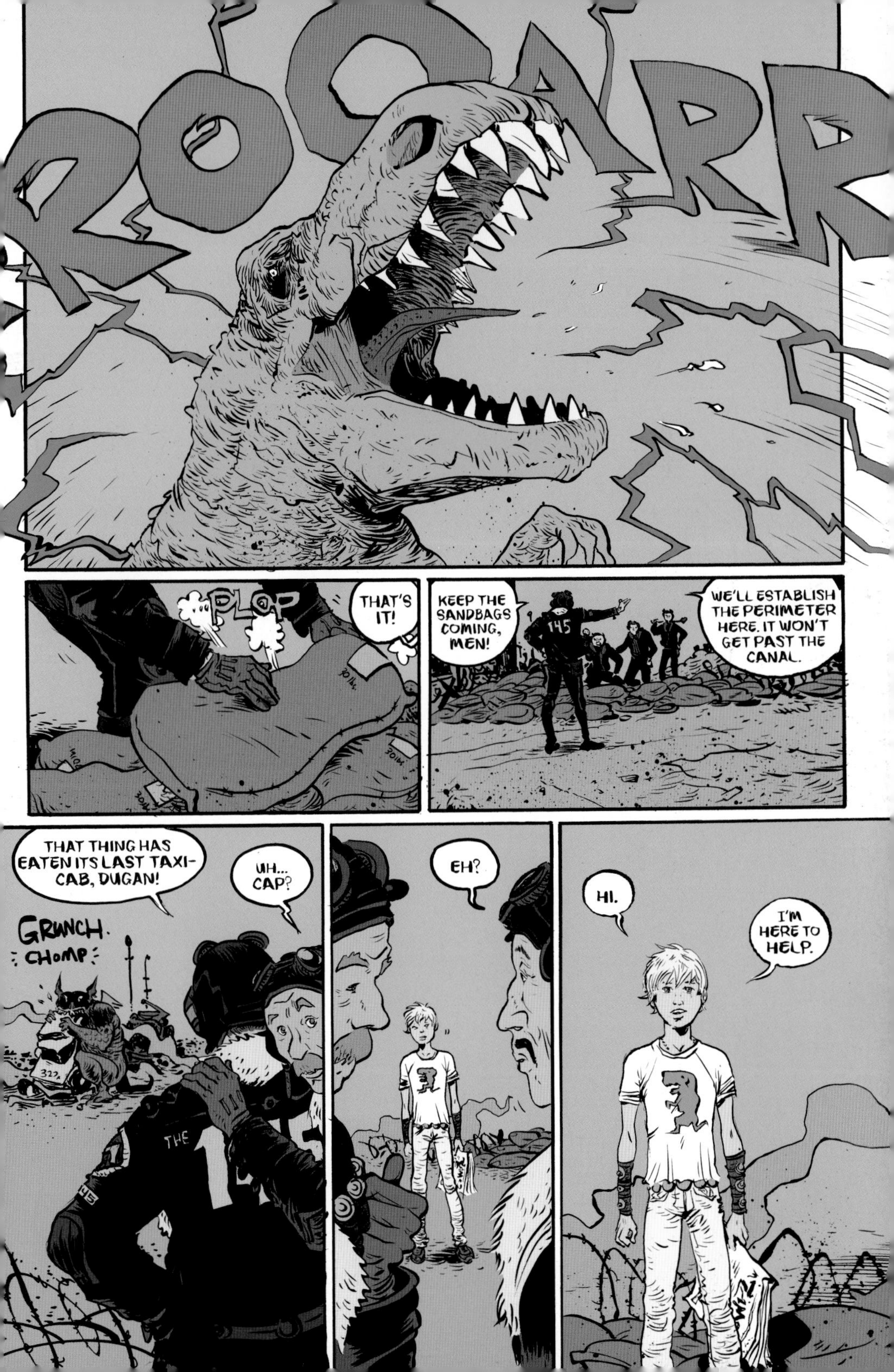
ROOARR
PLOP
THAT'S IT!
KEEP THE SANDBAGS COMING, MEN!
WE'LL ESTABLISH THE PERIMETER HERE. IT WON'T GET PAST THE CANAL.
THAT THING HAS EATEN ITS LAST TAXI-CAB, DUGAN!
UH... CAP?
GRUNCH
CHOMP
EH?
HI.
I'M HERE TO HELP.

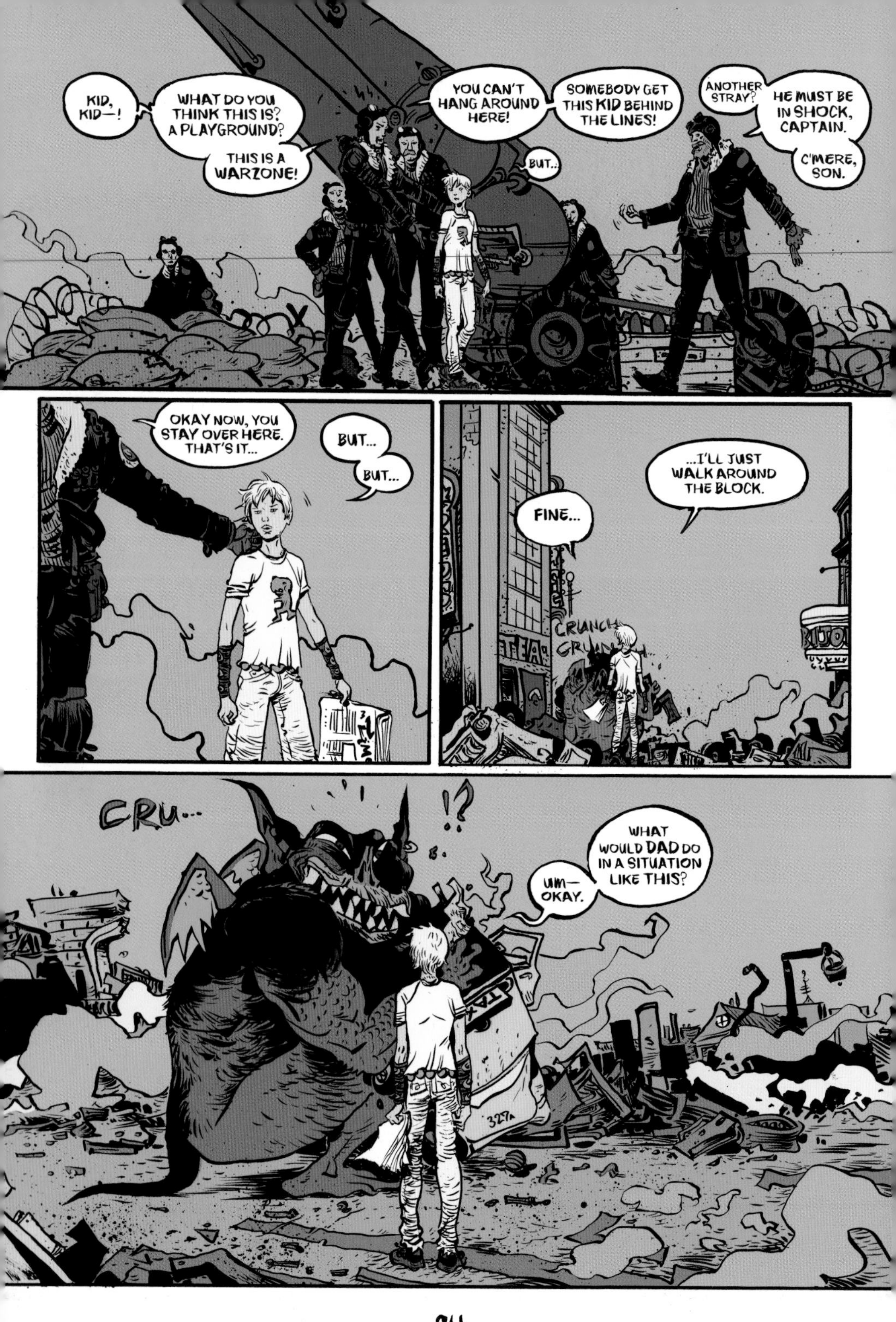
KID, KID—!
WHAT DO YOU THINK THIS IS? A PLAYGROUND?
THIS IS A WARZONE!
YOU CAN'T HANG AROUND HERE!
SOMEBODY GET THIS KID BEHIND THE LINES!
BUT...
ANOTHER STRAY?
HE MUST BE IN SHOCK, CAPTAIN.
C'MERE, SON.
OKAY NOW, YOU STAY OVER HERE. THAT'S IT...
BUT...
BUT...
FINE...
...I'LL JUST WALK AROUND THE BLOCK.
CRUNCH
CRUNCH
CRU...
!?
UM— OKAY.
WHAT WOULD DAD DO IN A SITUATION LIKE THIS?

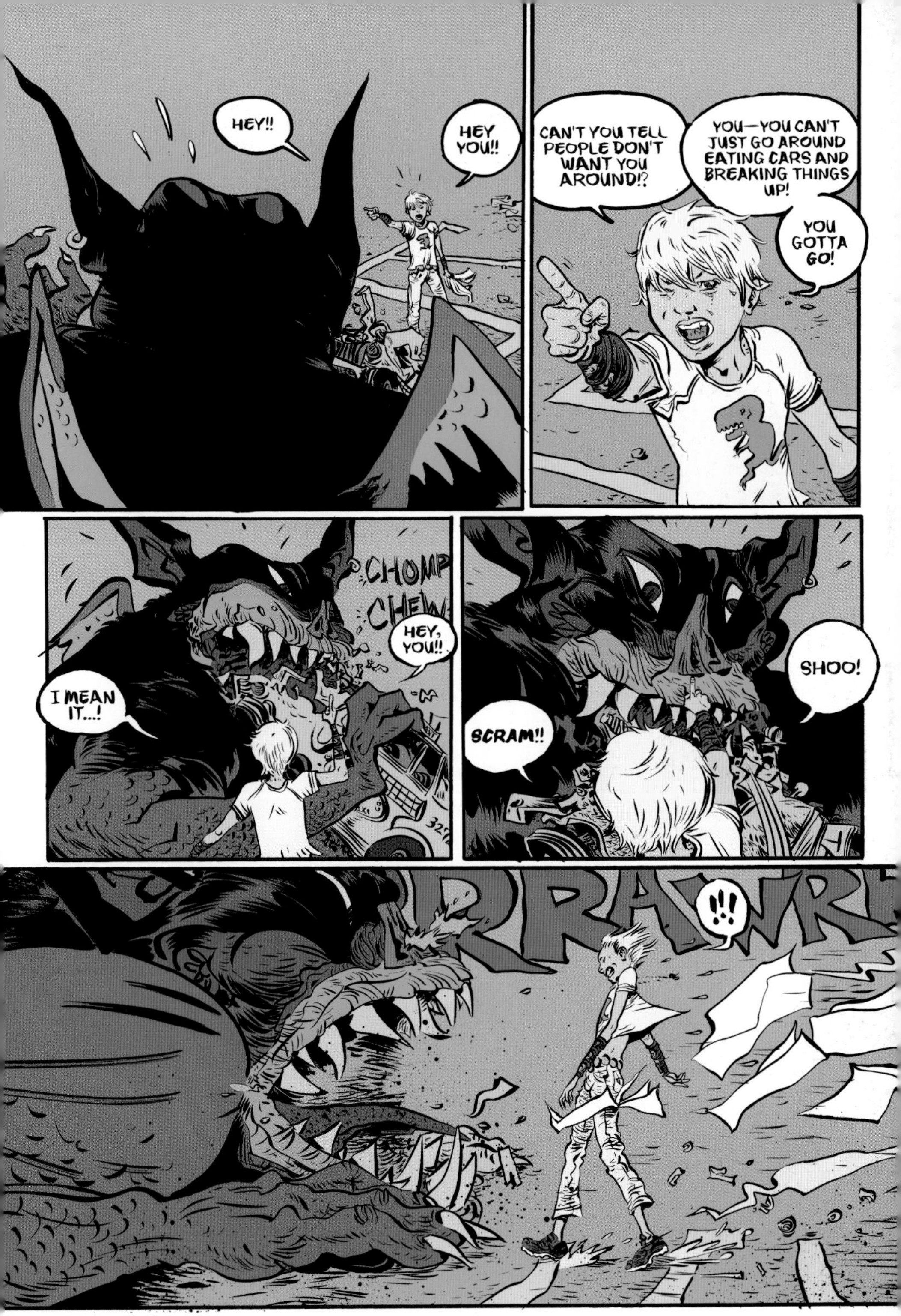
HEY!!
HEY YOU!!
CAN'T YOU TELL PEOPLE DON'T WANT YOU AROUND!?
YOU—YOU CAN'T JUST GO AROUND EATING CARS AND BREAKING THINGS UP!
YOU GOTTA GO!
CHOMP
CHEW
HEY, YOU!!
I MEAN IT...!
SHOO!
SCRAM!!
RRAWR
!!!

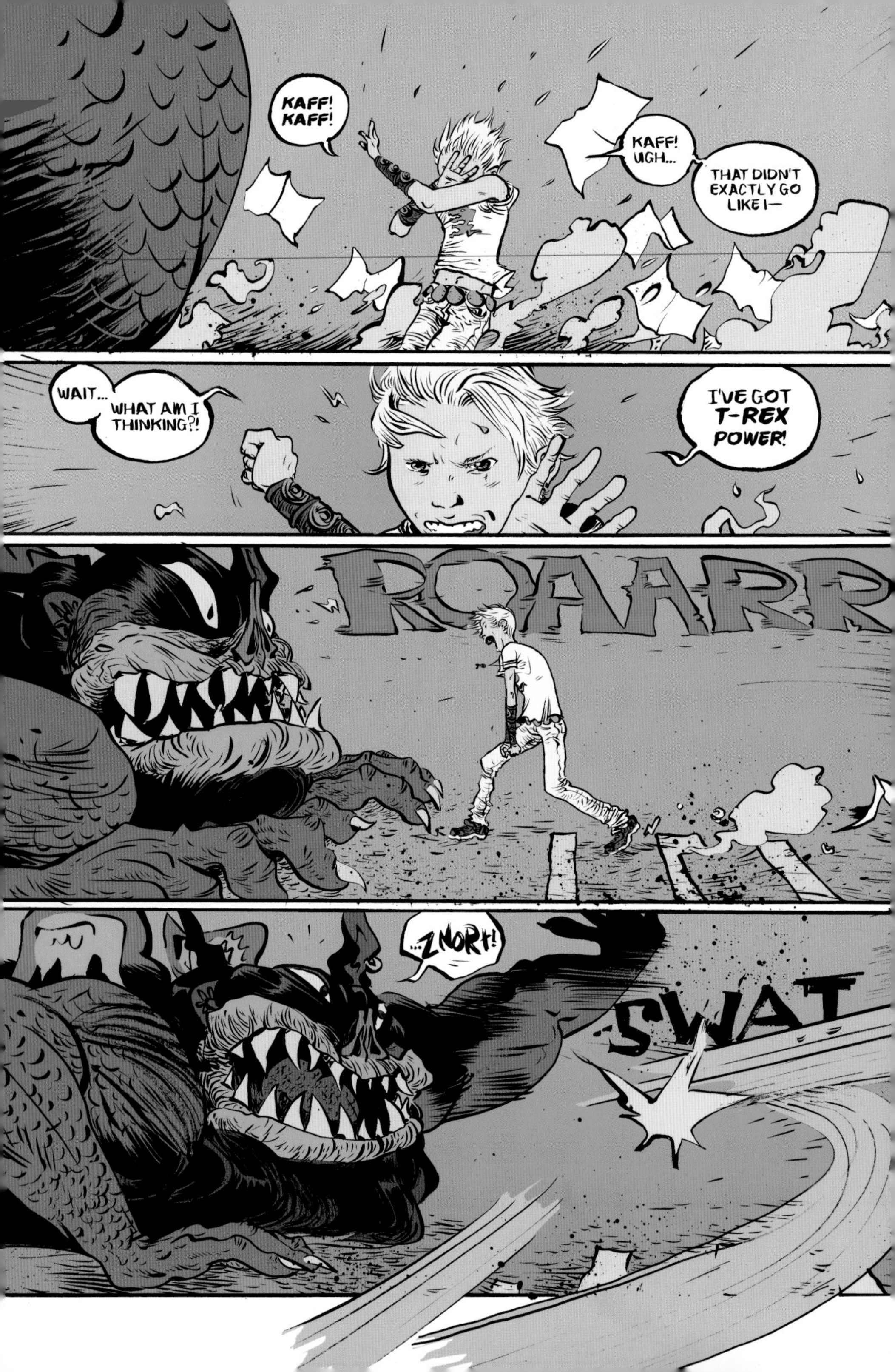
KAFF! KAFF!
KAFF! UGH...
THAT DIDN'T EXACTLY GO LIKE I—
WAIT... WHAT AM I THINKING?!
I'VE GOT T-REX POWER!
ROAARR
...ZNORT!
SWAT

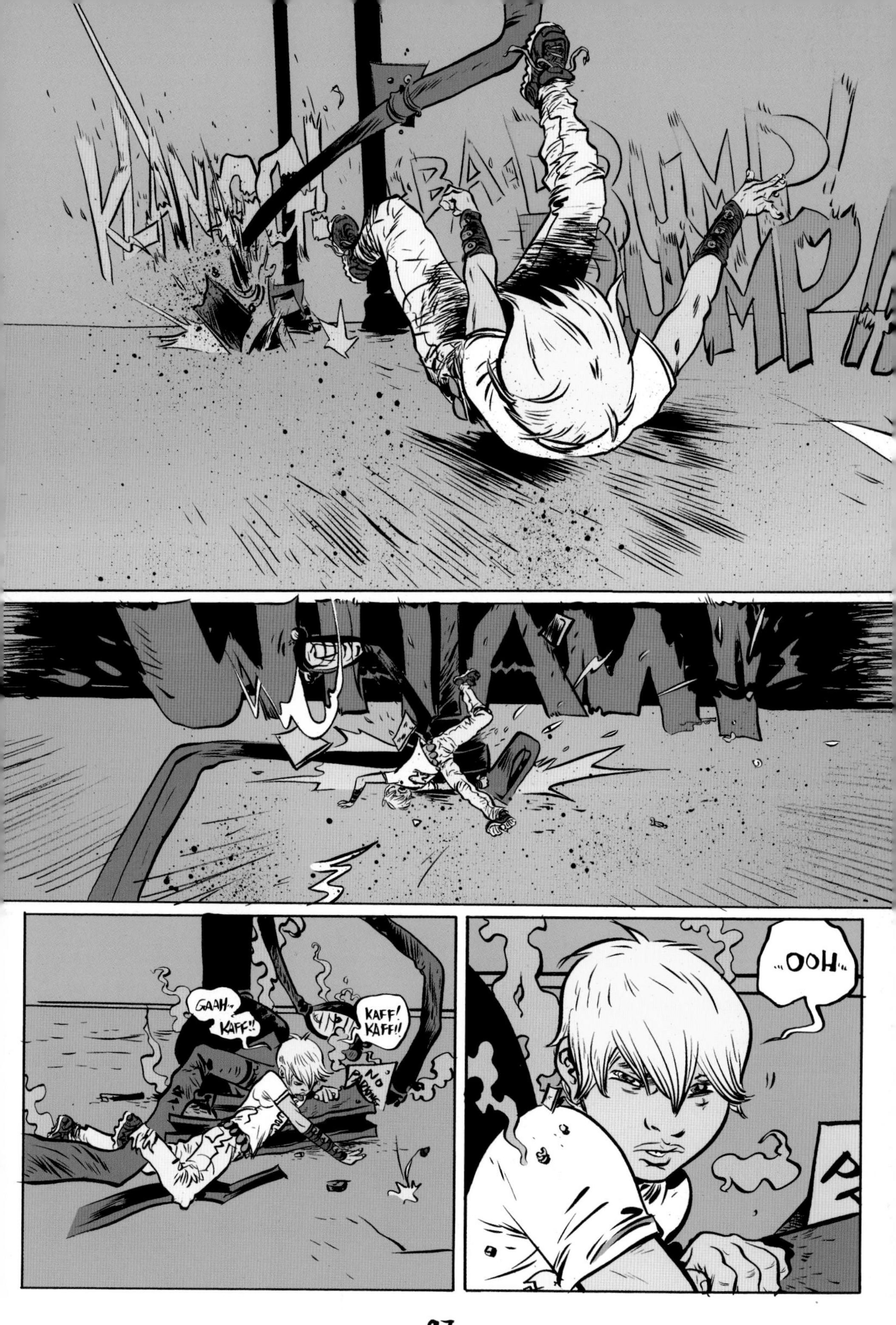
KLANGG!!
BA-LUMP!
BUMP!!
GAAH... KAFF!!
KAFF! KAFF!!
NO PARKING
...OOH...

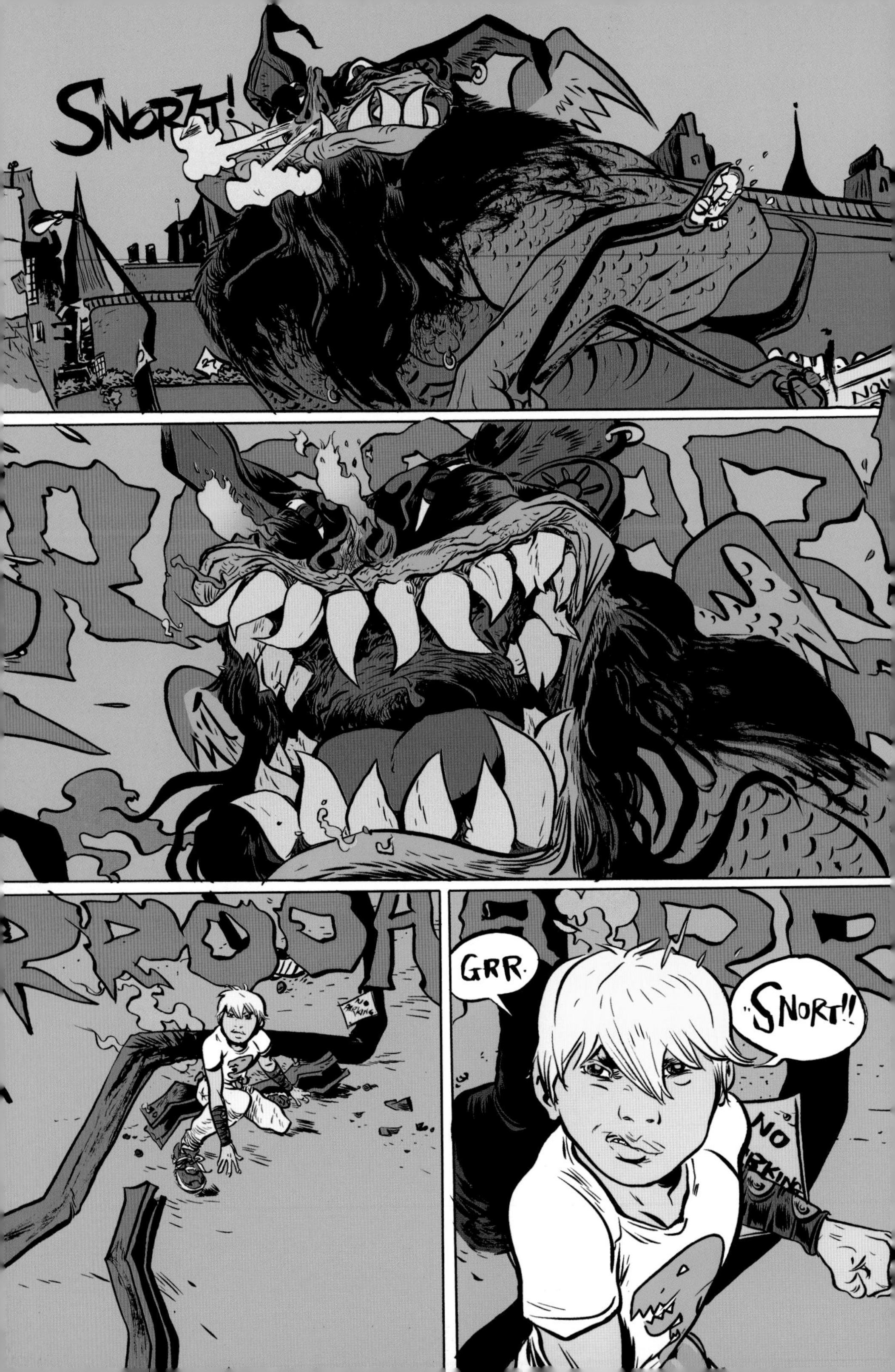
SNORZT!
NO PARKING
GRR.
SNORT!!

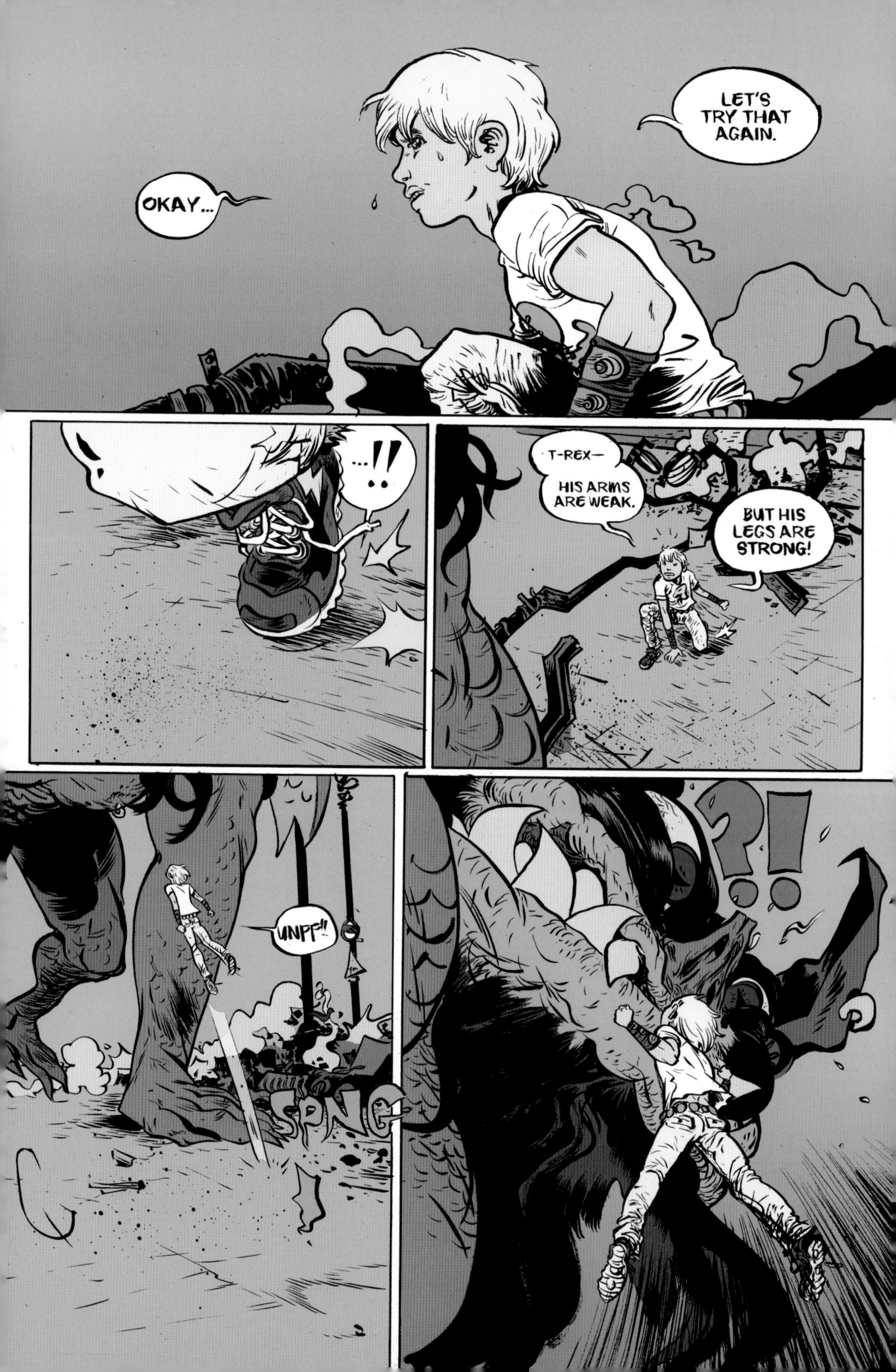
OKAY...
LET'S TRY THAT AGAIN.
...!!
T-REX—
HIS ARMS ARE WEAK.
BUT HIS LEGS ARE STRONG!
UNPF!!
SPNG
?!

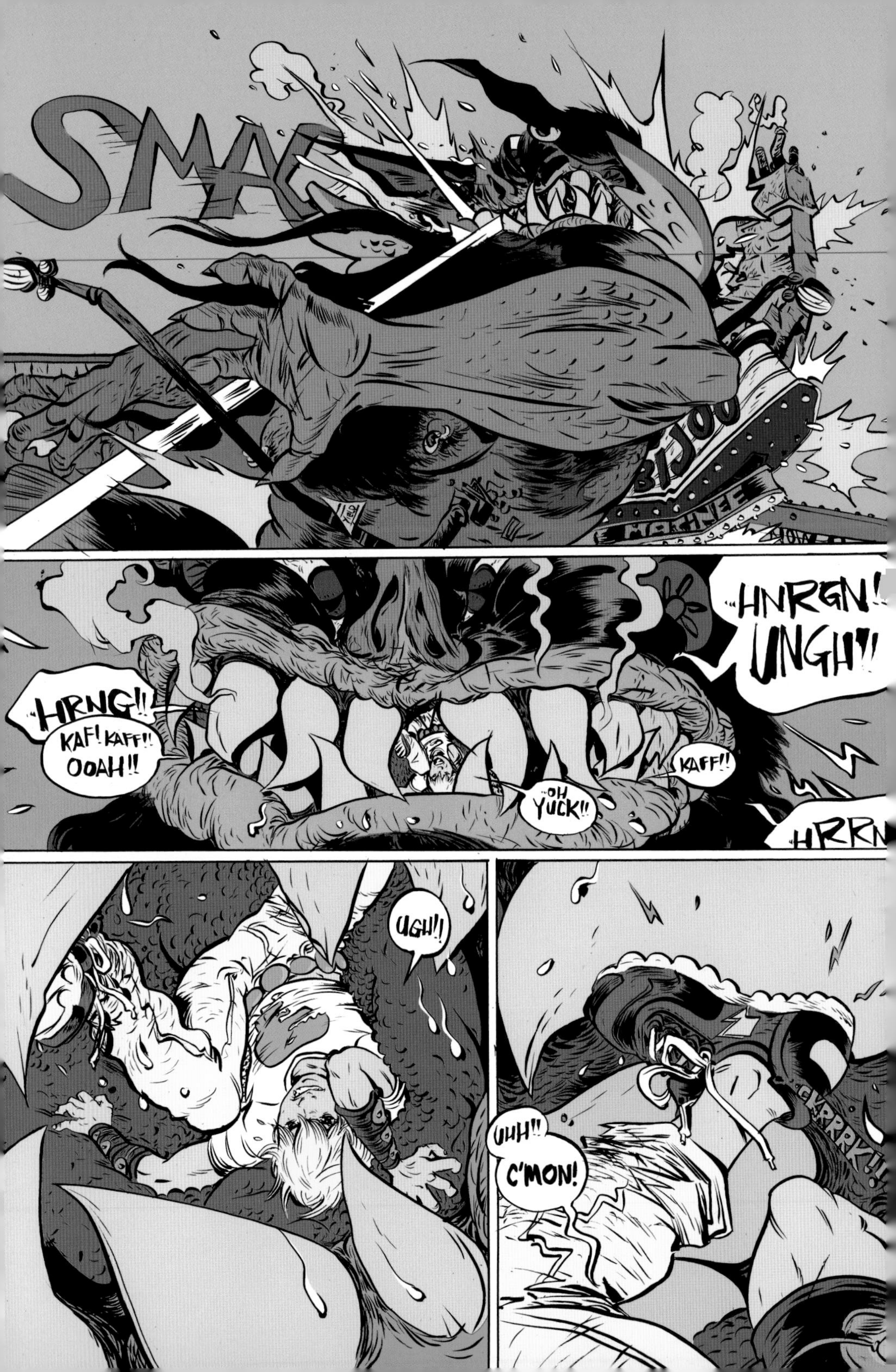
SMA
BIJOU
...HNRGN!! UNGH!!
...HRNG!!
KAF! KAFF!! OOAH!!
...OH YUCK!!
KAFF!!
...HRRN
UGH!!
UUH!! C'MON!
GKRRRK!!

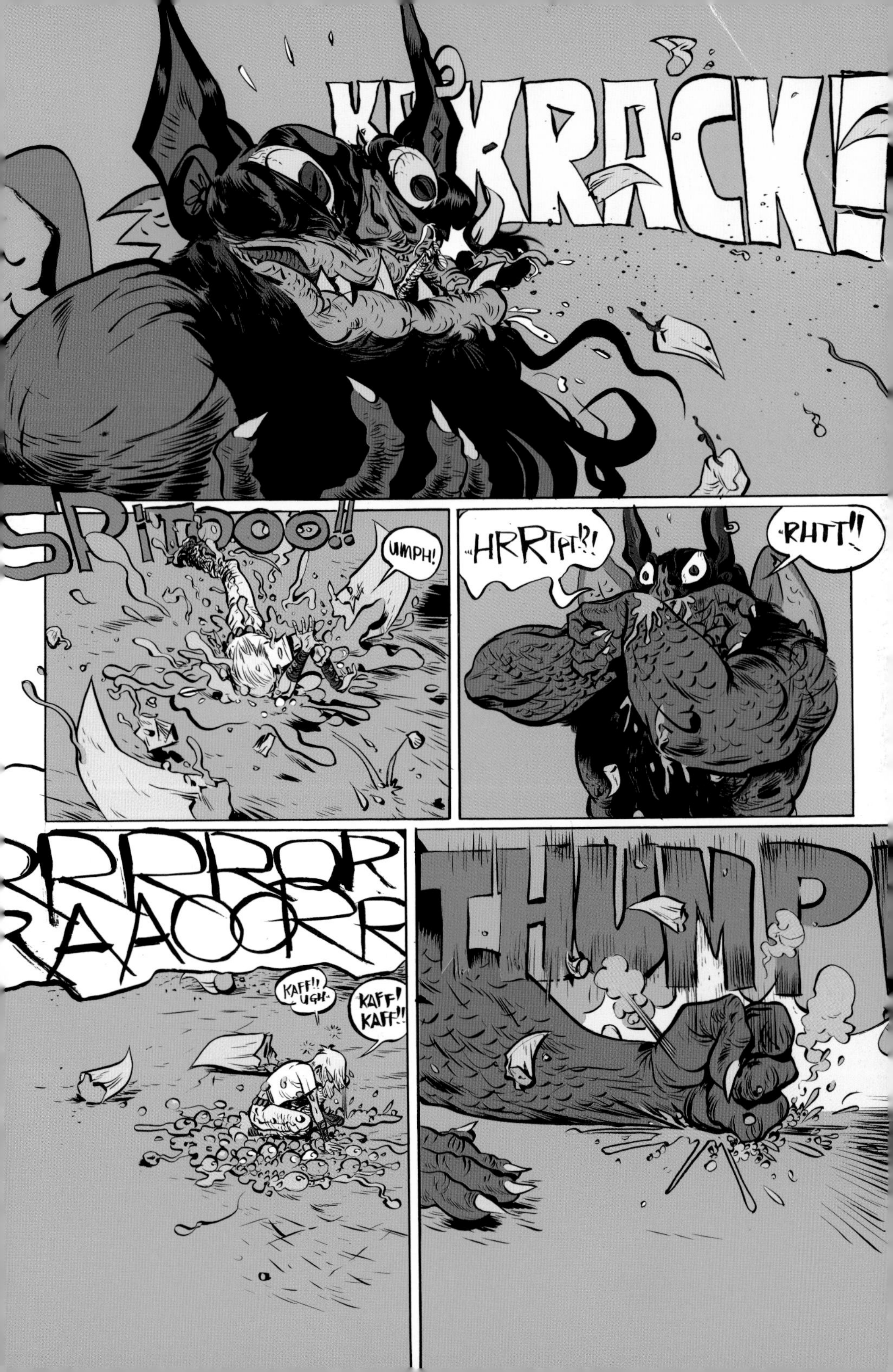

KRAKRACK!
SPITOOO!!
UMPH!
HRRTPT!?!
RHTT!!
RRRRRR RAAOORR
KAFF!! UGH
KAFF! KAFF!!
THUMP!

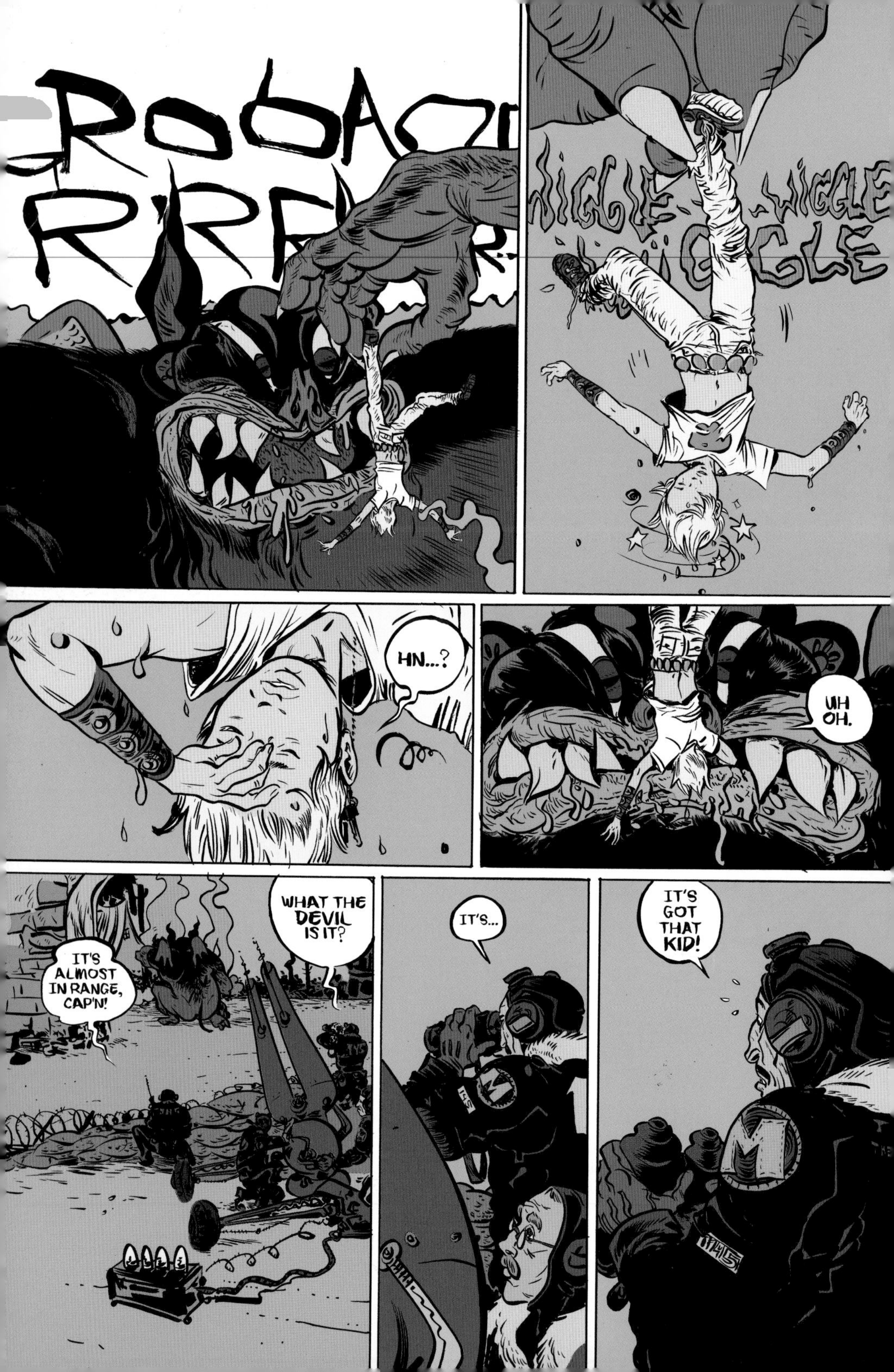

GROOAOR
R'RRR
WIGGLE WIGGLE
WIGGLE
HN...?
UH
OH.
IT'S
ALMOST
IN RANGE,
CAP'N!
WHAT THE
DEVIL
IS IT?
IT'S...
IT'S
GOT
THAT
KID!

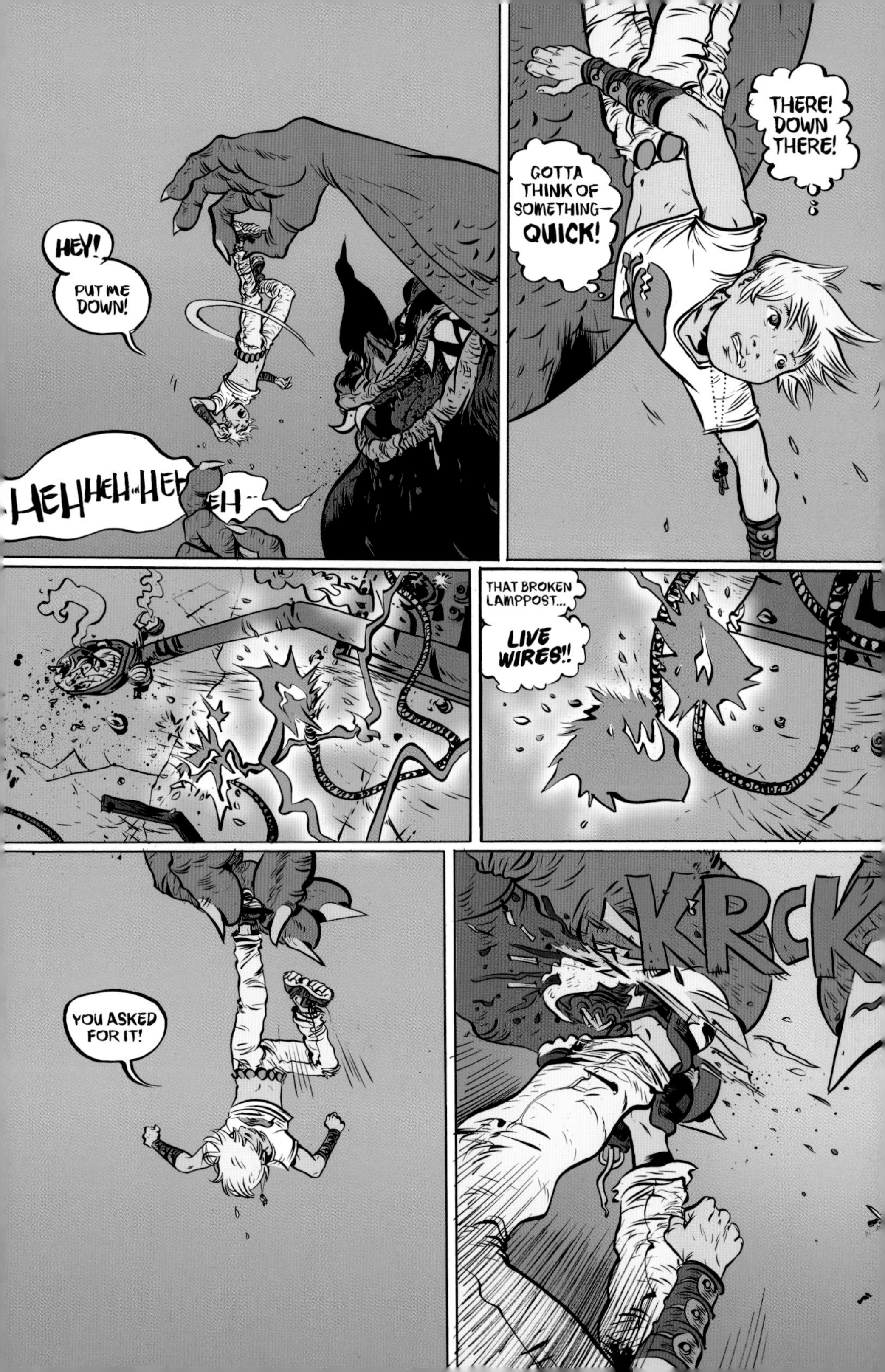
HEY!
PUT ME DOWN!
HEHHEH-HEHHEH...
GOTTA THINK OF SOMETHING— QUICK!
THERE! DOWN THERE!
THAT BROKEN LAMPPOST...
LIVE WIRES!!
YOU ASKED FOR IT!
KRCK

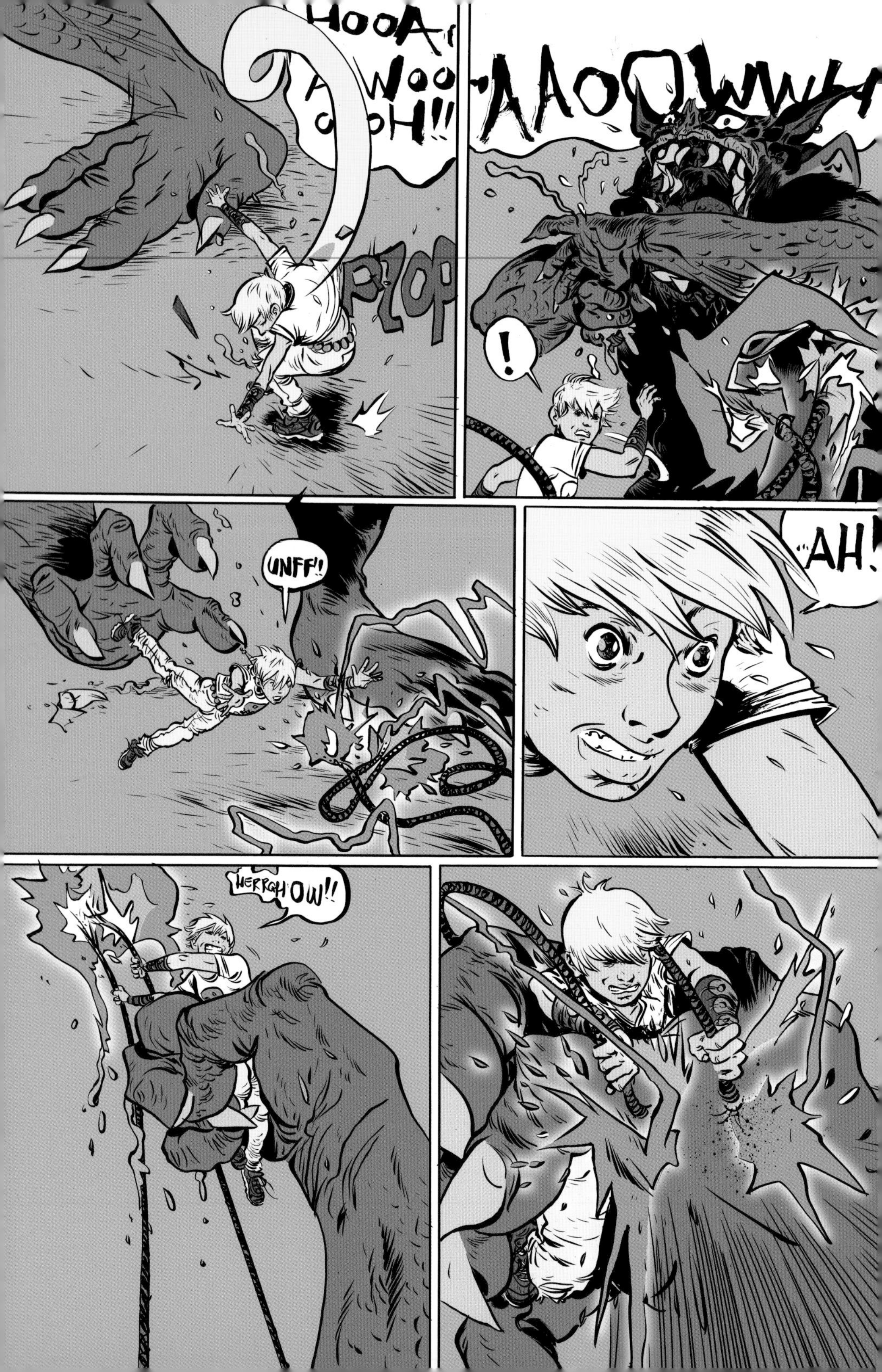
HOOAA WOOOOOH!!
PLOP
AAOOWWH
!
UNFF!
AH!
HERRGH OW!!

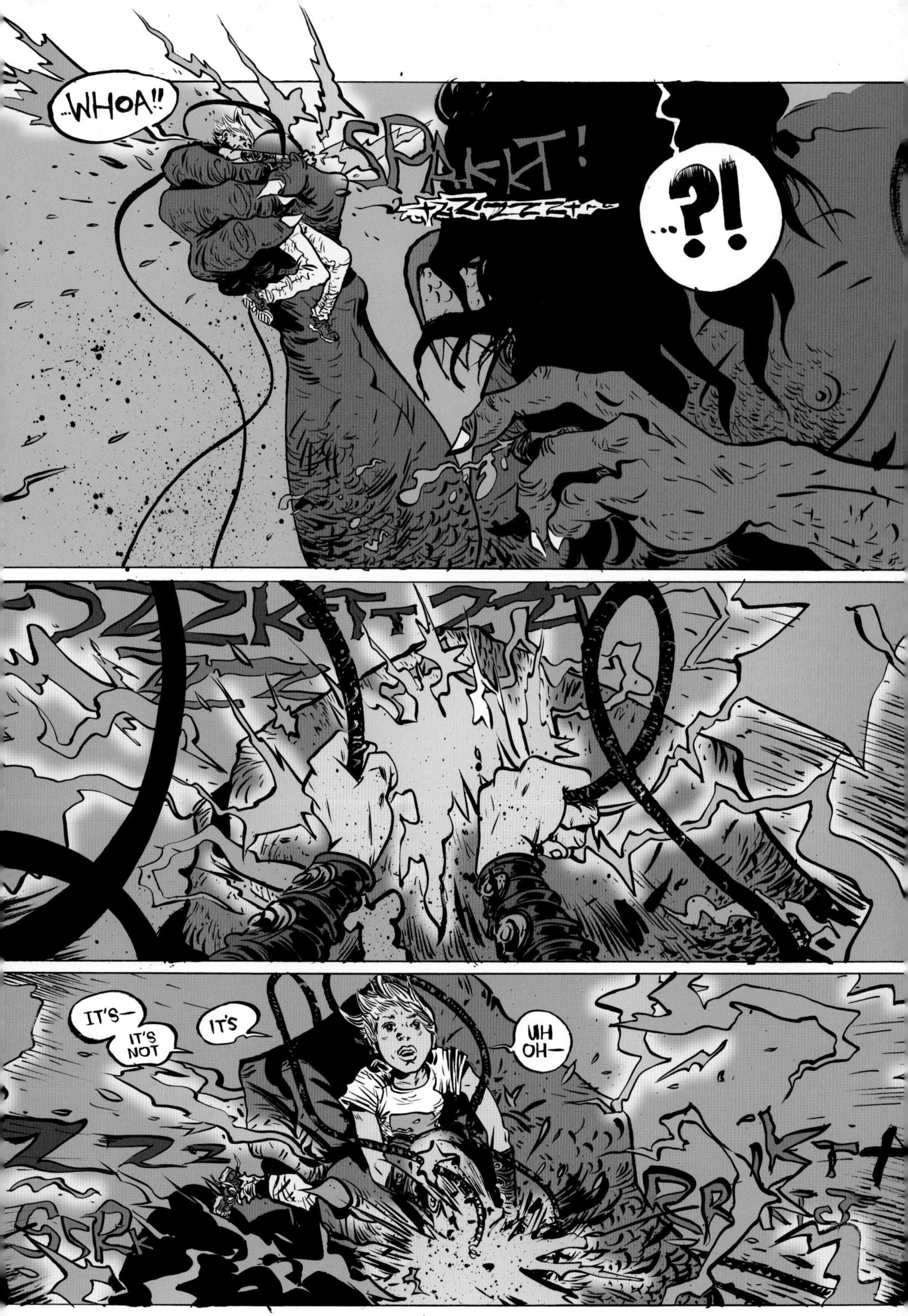
..WHOA!!
SPAKKT!
ZZZZZZ
...?!
ZZZKTT ZZZ
IT'S—
IT'S NOT
IT'S
UH OH—
ZZZ
SSRK
PRKT

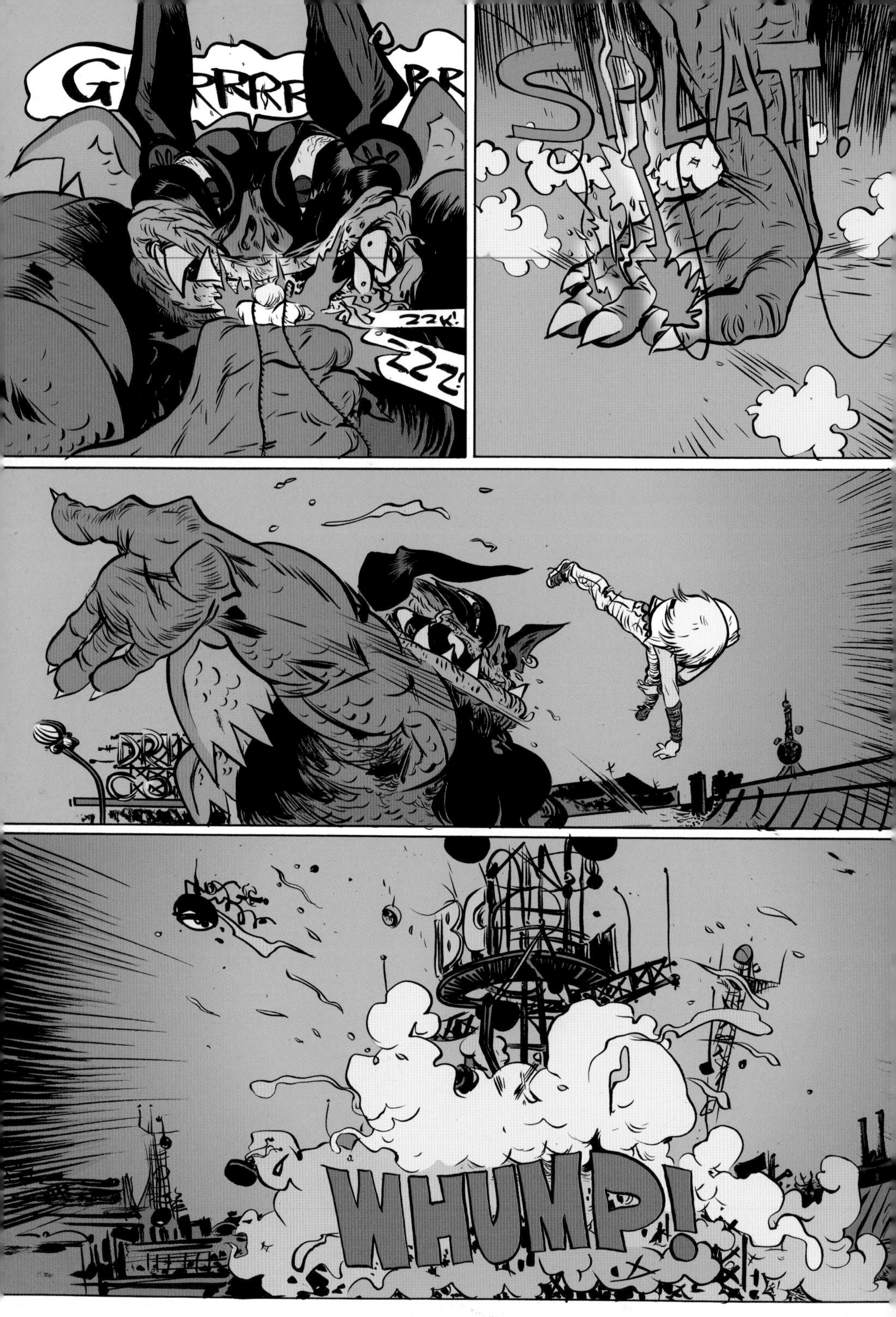
GRRRRRRRRR
ZZK!
ZZZ!
SPLAT!
WHUMP!

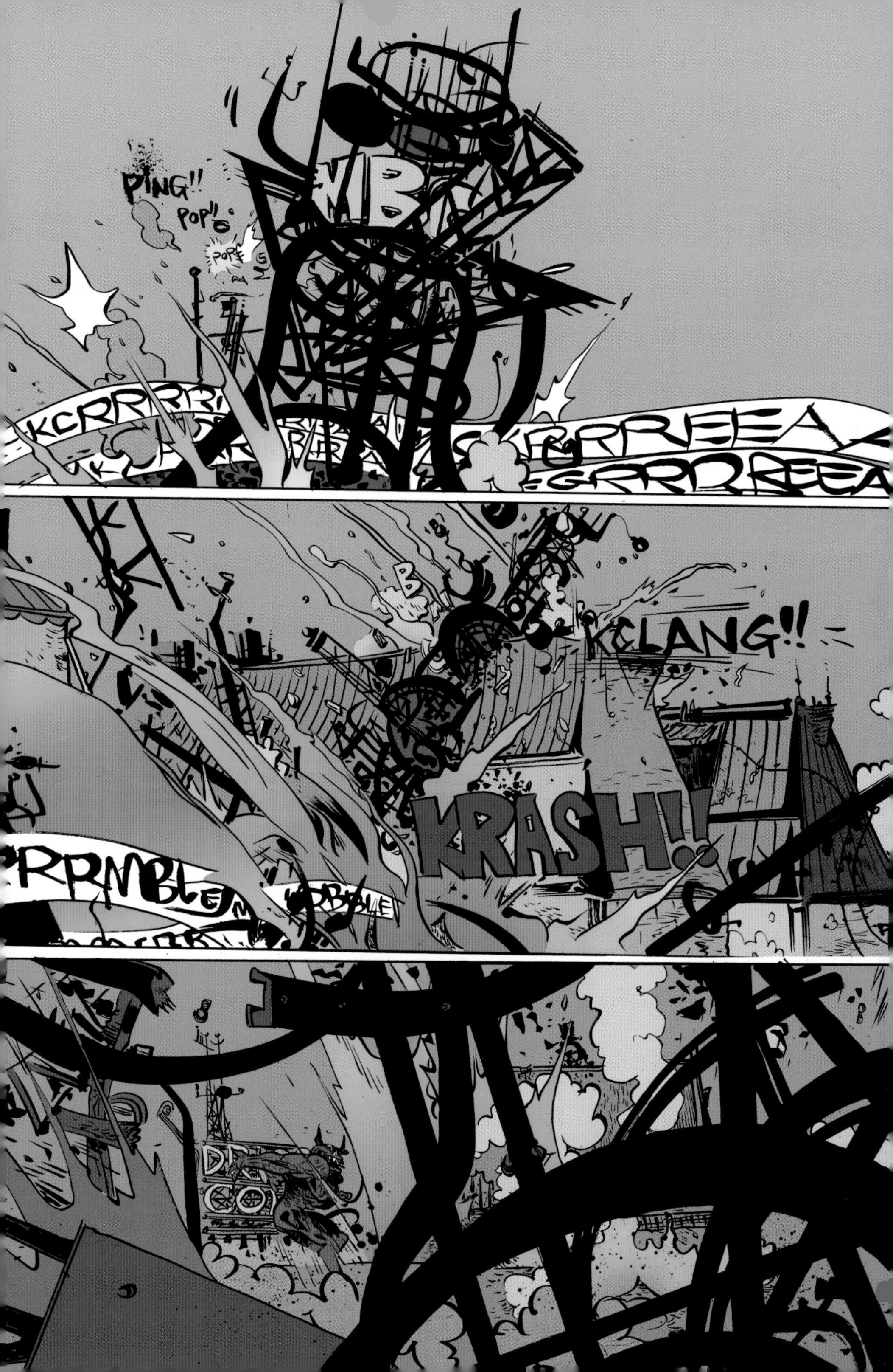

PING!!
POP!!
POP!
KCRRRRR
GRRRREEA
GRRRRREEA
KLANG!!
KRASH!!
RRRMBLE

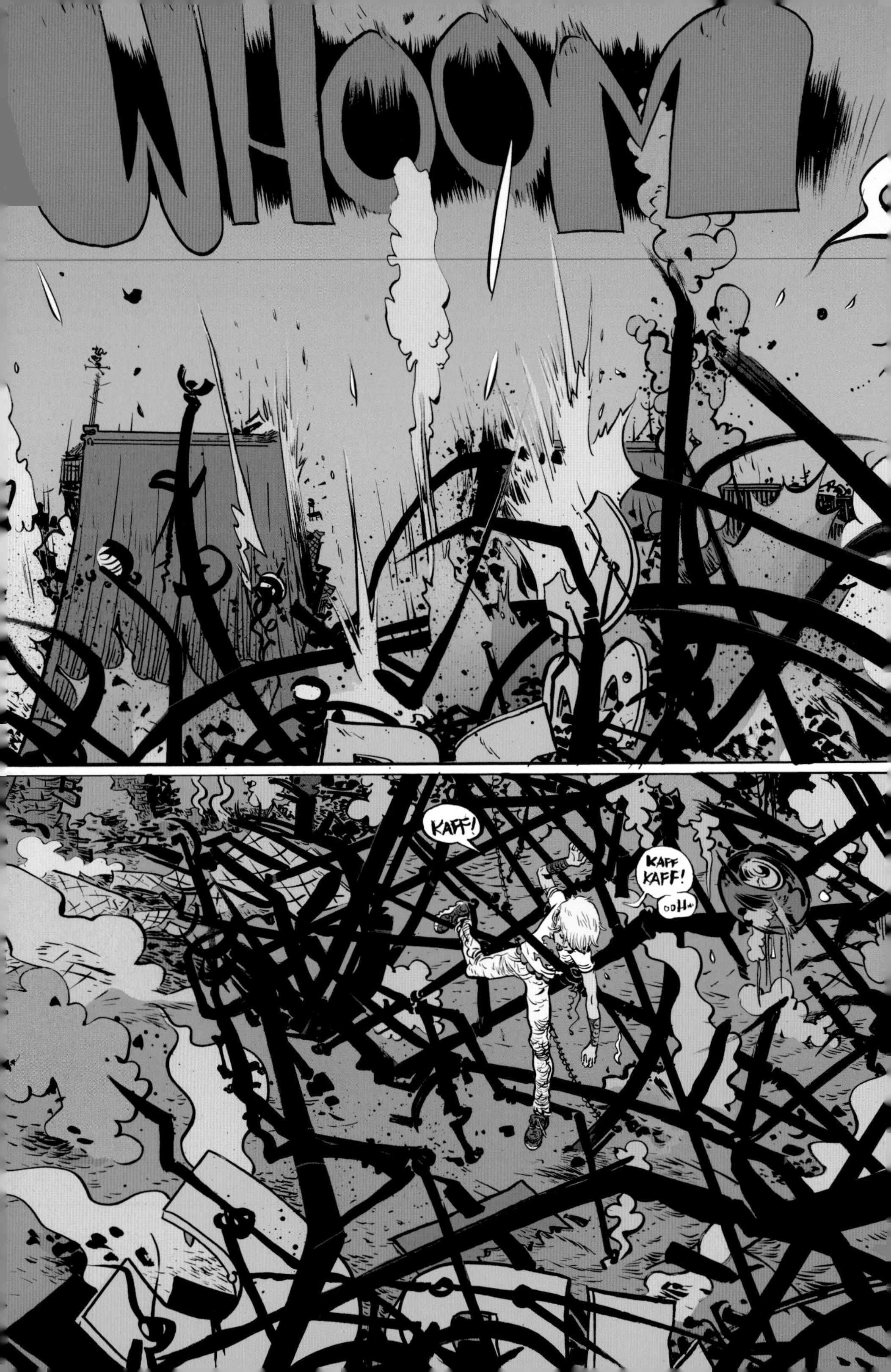
WHOOM
KAFF!
KAFF KAFF!
OOH...

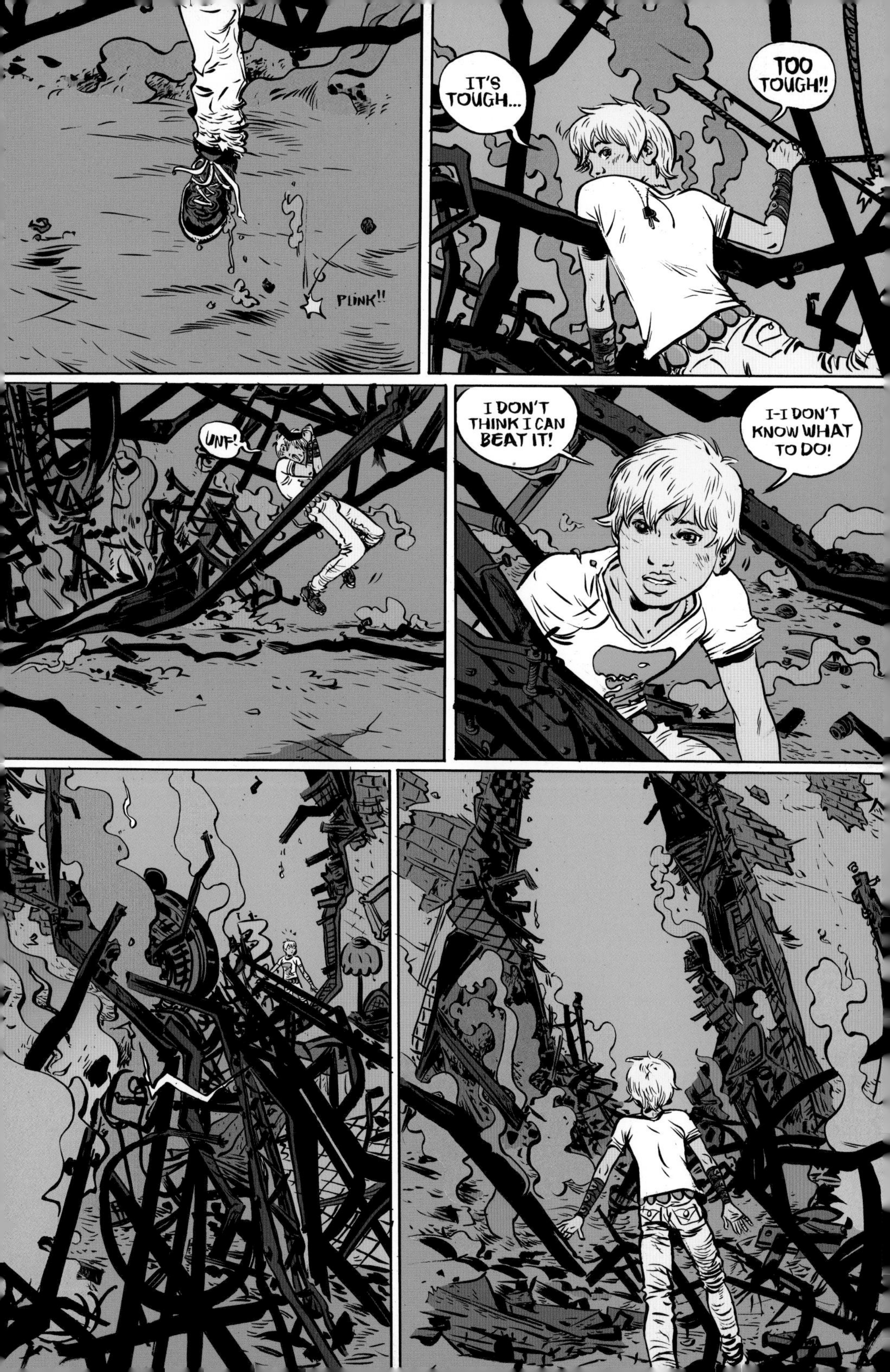
PLINK!!
IT'S TOUGH...
TOO TOUGH!!
UNF!
I DON'T THINK I CAN BEAT IT!
I-I DON'T KNOW WHAT TO DO!

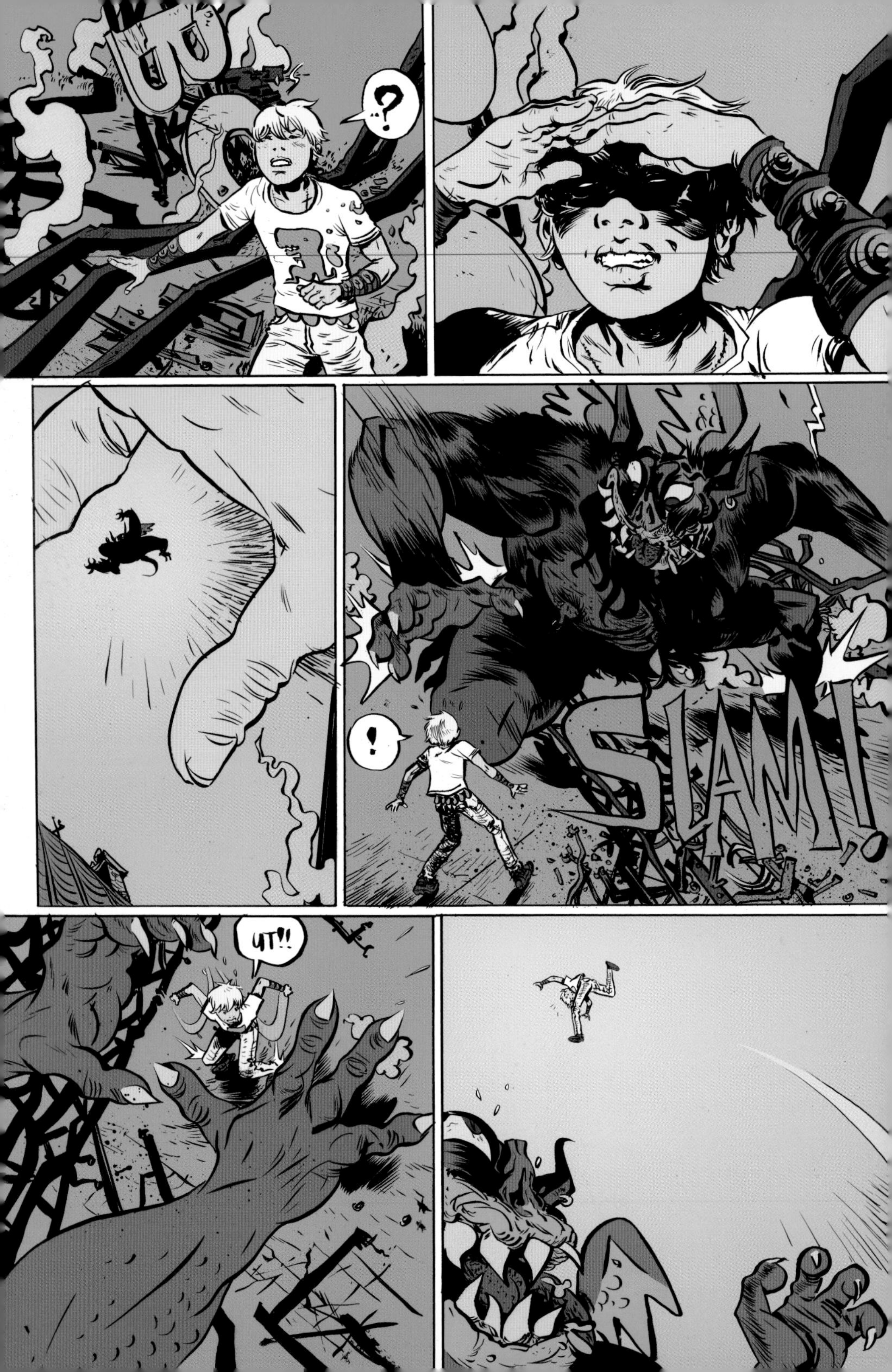
?
!
SLAM!
UT!!

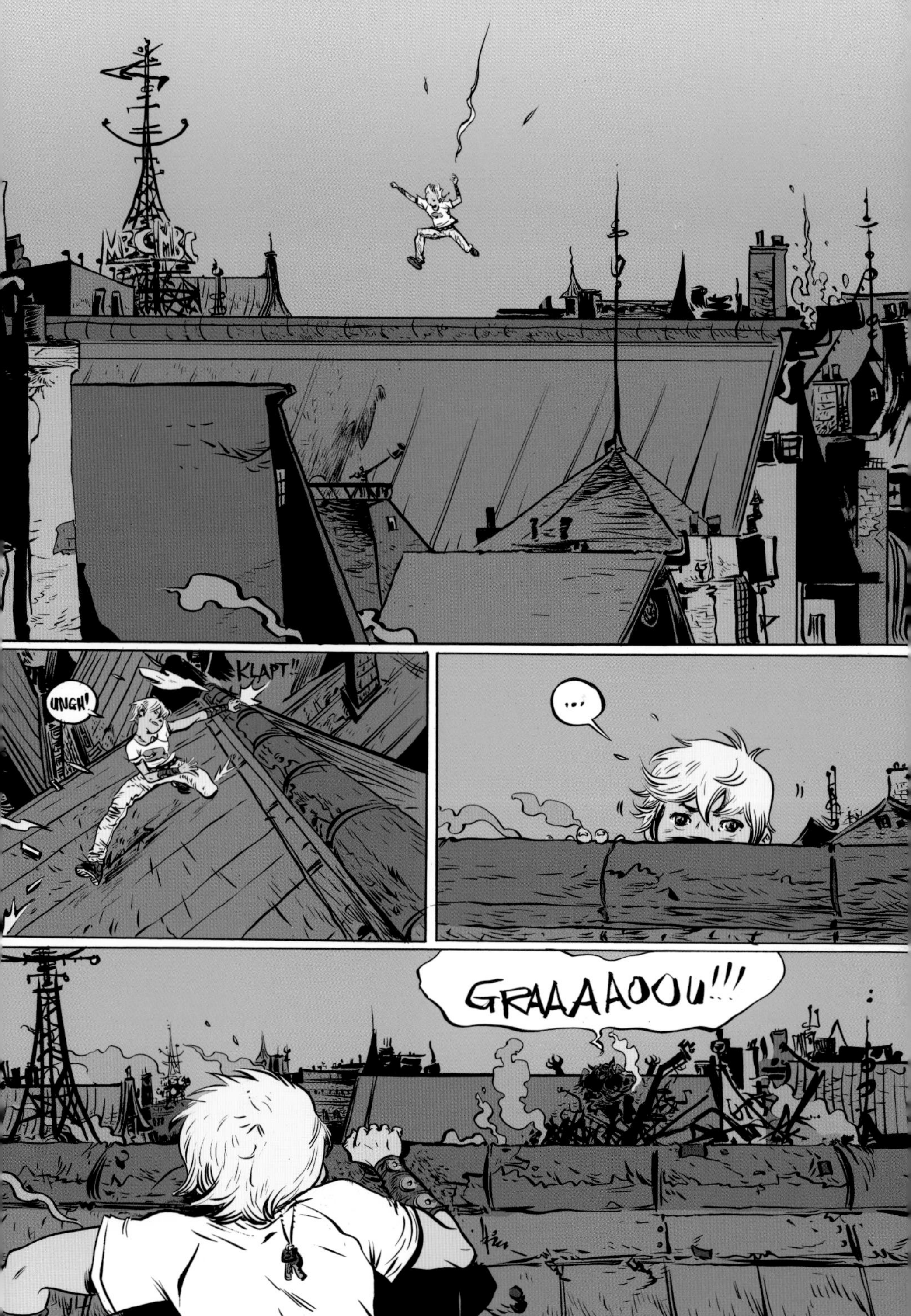

UNGH!
KLAPT!!
...
GRAAAAOOU!!!

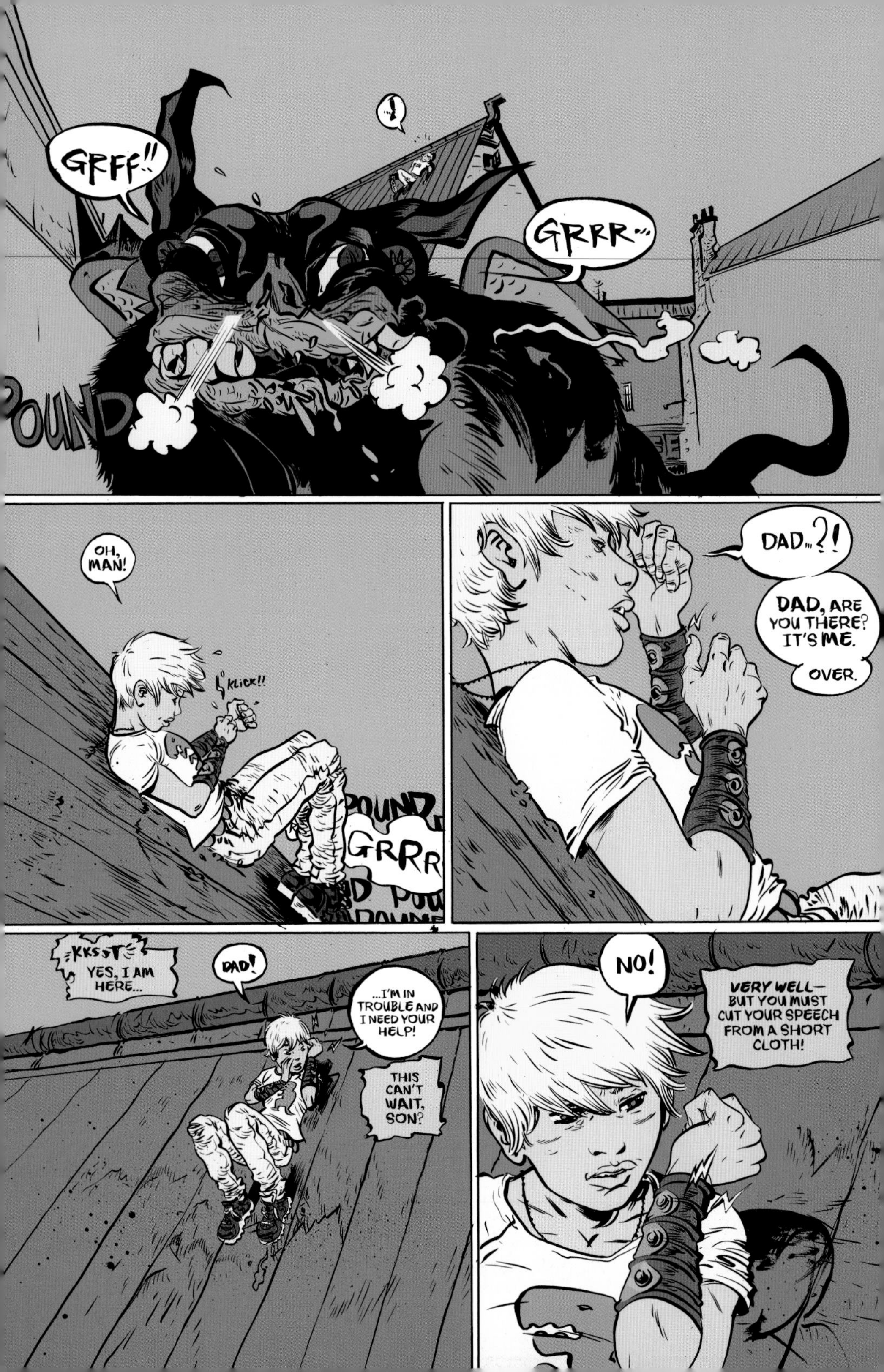
GRFF!!
!
GRRR...
POUND
OH, MAN!
KLICK!!
POUND
GRRR
DAD...?!
DAD, ARE YOU THERE? IT'S ME.
OVER.
KKSST
YES, I AM HERE...
DAD!
...I'M IN TROUBLE AND I NEED YOUR HELP!
THIS CAN'T WAIT, SON?
NO!
VERY WELL— BUT YOU MUST CUT YOUR SPEECH FROM A SHORT CLOTH!

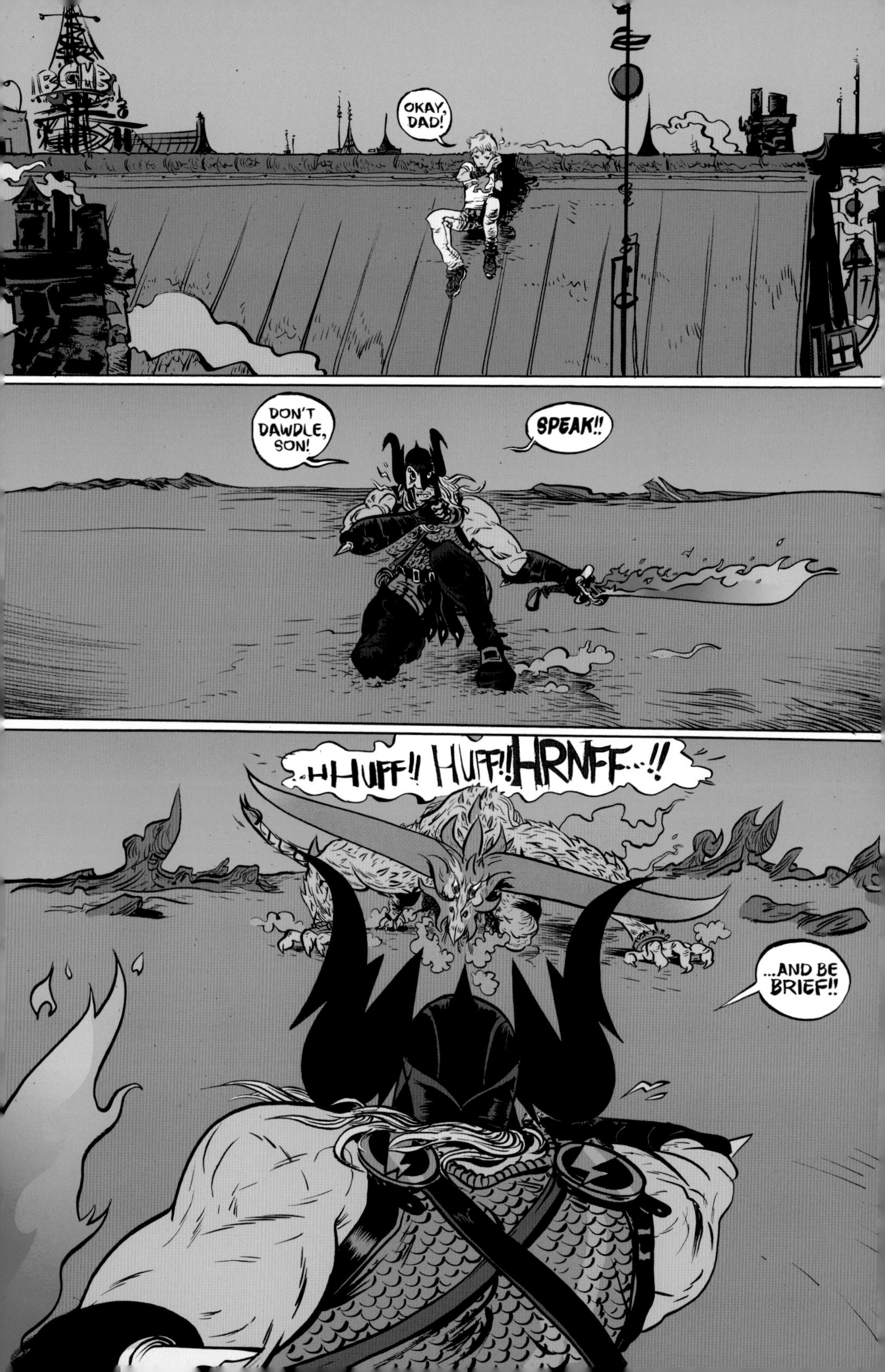

OKAY, DAD!
DON'T DAWDLE, SON!
SPEAK!!
..HHUFF!! HUFF!! HRNFF...!!
...AND BE BRIEF!!

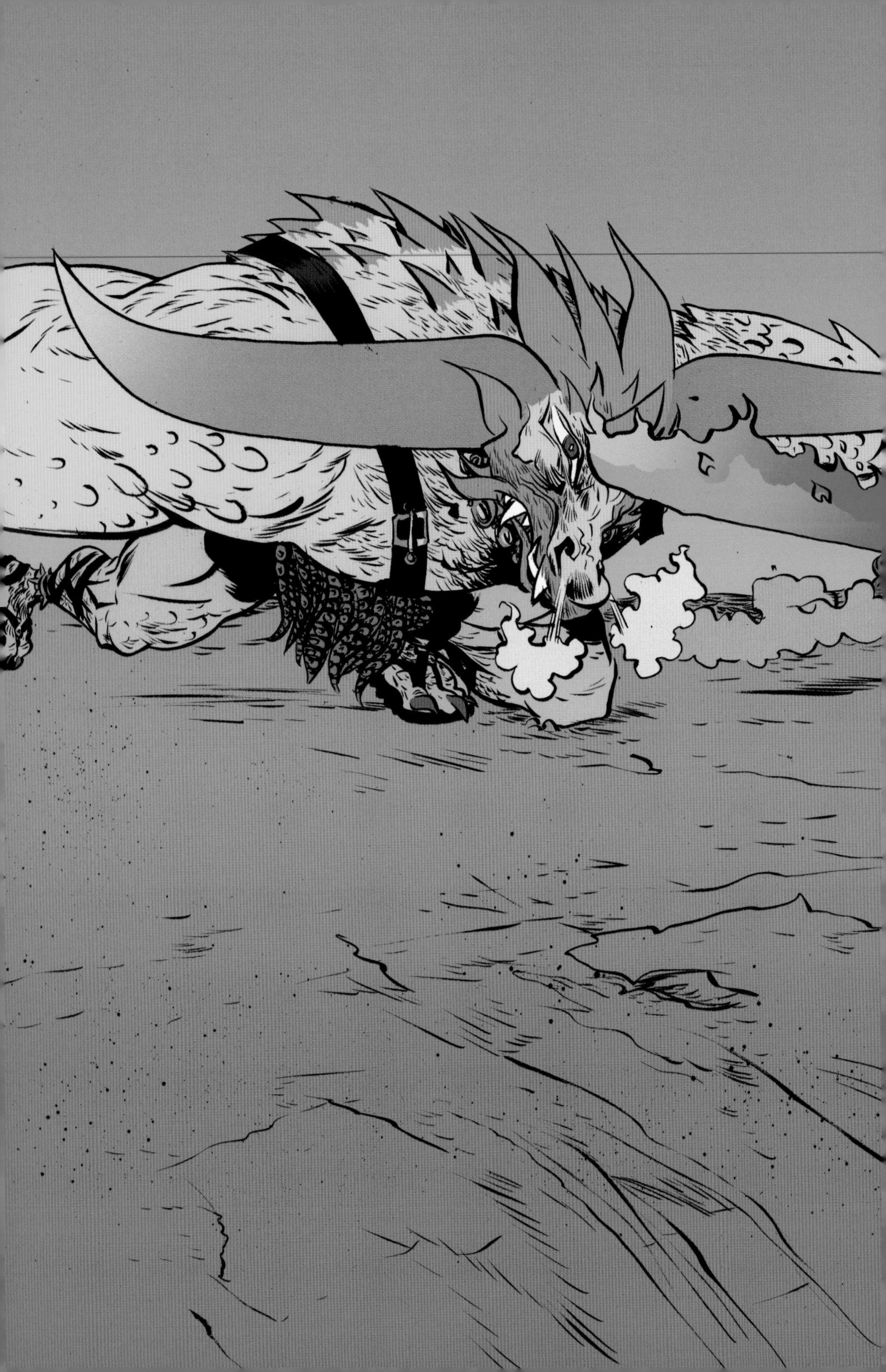

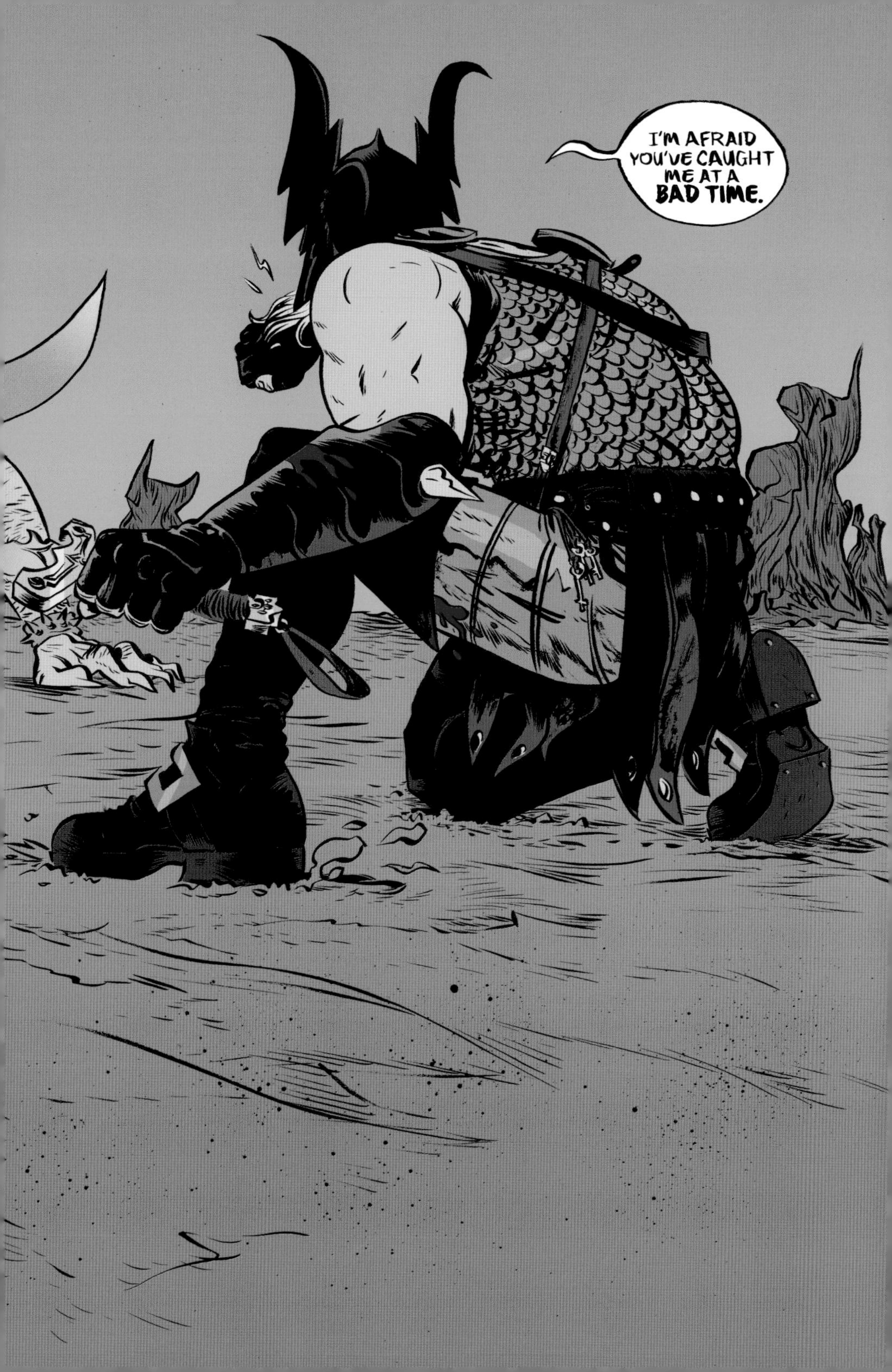
I'M AFRAID YOU'VE CAUGHT ME AT A BAD TIME.

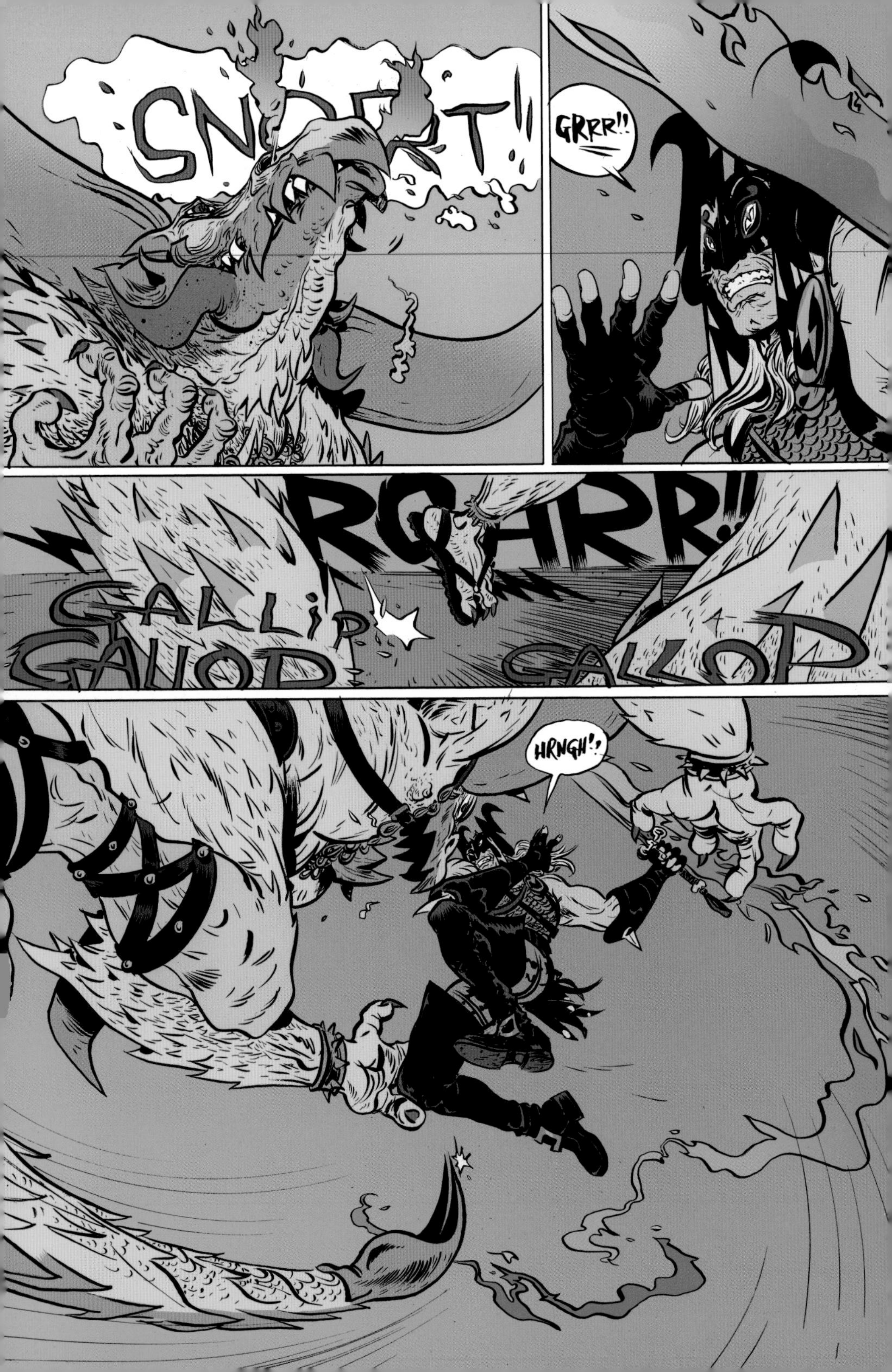
GRRR!!
GALLIP
GALLOP
HRNGH!?

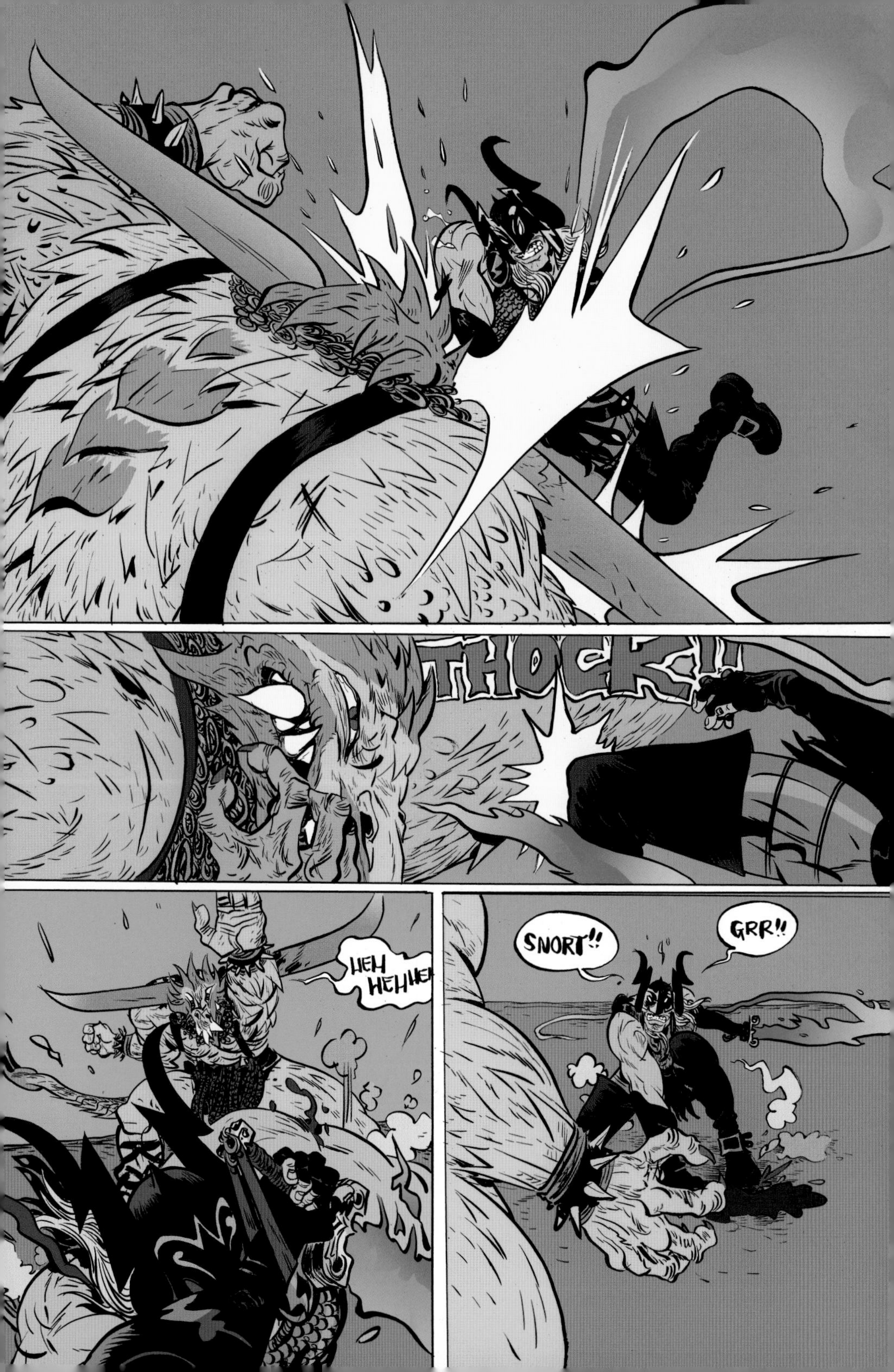
THOCK!!
HEH HEHHE
SNORT!!
GRR!!

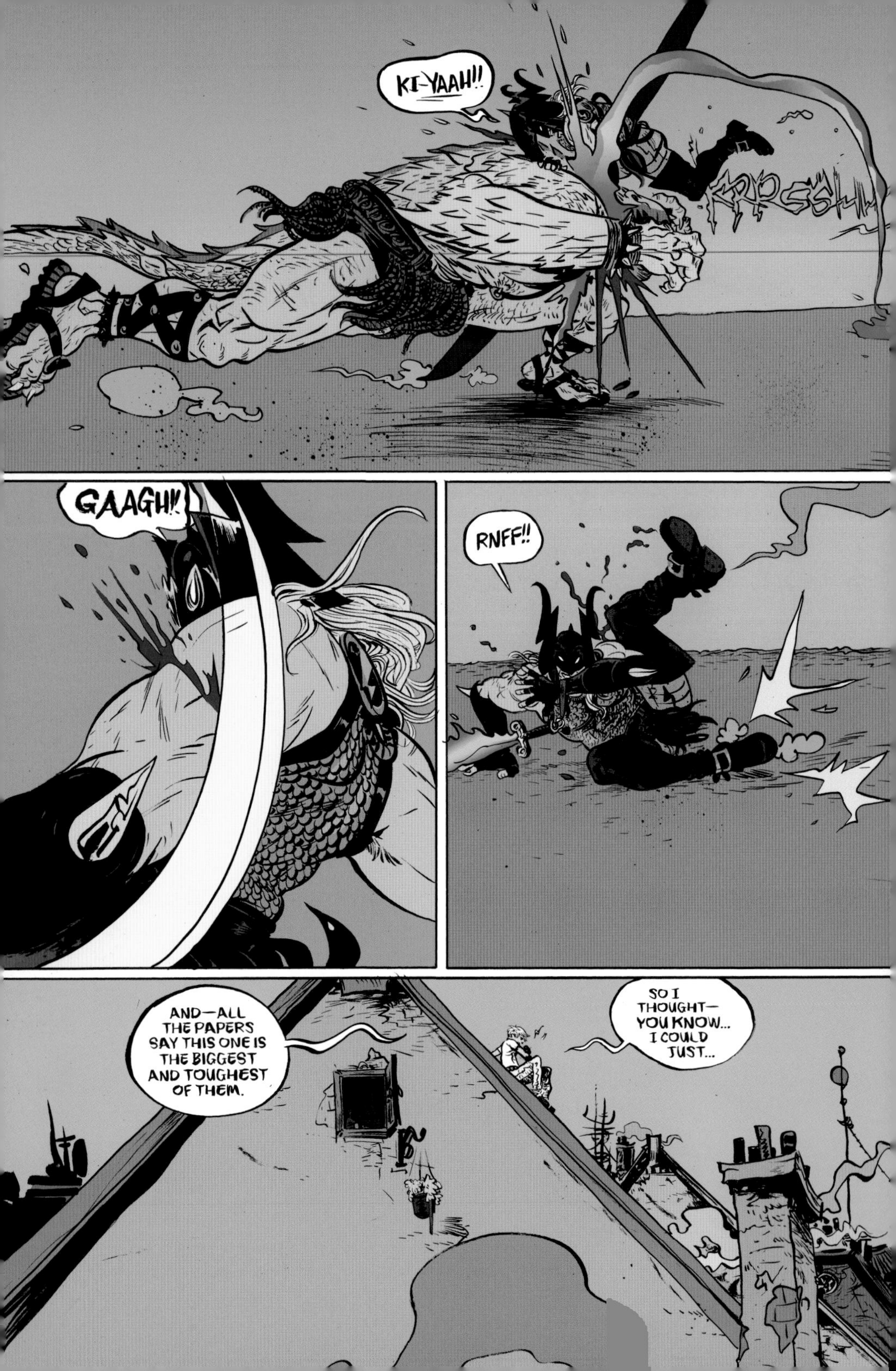
KI-YAAH!!
KRASSH
GAAGH!!
RNFF!!
AND—ALL THE PAPERS SAY THIS ONE IS THE BIGGEST AND TOUGHEST OF THEM.
SO I THOUGHT—YOU KNOW... I COULD JUST...

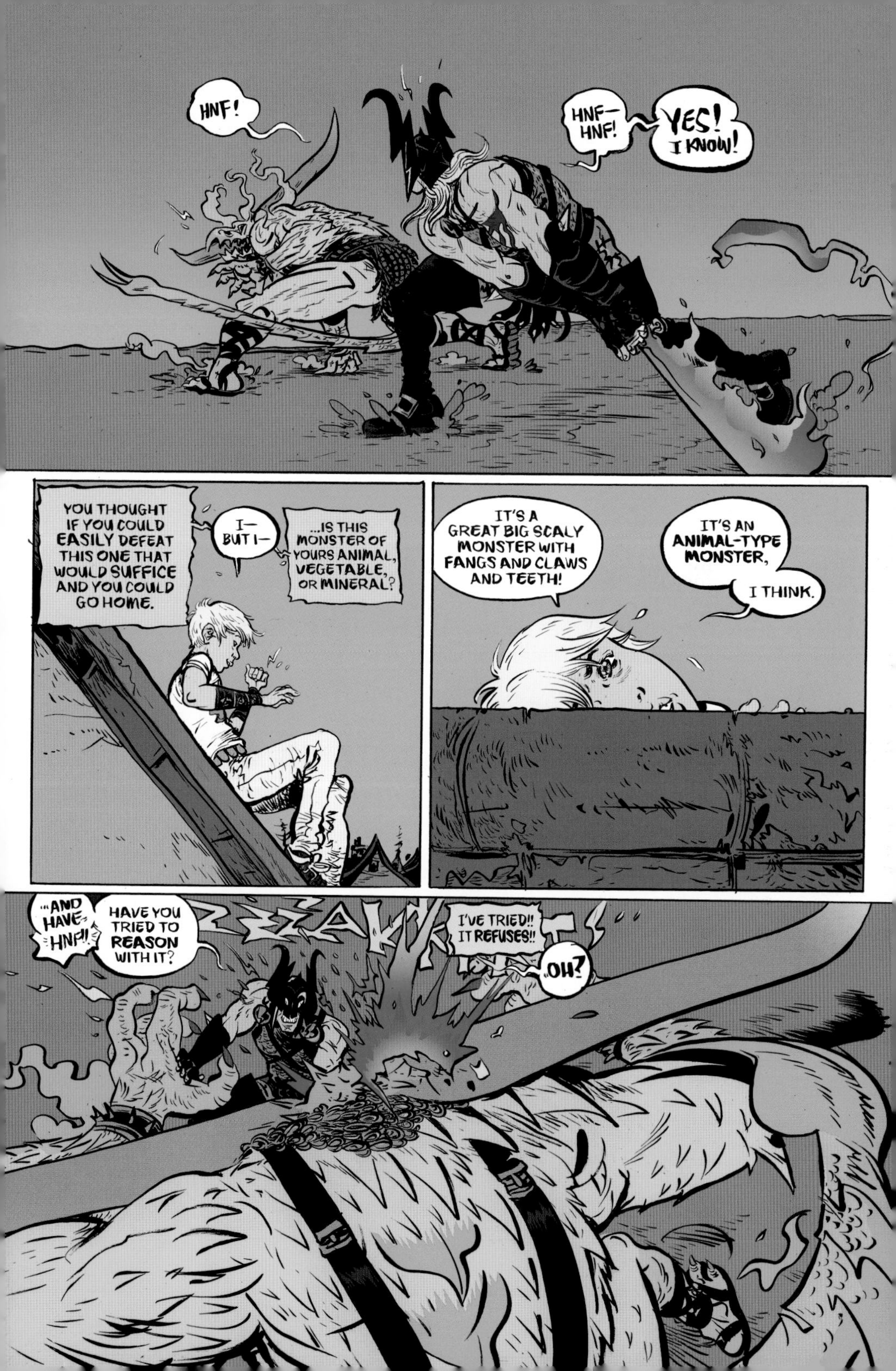
HNF!
HNF— HNF!
YES! I KNOW!
YOU THOUGHT IF YOU COULD EASILY DEFEAT THIS ONE THAT WOULD SUFFICE AND YOU COULD GO HOME.
I— BUT I—
...IS THIS MONSTER OF YOURS ANIMAL, VEGETABLE, OR MINERAL?
IT'S A GREAT BIG SCALY MONSTER WITH FANGS AND CLAWS AND TEETH!
IT'S AN ANIMAL-TYPE MONSTER,
I THINK.
...AND HAVE— HNF!!
HAVE YOU TRIED TO REASON WITH IT?
I'VE TRIED!! IT REFUSES!!
OH?

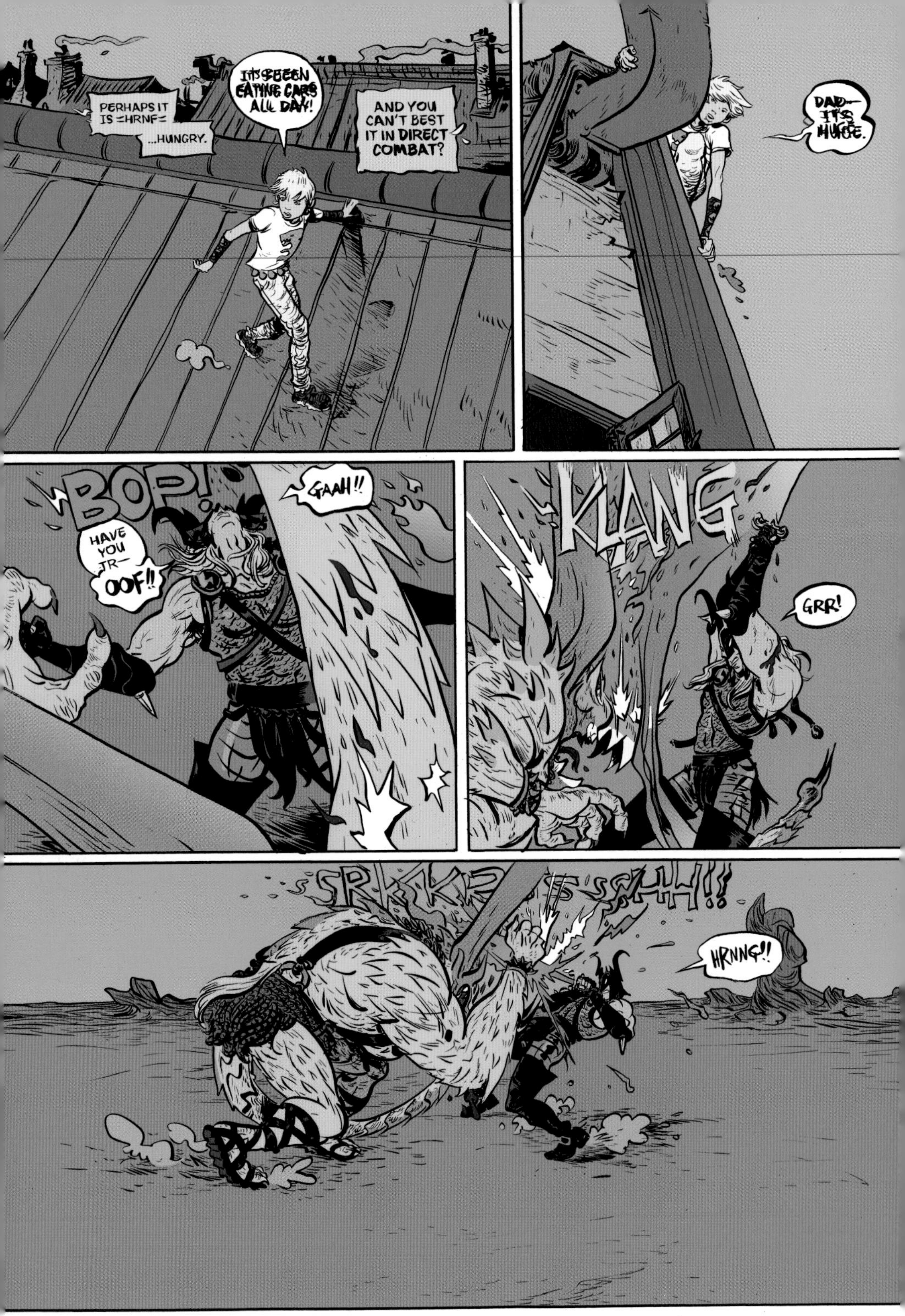

PERHAPS IT IS =HRNF=
...HUNGRY.
IT'S BEEN EATING CARS ALL DAY!
AND YOU CAN'T BEST IT IN DIRECT COMBAT?
DAD— IT'S HUGE.
BOP!
GAAH!!
HAVE YOU TR—
OOF!!
KLANG
GRR!
SRKKKSSSHH!!
HRNNG!!

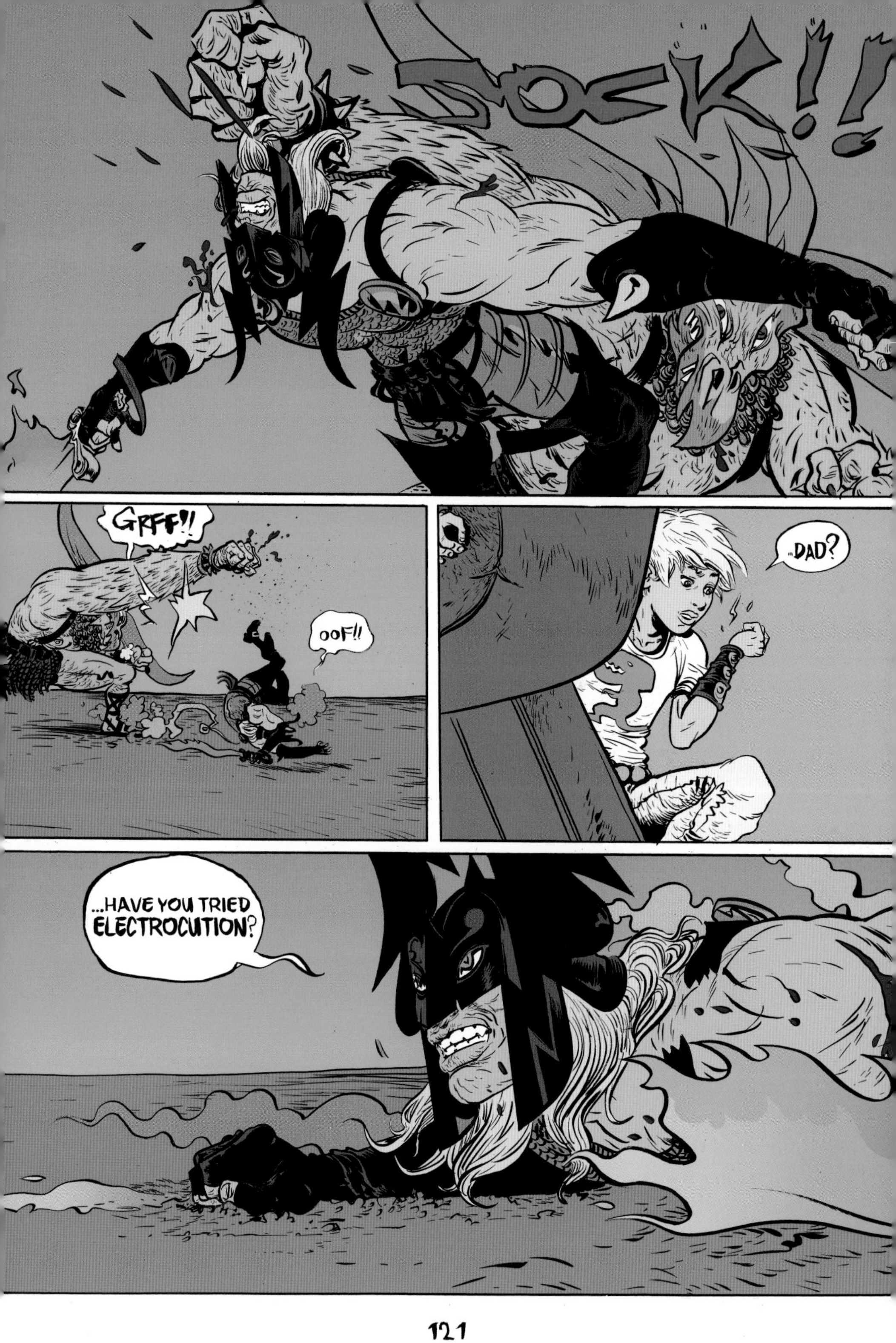
SOCK!!
GRFF!!
OOF!!
...DAD?
...HAVE YOU TRIED ELECTROCUTION?

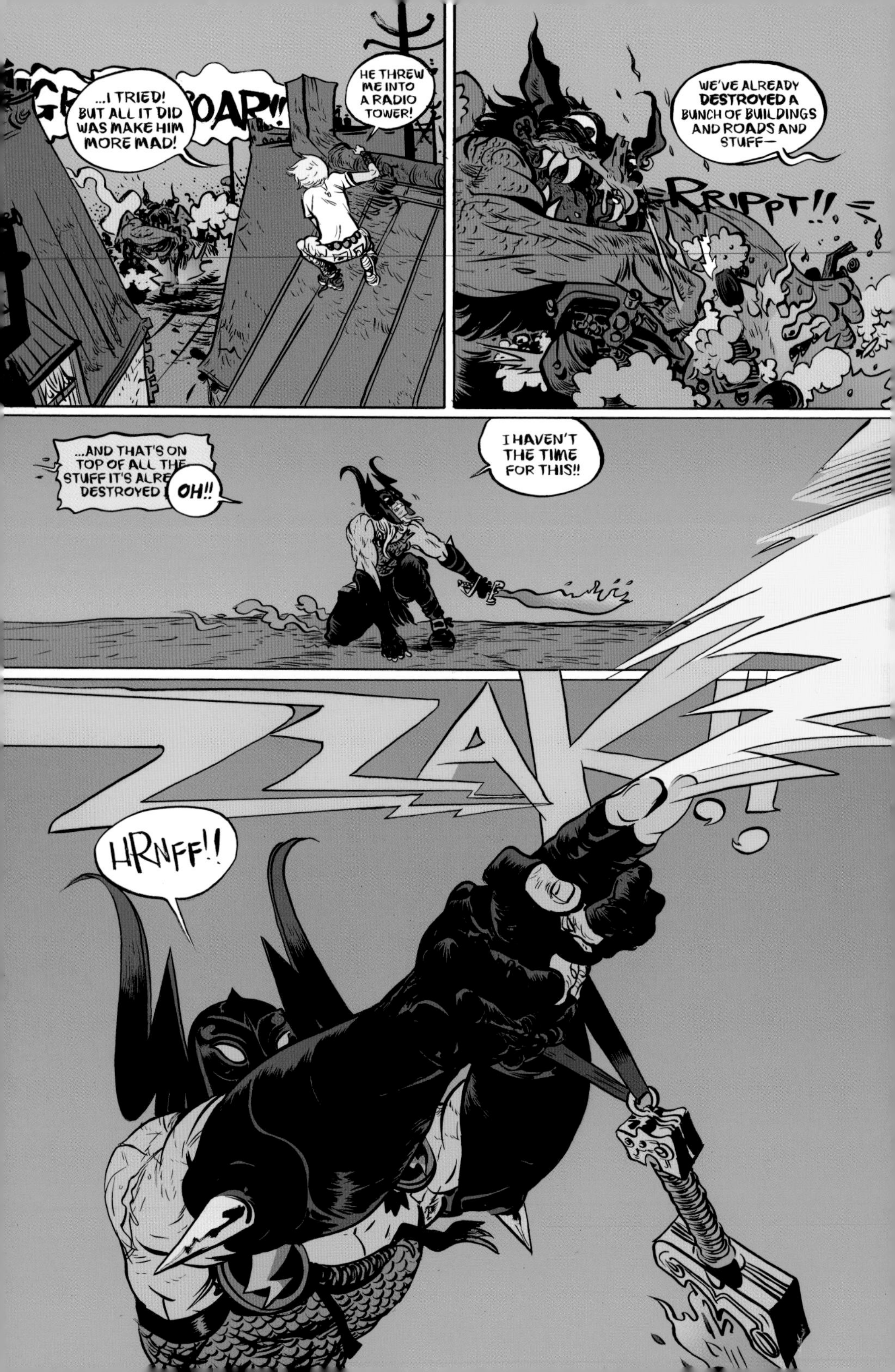

...I TRIED! BUT ALL IT DID WAS MAKE HIM MORE MAD!
HE THREW ME INTO A RADIO TOWER!
WE'VE ALREADY **DESTROYED** A BUNCH OF BUILDINGS AND ROADS AND STUFF—
RRIPPT!!
...AND THAT'S ON TOP OF ALL THE STUFF IT'S ALRE
DESTROYED
OH!!
I HAVEN'T THE TIME FOR THIS!!
ZAK
HRNFF!!

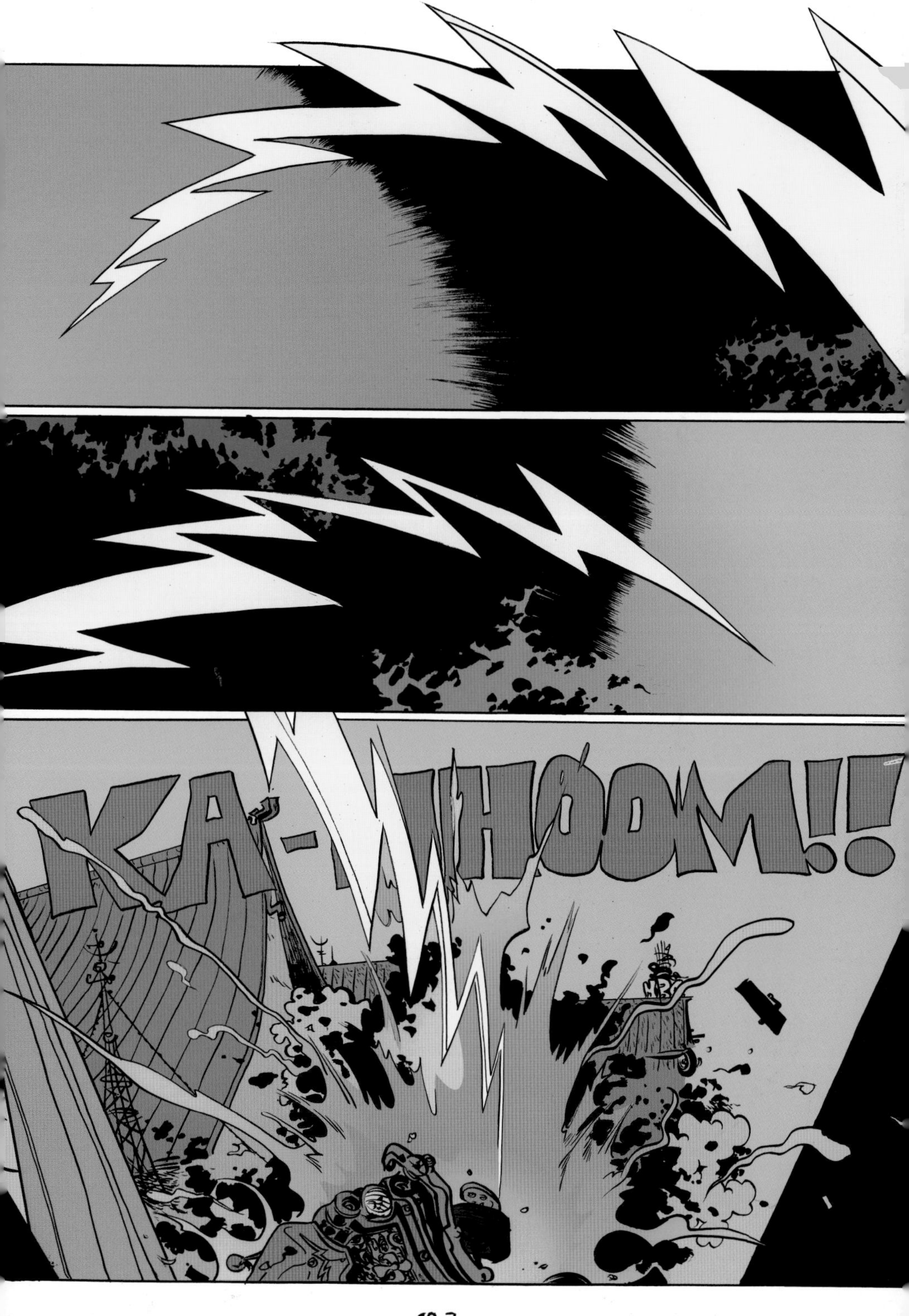
KA-WHOOM!!

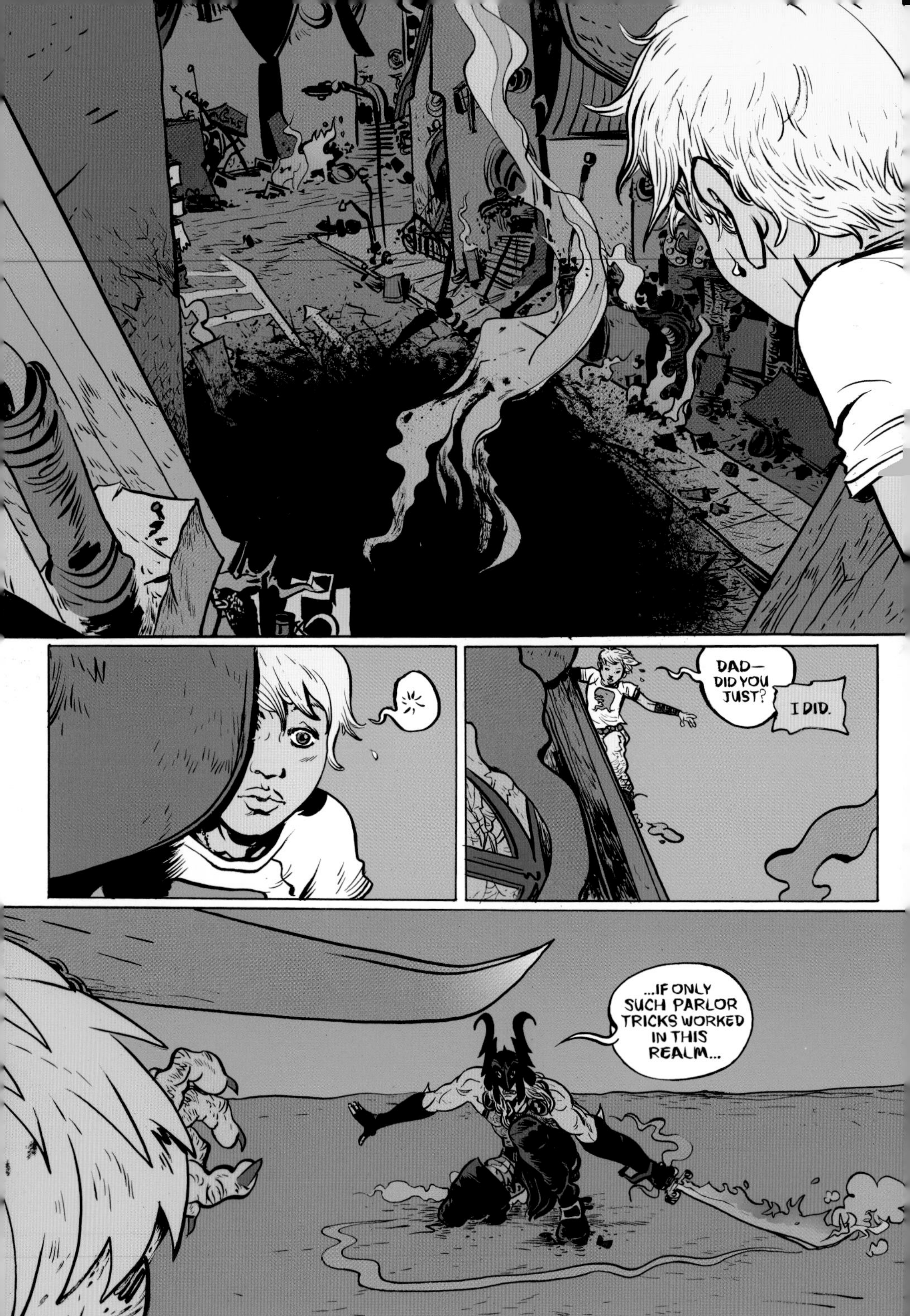
DAD— DID YOU JUST?
I DID.
...IF ONLY SUCH PARLOR TRICKS WORKED IN THIS REALM...

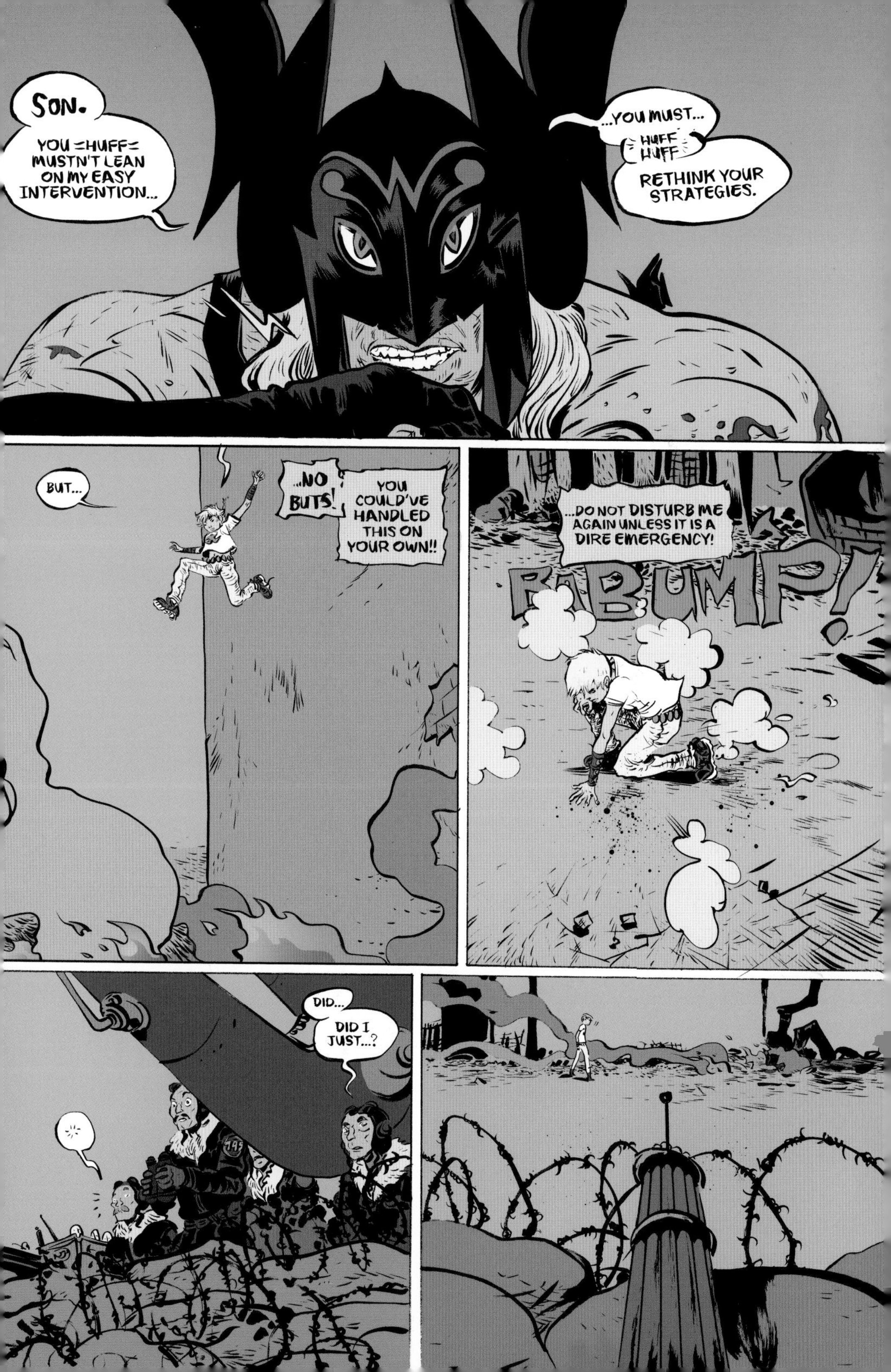
SON.
YOU =HUFF= MUSTN'T LEAN ON MY EASY INTERVENTION...
...YOU MUST...
HUFF HUFF
RETHINK YOUR STRATEGIES.
BUT...
...NO BUTS!
YOU COULD'VE HANDLED THIS ON YOUR OWN!!
...DO NOT DISTURB ME AGAIN UNLESS IT IS A DIRE EMERGENCY!
BABUMP!
DID...
DID I JUST...?

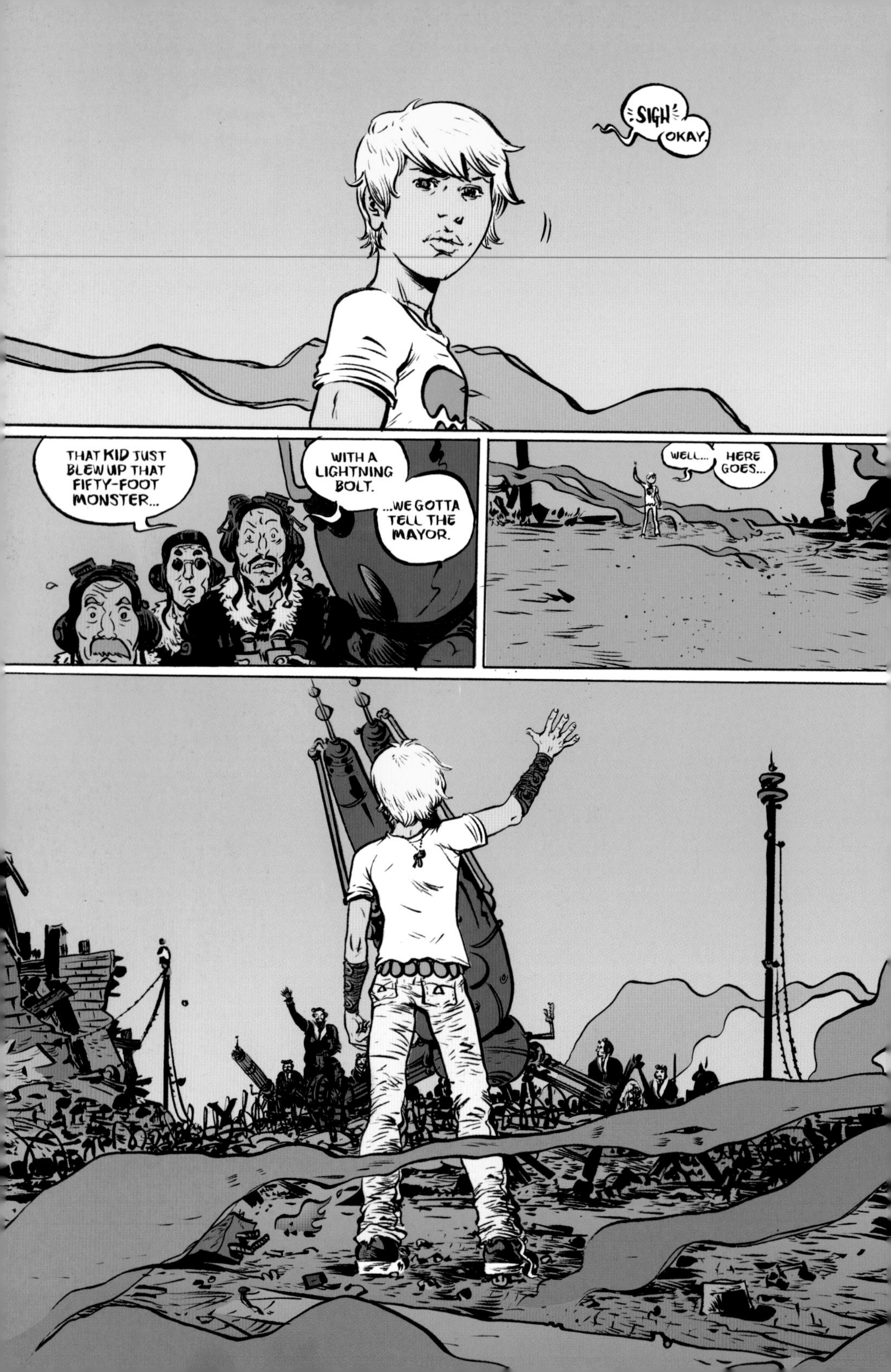
SIGH
OKAY.
THAT KID JUST BLEW UP THAT FIFTY-FOOT MONSTER...
WITH A LIGHTNING BOLT.
...WE GOTTA TELL THE MAYOR.
WELL...
HERE GOES...

AURORA—
PASS ME
THAT TWENTY
MILLIMETER
SPANNER,
WILL YOU?

...WHEN THE
ASSEMBLY
MEETS
LATER THIS
WEEK.

CRANK
CRANK

AURORA—
THE SPANNER.

TWENTY
MIL.

...AURORA!!

IN OTHER BREAKING NEWS,
THERE IS SOME PROGRESS
TONIGHT IN THE WAR
AGAINST THE MONS— OH!

YOU'RE NOT PAYING ATTENTION.

WE NEED TO REMOVE THESE MOTOR MOUNTS.

...ORDE... TO... SE...

SORRY.

...A NEW HERO EMERGED TODAY, AND, WITH THE ASSISTANCE OF THE MEN OF THE 145TH, DEFEATED...

NEW H—?

THE STRANGE NEW MONSTER KNOWN ONLY AS "HUMBABA."

MBC
NEW HERO ARC 9 PO...

THIS YOUNG MAN IS SAID TO HAVE EXHIBITED SUPERHUMAN ABILITIES, AND—

RO

ACCORDING TO EYEWITNESSES CALLED—AH—LIGHTNING DOWN FROM THE SKY, A, UM, FEAT WHICH CAUSED THE...

SUPERHU—? LIGHTNING?

MS. G—ARE YOU SEEING THIS?

LED TO THE DESTRUCTION OF THE MONSTER.

DETAILS ARE YET TO EMERGE AS TO THE IDENTITY OF—

THIS NEW CHAMPION.

WHAT!?

NEW CHAMPION?

A STATEMENT FROM OFFICIALS IS STILL FORTHCOMING.

128

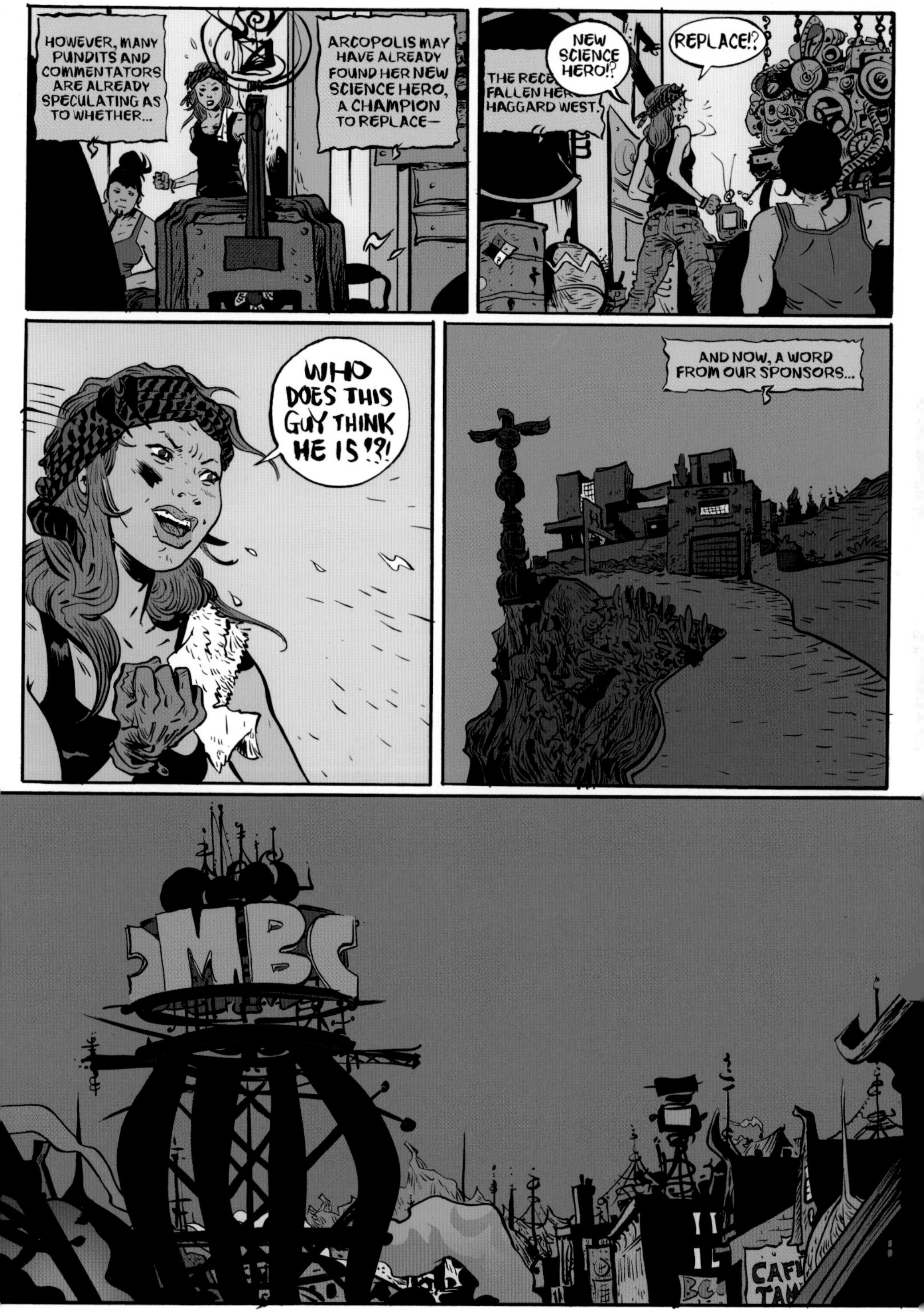
HOWEVER, MANY PUNDITS AND COMMENTATORS ARE ALREADY SPECULATING AS TO WHETHER...
ARCOPOLIS MAY HAVE ALREADY FOUND HER NEW SCIENCE HERO, A CHAMPION TO REPLACE—
NEW SCIENCE HERO!?
REPLACE!?
WHO DOES THIS GUY THINK HE IS!?!
AND NOW, A WORD FROM OUR SPONSORS...
MBC

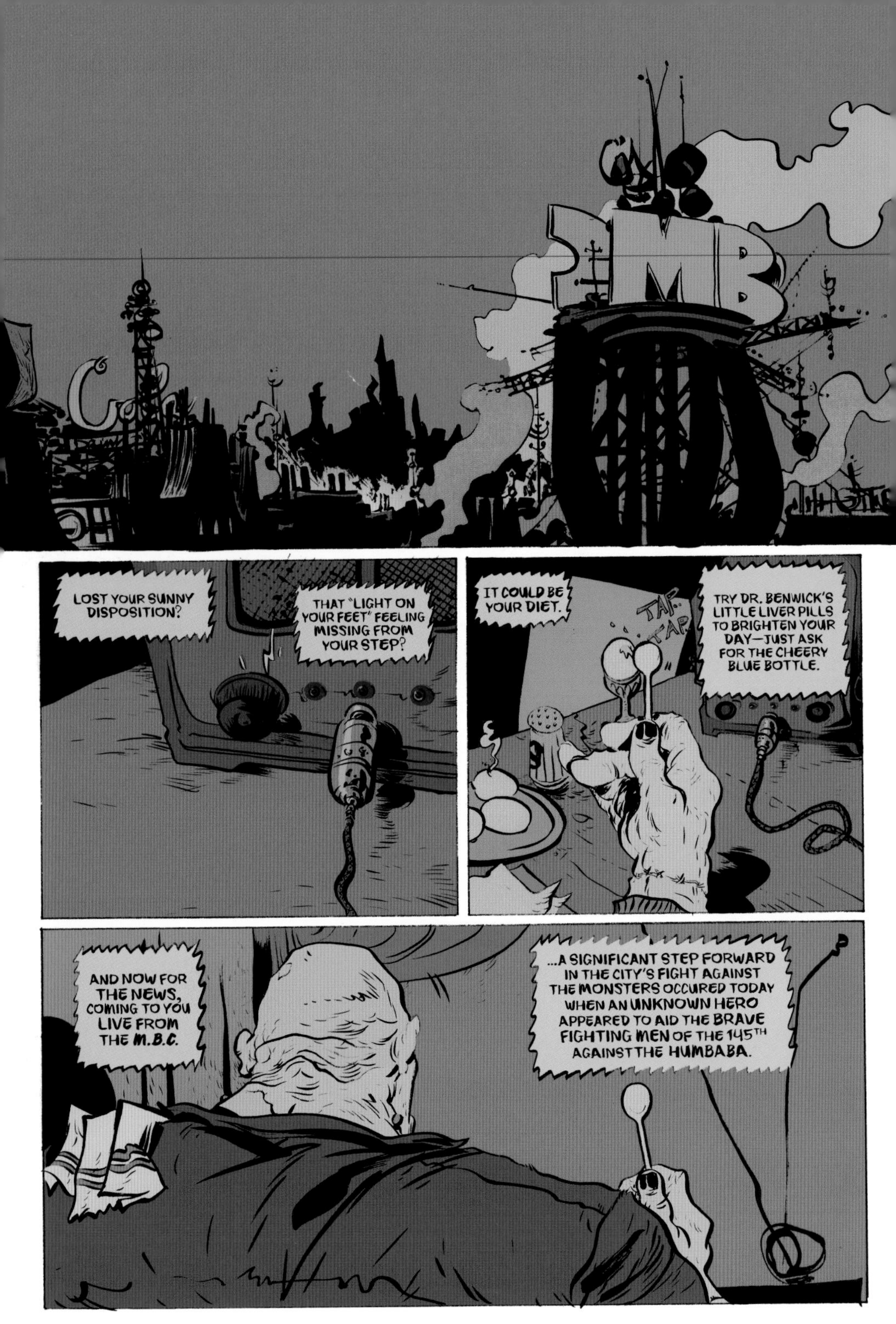

LOST YOUR SUNNY DISPOSITION?
THAT "LIGHT ON YOUR FEET" FEELING MISSING FROM YOUR STEP?
IT COULD BE YOUR DIET.
TAP TAP
TRY DR. BENWICK'S LITTLE LIVER PILLS TO BRIGHTEN YOUR DAY—JUST ASK FOR THE CHEERY BLUE BOTTLE.
AND NOW FOR THE NEWS, COMING TO YOU LIVE FROM THE M.B.C.
...A SIGNIFICANT STEP FORWARD IN THE CITY'S FIGHT AGAINST THE MONSTERS OCCURED TODAY WHEN AN UNKNOWN HERO APPEARED TO AID THE BRAVE FIGHTING MEN OF THE 145TH AGAINST THE HUMBABA.

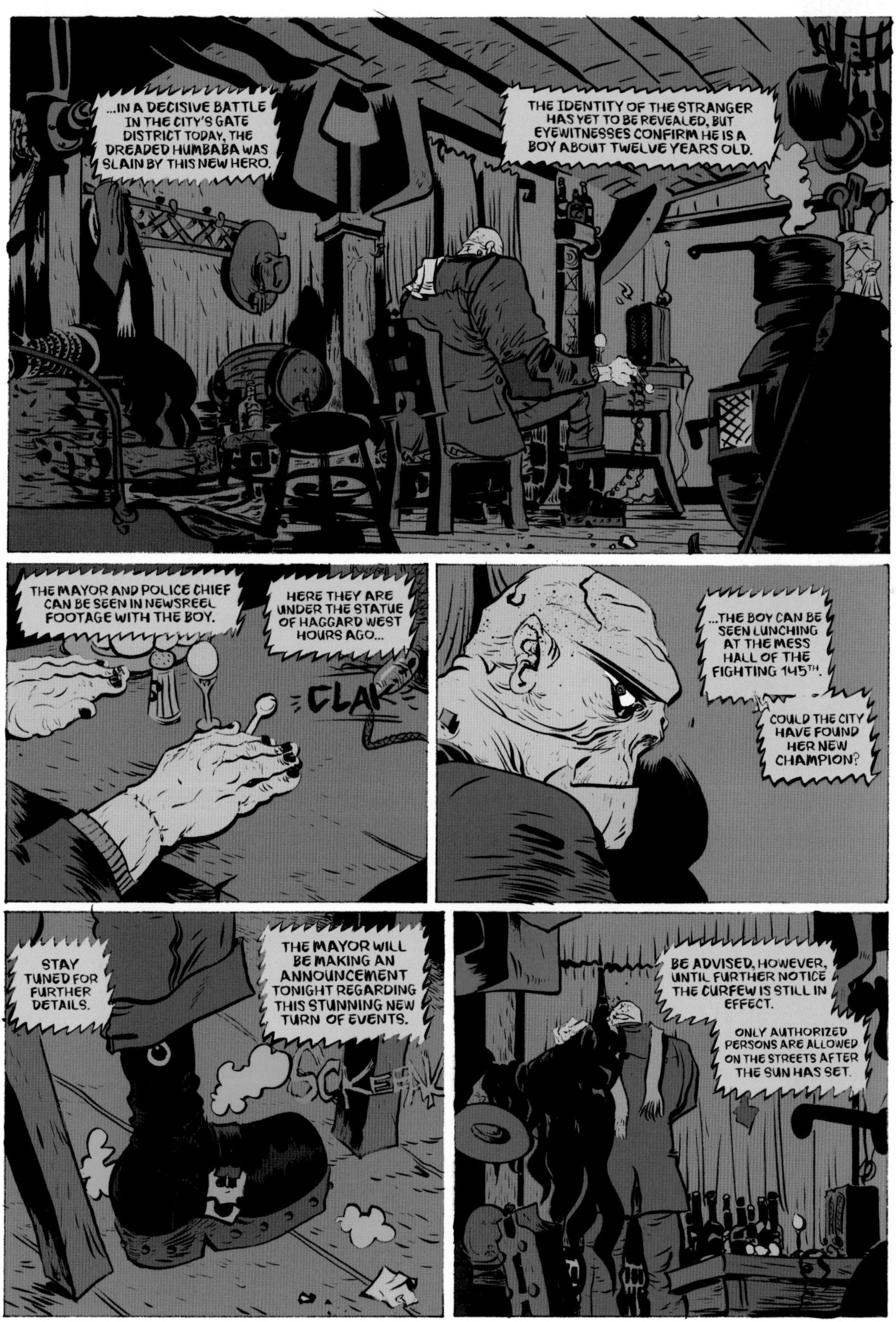
...IN A DECISIVE BATTLE IN THE CITY'S GATE DISTRICT TODAY, THE DREADED HUMBABA WAS SLAIN BY THIS NEW HERO.
THE IDENTITY OF THE STRANGER HAS YET TO BE REVEALED, BUT EYEWITNESSES CONFIRM HE IS A BOY ABOUT TWELVE YEARS OLD.
THE MAYOR AND POLICE CHIEF CAN BE SEEN IN NEWSREEL FOOTAGE WITH THE BOY.
HERE THEY ARE UNDER THE STATUE OF HAGGARD WEST HOURS AGO...
CLAK
...THE BOY CAN BE SEEN LUNCHING AT THE MESS HALL OF THE FIGHTING 145TH.
COULD THE CITY HAVE FOUND HER NEW CHAMPION?
STAY TUNED FOR FURTHER DETAILS.
THE MAYOR WILL BE MAKING AN ANNOUNCEMENT TONIGHT REGARDING THIS STUNNING NEW TURN OF EVENTS.
SCKEEK
BE ADVISED, HOWEVER, UNTIL FURTHER NOTICE THE CURFEW IS STILL IN EFFECT.
ONLY AUTHORIZED PERSONS ARE ALLOWED ON THE STREETS AFTER THE SUN HAS SET.

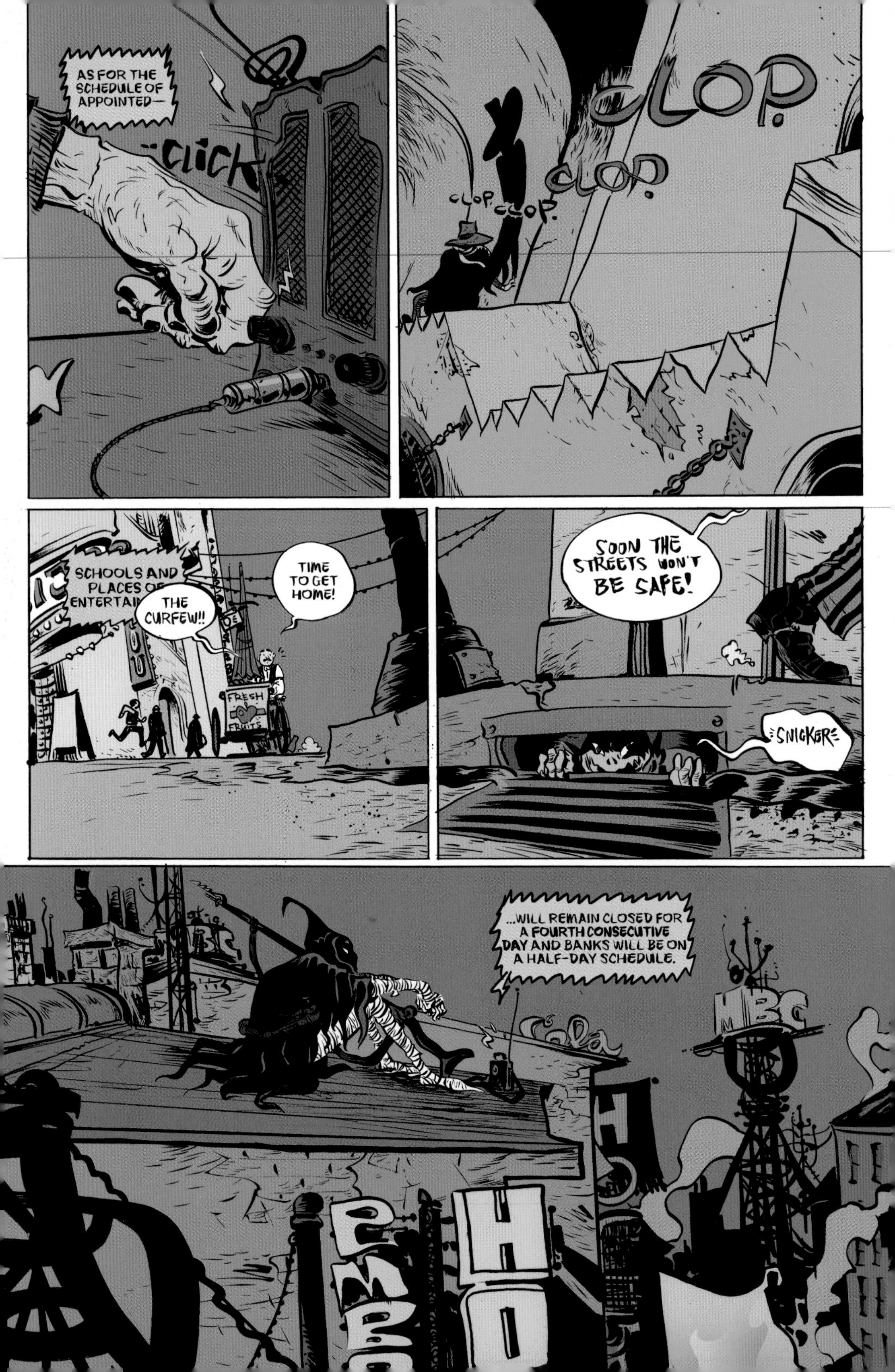
AS FOR THE SCHEDULE OF APPOINTED—
CLICK
CLOP.
CLOP.
CLOP.CLOP.
SCHOOLS AND PLACES OF ENTERTAIN
THE CURFEW!!
TIME TO GET HOME!
FRESH FRUITS
SOON THE STREETS WON'T BE SAFE!
SNICKER
...WILL REMAIN CLOSED FOR A FOURTH CONSECUTIVE DAY AND BANKS WILL BE ON A HALF-DAY SCHEDULE.

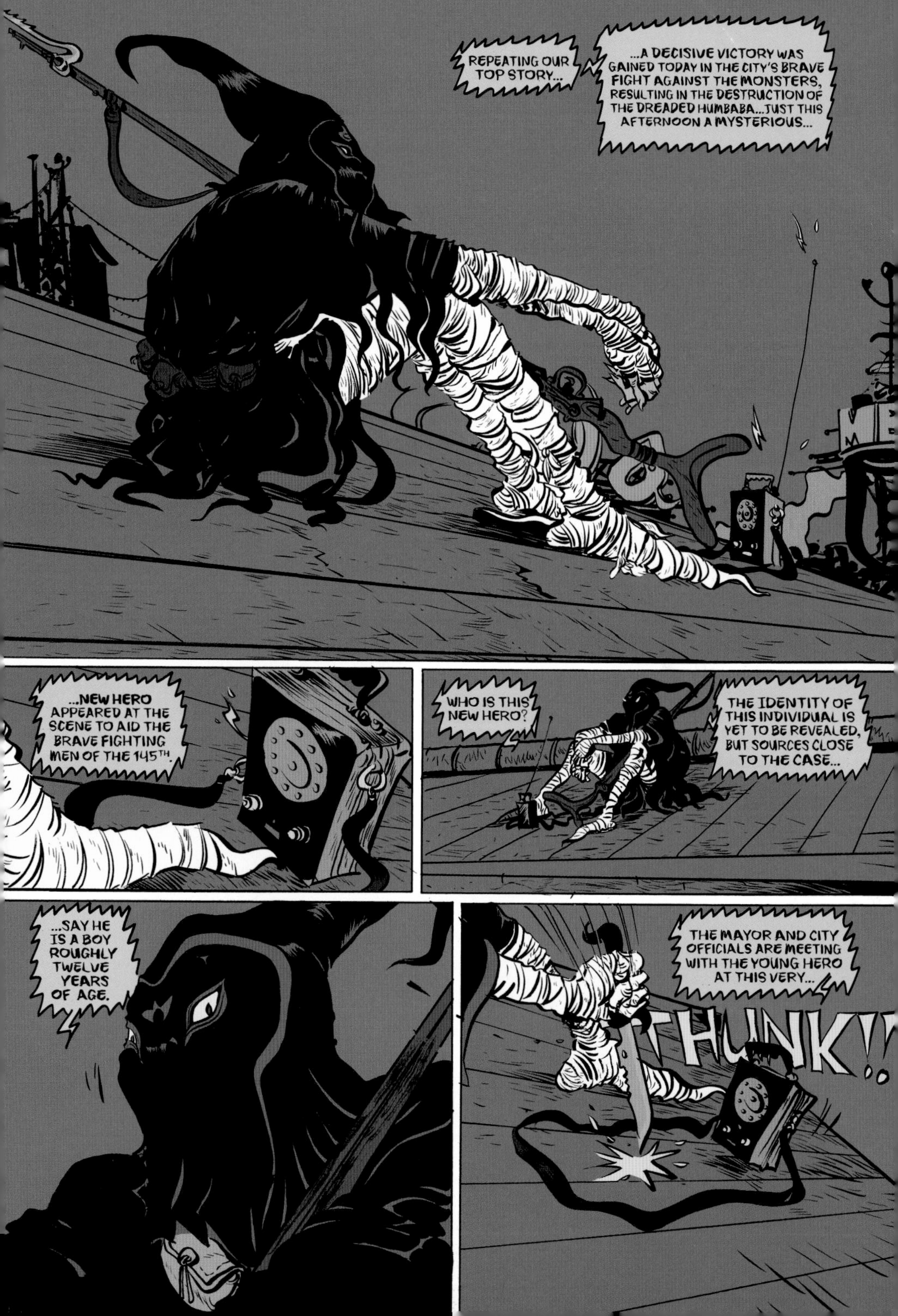
REPEATING OUR TOP STORY...
...A DECISIVE VICTORY WAS GAINED TODAY IN THE CITY'S BRAVE FIGHT AGAINST THE MONSTERS, RESULTING IN THE DESTRUCTION OF THE DREADED HUMBABA...JUST THIS AFTERNOON A MYSTERIOUS...
...NEW HERO APPEARED AT THE SCENE TO AID THE BRAVE FIGHTING MEN OF THE 145TH.
WHO IS THIS NEW HERO?
THE IDENTITY OF THIS INDIVIDUAL IS YET TO BE REVEALED, BUT SOURCES CLOSE TO THE CASE...
...SAY HE IS A BOY ROUGHLY TWELVE YEARS OF AGE.
THE MAYOR AND CITY OFFICIALS ARE MEETING WITH THE YOUNG HERO AT THIS VERY...
THUNK!!

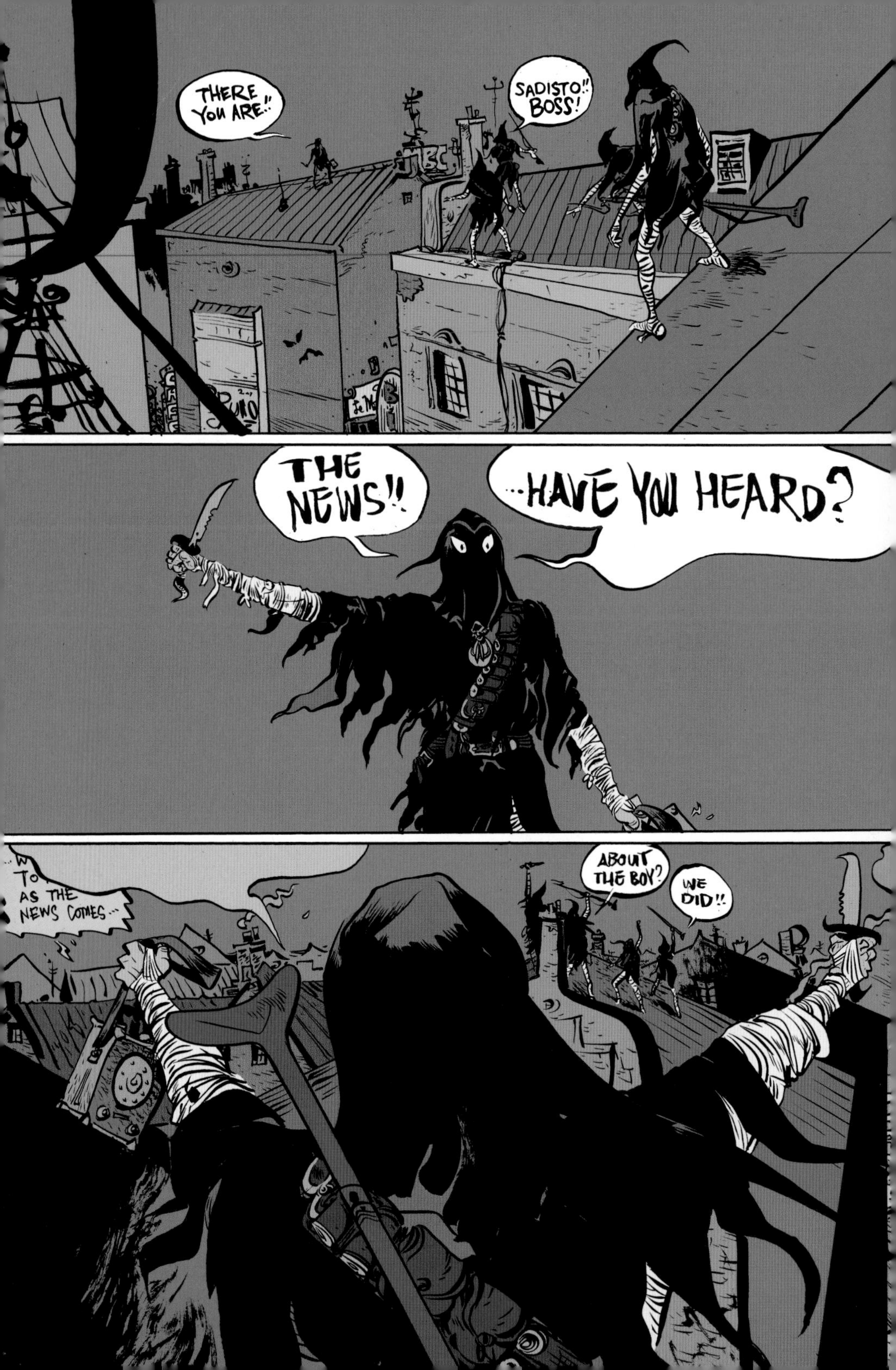
THERE YOU ARE!!
SADISTO!! BOSS!
THE NEWS!!
...HAVE YOU HEARD?
...W TO AS THE NEWS COMES...
ABOUT THE BOY?
WE DID!!

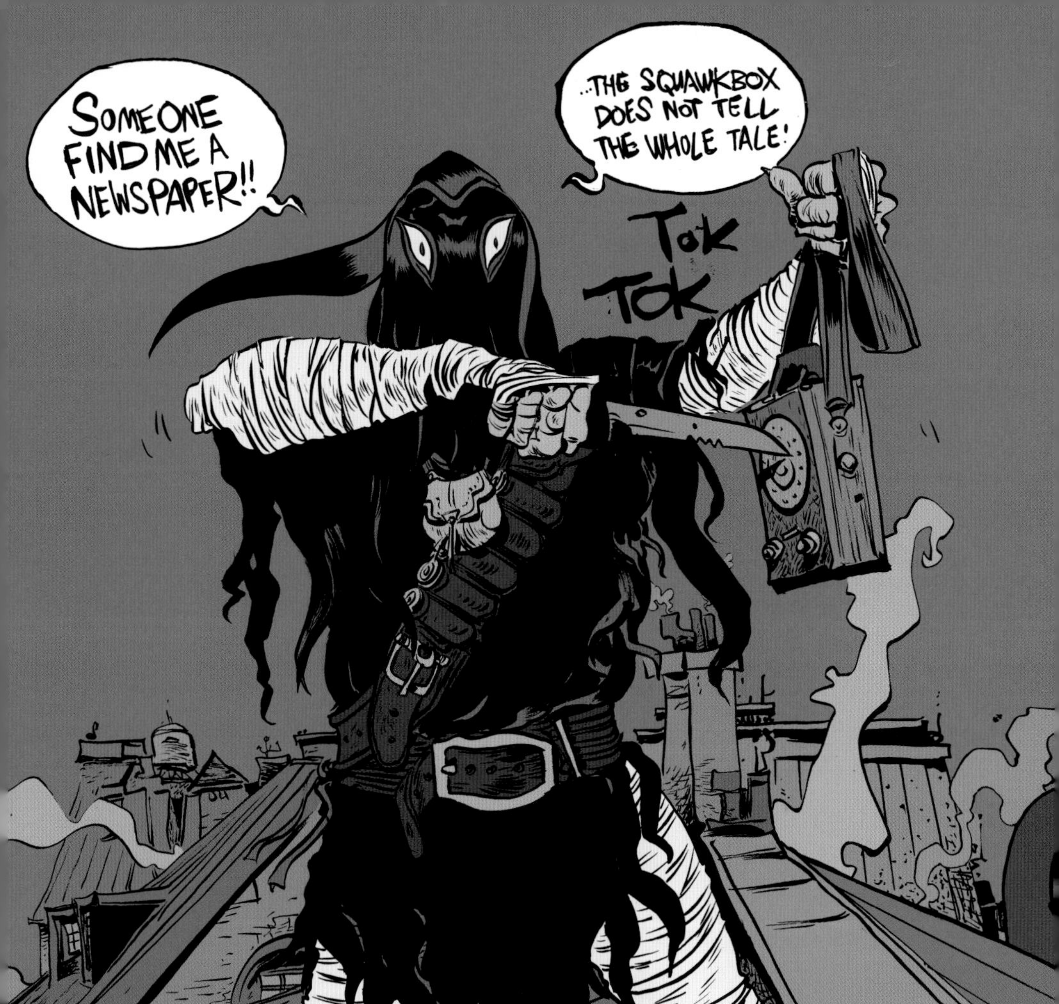
SOMEONE FIND ME A NEWSPAPER!!
...THE SQUAWKBOX DOES NOT TELL THE WHOLE TALE!
TOK TOK

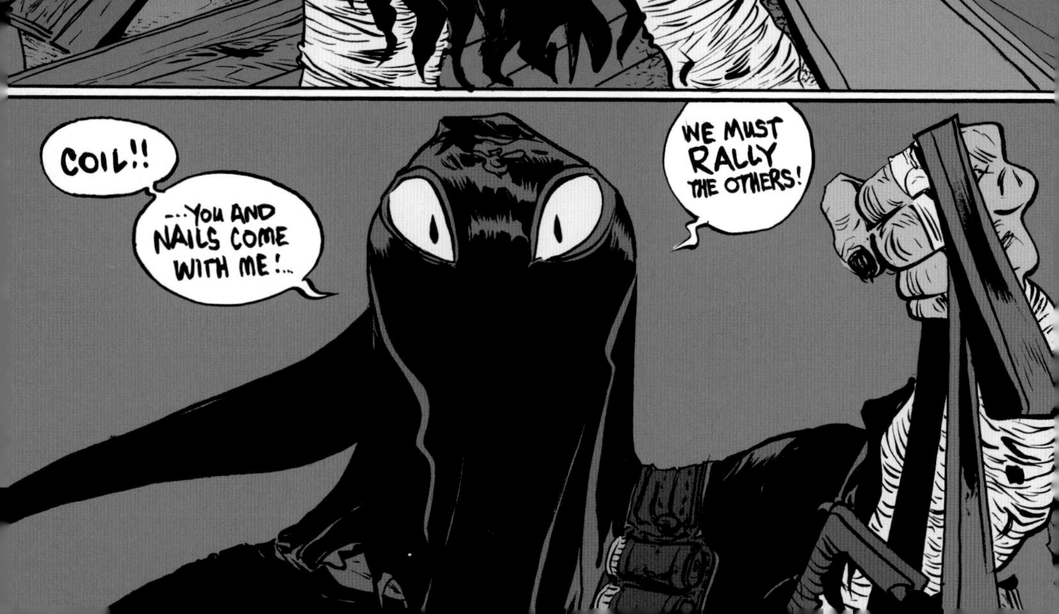
COIL!!
...YOU AND NAILS COME WITH ME!...
WE MUST RALLY THE OTHERS!

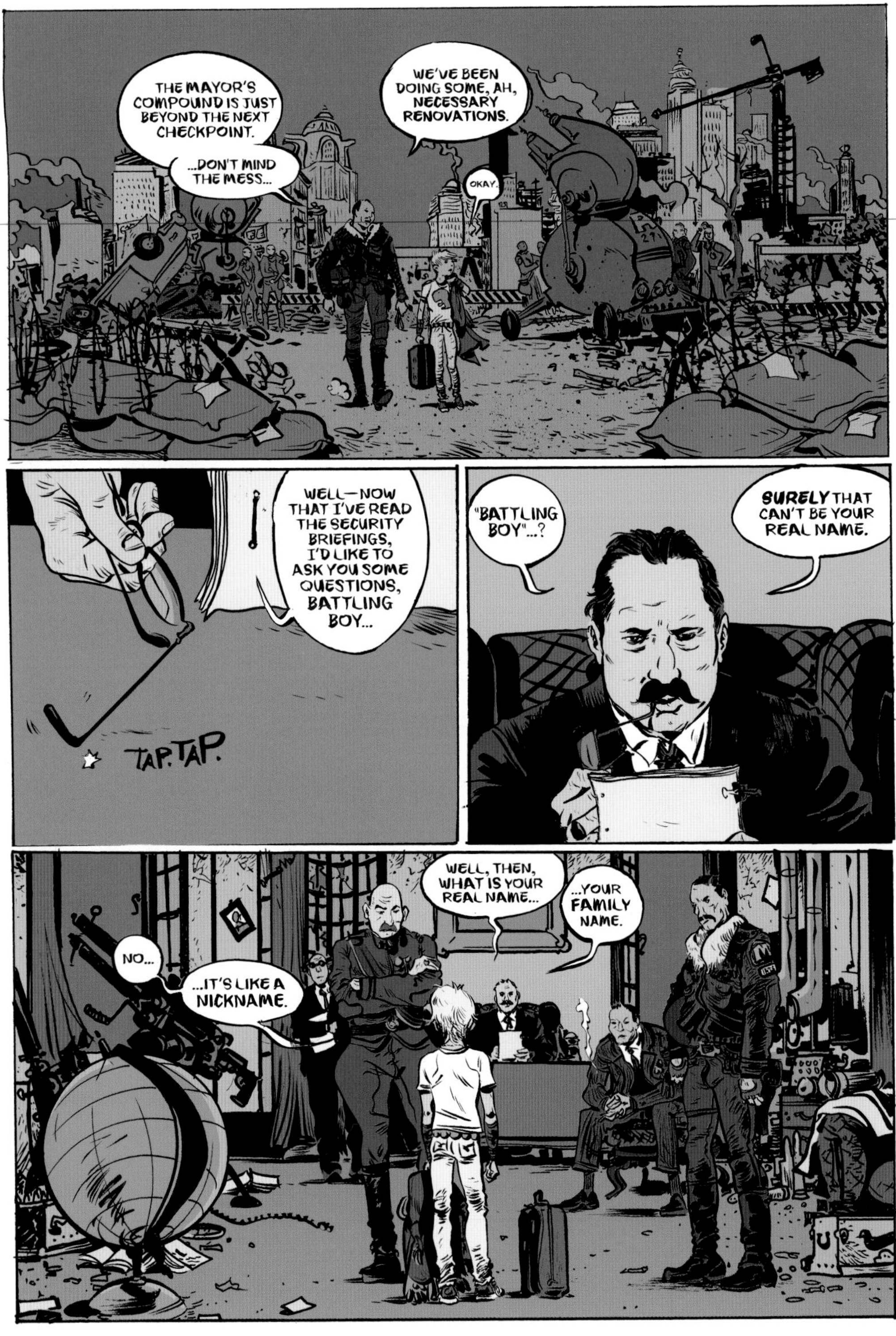
THE MAYOR'S COMPOUND IS JUST BEYOND THE NEXT CHECKPOINT.
...DON'T MIND THE MESS...
WE'VE BEEN DOING SOME, AH, NECESSARY RENOVATIONS.
OKAY.
WELL—NOW THAT I'VE READ THE SECURITY BRIEFINGS, I'D LIKE TO ASK YOU SOME QUESTIONS, BATTLING BOY...
TAP. TAP.
"BATTLING BOY"...?
SURELY THAT CAN'T BE YOUR REAL NAME.
NO...
...IT'S LIKE A NICKNAME.
WELL, THEN, WHAT IS YOUR REAL NAME...
...YOUR FAMILY NAME.

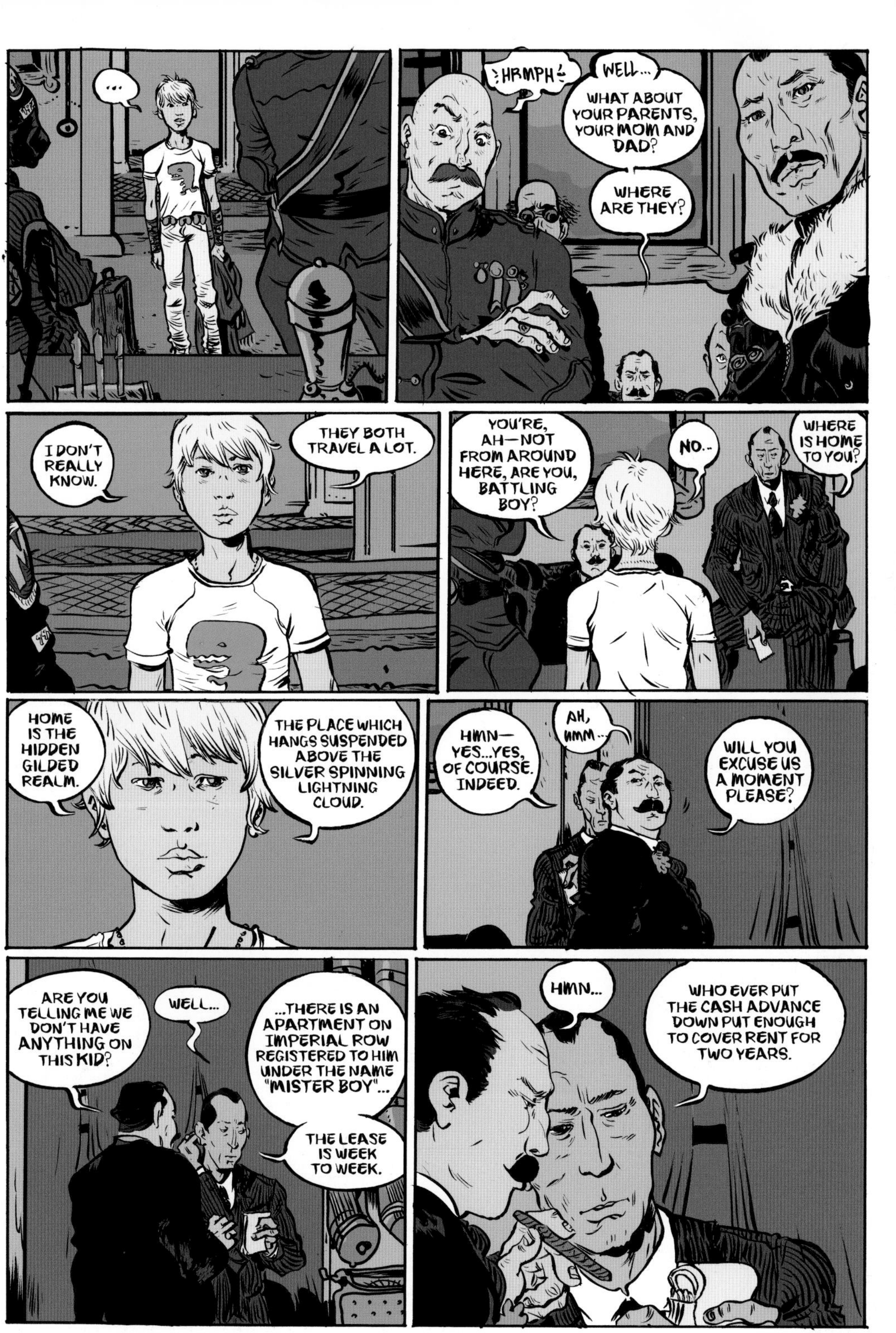
...
HRMPH
WELL...
WHAT ABOUT YOUR PARENTS, YOUR MOM AND DAD?
WHERE ARE THEY?
I DON'T REALLY KNOW.
THEY BOTH TRAVEL A LOT.
YOU'RE, AH—NOT FROM AROUND HERE, ARE YOU, BATTLING BOY?
NO..
WHERE IS HOME TO YOU?
HOME IS THE HIDDEN GILDED REALM.
THE PLACE WHICH HANGS SUSPENDED ABOVE THE SILVER SPINNING LIGHTNING CLOUD.
HMN— YES...YES, OF COURSE. INDEED.
AH, UMM...
WILL YOU EXCUSE US A MOMENT PLEASE?
ARE YOU TELLING ME WE DON'T HAVE ANYTHING ON THIS KID?
WELL...
...THERE IS AN APARTMENT ON IMPERIAL ROW REGISTERED TO HIM UNDER THE NAME "MISTER BOY"...
THE LEASE IS WEEK TO WEEK.
HMN...
WHO EVER PUT THE CASH ADVANCE DOWN PUT ENOUGH TO COVER RENT FOR TWO YEARS.

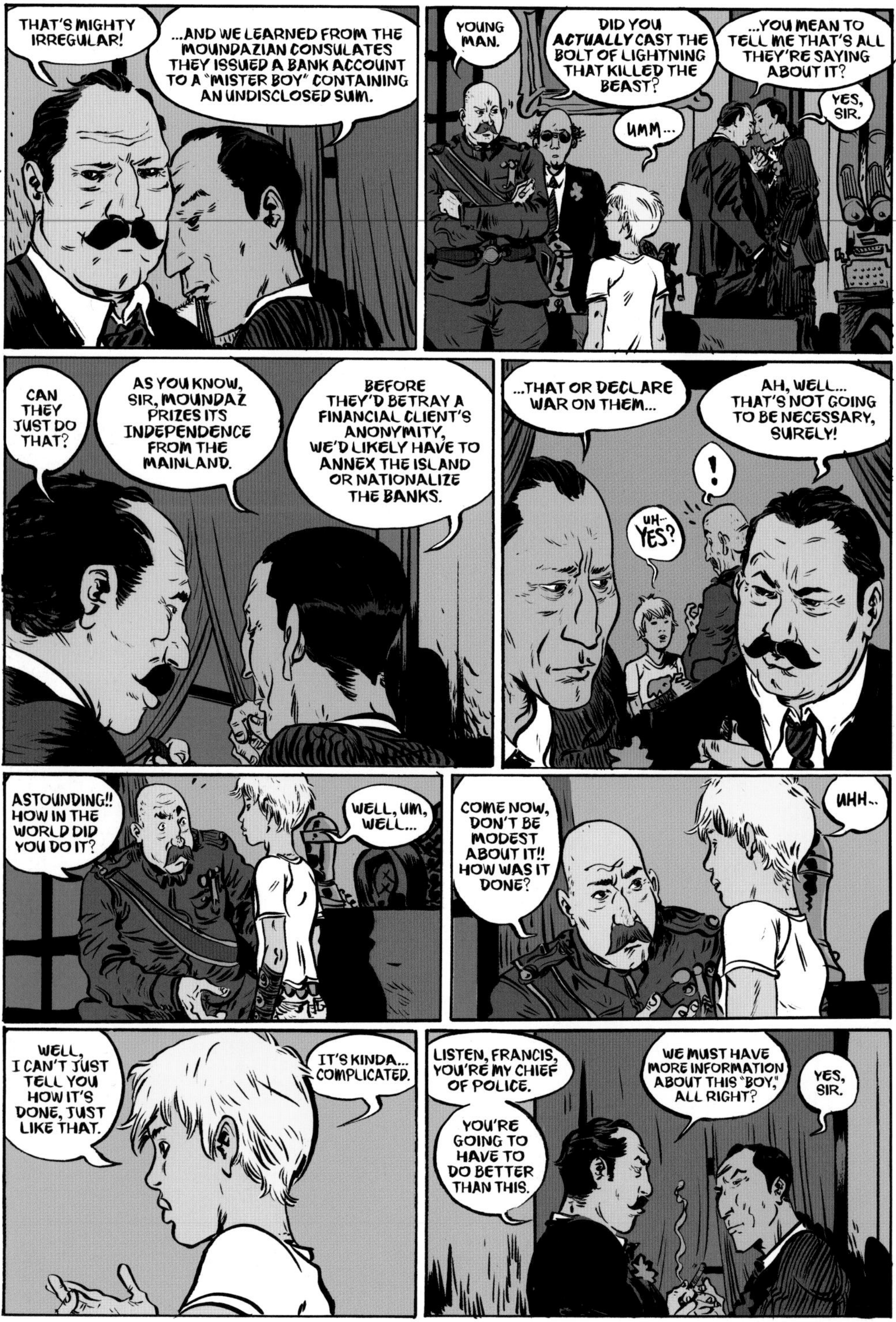
THAT'S MIGHTY IRREGULAR!
...AND WE LEARNED FROM THE MOUNDAZIAN CONSULATES THEY ISSUED A BANK ACCOUNT TO A "MISTER BOY" CONTAINING AN UNDISCLOSED SUM.
YOUNG MAN.
DID YOU ACTUALLY CAST THE BOLT OF LIGHTNING THAT KILLED THE BEAST?
UMM...
...YOU MEAN TO TELL ME THAT'S ALL THEY'RE SAYING ABOUT IT?
YES, SIR.
CAN THEY JUST DO THAT?
AS YOU KNOW, SIR, MOUNDAZ PRIZES ITS INDEPENDENCE FROM THE MAINLAND.
BEFORE THEY'D BETRAY A FINANCIAL CLIENT'S ANONYMITY, WE'D LIKELY HAVE TO ANNEX THE ISLAND OR NATIONALIZE THE BANKS.
...THAT OR DECLARE WAR ON THEM...
AH, WELL... THAT'S NOT GOING TO BE NECESSARY, SURELY!
!
UH... YES?
ASTOUNDING!! HOW IN THE WORLD DID YOU DO IT?
WELL, UM, WELL...
COME NOW, DON'T BE MODEST ABOUT IT!! HOW WAS IT DONE?
UHH..
WELL, I CAN'T JUST TELL YOU HOW IT'S DONE, JUST LIKE THAT.
IT'S KINDA... COMPLICATED.
LISTEN, FRANCIS, YOU'RE MY CHIEF OF POLICE.
YOU'RE GOING TO HAVE TO DO BETTER THAN THIS.
WE MUST HAVE MORE INFORMATION ABOUT THIS "BOY," ALL RIGHT?
YES, SIR.

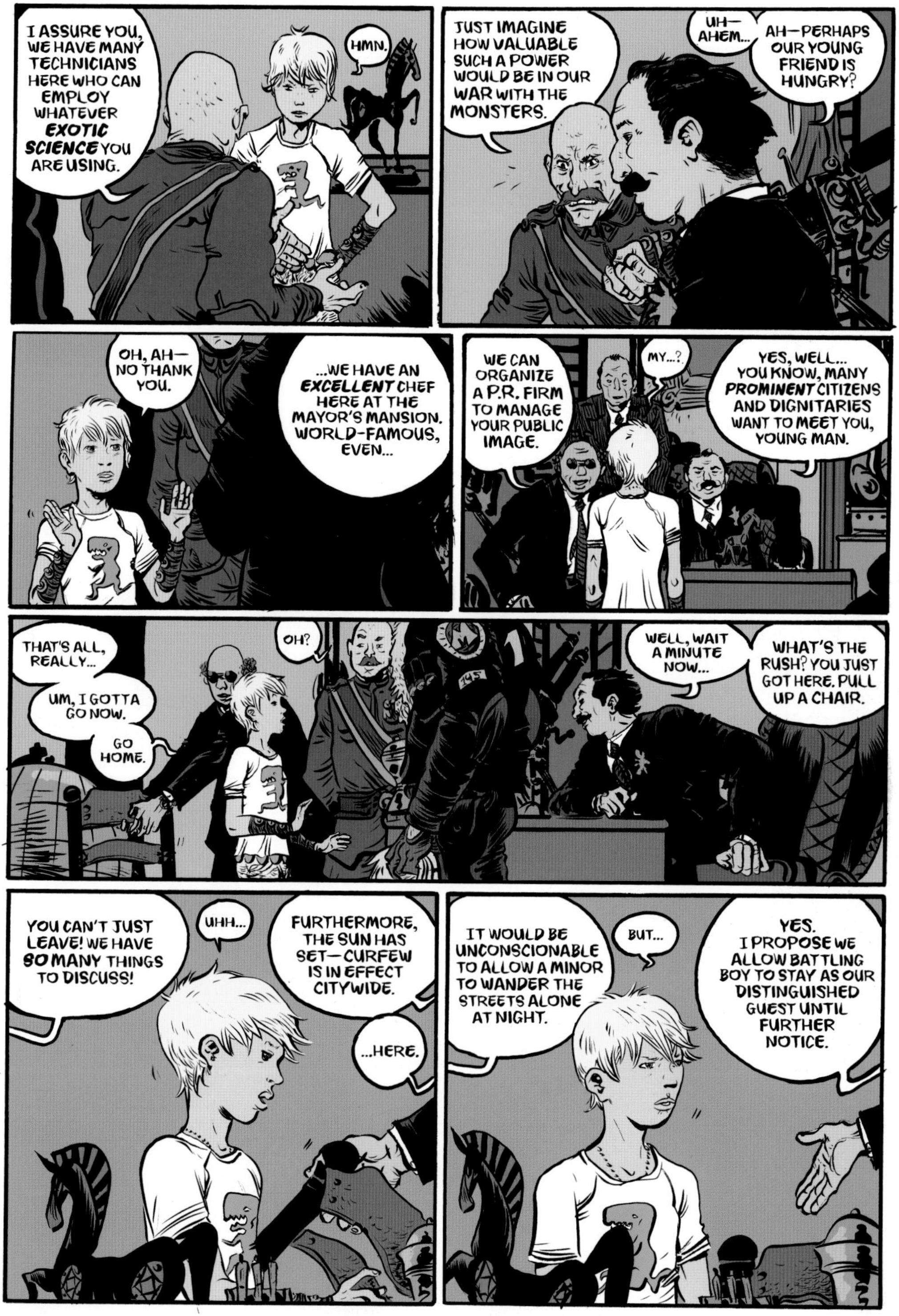

I ASSURE YOU, WE HAVE MANY TECHNICIANS HERE WHO CAN EMPLOY WHATEVER EXOTIC SCIENCE YOU ARE USING.
HMN.
JUST IMAGINE HOW VALUABLE SUCH A POWER WOULD BE IN OUR WAR WITH THE MONSTERS.
UH— AHEM...
AH—PERHAPS OUR YOUNG FRIEND IS HUNGRY?
OH, AH— NO THANK YOU.
...WE HAVE AN EXCELLENT CHEF HERE AT THE MAYOR'S MANSION. WORLD-FAMOUS, EVEN...
WE CAN ORGANIZE A P.R. FIRM TO MANAGE YOUR PUBLIC IMAGE.
MY...?
YES, WELL... YOU KNOW, MANY PROMINENT CITIZENS AND DIGNITARIES WANT TO MEET YOU, YOUNG MAN.
THAT'S ALL, REALLY...
UM, I GOTTA GO NOW.
GO HOME.
OH?
WELL, WAIT A MINUTE NOW...
WHAT'S THE RUSH? YOU JUST GOT HERE. PULL UP A CHAIR.
YOU CAN'T JUST LEAVE! WE HAVE SO MANY THINGS TO DISCUSS!
UHH...
FURTHERMORE, THE SUN HAS SET—CURFEW IS IN EFFECT CITYWIDE.
...HERE.
IT WOULD BE UNCONSCIONABLE TO ALLOW A MINOR TO WANDER THE STREETS ALONE AT NIGHT.
BUT...
YES. I PROPOSE WE ALLOW BATTLING BOY TO STAY AS OUR DISTINGUISHED GUEST UNTIL FURTHER NOTICE.

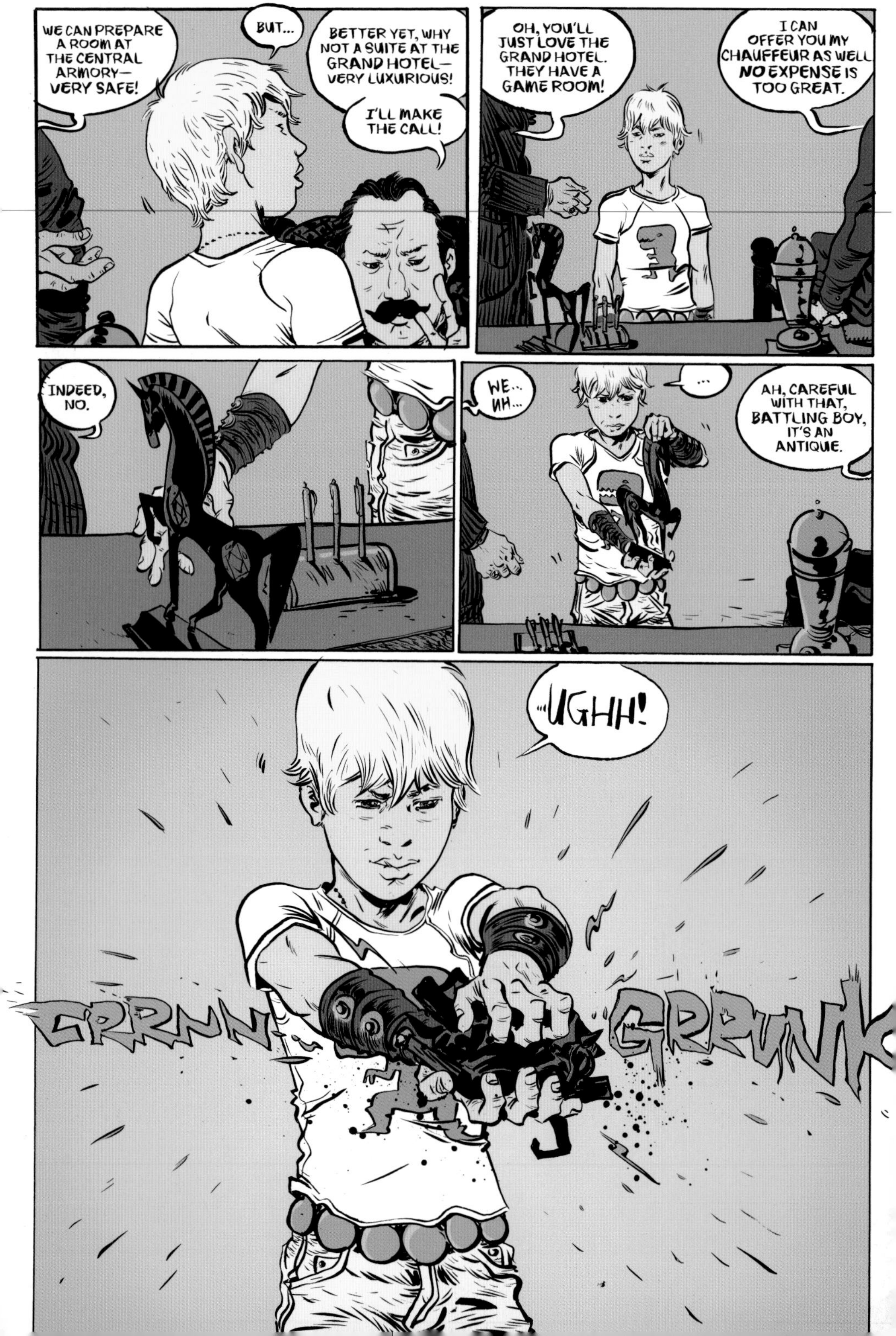
WE CAN PREPARE A ROOM AT THE CENTRAL ARMORY— VERY SAFE!
BUT...
BETTER YET, WHY NOT A SUITE AT THE GRAND HOTEL— VERY LUXURIOUS!
I'LL MAKE THE CALL!
OH, YOU'LL JUST LOVE THE GRAND HOTEL. THEY HAVE A GAME ROOM!
I CAN OFFER YOU MY CHAUFFEUR AS WELL. NO EXPENSE IS TOO GREAT.
INDEED, NO.
WE... UH...
...
AH, CAREFUL WITH THAT, BATTLING BOY, IT'S AN ANTIQUE.
UGHH!
GRRNN
GRRUNK

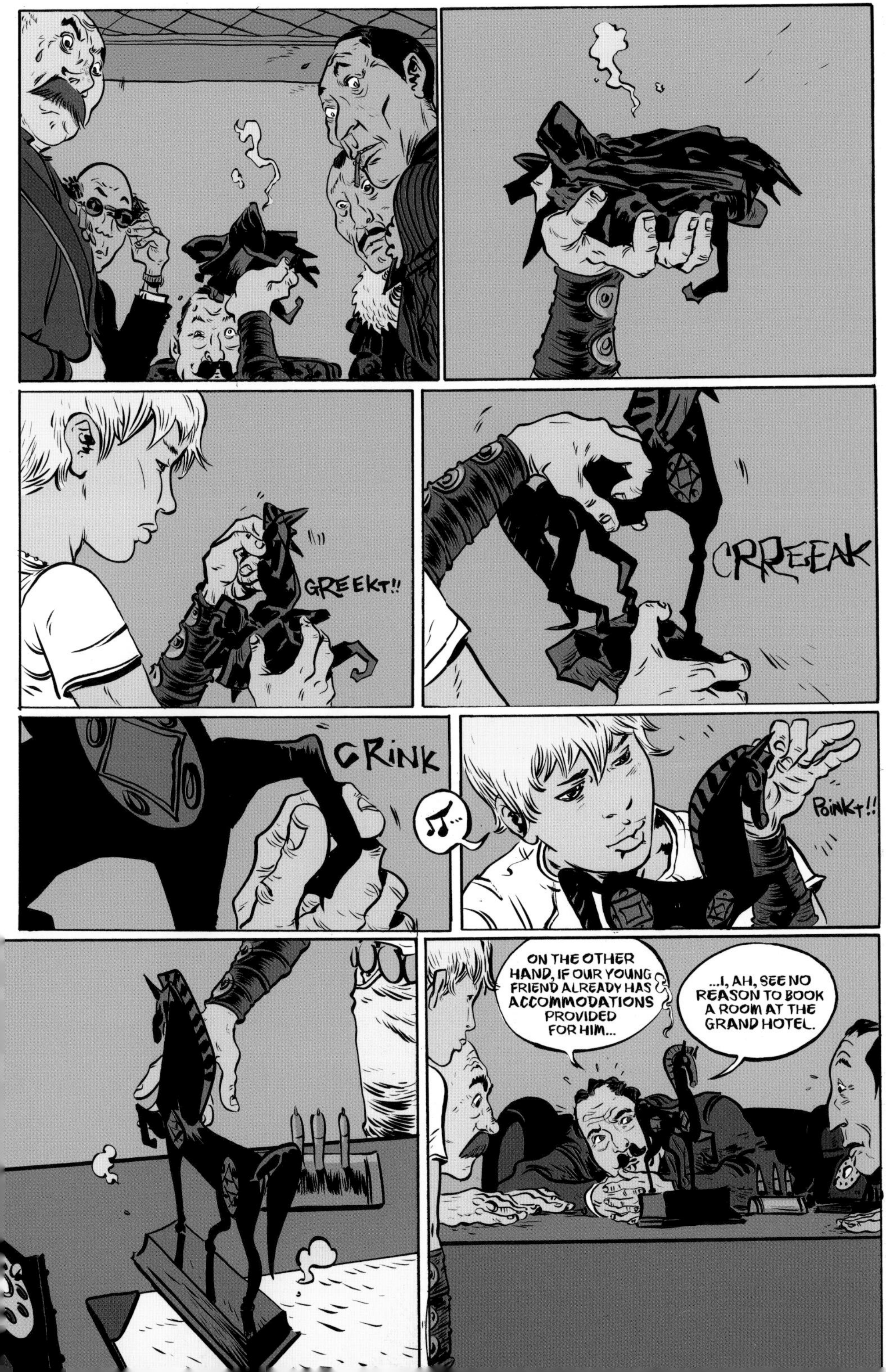
GREEKT!!
CRREEAK
GRINK
♫...
POINKT!!
ON THE OTHER HAND, IF OUR YOUNG FRIEND ALREADY HAS ACCOMMODATIONS PROVIDED FOR HIM...
...I, AH, SEE NO REASON TO BOOK A ROOM AT THE GRAND HOTEL.

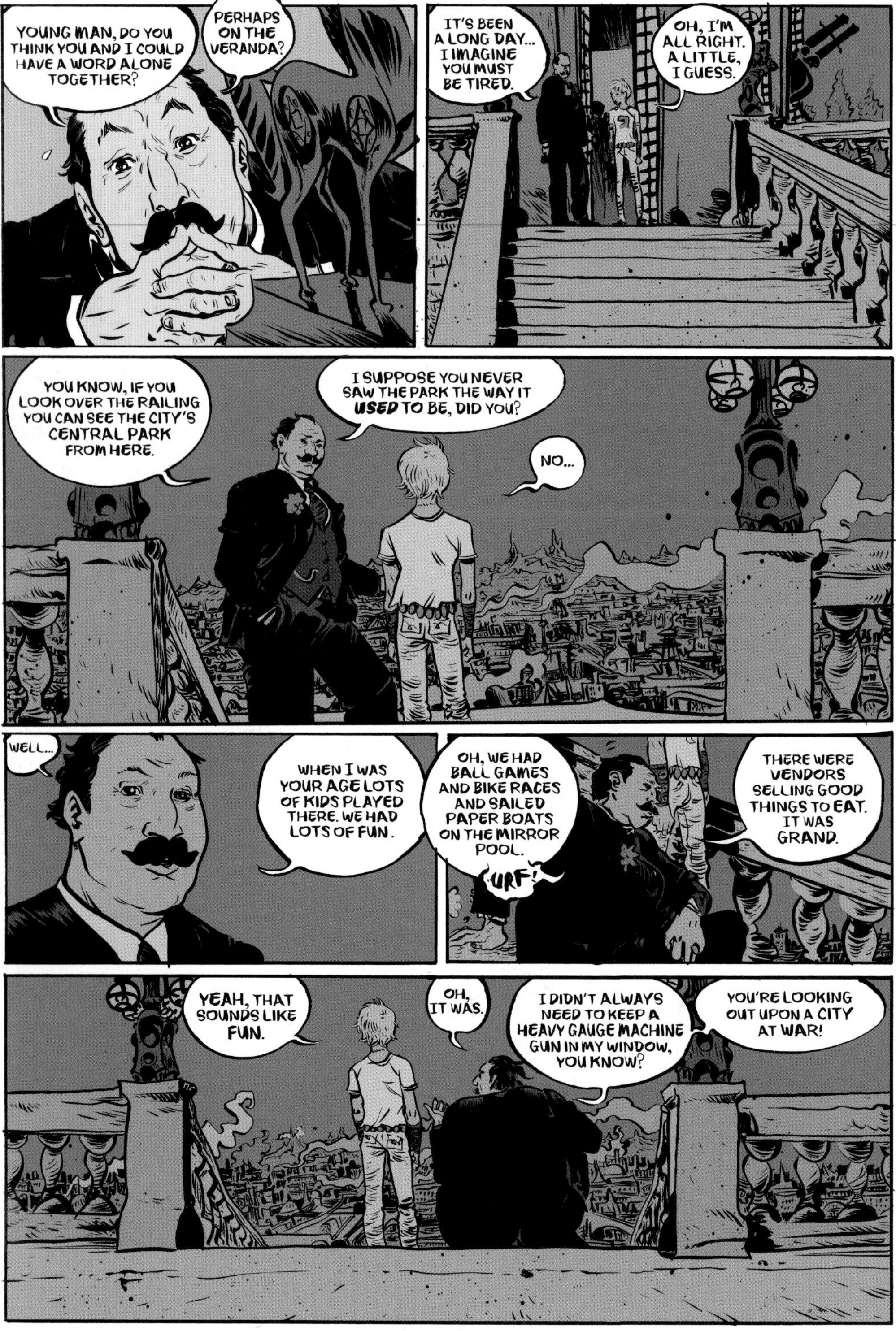

YOUNG MAN, DO YOU THINK YOU AND I COULD HAVE A WORD ALONE TOGETHER?
PERHAPS ON THE VERANDA?
IT'S BEEN A LONG DAY... I IMAGINE YOU MUST BE TIRED.
OH, I'M ALL RIGHT. A LITTLE, I GUESS.
YOU KNOW, IF YOU LOOK OVER THE RAILING YOU CAN SEE THE CITY'S CENTRAL PARK FROM HERE.
I SUPPOSE YOU NEVER SAW THE PARK THE WAY IT USED TO BE, DID YOU?
NO...
WELL...
WHEN I WAS YOUR AGE LOTS OF KIDS PLAYED THERE. WE HAD LOTS OF FUN.
OH, WE HAD BALL GAMES AND BIKE RACES AND SAILED PAPER BOATS ON THE MIRROR POOL.
URF!
THERE WERE VENDORS SELLING GOOD THINGS TO EAT. IT WAS GRAND.
YEAH, THAT SOUNDS LIKE FUN.
OH, IT WAS.
I DIDN'T ALWAYS NEED TO KEEP A HEAVY GAUGE MACHINE GUN IN MY WINDOW, YOU KNOW?
YOU'RE LOOKING OUT UPON A CITY AT WAR!

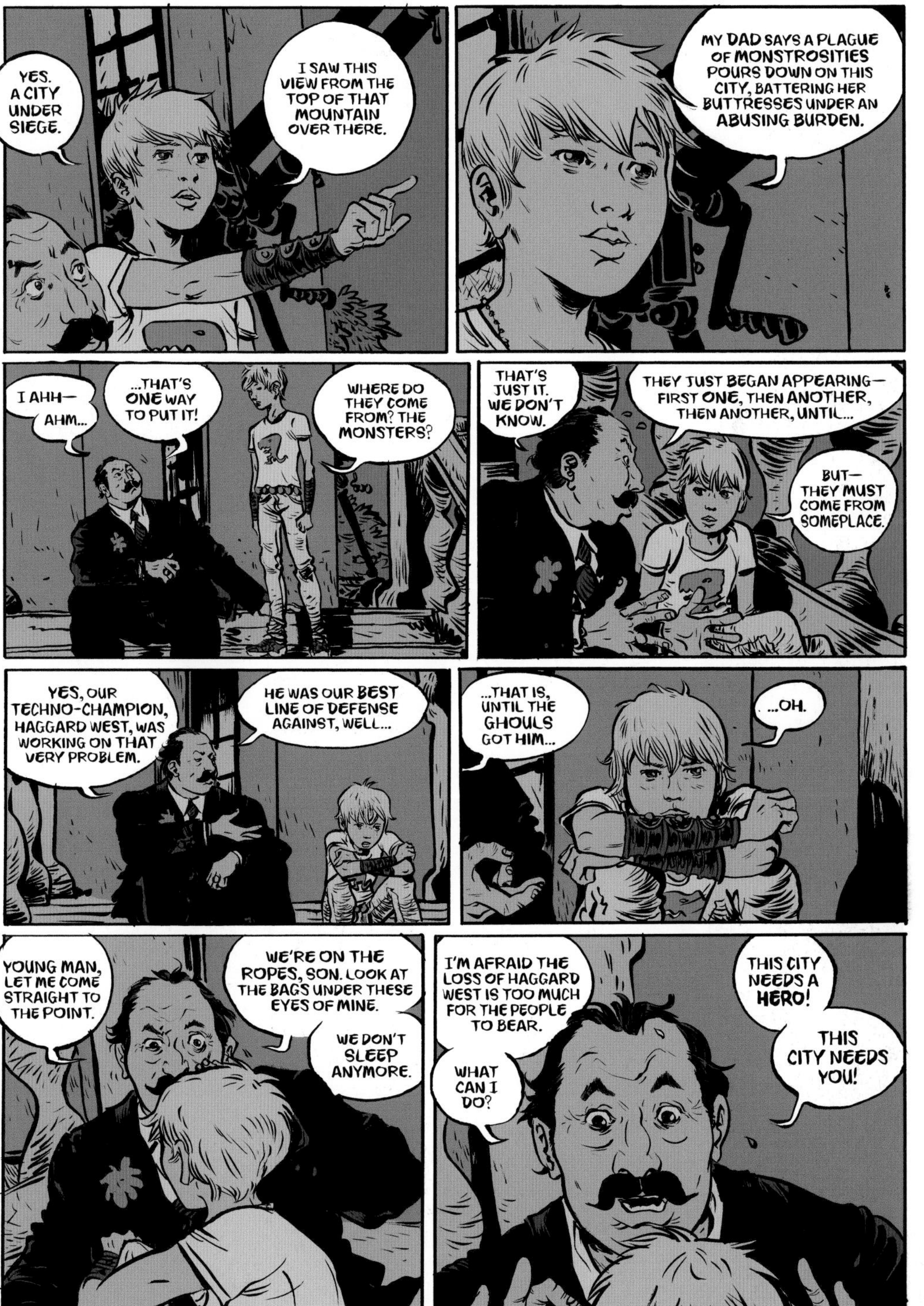
YES. A CITY UNDER SIEGE.
I SAW THIS VIEW FROM THE TOP OF THAT MOUNTAIN OVER THERE.
MY DAD SAYS A PLAGUE OF MONSTROSITIES POURS DOWN ON THIS CITY, BATTERING HER BUTTRESSES UNDER AN ABUSING BURDEN.
I AHH— AHM...
...THAT'S ONE WAY TO PUT IT!
WHERE DO THEY COME FROM? THE MONSTERS?
THAT'S JUST IT. WE DON'T KNOW.
THEY JUST BEGAN APPEARING— FIRST ONE, THEN ANOTHER, THEN ANOTHER, UNTIL...
BUT— THEY MUST COME FROM SOMEPLACE.
YES, OUR TECHNO-CHAMPION, HAGGARD WEST, WAS WORKING ON THAT VERY PROBLEM.
HE WAS OUR BEST LINE OF DEFENSE AGAINST, WELL...
...THAT IS, UNTIL THE GHOULS GOT HIM...
...OH.
YOUNG MAN, LET ME COME STRAIGHT TO THE POINT.
WE'RE ON THE ROPES, SON. LOOK AT THE BAGS UNDER THESE EYES OF MINE.
WE DON'T SLEEP ANYMORE.
I'M AFRAID THE LOSS OF HAGGARD WEST IS TOO MUCH FOR THE PEOPLE TO BEAR.
WHAT CAN I DO?
THIS CITY NEEDS A HERO!
THIS CITY NEEDS YOU!

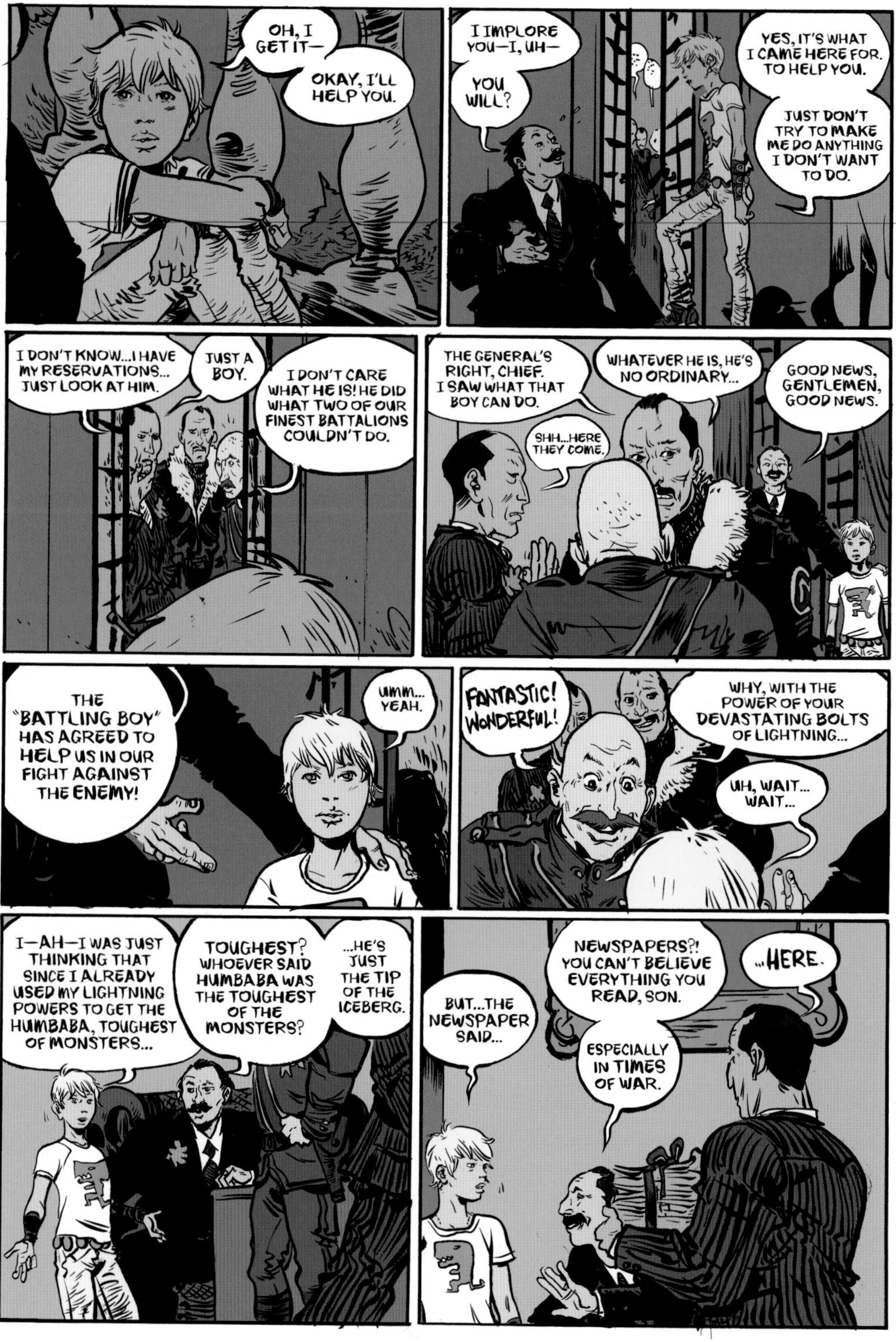
OH, I GET IT—
OKAY, I'LL HELP YOU.
I IMPLORE YOU—I, UH—
YOU WILL?
YES, IT'S WHAT I CAME HERE FOR. TO HELP YOU.
JUST DON'T TRY TO MAKE ME DO ANYTHING I DON'T WANT TO DO.
I DON'T KNOW...I HAVE MY RESERVATIONS... JUST LOOK AT HIM.
JUST A BOY.
I DON'T CARE WHAT HE IS! HE DID WHAT TWO OF OUR FINEST BATTALIONS COULDN'T DO.
THE GENERAL'S RIGHT, CHIEF. I SAW WHAT THAT BOY CAN DO.
WHATEVER HE IS, HE'S NO ORDINARY...
SHH...HERE THEY COME.
GOOD NEWS, GENTLEMEN, GOOD NEWS.
THE "BATTLING BOY" HAS AGREED TO HELP US IN OUR FIGHT AGAINST THE ENEMY!
UMM... YEAH.
FANTASTIC! WONDERFUL!
WHY, WITH THE POWER OF YOUR DEVASTATING BOLTS OF LIGHTNING...
UH, WAIT... WAIT...
I—AH—I WAS JUST THINKING THAT SINCE I ALREADY USED MY LIGHTNING POWERS TO GET THE HUMBABA, TOUGHEST OF MONSTERS...
TOUGHEST? WHOEVER SAID HUMBABA WAS THE TOUGHEST OF THE MONSTERS?
...HE'S JUST THE TIP OF THE ICEBERG.
BUT...THE NEWSPAPER SAID...
NEWSPAPERS?! YOU CAN'T BELIEVE EVERYTHING YOU READ, SON.
ESPECIALLY IN TIMES OF WAR.
...HERE.

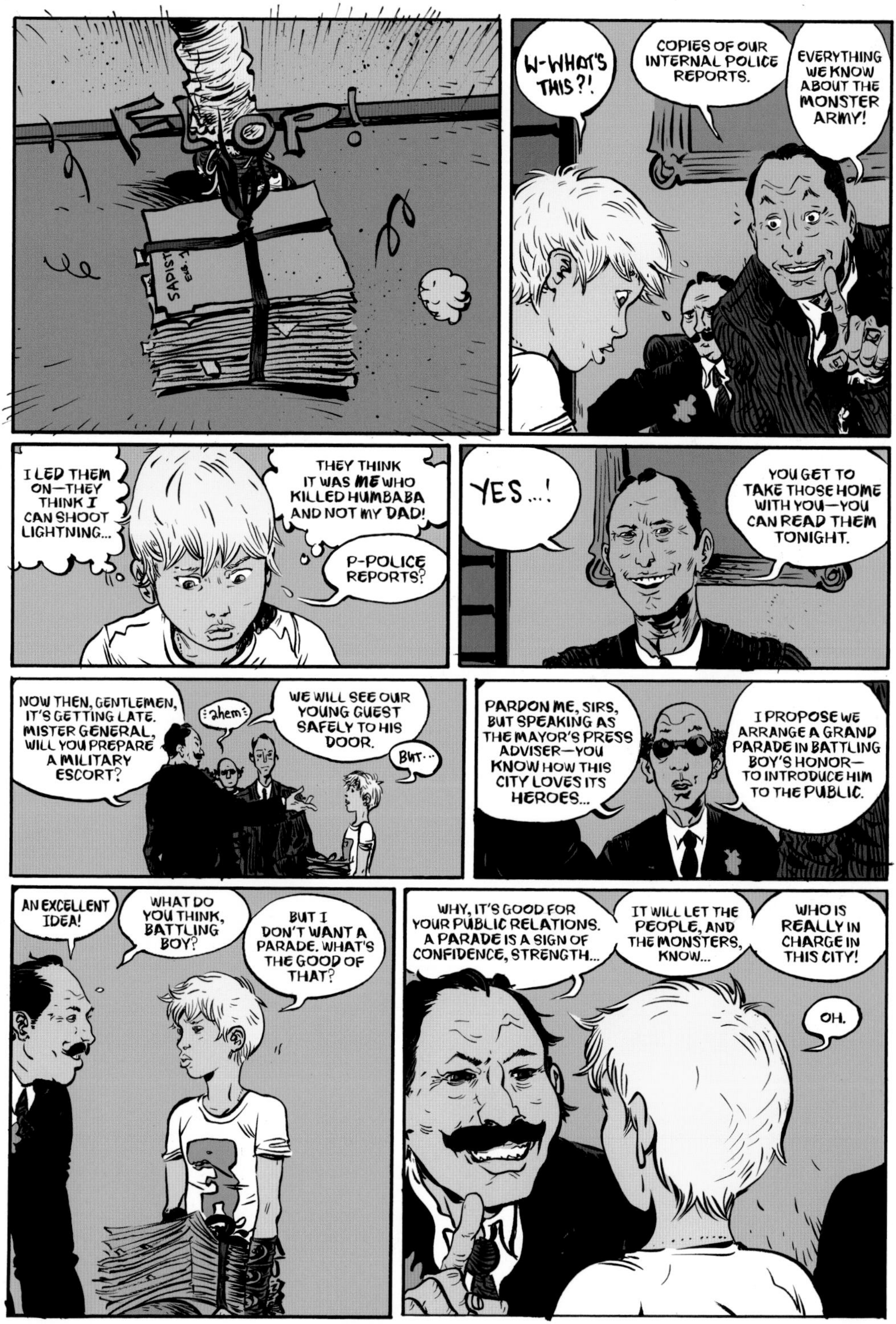
FLOOP!
SADIST
W-WHAT'S THIS?!
COPIES OF OUR INTERNAL POLICE REPORTS.
EVERYTHING WE KNOW ABOUT THE MONSTER ARMY!
I LED THEM ON—THEY THINK I CAN SHOOT LIGHTNING...
THEY THINK IT WAS ME WHO KILLED HUMBABA AND NOT MY DAD!
P-POLICE REPORTS?
YES...!
YOU GET TO TAKE THOSE HOME WITH YOU—YOU CAN READ THEM TONIGHT.
NOW THEN, GENTLEMEN, IT'S GETTING LATE. MISTER GENERAL, WILL YOU PREPARE A MILITARY ESCORT?
ahem
WE WILL SEE OUR YOUNG GUEST SAFELY TO HIS DOOR.
BUT...
PARDON ME, SIRS, BUT SPEAKING AS THE MAYOR'S PRESS ADVISER—YOU KNOW HOW THIS CITY LOVES ITS HEROES...
I PROPOSE WE ARRANGE A GRAND PARADE IN BATTLING BOY'S HONOR—TO INTRODUCE HIM TO THE PUBLIC.
AN EXCELLENT IDEA!
WHAT DO YOU THINK, BATTLING BOY?
BUT I DON'T WANT A PARADE. WHAT'S THE GOOD OF THAT?
WHY, IT'S GOOD FOR YOUR PUBLIC RELATIONS. A PARADE IS A SIGN OF CONFIDENCE, STRENGTH...
IT WILL LET THE PEOPLE, AND THE MONSTERS, KNOW...
WHO IS REALLY IN CHARGE IN THIS CITY!
OH.

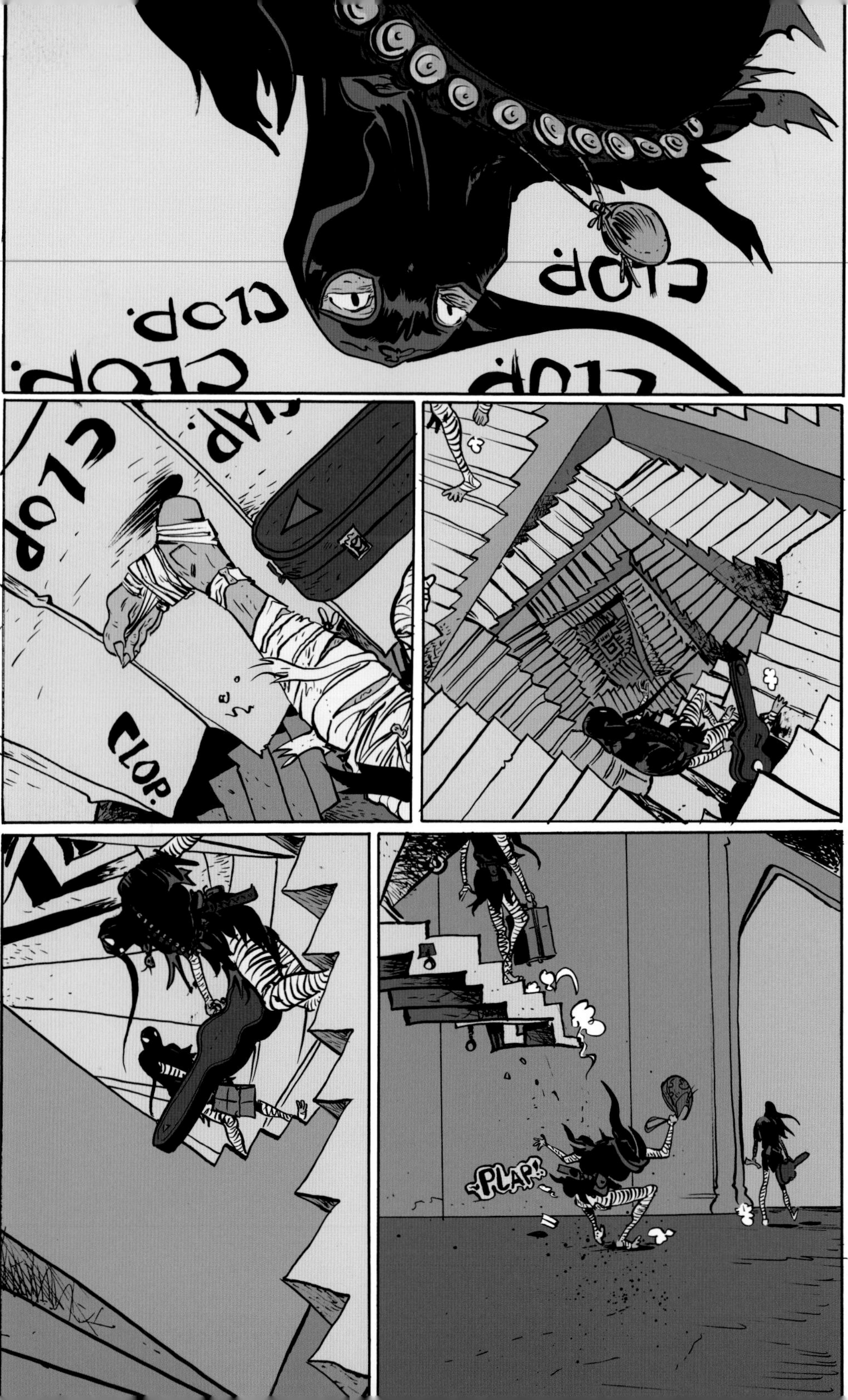

CLOP.
CLOP.
CLOP.
CLOP.
CLOP.
CLOP.
PLAP!

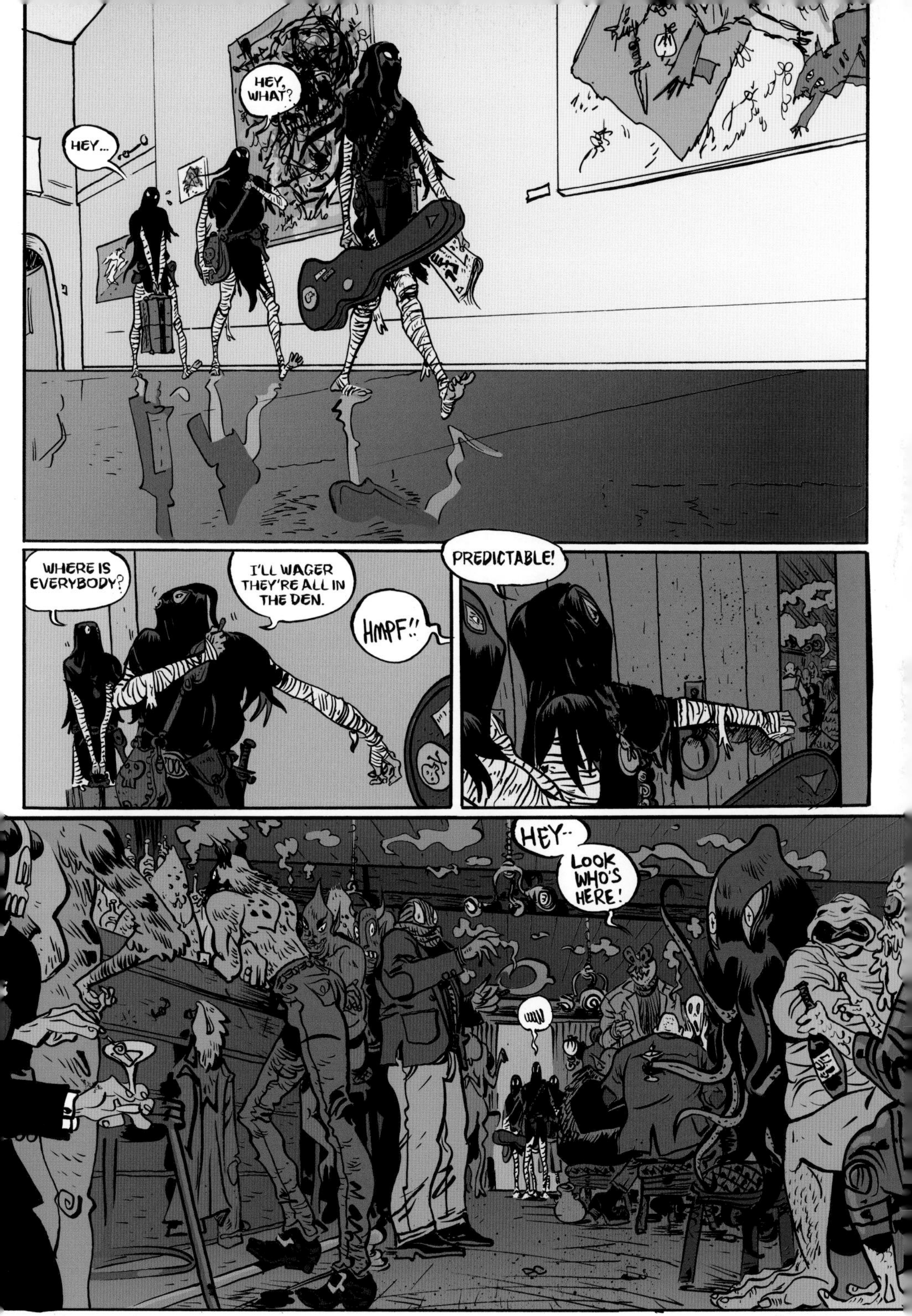
HEY...
HEY, WHAT?
WHERE IS EVERYBODY?
I'LL WAGER THEY'RE ALL IN THE DEN.
HMPF!!
PREDICTABLE!
HEY--
LOOK WHO'S HERE!

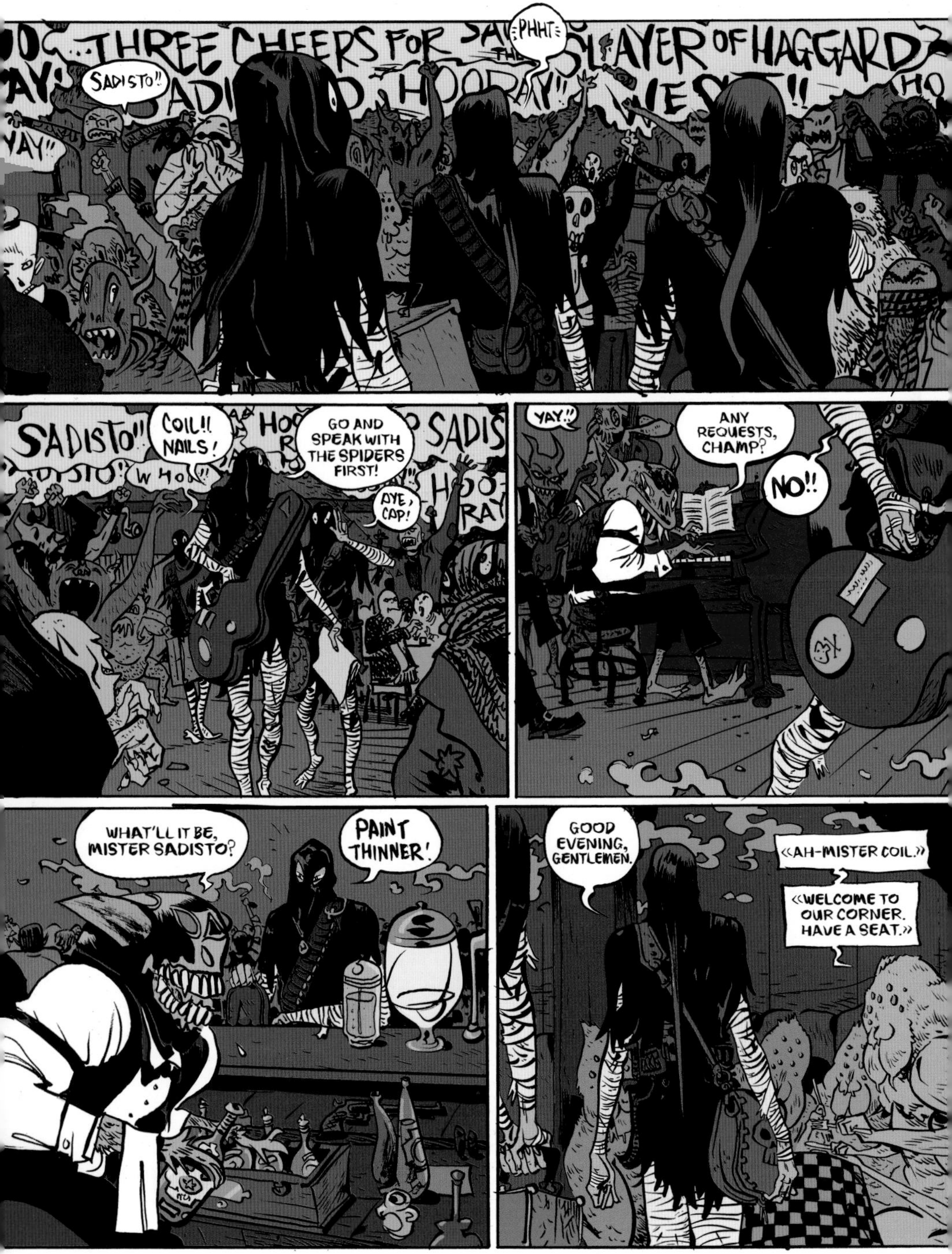
THREE CHEERS FOR SA... THE SLAYER OF HAGGARD WEST!!
PHHT
SADISTO!!
HOORAY!!
YAY!!
SADISTO!!
COIL!! NAILS!
GO AND SPEAK WITH THE SPIDERS FIRST!
AYE, CAP!
HOORAY
YAY!!
ANY REQUESTS, CHAMP?
NO!!
WHAT'LL IT BE, MISTER SADISTO?
PAINT THINNER!
GOOD EVENING, GENTLEMEN.
«AH-MISTER COIL.»
«WELCOME TO OUR CORNER. HAVE A SEAT.»

VERY WELL.

THAT IS, IF YOU'RE NOT OPPOSED TO A LITTLE BUSINESS OVER DINNER.

PLAP!!

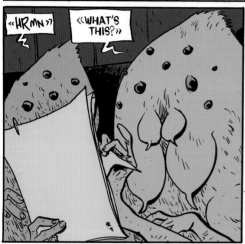

«HRMN»

«WHAT'S THIS?»

BLUEPRINTS! FOR NEW RAGS!!

WE LOST HALF OUR GANG IN THE BATTLE WITH HAGGARD WEST.

WE DECIDED THE ROBES ARE AN... OCCUPATIONAL HAZARD.

«HMN. YES.»

«I SEE.»

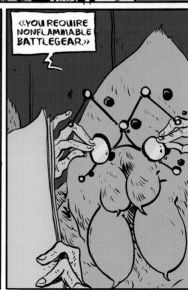

«YOU REQUIRE NONFLAMMABLE BATTLEGEAR.»

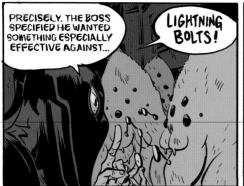

PRECISELY. THE BOSS SPECIFIED HE WANTED SOMETHING ESPECIALLY EFFECTIVE AGAINST...

LIGHTNING BOLTS!

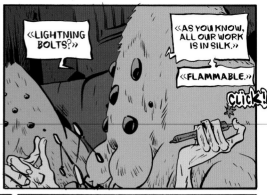

«LIGHTNING BOLTS?»

«AS YOU KNOW, ALL OUR WORK IS IN SILK.»

«FLAMMABLE.»

CLICK!

«STILL, WE COULD INTERWEAVE THREADS OF BLACK ASBESTOS...»

«REINFORCE IT WITH A RUBBER FILAMENT...»

«HMM, THIS COULD GET EXPENSIVE.»

A URANIUM GUMBALL WITH THAT, TOO!

O-OKAY.

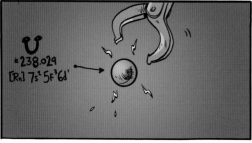

$\#238.029$
$[R_n]\ 7s^2\ 5f^3\ 6d^1$

WHOOM!

150

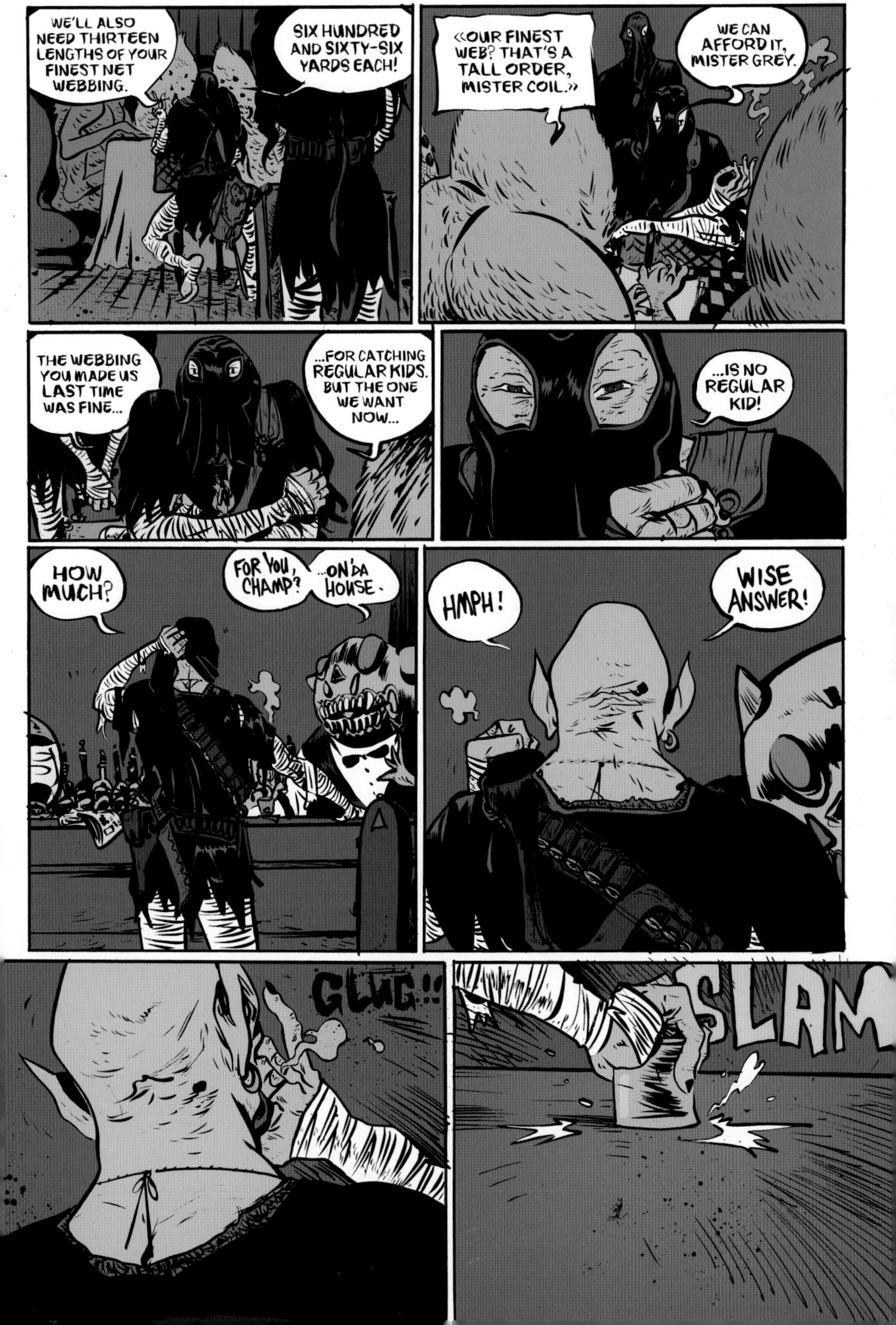
WE'LL ALSO NEED THIRTEEN LENGTHS OF YOUR FINEST NET WEBBING.
SIX HUNDRED AND SIXTY-SIX YARDS EACH!
«OUR FINEST WEB? THAT'S A TALL ORDER, MISTER COIL.»
WE CAN AFFORD IT, MISTER GREY.
THE WEBBING YOU MADE US LAST TIME WAS FINE...
...FOR CATCHING REGULAR KIDS. BUT THE ONE WE WANT NOW...
...IS NO REGULAR KID!
HOW MUCH?
FOR YOU, CHAMP?
...ON'DA HOUSE.
HMPH!
WISE ANSWER!
GLUG!!
SLAM

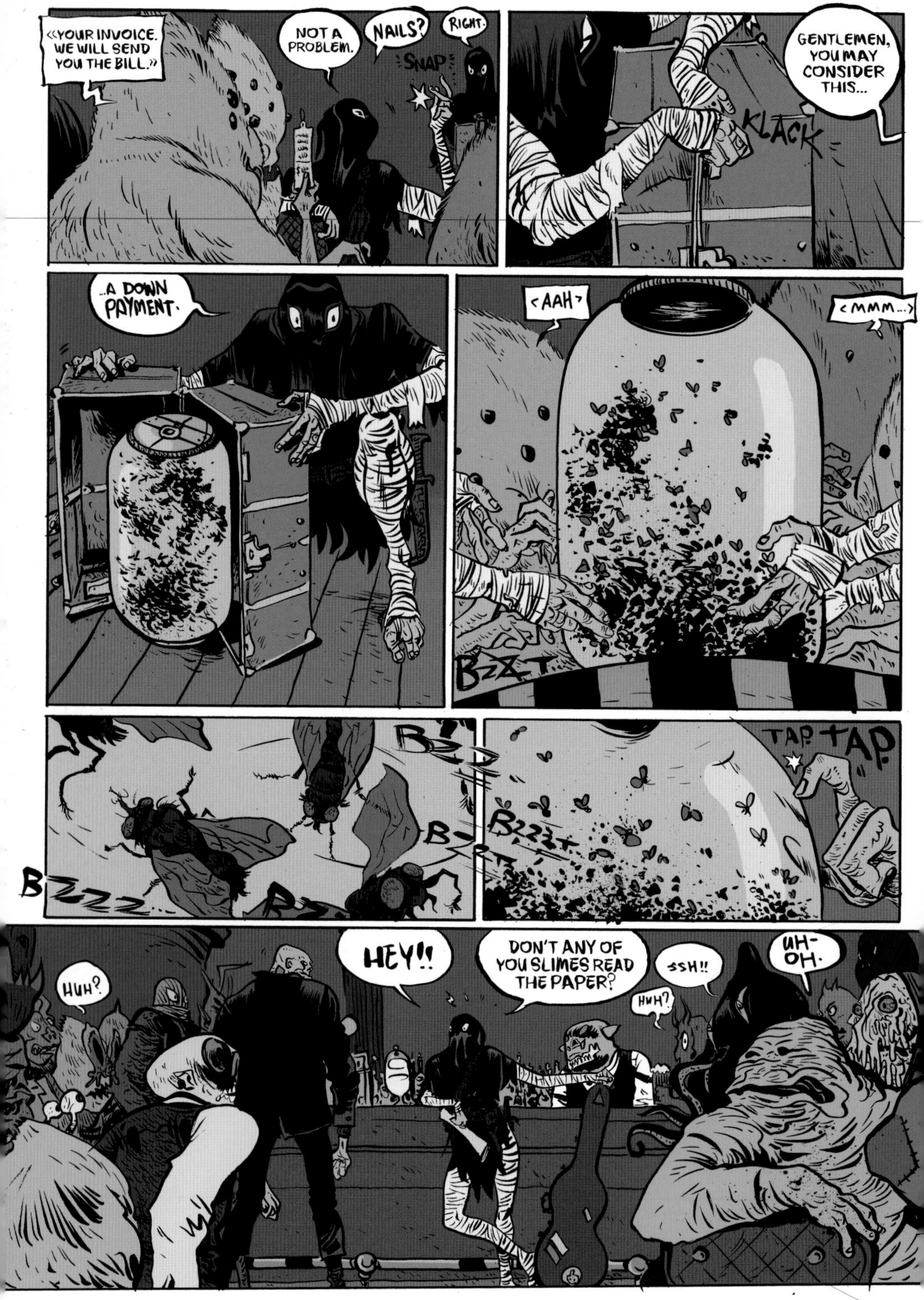

«YOUR INVOICE. WE WILL SEND YOU THE BILL.»
NOT A PROBLEM.
NAILS?
RIGHT.
SNAP
GENTLEMEN, YOU MAY CONSIDER THIS...
KLACK
...A DOWN PAYMENT.
<AAH>
<MMM...>
BZZT
BZZZZ
TAP TAP
HUH?
HEY!!
DON'T ANY OF YOU SLIMES READ THE PAPER?
SSH!!
HUH?
UH-OH.

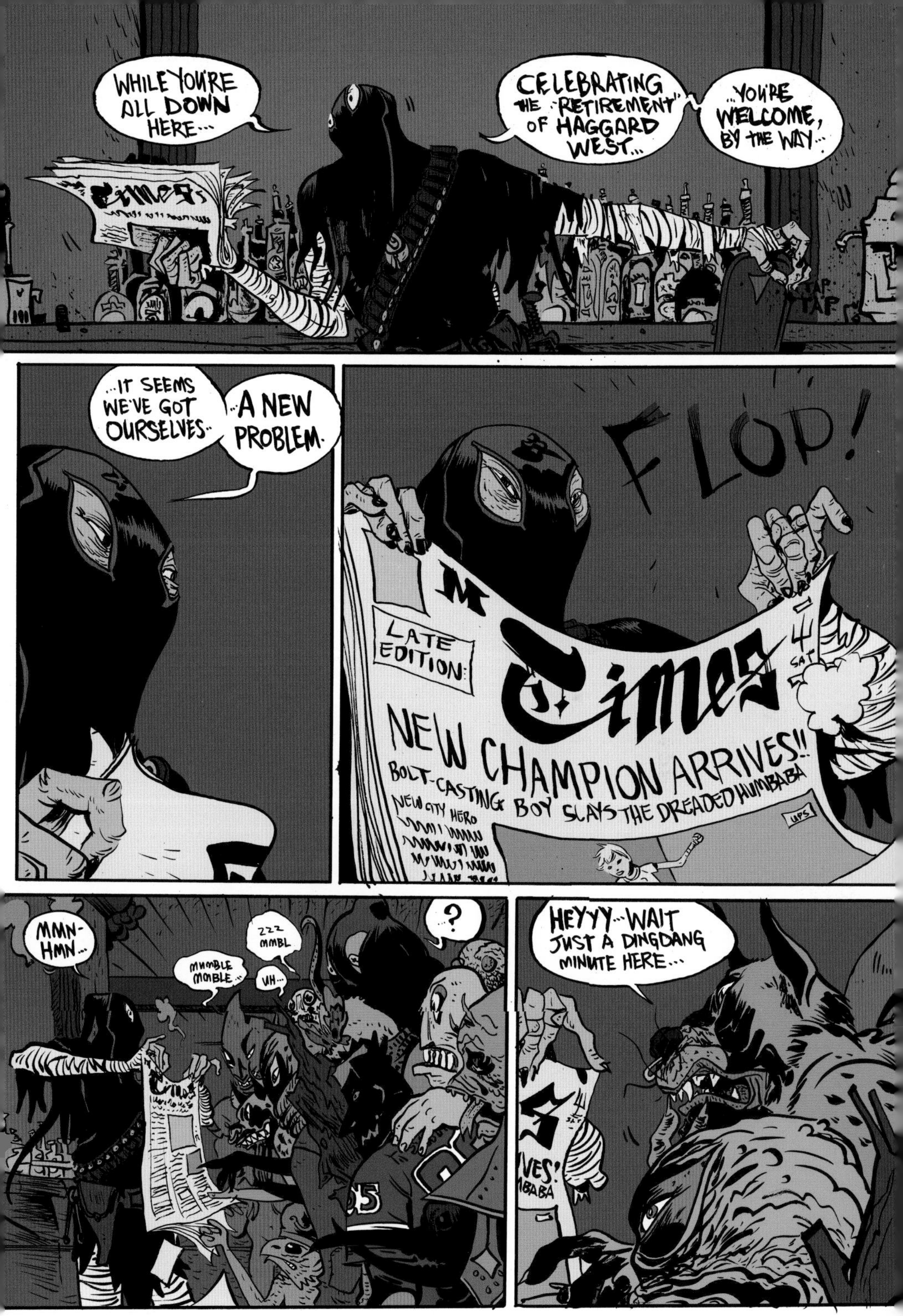
WHILE YOU'RE ALL DOWN HERE...
CELEBRATING THE "RETIREMENT" OF HAGGARD WEST...
...YOU'RE WELCOME, BY THE WAY...
TAP TAP
...IT SEEMS WE'VE GOT OURSELVES...
...A NEW PROBLEM.
FLOP!
LATE EDITION
Times
NEW CHAMPION ARRIVES!!
BOLT-CASTING BOY SLAYS THE DREADED HUMBABA
NEW CITY HERO
MMN-HMN...
MUMBLE MMBLE...
ZZZ MMBL
UH...
...?
HEYYY...WAIT JUST A DINGDANG MINUTE HERE...

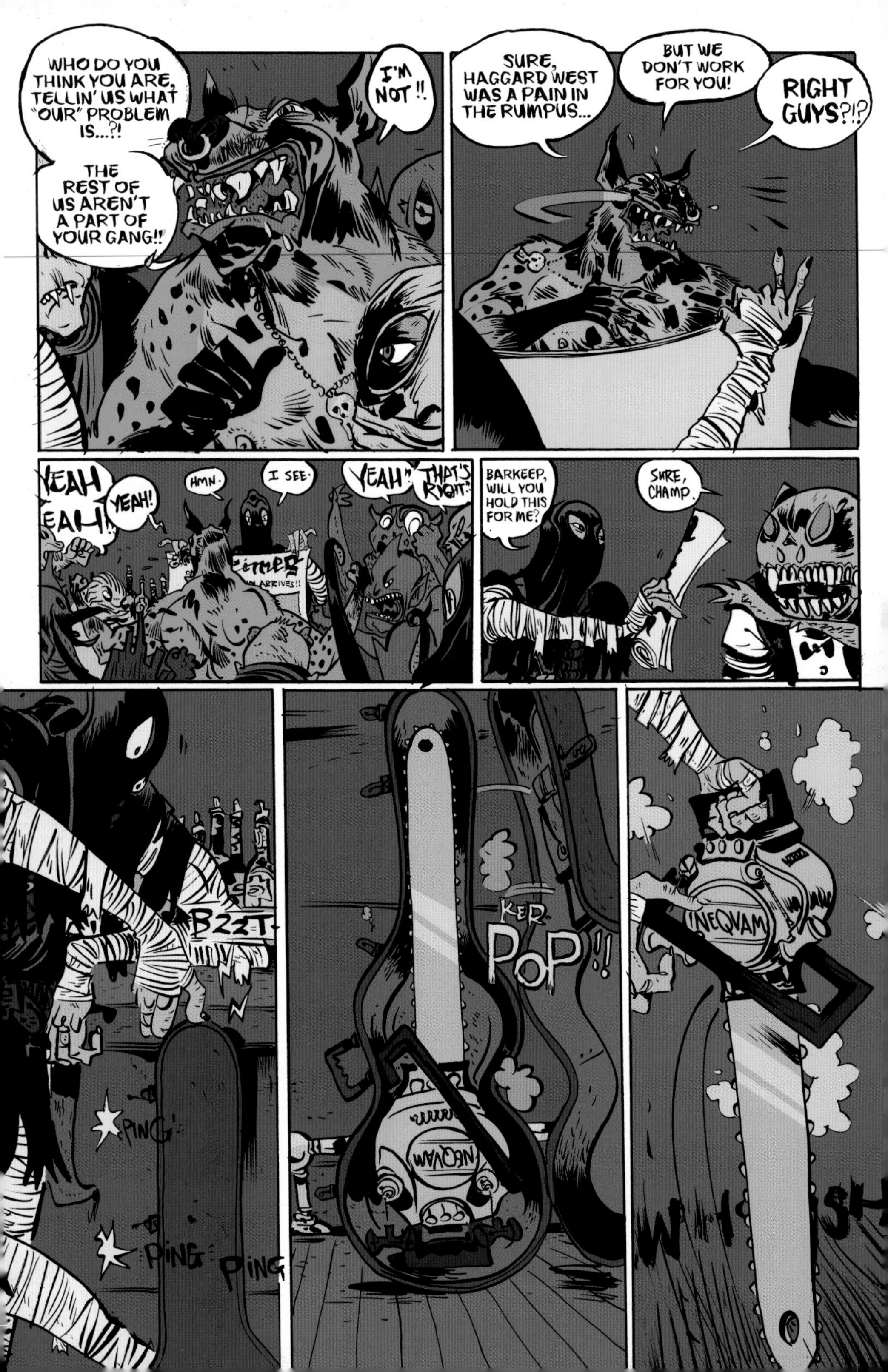
WHO DO YOU THINK YOU ARE, TELLIN' US WHAT "OUR" PROBLEM IS...?!
THE REST OF US AREN'T A PART OF YOUR GANG!!
I'M NOT!!
SURE, HAGGARD WEST WAS A PAIN IN THE RUMPUS...
BUT WE DON'T WORK FOR YOU!
RIGHT GUYS?!?
YEAH
YEAH!
YEAH!
HMN.
I SEE.
YEAH!
THAT'S RIGHT!
BARKEEP, WILL YOU HOLD THIS FOR ME?
SURE, CHAMP.
BZZT
PING
PING
PING
KER POP!!
NEQVAM
NEQVAM

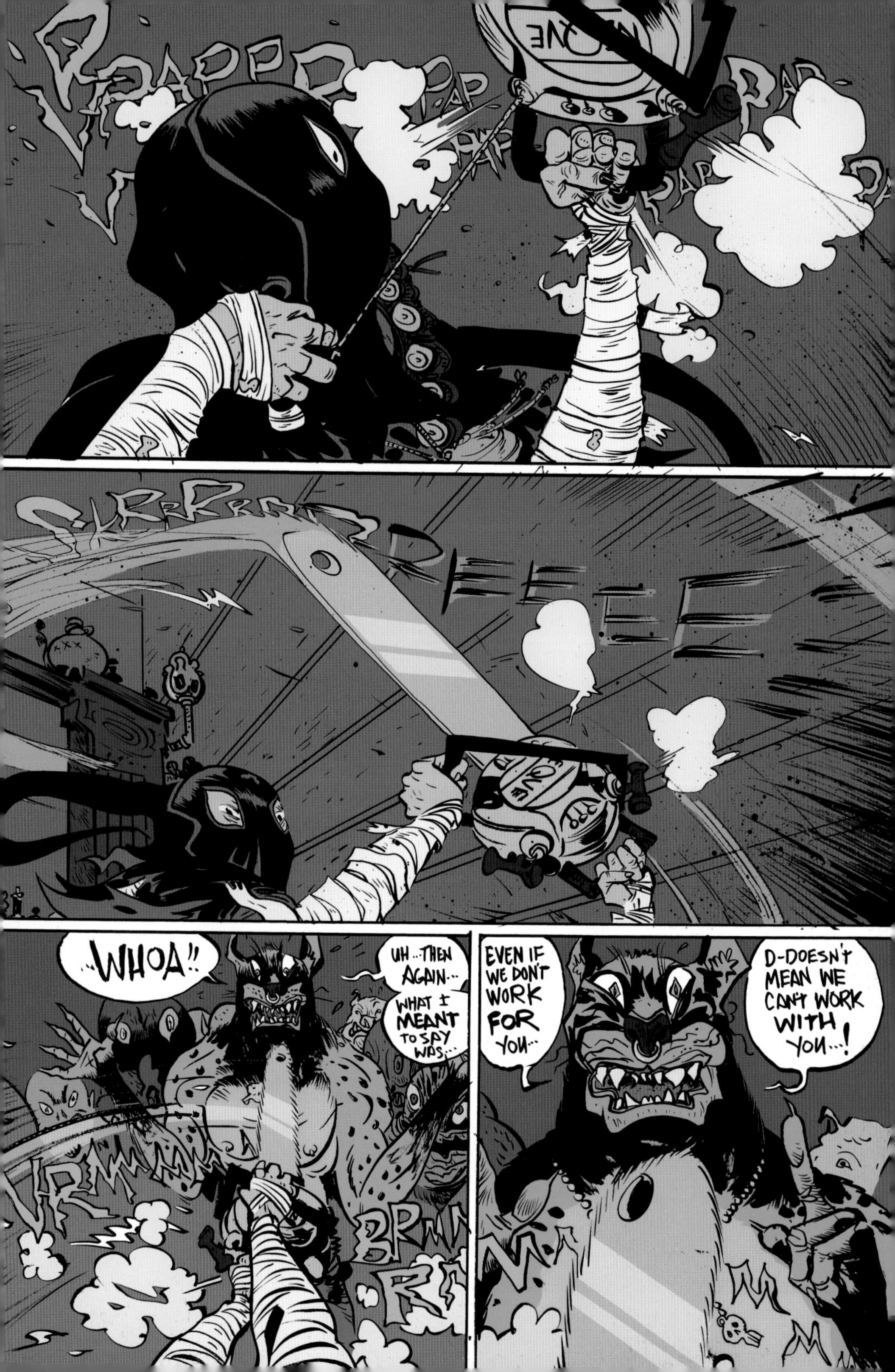
..WHOA!!
UH...THEN AGAIN...
WHAT I MEANT TO SAY WAS...
EVEN IF WE DON'T WORK FOR YOU...
D-DOESN'T MEAN WE CAN'T WORK WITH YOU...!

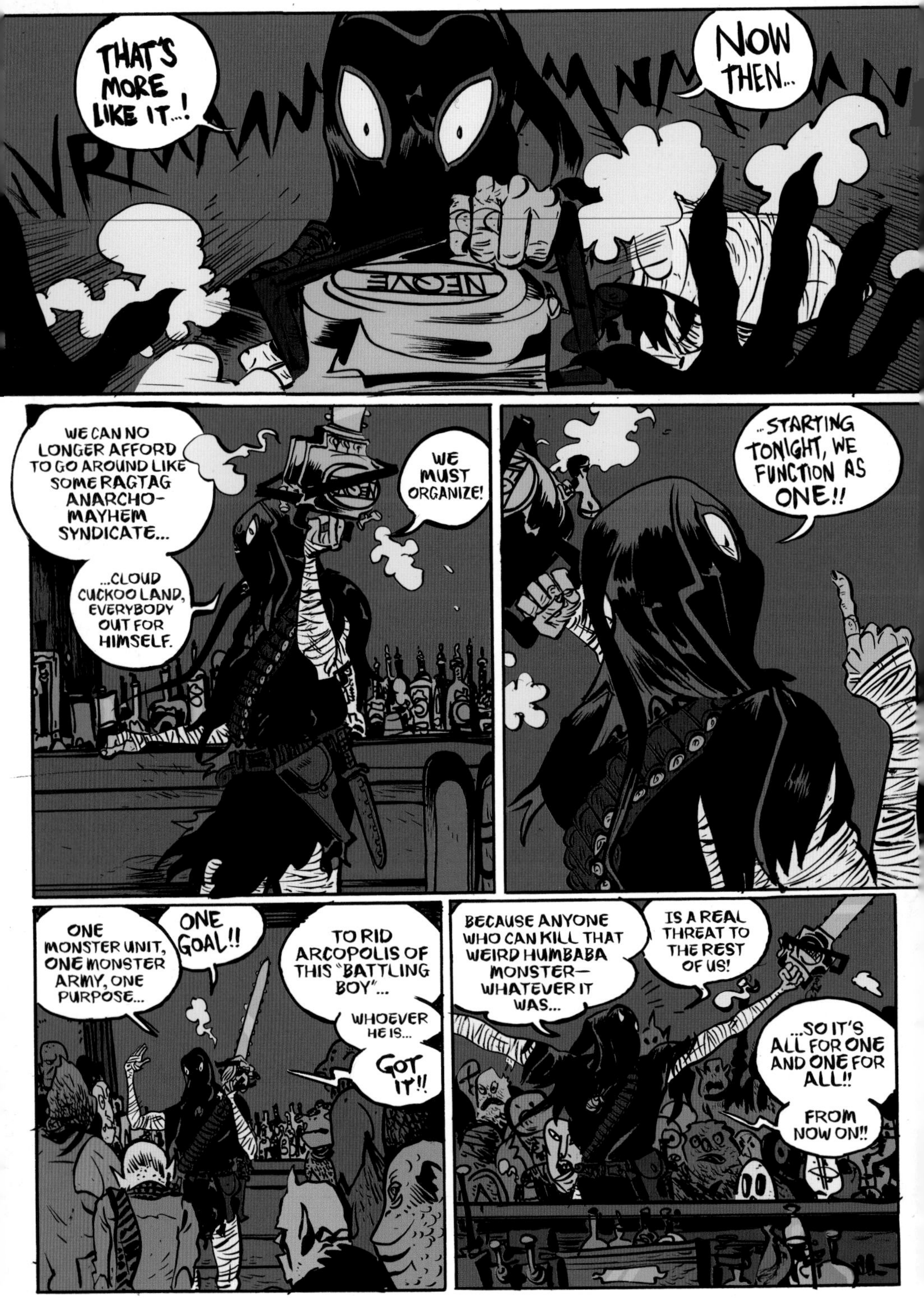
THAT'S MORE LIKE IT...!
NOW THEN...
WE CAN NO LONGER AFFORD TO GO AROUND LIKE SOME RAGTAG ANARCHO-MAYHEM SYNDICATE...
...CLOUD CUCKOO LAND, EVERYBODY OUT FOR HIMSELF.
WE MUST ORGANIZE!
...STARTING TONIGHT, WE FUNCTION AS ONE!!
ONE MONSTER UNIT, ONE MONSTER ARMY, ONE PURPOSE...
ONE GOAL!!
TO RID ARCOPOLIS OF THIS "BATTLING BOY"...
WHOEVER HE IS...
GOT IT!!
BECAUSE ANYONE WHO CAN KILL THAT WEIRD HUMBABA MONSTER— WHATEVER IT WAS...
IS A REAL THREAT TO THE REST OF US!
...SO IT'S ALL FOR ONE AND ONE FOR ALL!!
FROM NOW ON!!

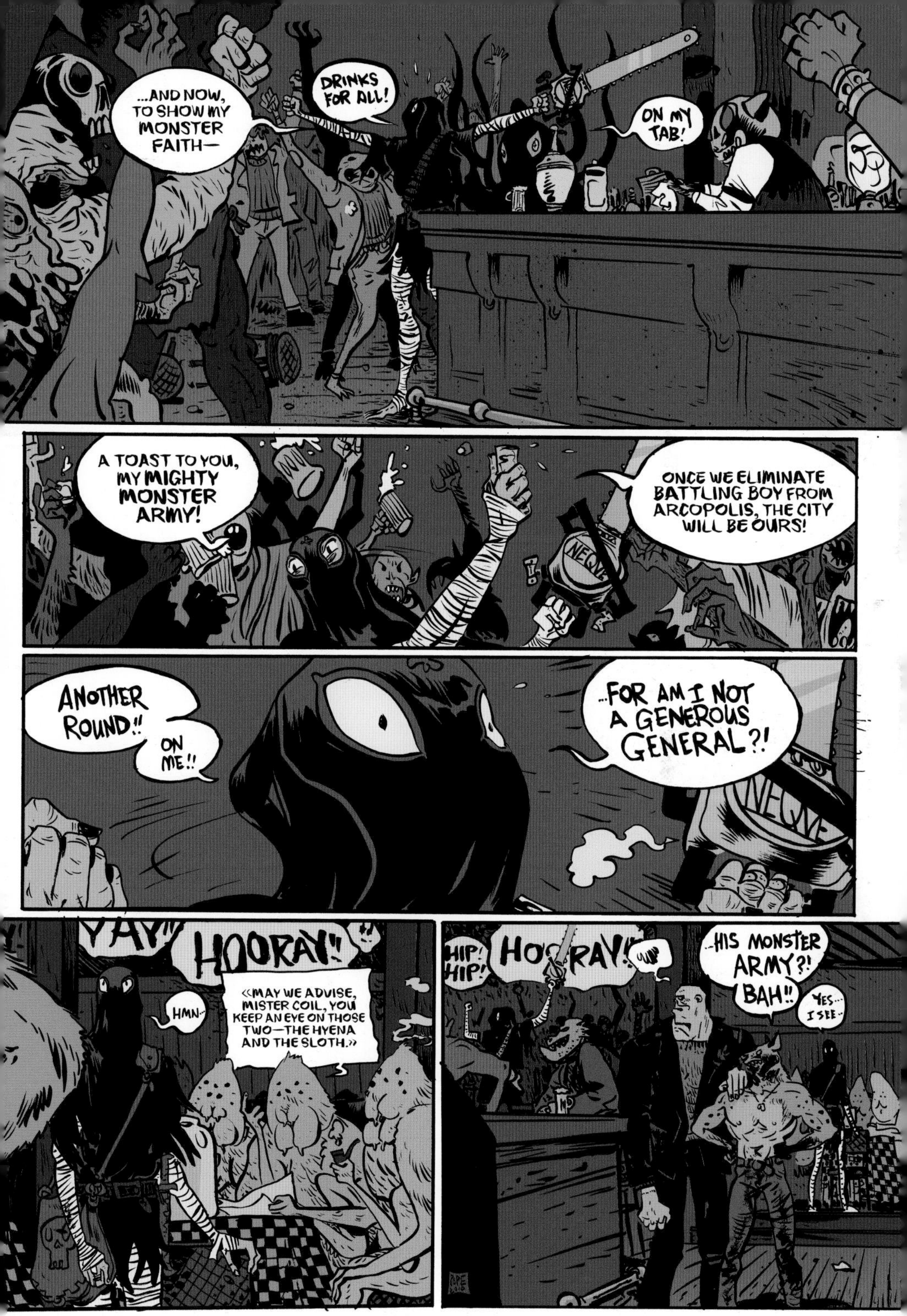
...AND NOW, TO SHOW MY MONSTER FAITH—
DRINKS FOR ALL!
ON MY TAB!
A TOAST TO YOU, MY MIGHTY MONSTER ARMY!
ONCE WE ELIMINATE BATTLING BOY FROM ARCOPOLIS, THE CITY WILL BE OURS!
ANOTHER ROUND!!
ON ME!!
...FOR AM I NOT A GENEROUS GENERAL?!
YAY!
HOORAY!
HMN...
«MAY WE ADVISE, MISTER COIL, YOU KEEP AN EYE ON THOSE TWO—THE HYENA AND THE SLOTH.»
HIP! HIP!
HOORAY!
...HIS MONSTER ARMY?! BAH!!
YES... I SEE...

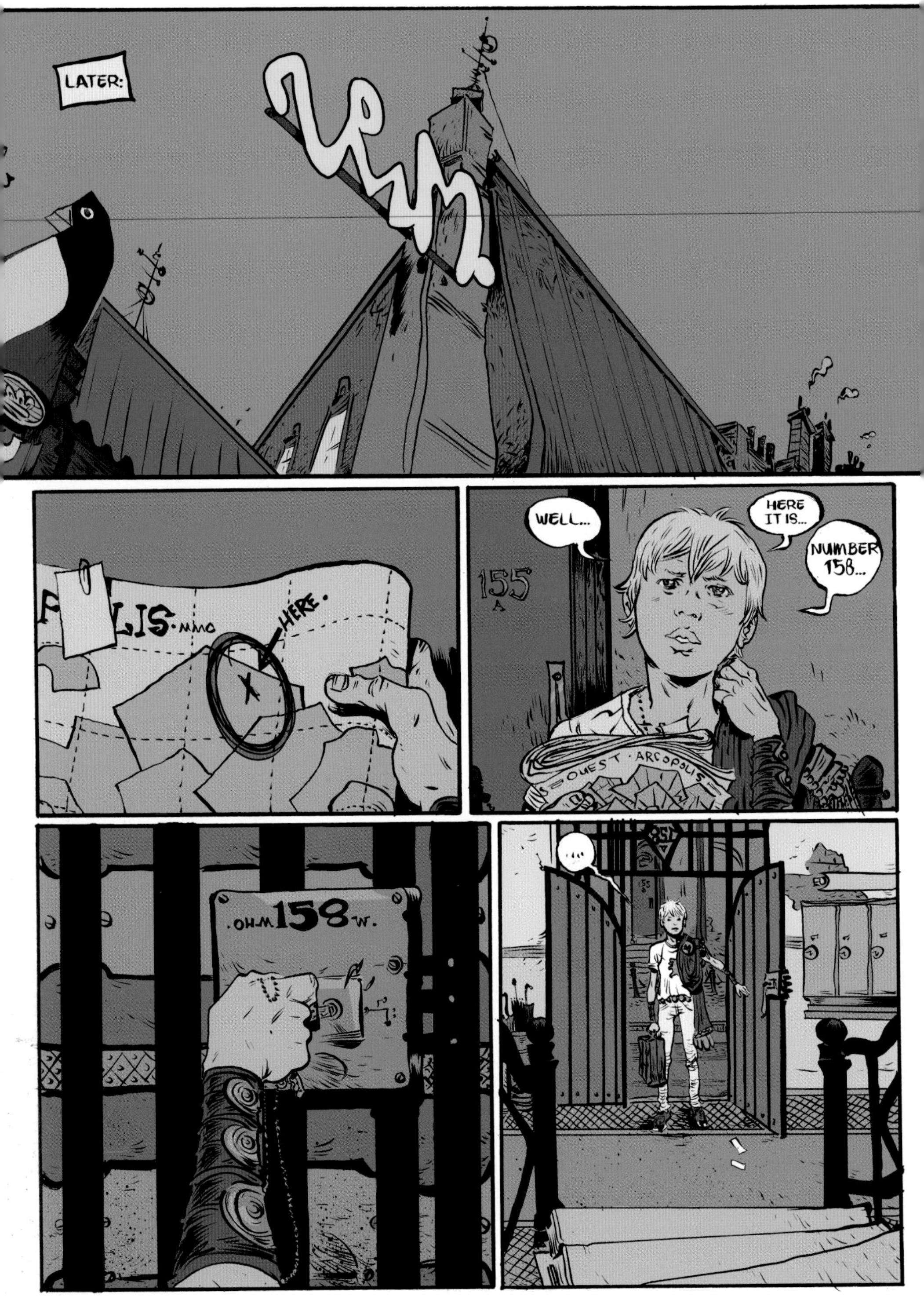
LATER:
LIS·MMC
HERE.
X
WELL...
HERE IT IS...
NUMBER 158...
155 A
OUEST · ARCOPOLIS
.OHM 158 W.

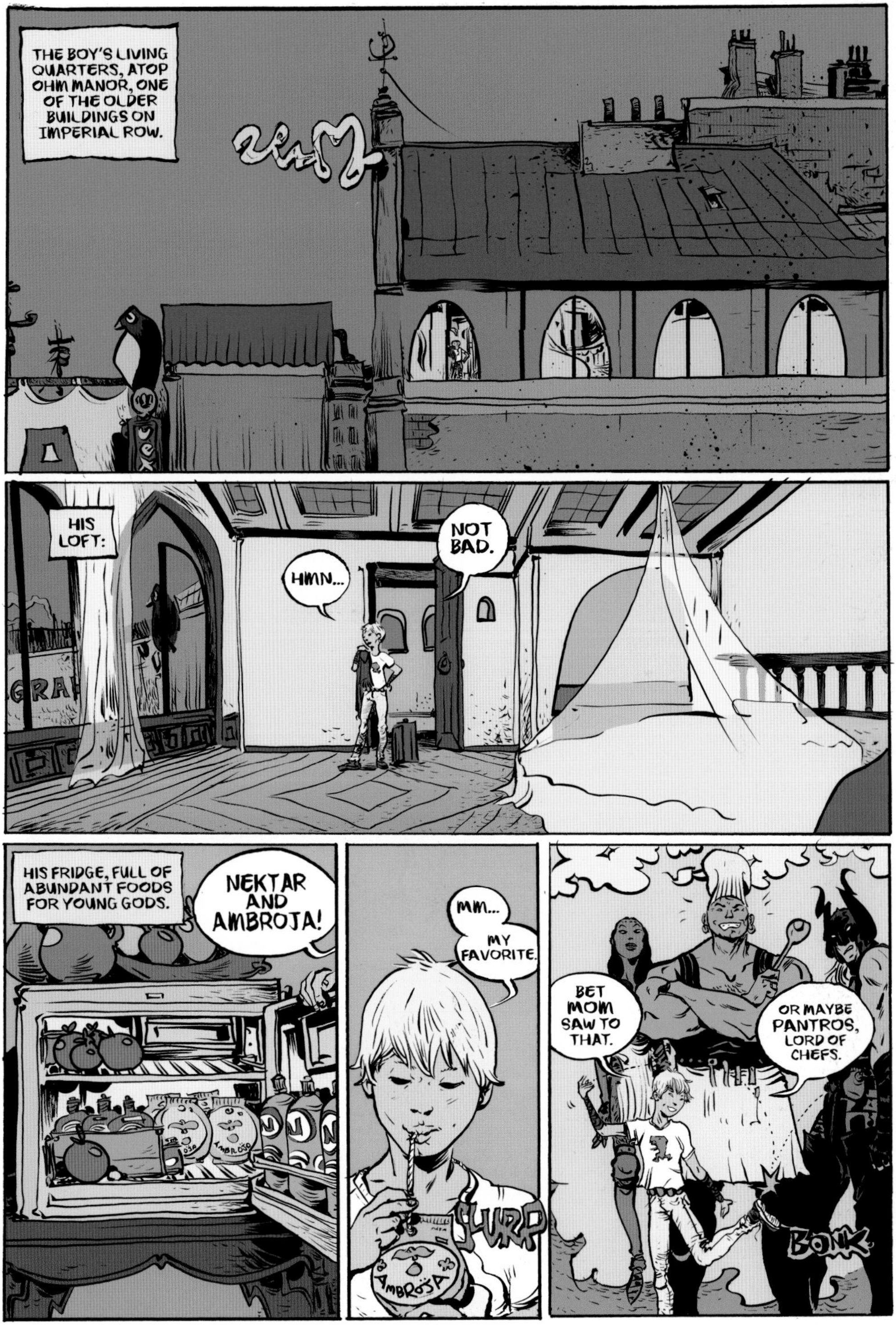
THE BOY'S LIVING QUARTERS, ATOP OHM MANOR, ONE OF THE OLDER BUILDINGS ON IMPERIAL ROW.
HIS LOFT:
HMN...
NOT BAD.
HIS FRIDGE, FULL OF ABUNDANT FOODS FOR YOUNG GODS.
NEKTAR AND AMBROJA!
MM... MY FAVORITE.
SLURP
AMBRÖSA
BET MOM SAW TO THAT.
OR MAYBE PANTROS, LORD OF CHEFS.
BONK

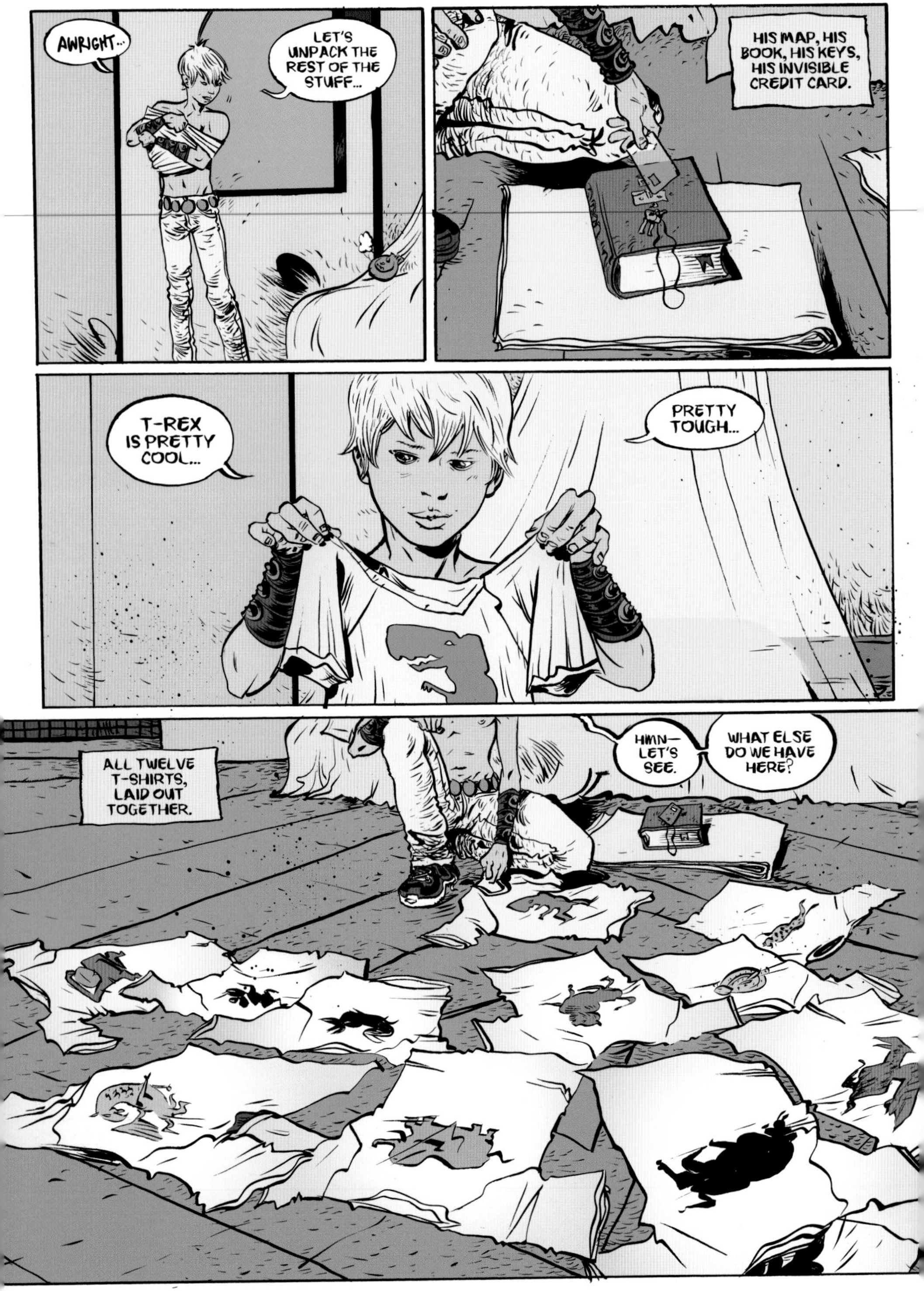
AWRIGHT...
LET'S UNPACK THE REST OF THE STUFF...
HIS MAP, HIS BOOK, HIS KEYS, HIS INVISIBLE CREDIT CARD.
T-REX IS PRETTY COOL...
PRETTY TOUGH...
ALL TWELVE T-SHIRTS, LAID OUT TOGETHER.
HMN— LET'S SEE.
WHAT ELSE DO WE HAVE HERE?

KING LION.

KING LEOPARD.

CURIOUS ORANGUTAN.

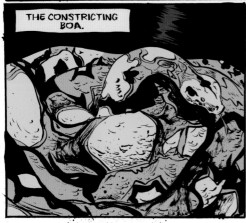

THE CONSTRICTING BOA.

THE SLY, SILENT FOX.

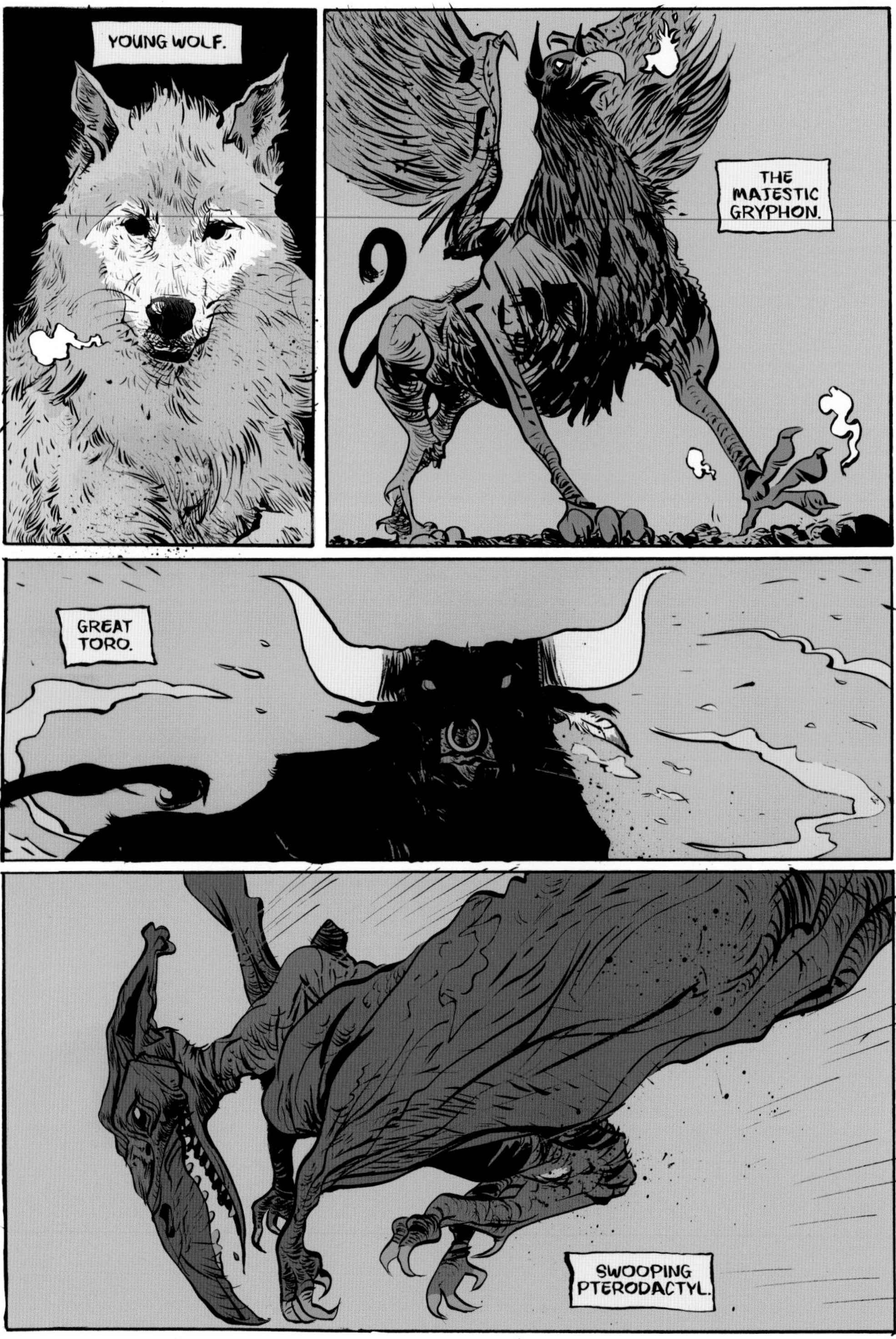
YOUNG WOLF.
THE MAJESTIC GRYPHON.
GREAT TORO.
SWOOPING PTERODACTYL.

T-REX, HE WITH THE COLD EYE.

KING ELEPHANT.

...AND THE FIELD MOUSE.

A MOUSE?!

WHAT GOOD IS A MOUSE?

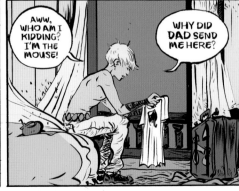

AWW, WHO AM I KIDDING? I'M THE MOUSE!

WHY DID DAD SEND ME HERE?

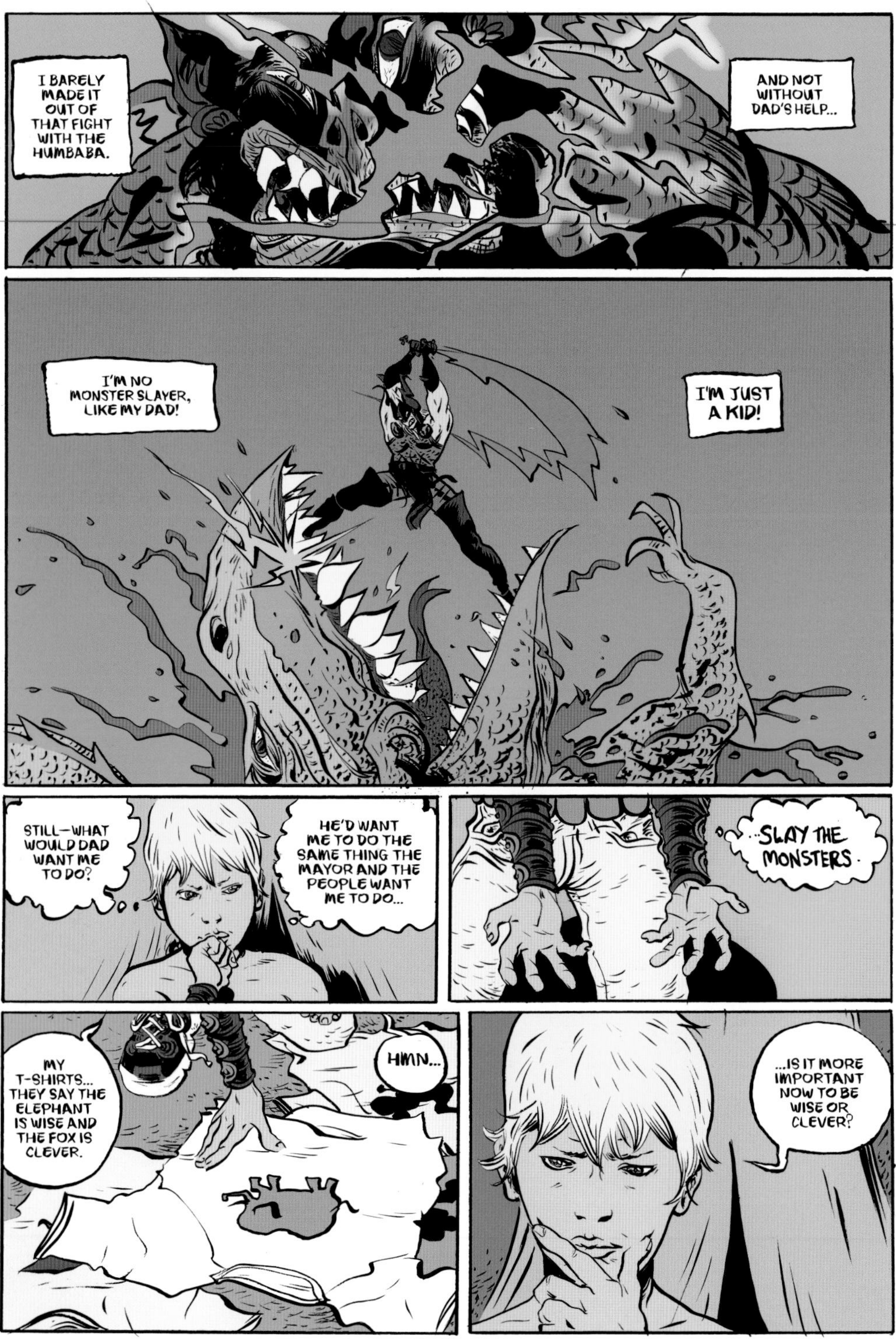
I BARELY MADE IT OUT OF THAT FIGHT WITH THE HUMBABA.
AND NOT WITHOUT DAD'S HELP...
I'M NO MONSTER SLAYER, LIKE MY DAD!
I'M JUST A KID!
STILL—WHAT WOULD DAD WANT ME TO DO?
HE'D WANT ME TO DO THE SAME THING THE MAYOR AND THE PEOPLE WANT ME TO DO...
...SLAY THE MONSTERS.
MY T-SHIRTS... THEY SAY THE ELEPHANT IS WISE AND THE FOX IS CLEVER.
HMN...
...IS IT MORE IMPORTANT NOW TO BE WISE OR CLEVER?

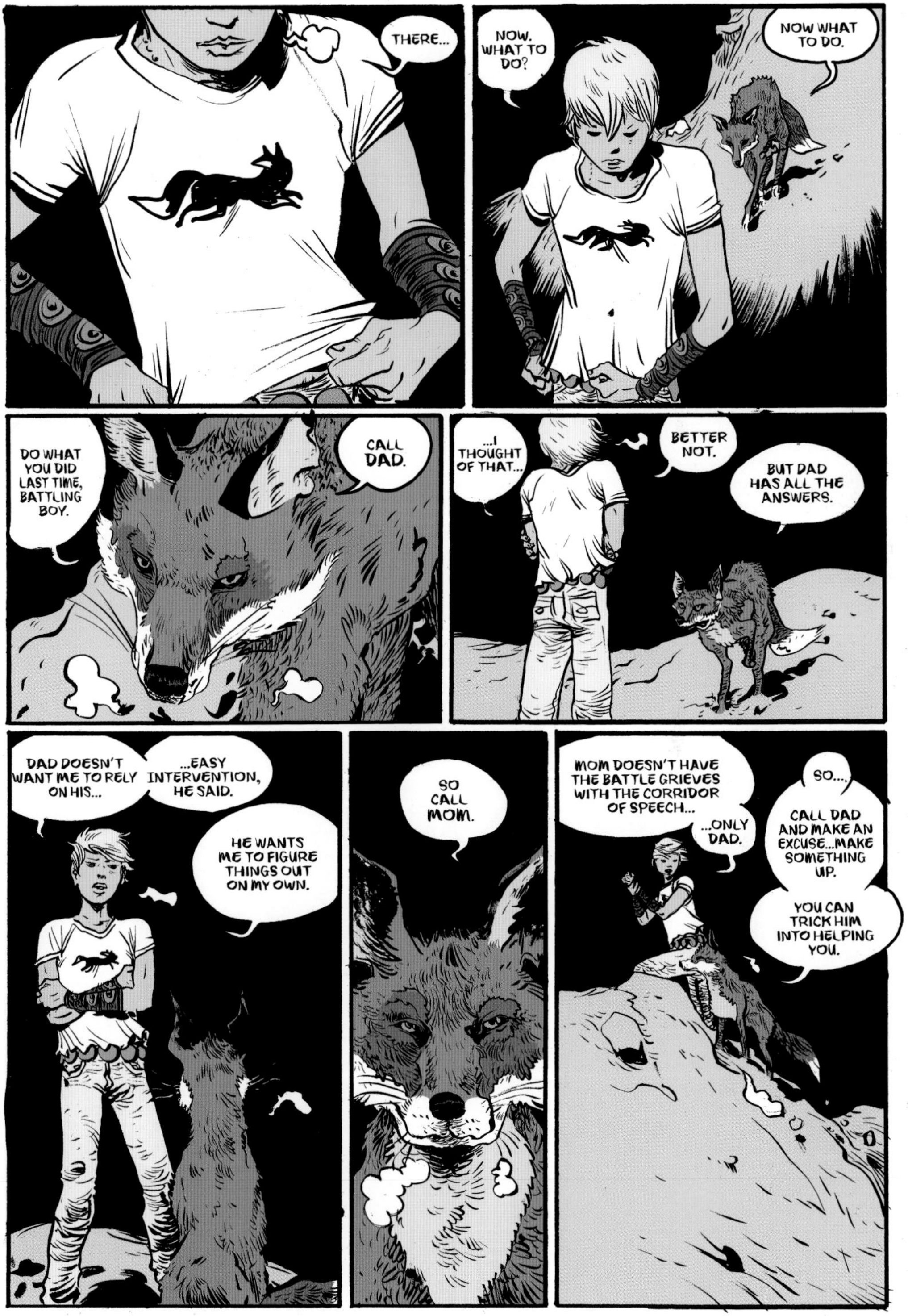
THERE...
NOW. WHAT TO DO?
NOW WHAT TO DO.
DO WHAT YOU DID LAST TIME, BATTLING BOY.
CALL DAD.
...I THOUGHT OF THAT...
BETTER NOT.
BUT DAD HAS ALL THE ANSWERS.
DAD DOESN'T WANT ME TO RELY ON HIS...
...EASY INTERVENTION, HE SAID.
HE WANTS ME TO FIGURE THINGS OUT ON MY OWN.
SO CALL MOM.
MOM DOESN'T HAVE THE BATTLE GRIEVES WITH THE CORRIDOR OF SPEECH...
...ONLY DAD.
SO....
CALL DAD AND MAKE AN EXCUSE...MAKE SOMETHING UP.
YOU CAN TRICK HIM INTO HELPING YOU.

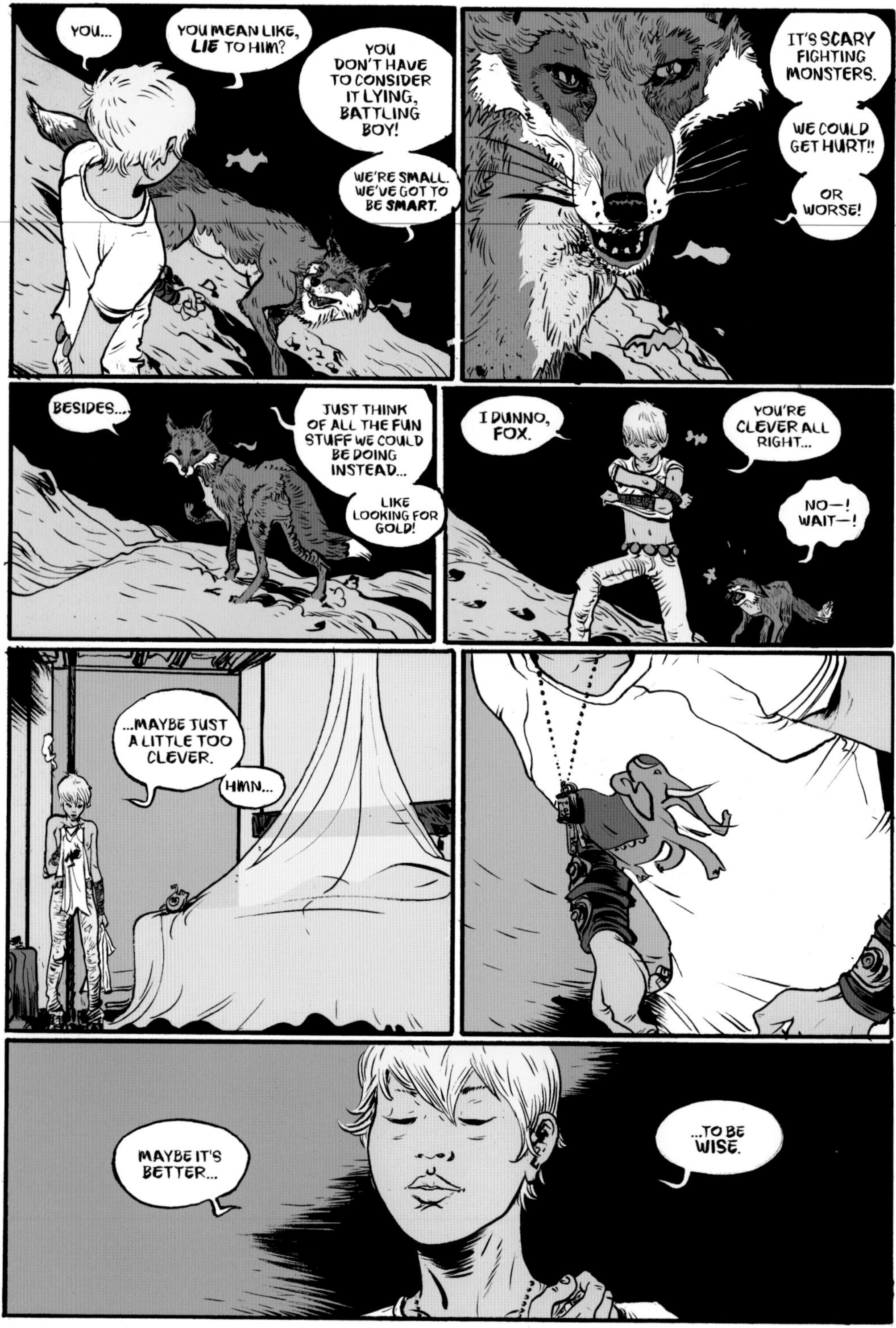
YOU...
YOU MEAN LIKE, LIE TO HIM?
YOU DON'T HAVE TO CONSIDER IT LYING, BATTLING BOY!
WE'RE SMALL. WE'VE GOT TO BE SMART.
IT'S SCARY FIGHTING MONSTERS.
WE COULD GET HURT!!
OR WORSE!
BESIDES...
JUST THINK OF ALL THE FUN STUFF WE COULD BE DOING INSTEAD...
LIKE LOOKING FOR GOLD!
I DUNNO, FOX.
YOU'RE CLEVER ALL RIGHT...
NO—! WAIT—!
...MAYBE JUST A LITTLE TOO CLEVER.
HMN...
MAYBE IT'S BETTER...
...TO BE WISE.

HRMN...

...BATTLING BOY...

OH WOW!

KING ELEPHANT, I...

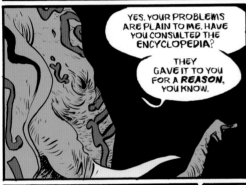

YES. YOUR PROBLEMS ARE PLAIN TO ME. HAVE YOU CONSULTED THE ENCYCLOPEDIA?

THEY GAVE IT TO YOU FOR A **REASON**, YOU KNOW.

I-I DID! THERE'S NOTHING IN THERE ABOUT THE HUMBABA. I LOOKED AFTER THE FIGHT.

OH?

THAT IS... STRANGE.

THERE'S STUFF IN THERE ABOUT OTHER MONSTERS, THOUGH, LIKE...

WAIT A MINUTE!

HOW CAN I BE STANDING HERE TALKING TO AN ELEPHANT?

ELEPHANTS CAN'T TALK!

...AND NEITHER CAN FOXES...

...BUT YOU ARE NOT STANDING HERE TALKING TO THE ELEPHANT KING.

YOU ARE STANDING ALONE IN YOUR ROOM, THINKING OUT LOUD.

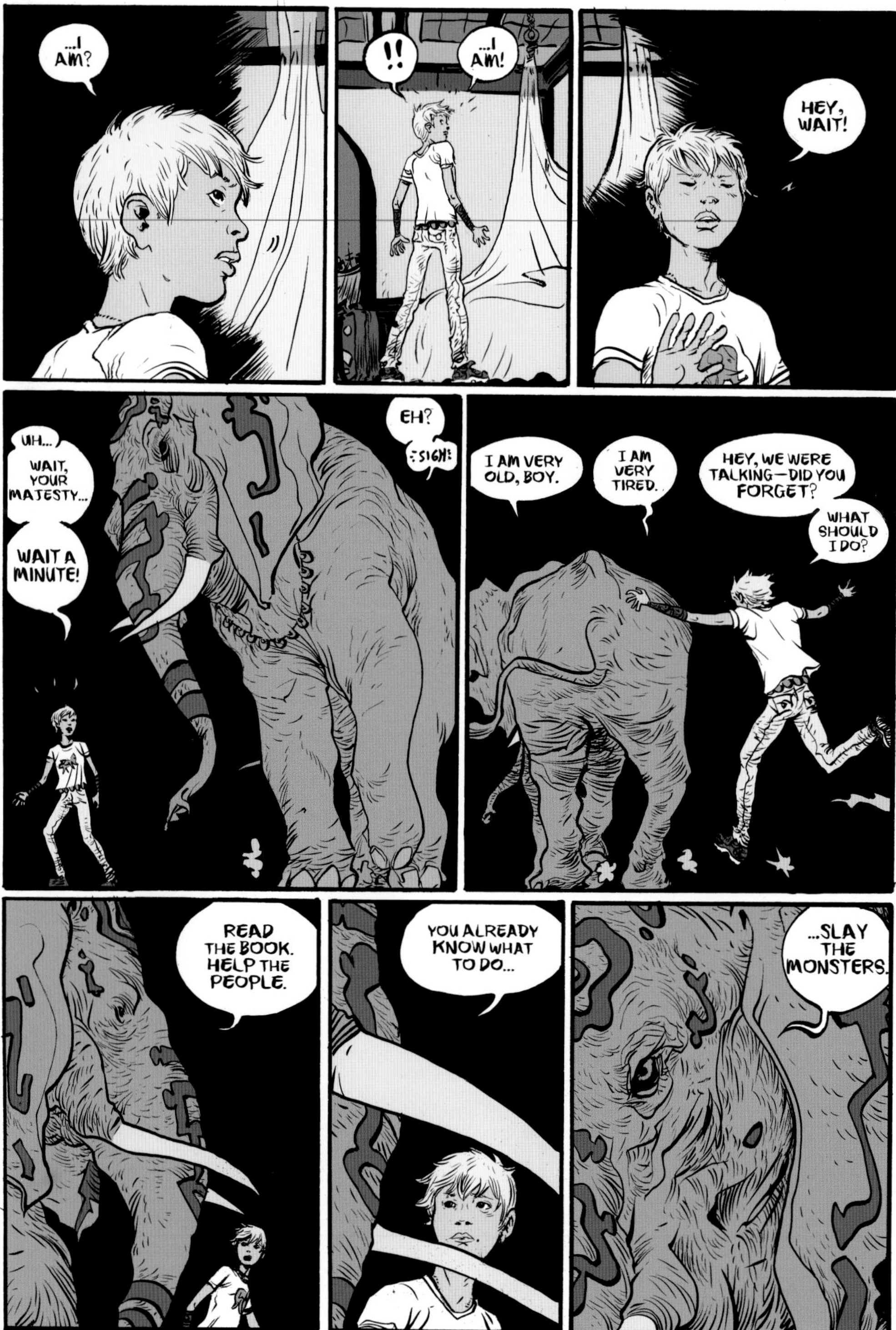
...I AM?
!!
...I AM!
HEY, WAIT!
UH... WAIT, YOUR MAJESTY...
WAIT A MINUTE!
EH?
:SIGH:
I AM VERY OLD, BOY.
I AM VERY TIRED.
HEY, WE WERE TALKING—DID YOU FORGET?
WHAT SHOULD I DO?
READ THE BOOK. HELP THE PEOPLE.
YOU ALREADY KNOW WHAT TO DO...
...SLAY THE MONSTERS.

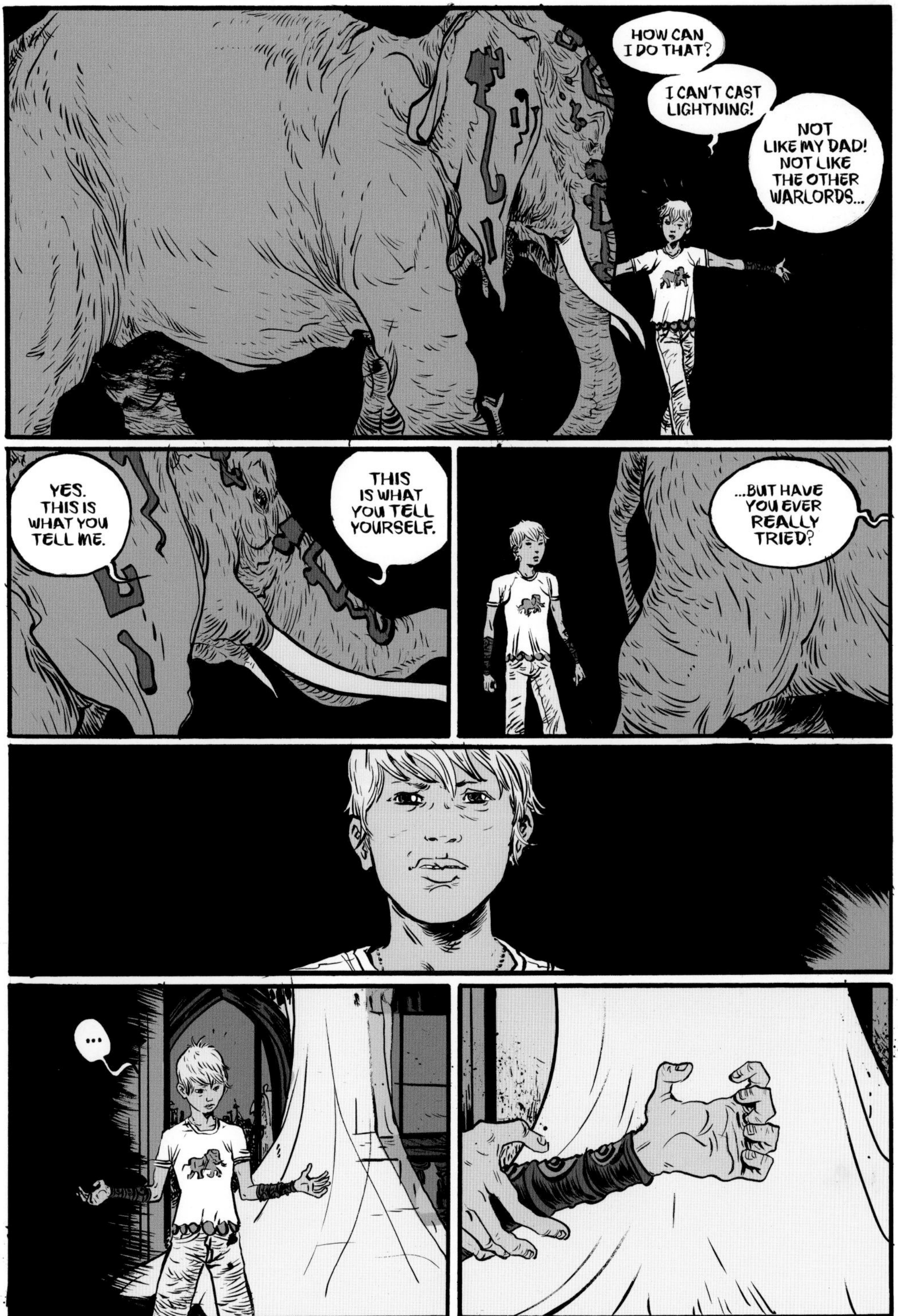
HOW CAN I DO THAT?
I CAN'T CAST LIGHTNING!
NOT LIKE MY DAD! NOT LIKE THE OTHER WARLORDS...
YES. THIS IS WHAT YOU TELL ME.
THIS IS WHAT YOU TELL YOURSELF.
...BUT HAVE YOU EVER REALLY TRIED?
...

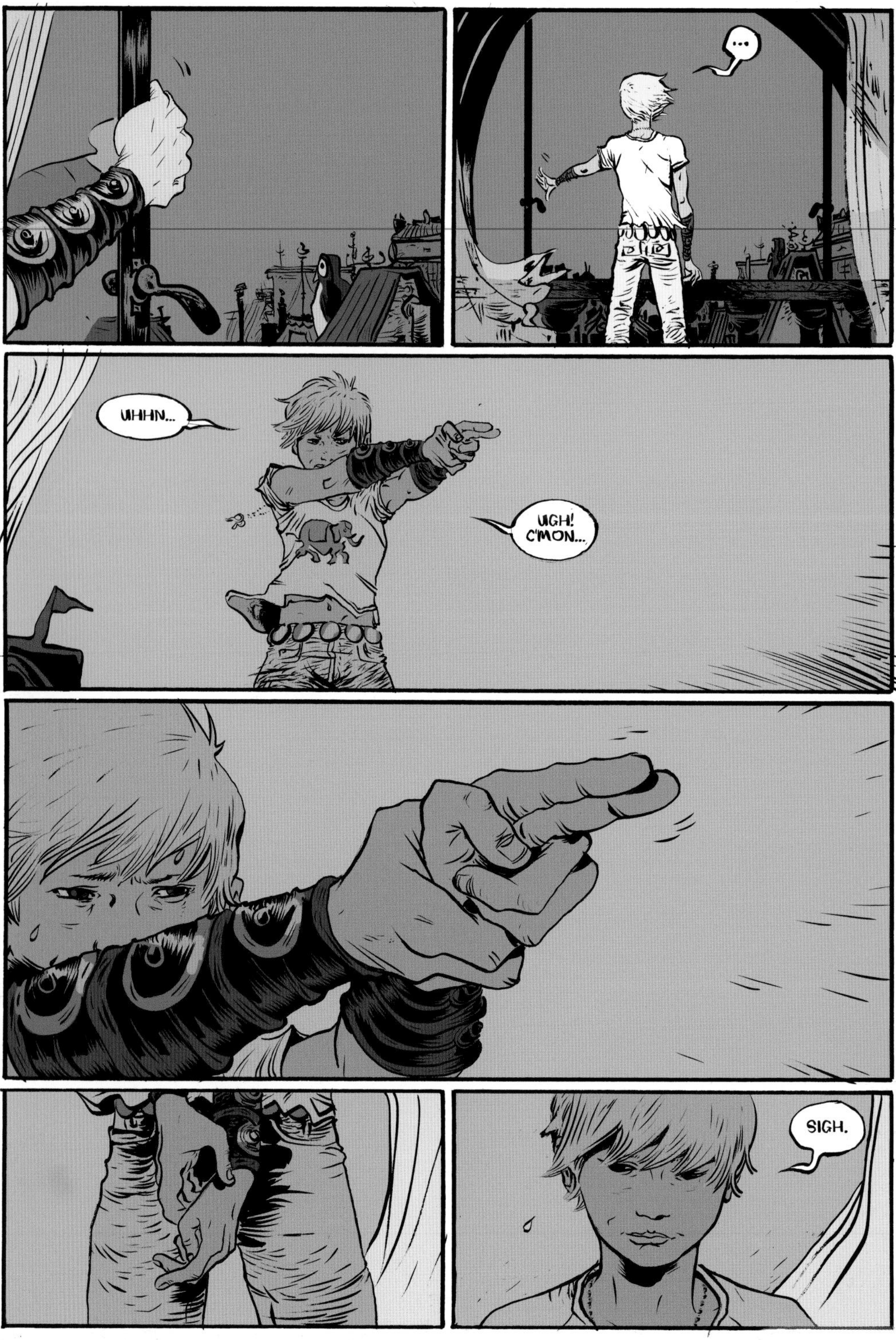
...
UHHN...
UGH! C'MON...
SIGH.

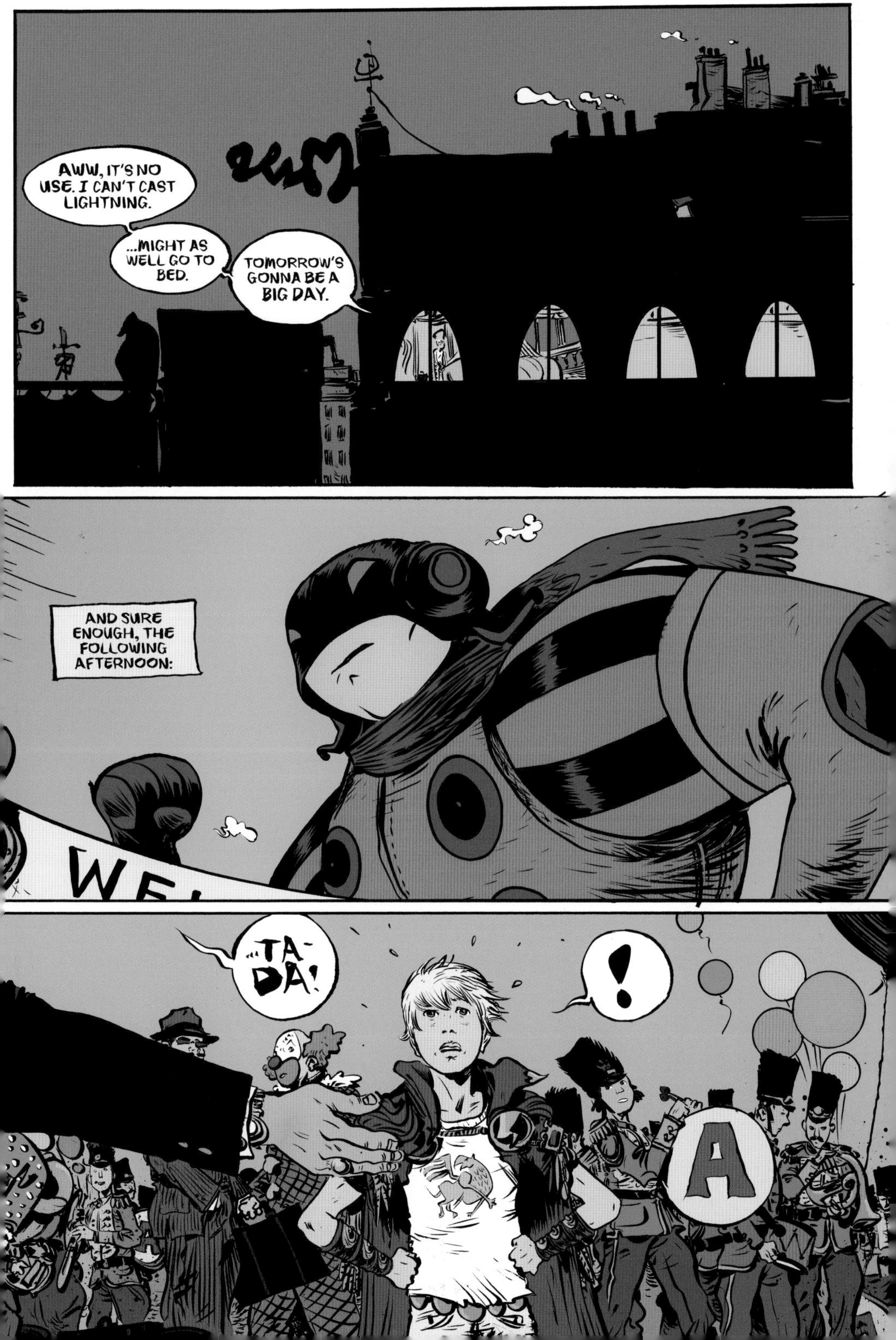
AWW, IT'S NO USE. I CAN'T CAST LIGHTNING.
...MIGHT AS WELL GO TO BED.
TOMORROW'S GONNA BE A BIG DAY.
AND SURE ENOUGH, THE FOLLOWING AFTERNOON:
WE
...TA-DA!
!
A

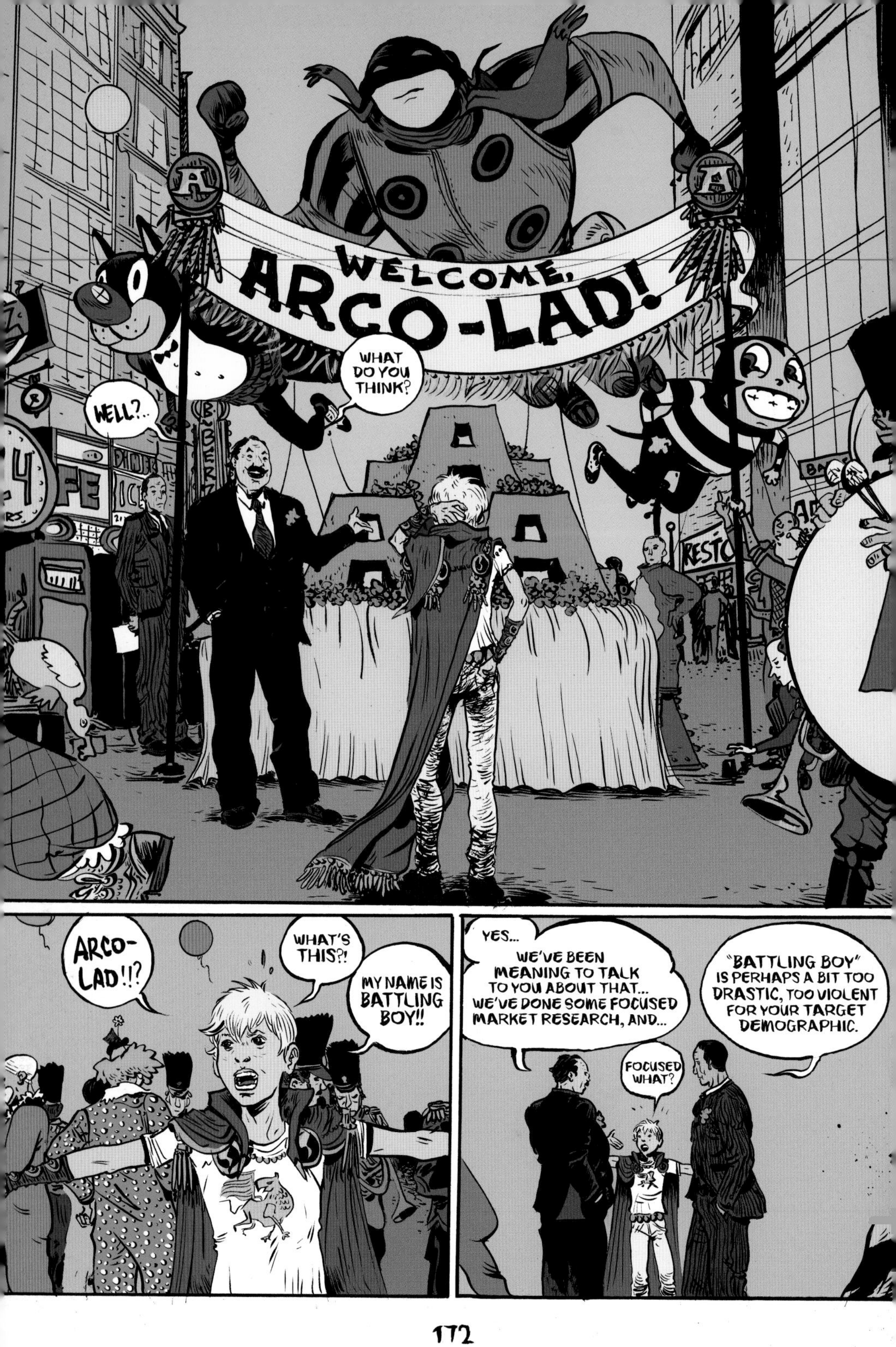
WELCOME, ARCO-LAD!
WHAT DO YOU THINK?
WELL?...
ARCO-LAD!!?
WHAT'S THIS?!
MY NAME IS BATTLING BOY!!
YES...
WE'VE BEEN MEANING TO TALK TO YOU ABOUT THAT... WE'VE DONE SOME FOCUSED MARKET RESEARCH, AND...
"BATTLING BOY" IS PERHAPS A BIT TOO DRASTIC, TOO VIOLENT FOR YOUR TARGET DEMOGRAPHIC.
FOCUSED WHAT?

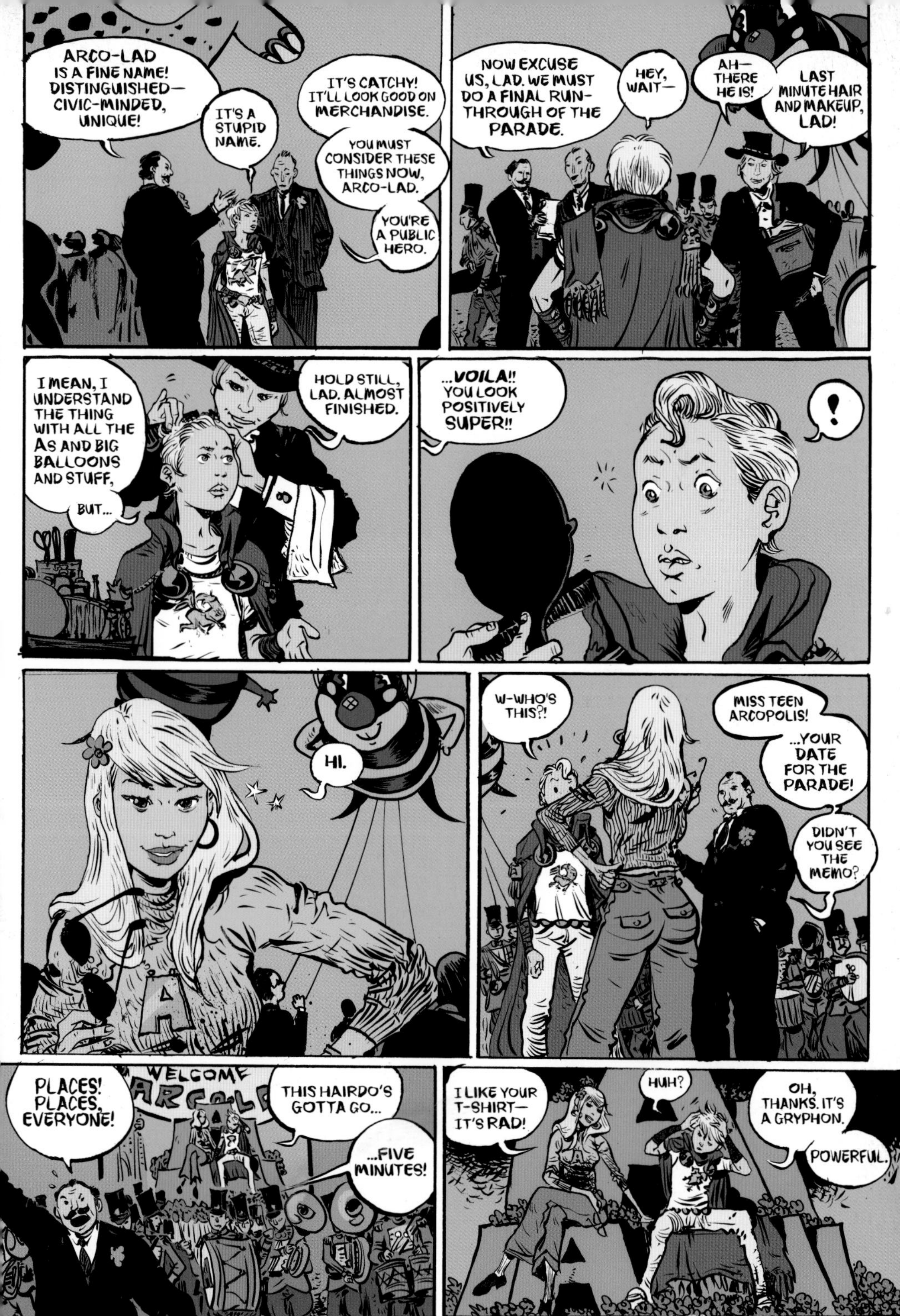
ARCO-LAD IS A FINE NAME! DISTINGUISHED— CIVIC-MINDED, UNIQUE!
IT'S A STUPID NAME.
IT'S CATCHY! IT'LL LOOK GOOD ON MERCHANDISE.
YOU MUST CONSIDER THESE THINGS NOW, ARCO-LAD.
YOU'RE A PUBLIC HERO.
NOW EXCUSE US, LAD. WE MUST DO A FINAL RUN-THROUGH OF THE PARADE.
HEY, WAIT—
AH— THERE HE IS!
LAST MINUTE HAIR AND MAKEUP, LAD!
I MEAN, I UNDERSTAND THE THING WITH ALL THE As AND BIG BALLOONS AND STUFF,
BUT...
HOLD STILL, LAD. ALMOST FINISHED.
...VOILA!! YOU LOOK POSITIVELY SUPER!!
!
HI.
W-WHO'S THIS?!
MISS TEEN ARCOPOLIS!
...YOUR DATE FOR THE PARADE!
DIDN'T YOU SEE THE MEMO?
WELCOME
PLACES! PLACES, EVERYONE!
THIS HAIRDO'S GOTTA GO...
...FIVE MINUTES!
I LIKE YOUR T-SHIRT— IT'S RAD!
HUH?
OH, THANKS. IT'S A GRYPHON.
POWERFUL.

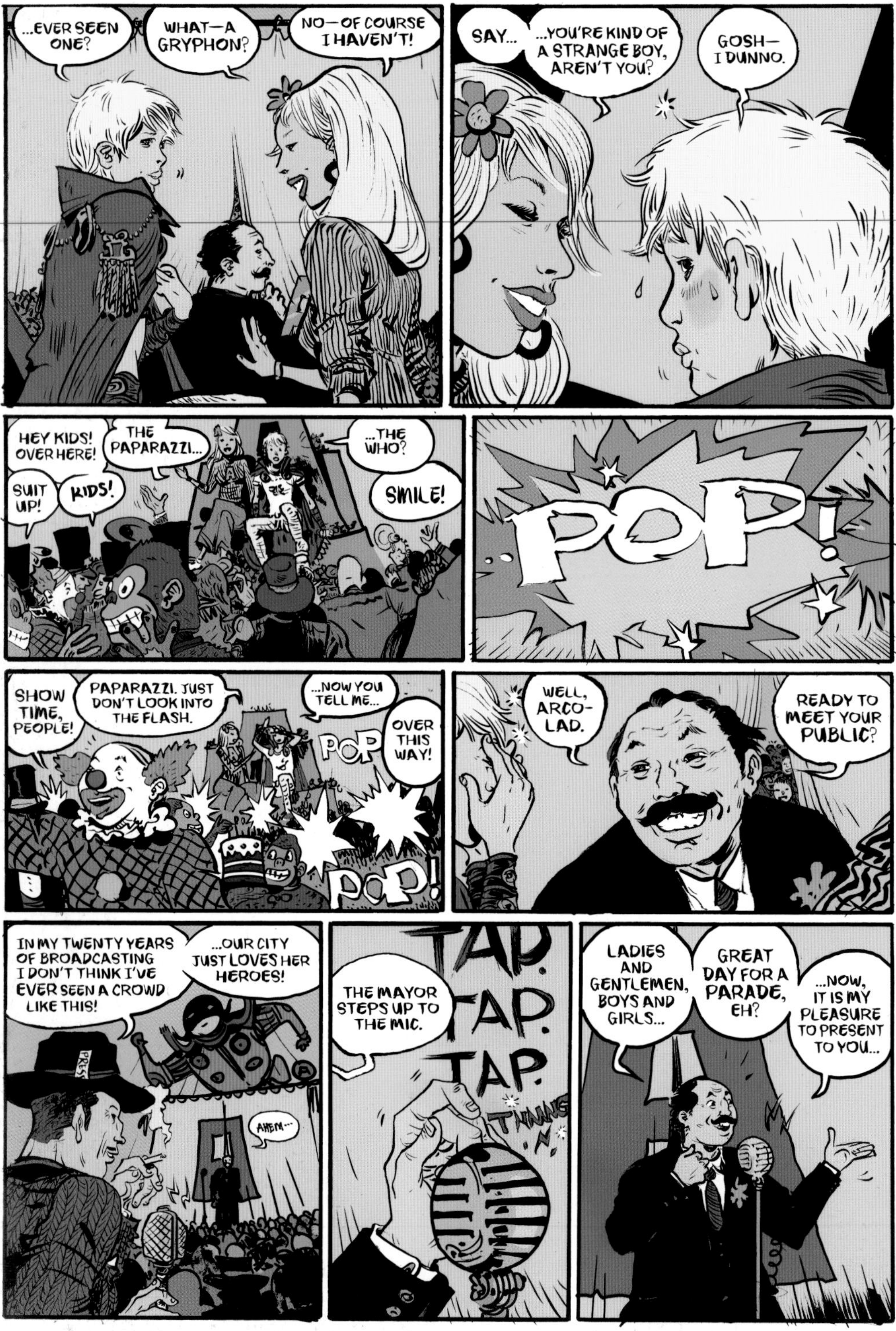
...EVER SEEN ONE?
WHAT—A GRYPHON?
NO—OF COURSE I HAVEN'T!
SAY...
...YOU'RE KIND OF A STRANGE BOY, AREN'T YOU?
GOSH— I DUNNO.
HEY KIDS! OVER HERE!
THE PAPARAZZI...
...THE WHO?
SUIT UP!
KIDS!
SMILE!
POP!
SHOW TIME, PEOPLE!
PAPARAZZI. JUST DON'T LOOK INTO THE FLASH.
...NOW YOU TELL ME...
OVER THIS WAY!
POP
POP!
WELL, ARCO-LAD.
READY TO MEET YOUR PUBLIC?
IN MY TWENTY YEARS OF BROADCASTING I DON'T THINK I'VE EVER SEEN A CROWD LIKE THIS!
...OUR CITY JUST LOVES HER HEROES!
AHEM...
TAP. TAP. TAP.
THE MAYOR STEPS UP TO THE MIC.
TINNNG
LADIES AND GENTLEMEN, BOYS AND GIRLS...
GREAT DAY FOR A PARADE, EH?
...NOW, IT IS MY PLEASURE TO PRESENT TO YOU...

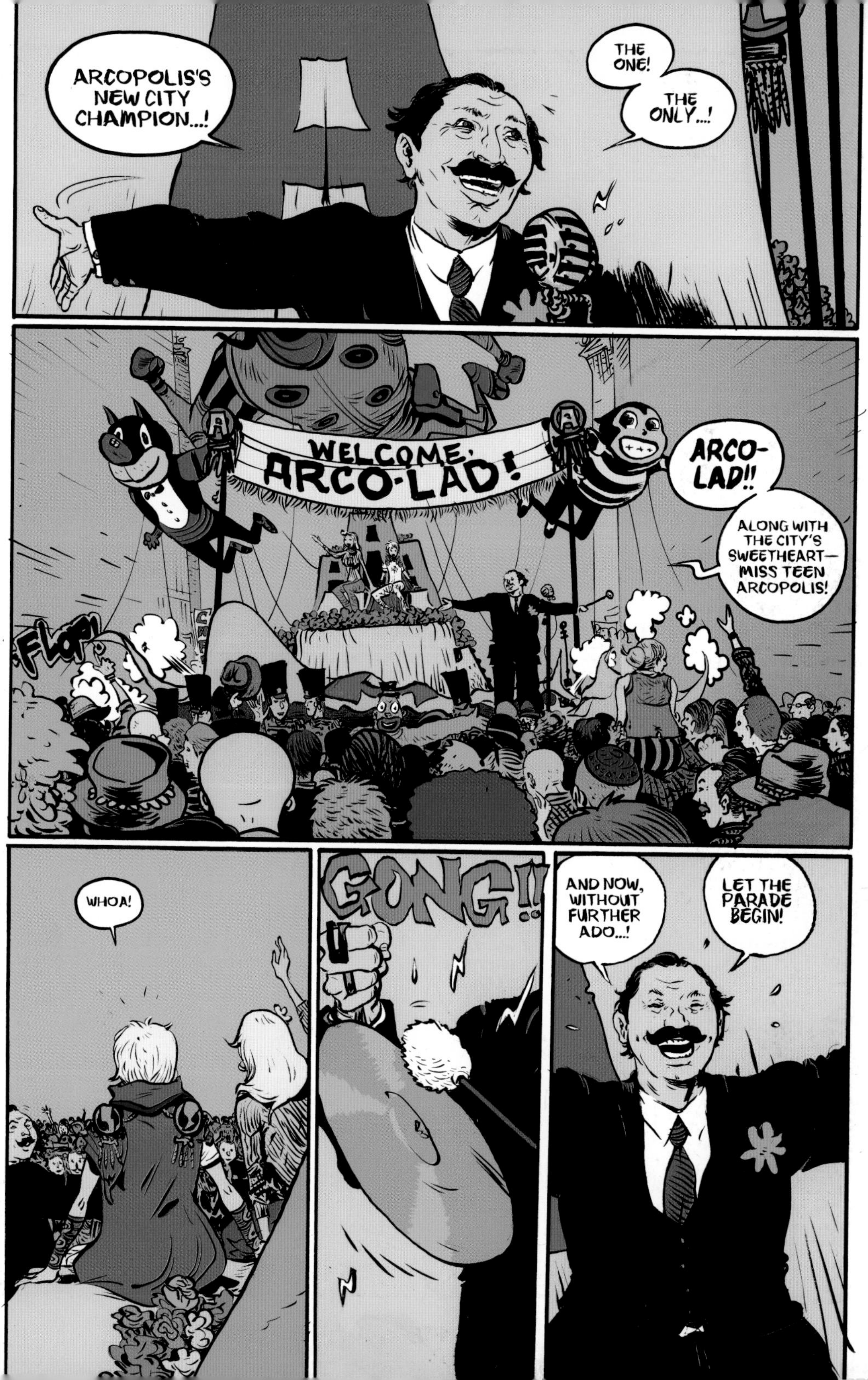
ARCOPOLIS'S NEW CITY CHAMPION...!
THE ONE!
THE ONLY...!
WELCOME, ARCO-LAD!
ARCO-LAD!!
ALONG WITH THE CITY'S SWEETHEART— MISS TEEN ARCOPOLIS!
FLOP!
WHOA!
GONG!!
AND NOW, WITHOUT FURTHER ADO...!
LET THE PARADE BEGIN!

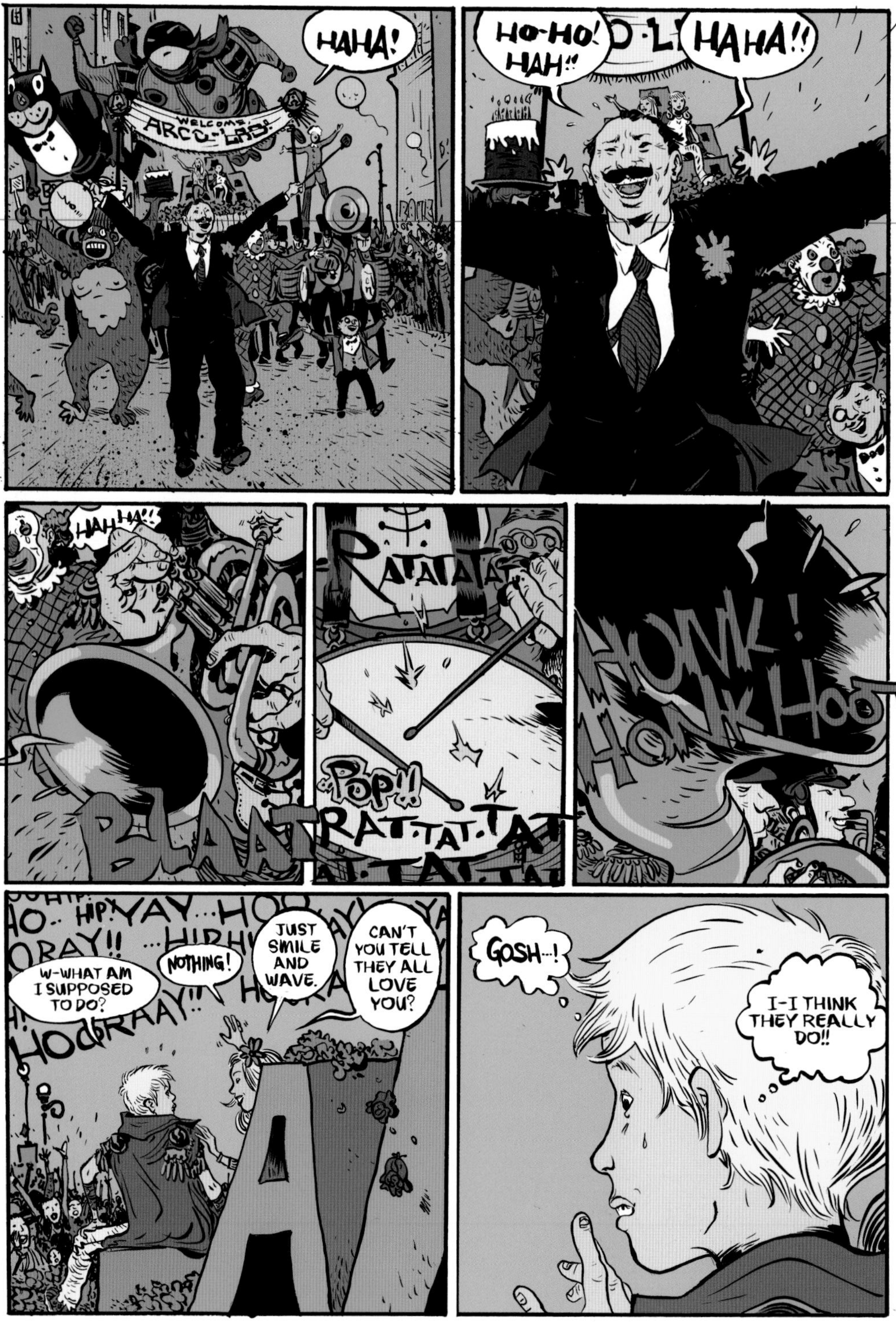
HAHA!
WELCOME, ARCO-LAD!
HO-HO! HAH!!
HAHA!!
HAH HA!!
RATATATAT
POP!!
BLAAT
RAT-TAT-TAT
HONK! HONK HOOT
HIP! YAY... HOORAY!!
W-WHAT AM I SUPPOSED TO DO?
NOTHING!
JUST SMILE AND WAVE.
CAN'T YOU TELL THEY ALL LOVE YOU?
GOSH...!
I-I THINK THEY REALLY DO!!

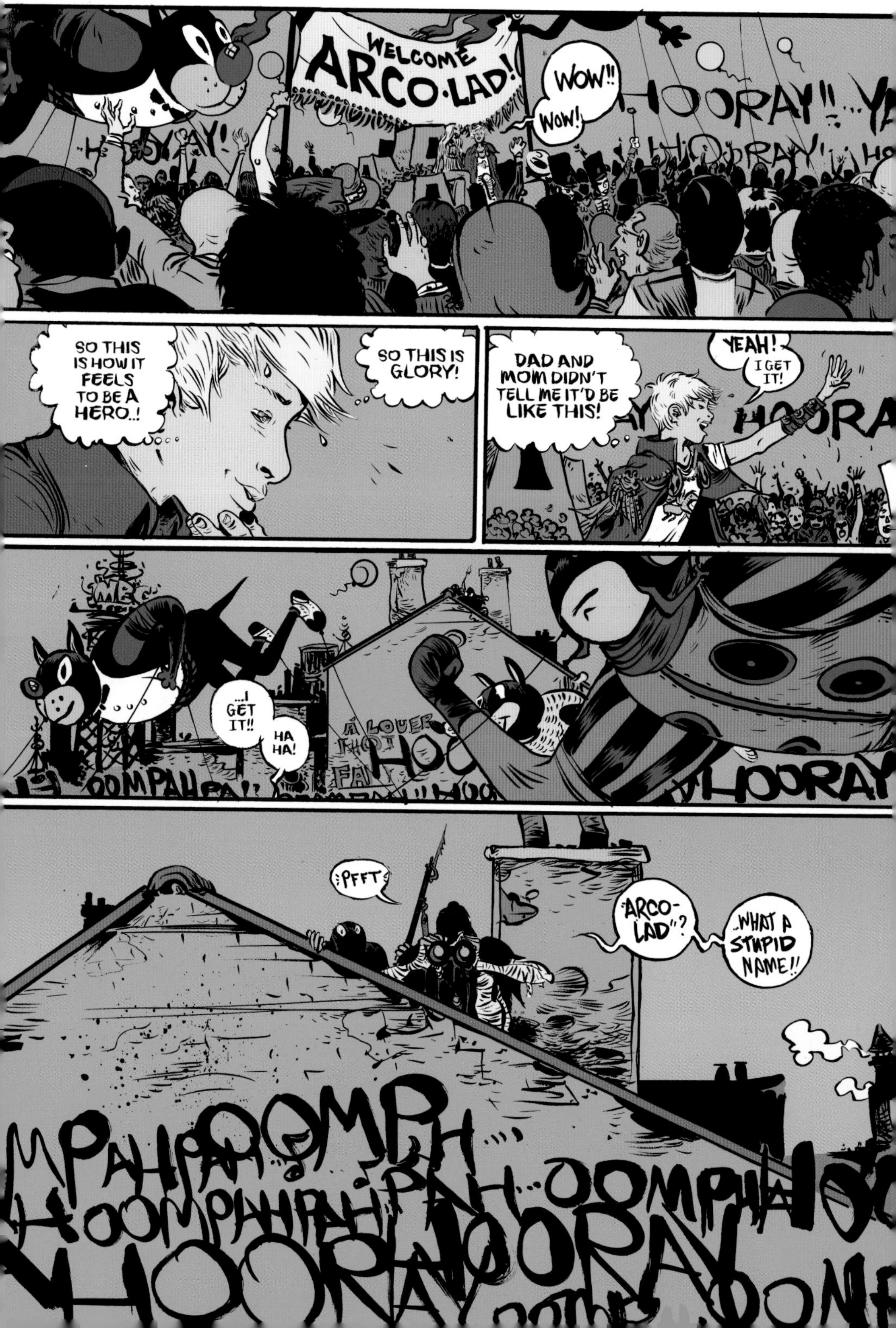
WELCOME ARCO-LAD!
WOW!!
WOW!
HOORAY!
HOORAY!! ...YA
HOORAY!
SO THIS IS HOW IT FEELS TO BE A HERO..!
SO THIS IS GLORY!
DAD AND MOM DIDN'T TELL ME IT'D BE LIKE THIS!
YEAH!
I GET IT!
HOORA
...I GET IT!!
HA HA!
À LOUER
OOMPAHPA!!
HOORAY
PFFT
"ARCO-LAD"?
...WHAT A STUPID NAME!!
OOMPH...
HOOMPAHPAH
OOMPHA
HOORAY
HOORA

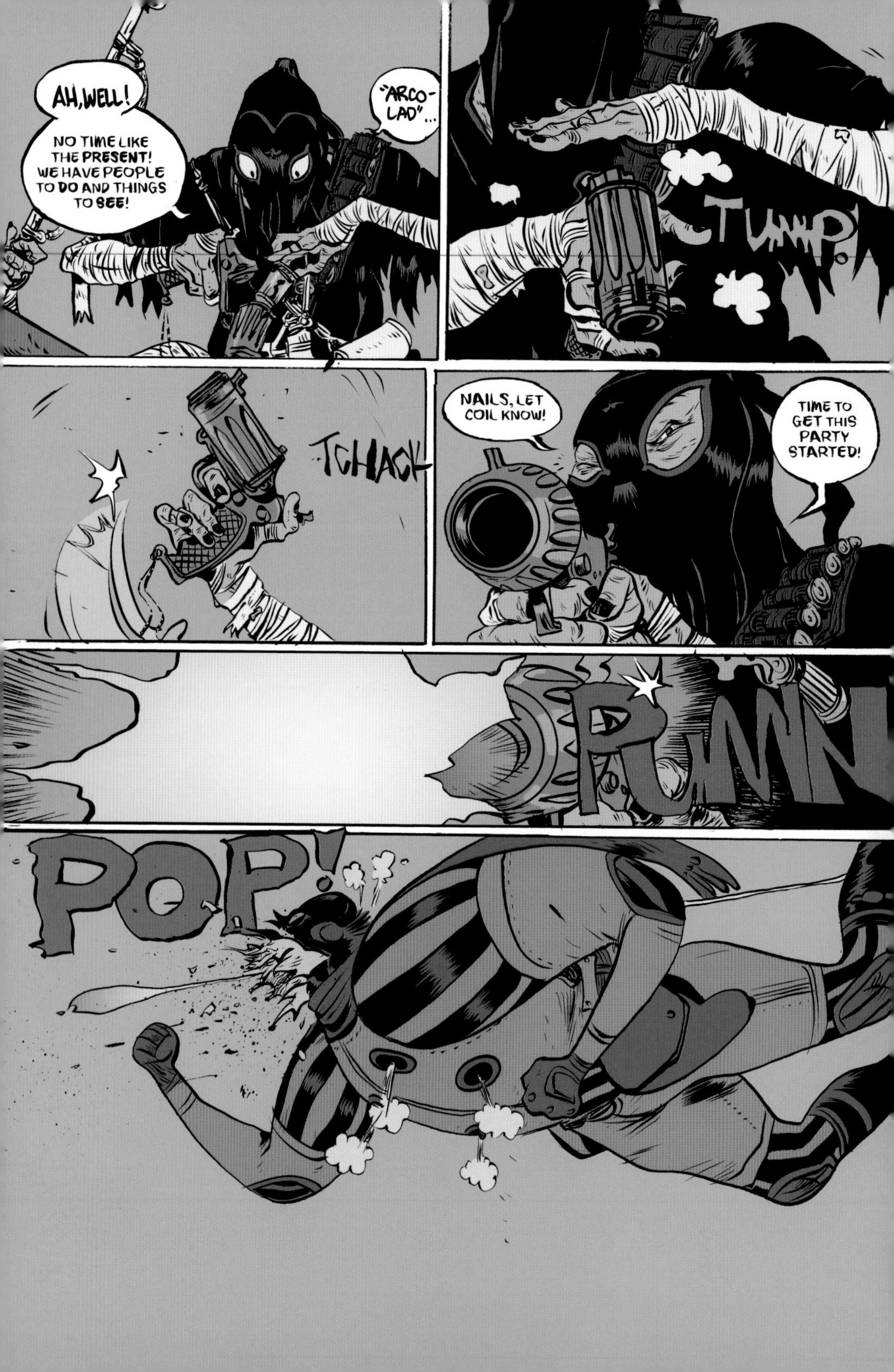
AH, WELL!
NO TIME LIKE THE PRESENT! WE HAVE PEOPLE TO DO AND THINGS TO SEE!
"ARCO-LAD"...
TUMP
TCHACK
NAILS, LET COIL KNOW!
TIME TO GET THIS PARTY STARTED!
PUMMN
POP!

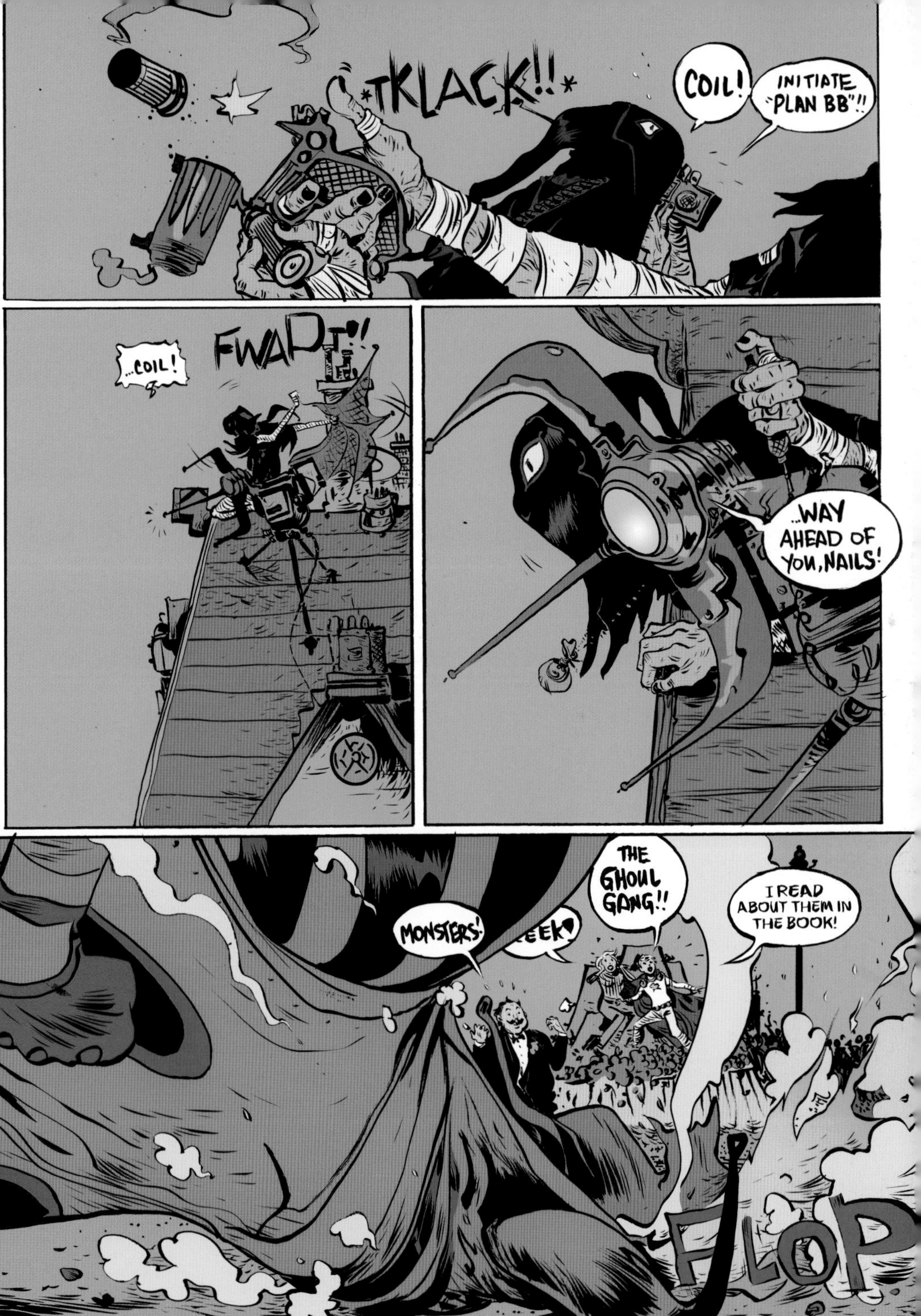
TKLACK!!
COIL!
INITIATE "PLAN BB"!!
...COIL!
FWAPT!!
...WAY AHEAD OF YOU, NAILS!
MONSTERS!
EEEK!
THE GHOUL GANG!!
I READ ABOUT THEM IN THE BOOK!
FLOP

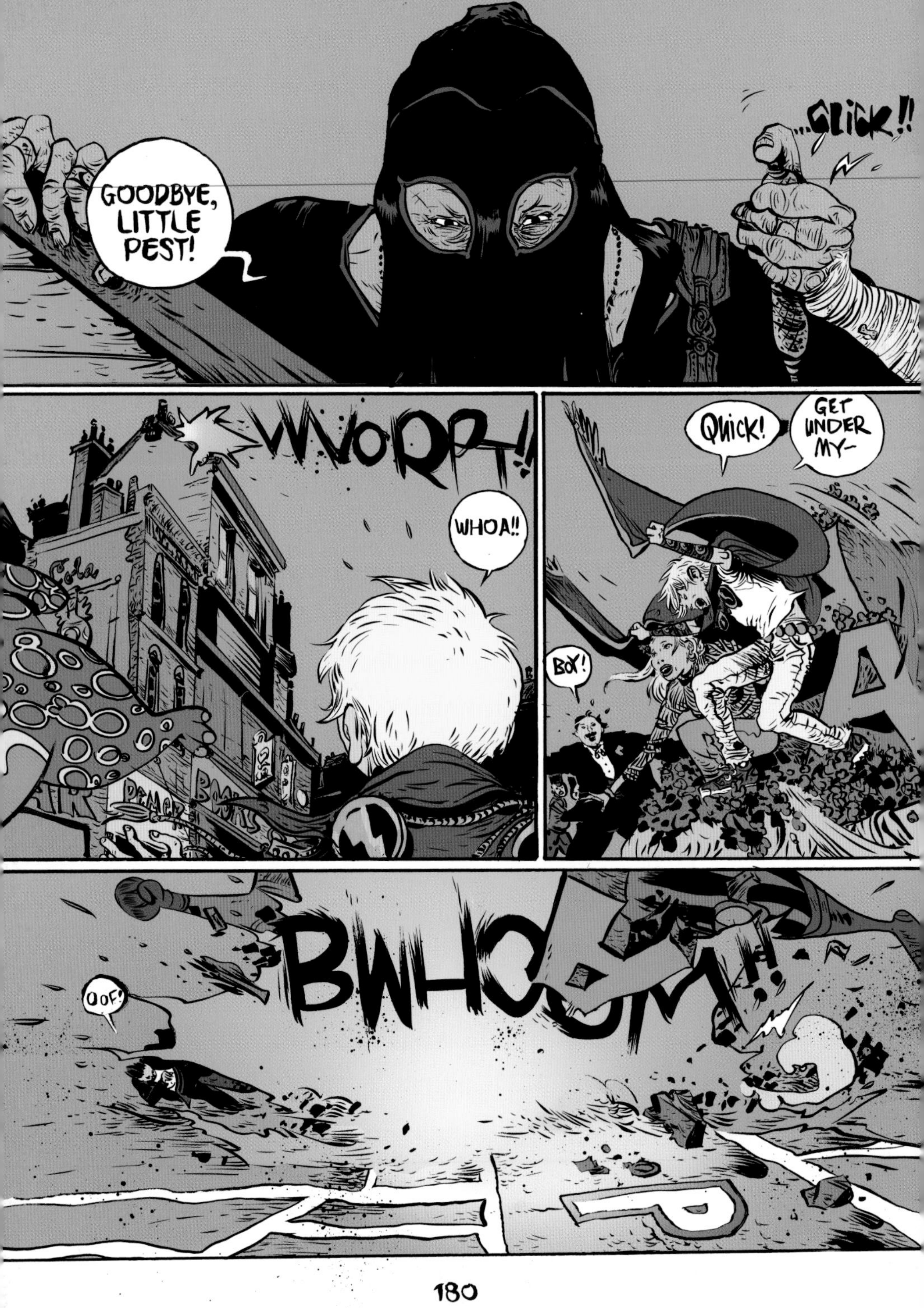
GOODBYE, LITTLE PEST!
...GLICK!!
WWORRT!!
WHOA!!
QUICK!
GET UNDER MY-
BOY!
BWHOOM!!
OOF!

KKHSSSS...

KFOOM

OOF!!

PLINK

PLINK

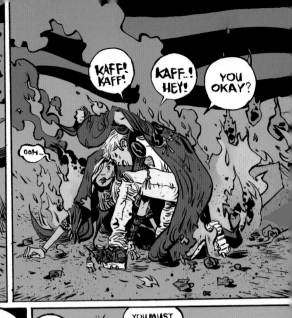

KAFF! KAFF!

KAFF..! HEY!

YOU OKAY?

OOH...

WHAT D'YA KNOW?

IT--IT WORKED!!

MISTER MAYOR, PLEASE...

YOU MUST COME WITH US, SIR.

BATTLING BOY!!

YOU MUST STOP THE MONSTERS!

:TSK: RESILIANT LITTLE BUGGER.

ONE MORE BLAST...

...YOU'RE THE CITY CHAMPION NOW!!

OKAY, CREEP!

YOU ASKED FOR IT!!

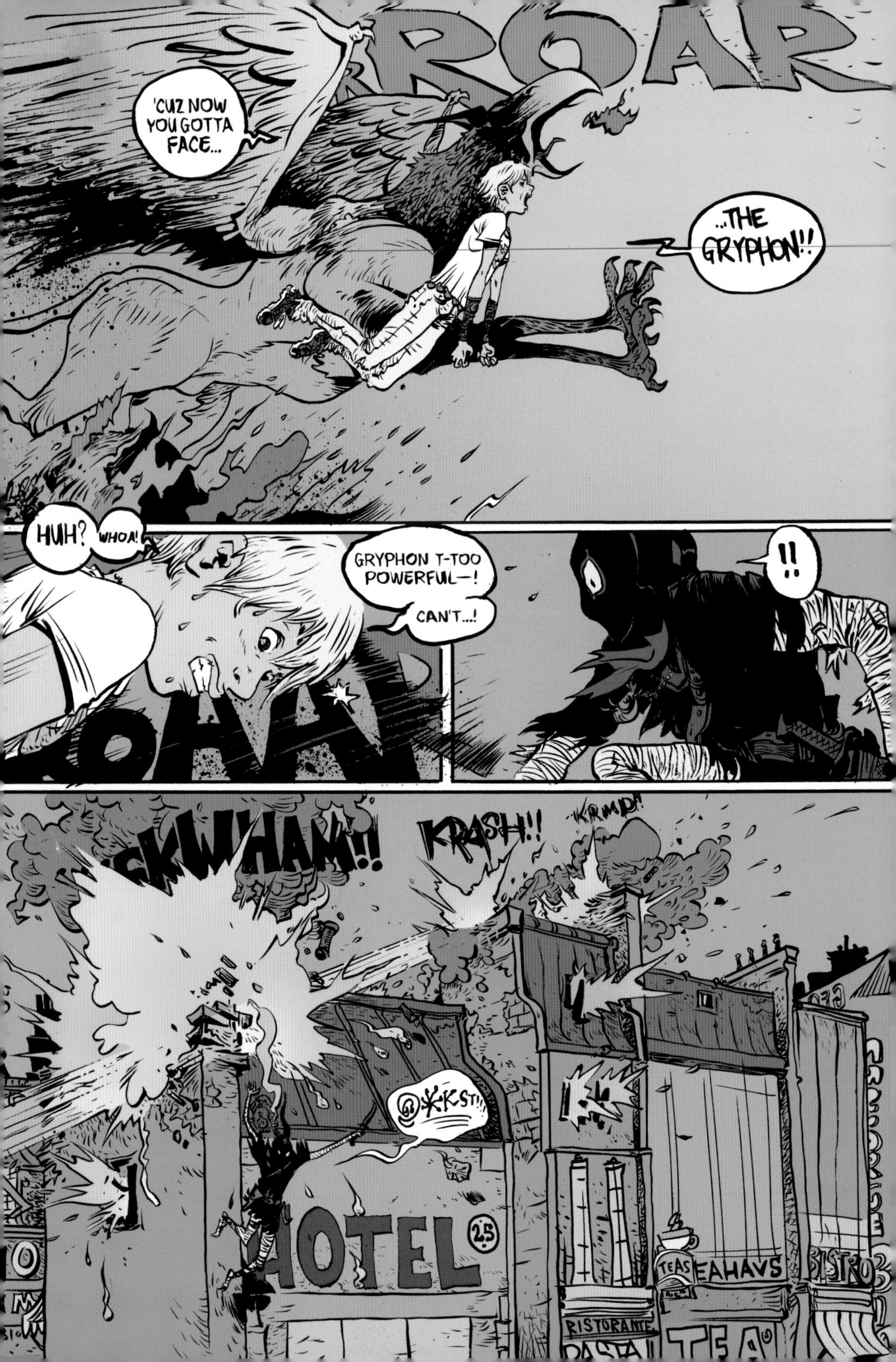
ROAR
'CUZ NOW YOU GOTTA FACE...
...THE GRYPHON!!
HUH?
WHOA!
GRYPHON T-TOO POWERFUL—!
CAN'T...!
!!
KWHAM!!
KRASH!!
KRMP!
@✻KST!!
HOTEL
25
TEAS
EAHAUS
BISTRO
RISTORANTE
PASTA
TEA

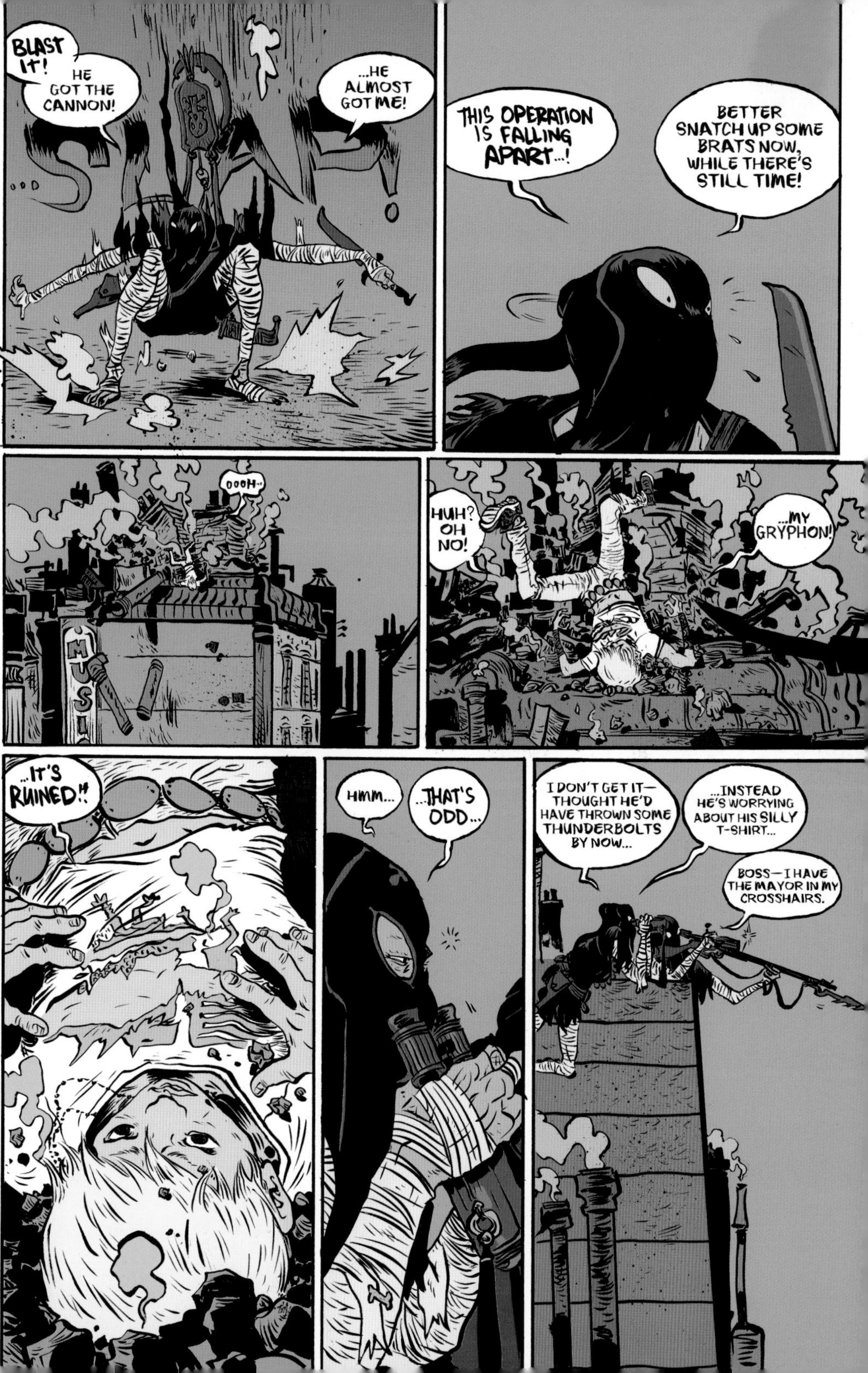
BLAST IT!
HE GOT THE CANNON!
...HE ALMOST GOT ME!
THIS OPERATION IS FALLING APART...!
BETTER SNATCH UP SOME BRATS NOW, WHILE THERE'S STILL TIME!
OOOH...
HUH? OH NO!
...MY GRYPHON!
...IT'S RUINED!!
HMM...
...THAT'S ODD...
I DON'T GET IT— THOUGHT HE'D HAVE THROWN SOME THUNDERBOLTS BY NOW...
...INSTEAD HE'S WORRYING ABOUT HIS SILLY T-SHIRT...
BOSS—I HAVE THE MAYOR IN MY CROSSHAIRS.

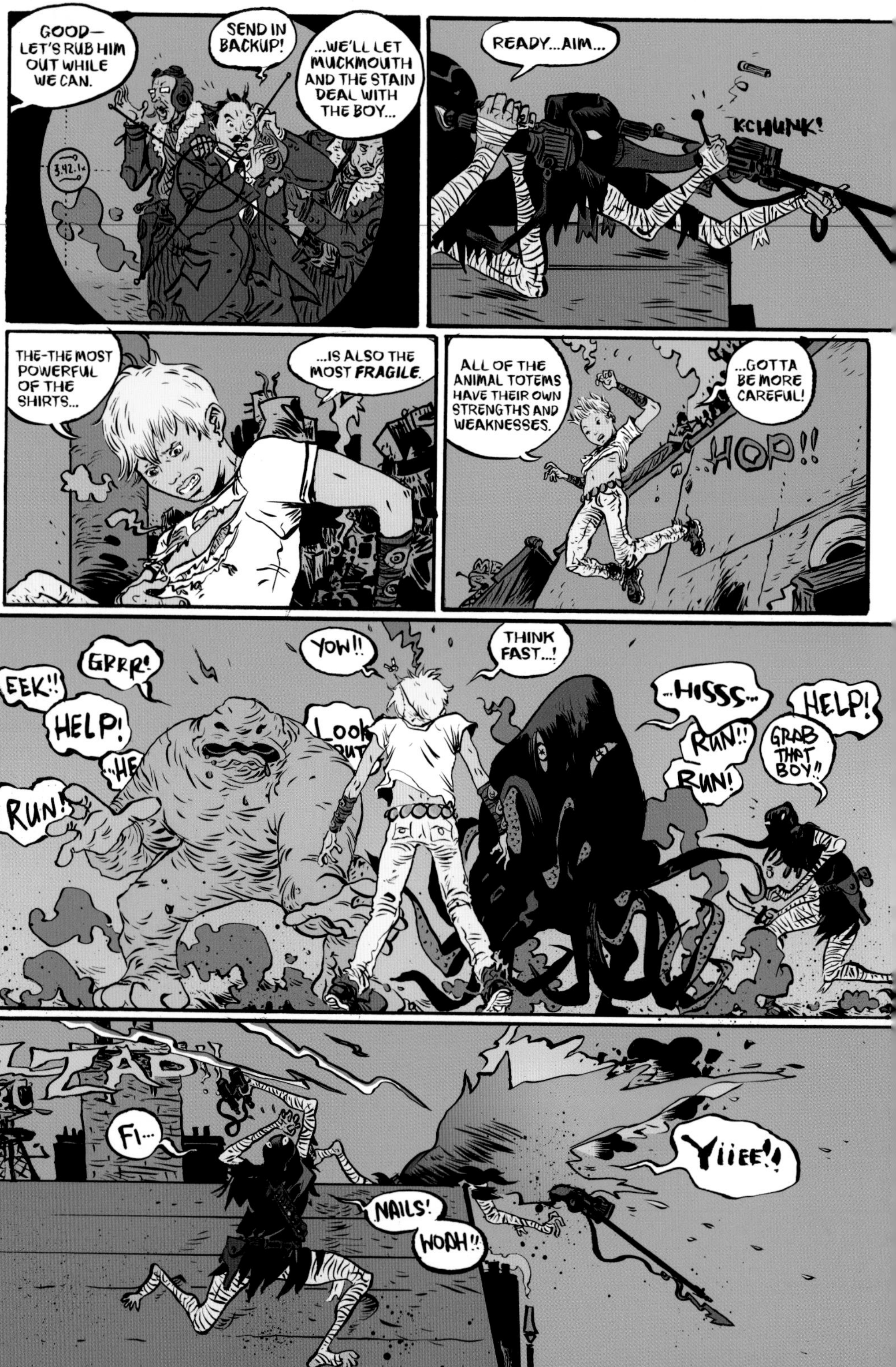
GOOD—
LET'S RUB HIM OUT WHILE WE CAN.
SEND IN BACKUP!
...WE'LL LET MUCKMOUTH AND THE STAIN DEAL WITH THE BOY...
3.42.1
READY...AIM...
K-CHUNK!
THE-THE MOST POWERFUL OF THE SHIRTS...
...IS ALSO THE MOST FRAGILE.
ALL OF THE ANIMAL TOTEMS HAVE THEIR OWN STRENGTHS AND WEAKNESSES.
...GOTTA BE MORE CAREFUL!
HOP!!
EEK!!
GRRR!
HELP!
YOW!!
THINK FAST...!
RUN!
...HISSS...
HELP!
RUN!!
RUN!
GRAB THAT BOY!!
Z-ZAP
FI...
Yiiee!!
NAILS!
WORH!!

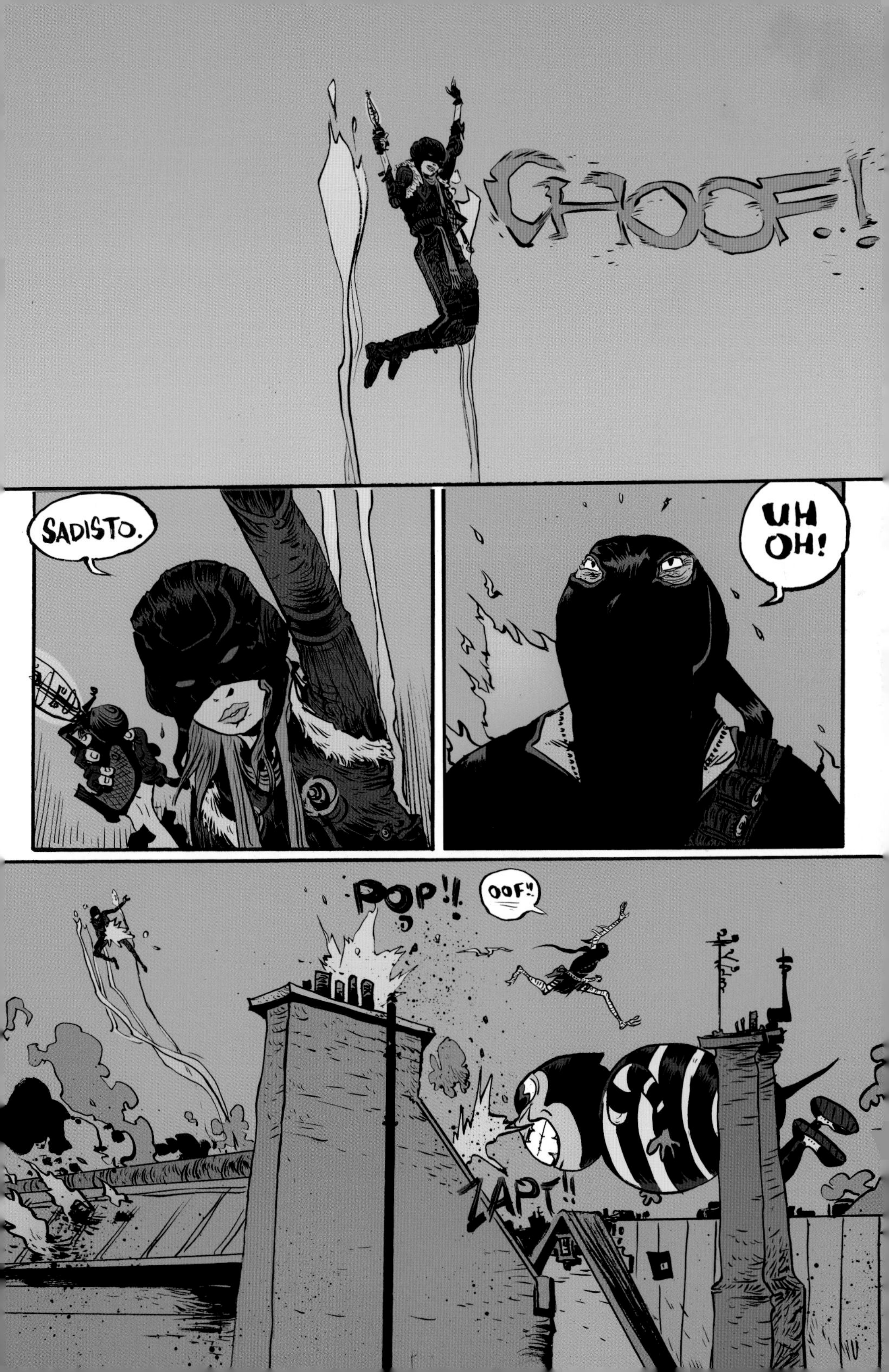
CHOOF!
SADISTO.
UH OH!
POP!!
OOF!!
ZAPT!!

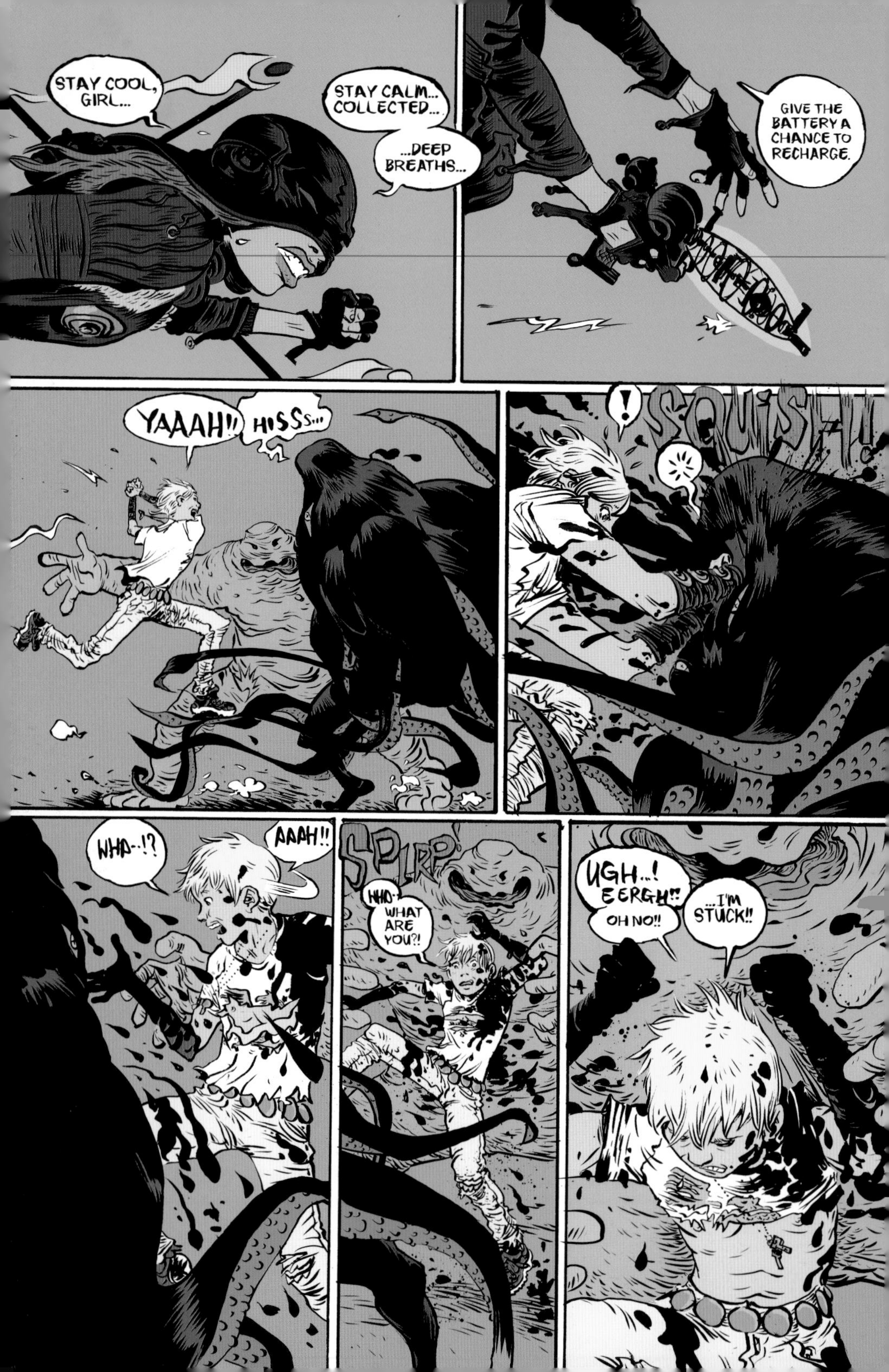
STAY COOL, GIRL...
STAY CALM... COLLECTED...
...DEEP BREATHS...
GIVE THE BATTERY A CHANCE TO RECHARGE.
YAAAH!!
HISSS...
!
SQUISH!!
WHA--!?
AAAH!!
SPLRP!
WHO-- WHAT ARE YOU?!
UGH...! EERGH!!
OH NO!!
...I'M STUCK!!

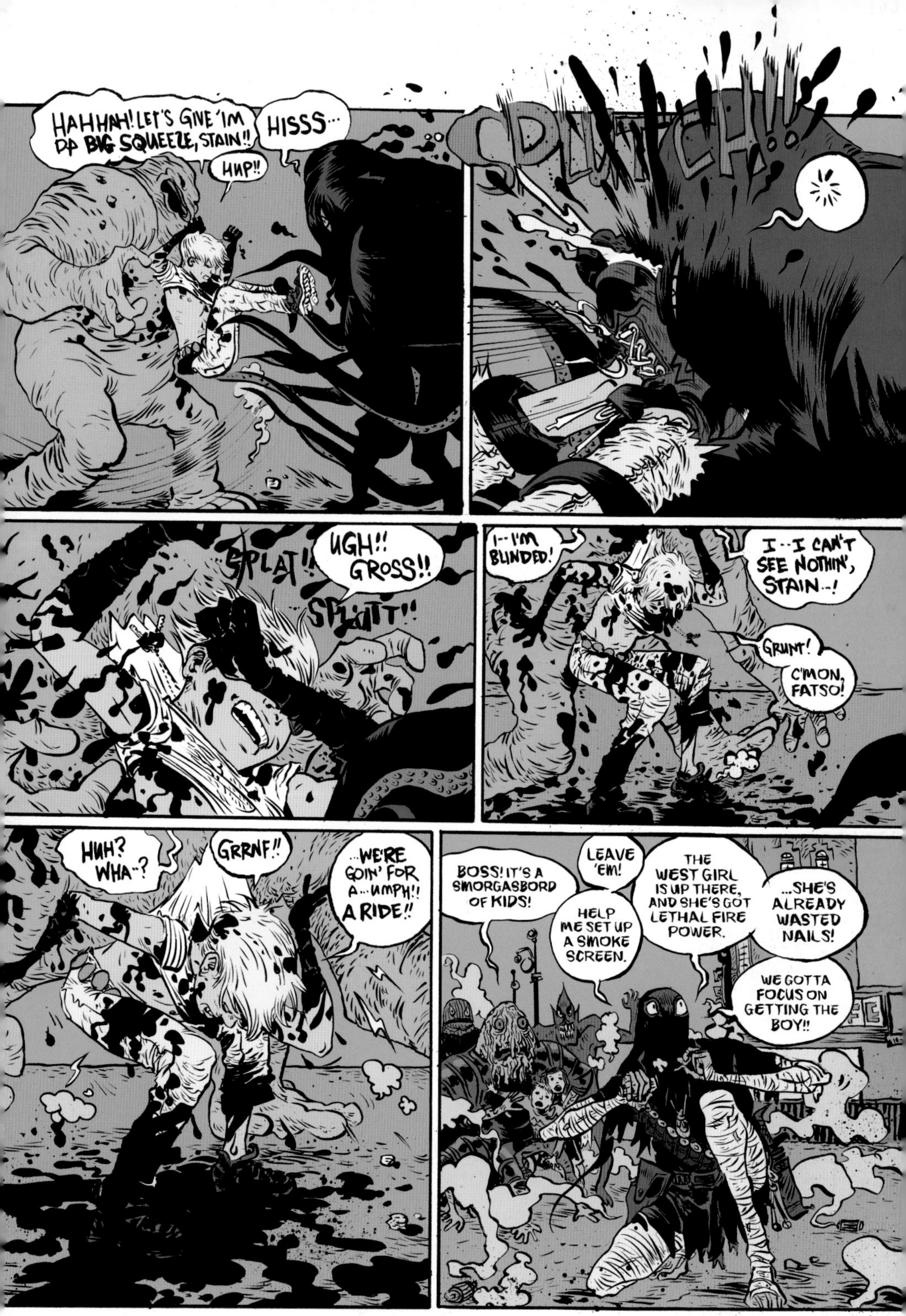
HAHHAH! LET'S GIVE 'IM DA BIG SQUEEZE, STAIN!!
HISSS...
HNP!!
SPLUTTCH!!
!
SPLAT!!
UGH!! GROSS!!
SPLUTT!!
I--I'M BLINDED!
I--I CAN'T SEE NOTHIN', STAIN--!
GRUNT!
C'MON, FATSO!
HUH? WHA--?
GRRNF!!
...WE'RE GOIN' FOR A...UMPH!! A RIDE!!
BOSS! IT'S A SMORGASBORD OF KIDS!
LEAVE 'EM!
HELP ME SET UP A SMOKE SCREEN.
THE WEST GIRL IS UP THERE, AND SHE'S GOT LETHAL FIRE POWER.
...SHE'S ALREADY WASTED NAILS!
WE GOTTA FOCUS ON GETTING THE BOY!!

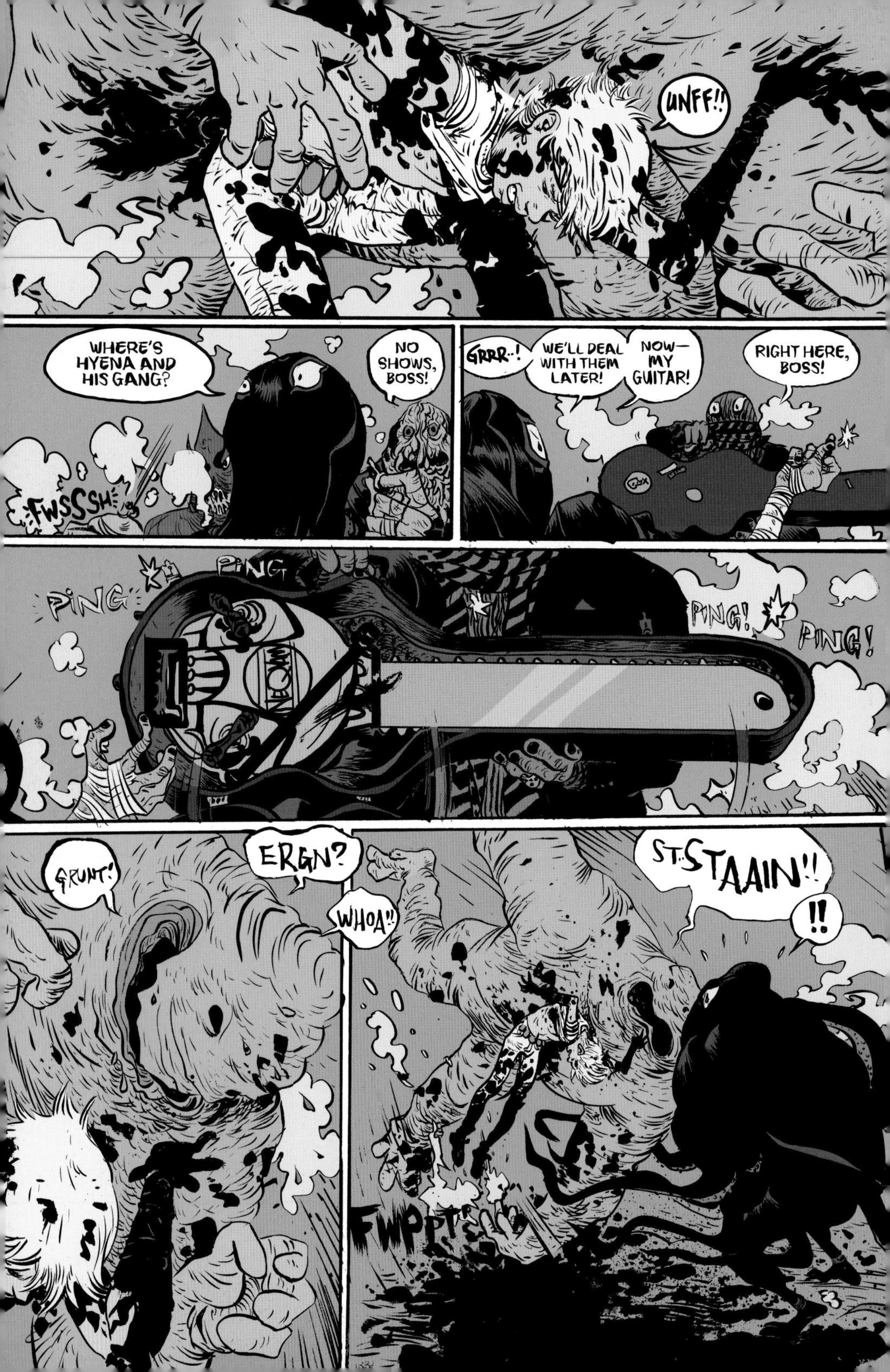
UNFF!!
WHERE'S HYENA AND HIS GANG?
NO SHOWS, BOSS!
FWSSSH!
GRRR..!
WE'LL DEAL WITH THEM LATER!
NOW— MY GUITAR!
RIGHT HERE, BOSS!
PING
PING
PING!
PING!
GRUNT!
ERGN?
WHOA!!
ST..STAAIN!!
!!
FWPPT

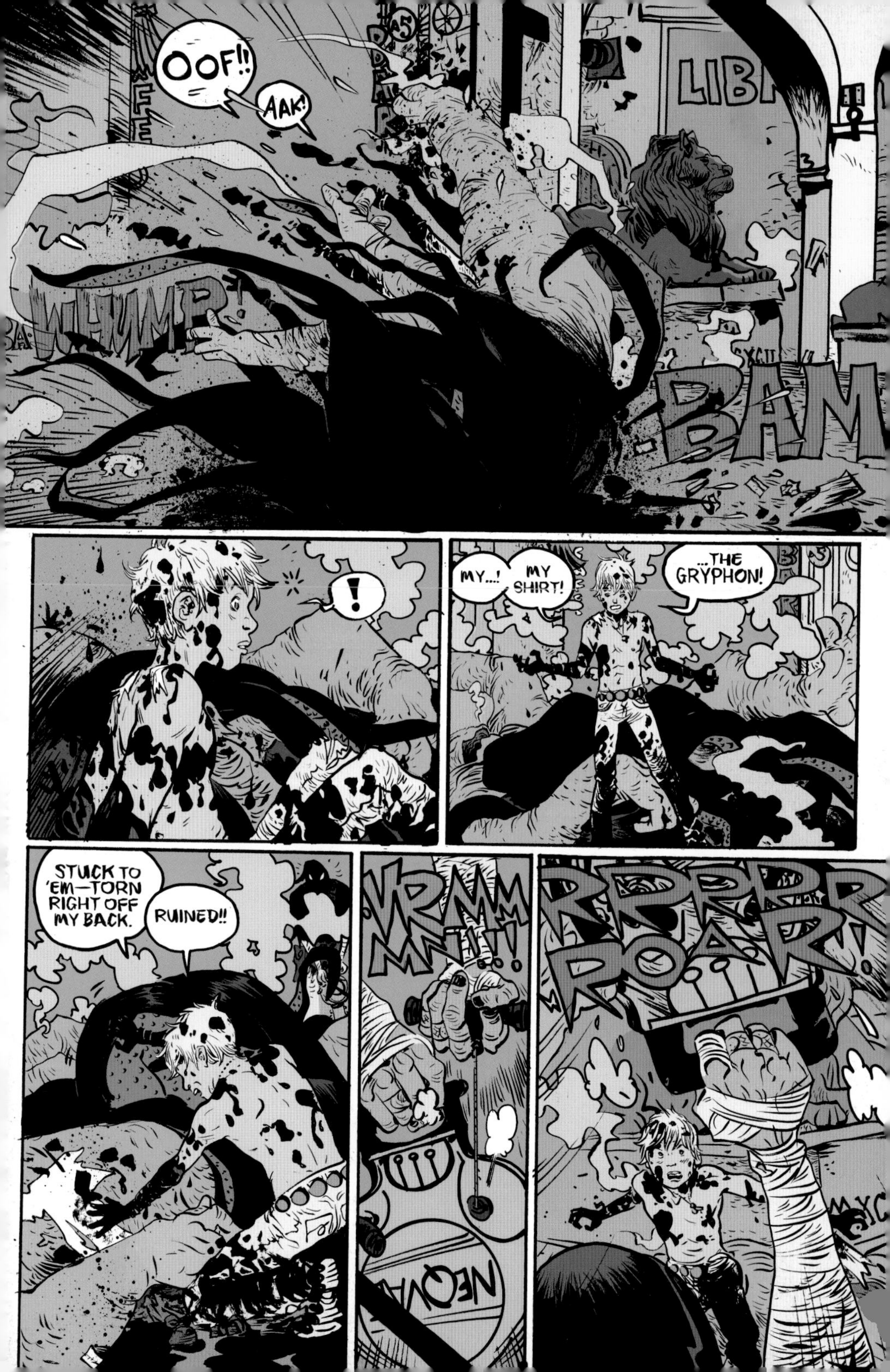
OOF!!
AAK!
WHUMP!
BAM
!
MY...!
MY SHIRT!
...THE GRYPHON!
STUCK TO 'EM—TORN RIGHT OFF MY BACK.
RUINED!!
VRMMMM!!!
RRRRRR ROAR!

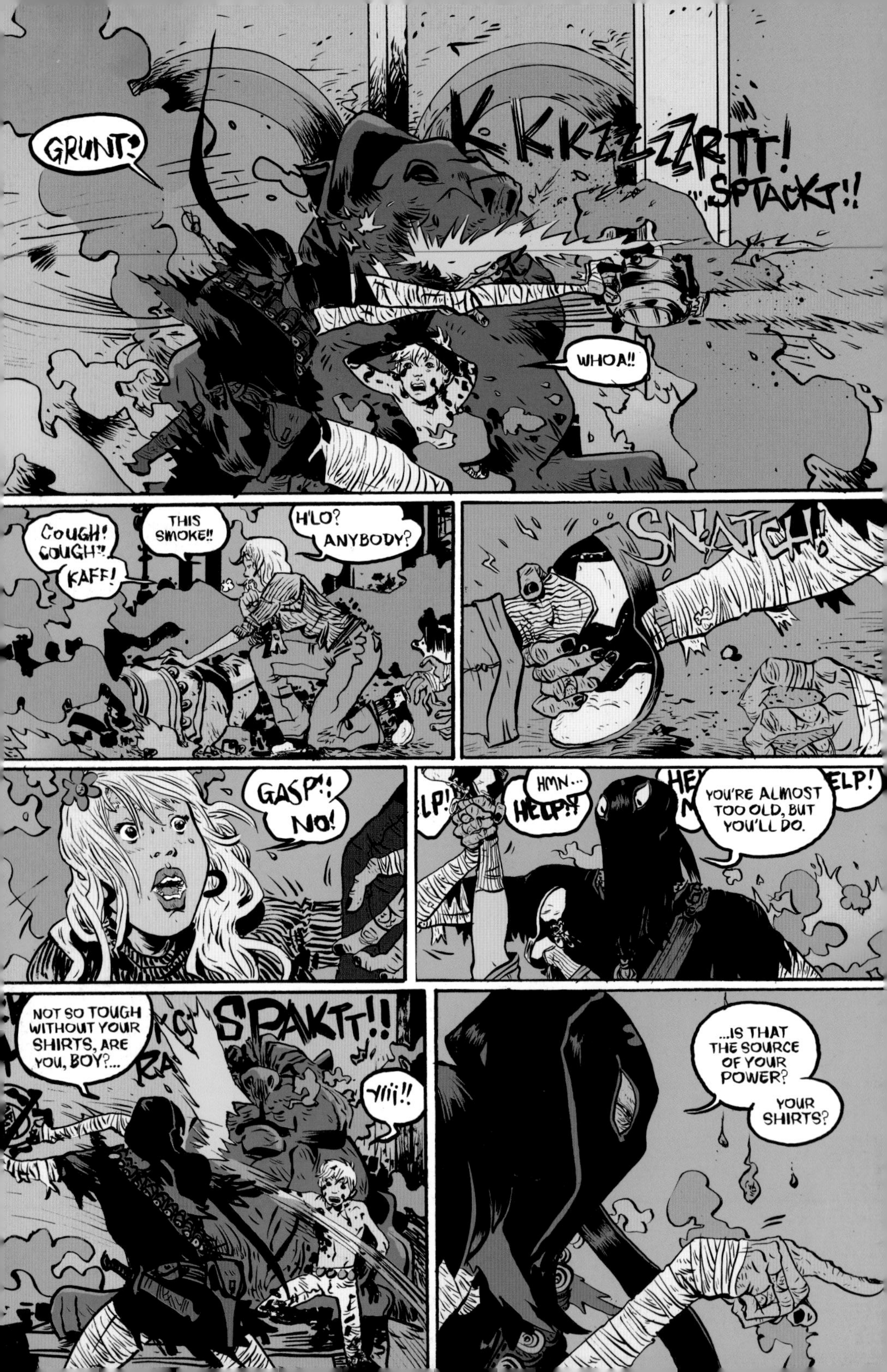

GRUNT!
KKKZZZRTT!
SPTACKT!!
WHOA!!
COUGH! COUGH!
KAFF!
THIS SMOKE!!
H'LO? ANYBODY?
SNATCH!
GASP!! NO!
HMN...
HELP!!
YOU'RE ALMOST TOO OLD, BUT YOU'LL DO.
NOT SO TOUGH WITHOUT YOUR SHIRTS, ARE YOU, BOY?...
SPAKTT!!
YIII!!
...IS THAT THE SOURCE OF YOUR POWER?
YOUR SHIRTS?

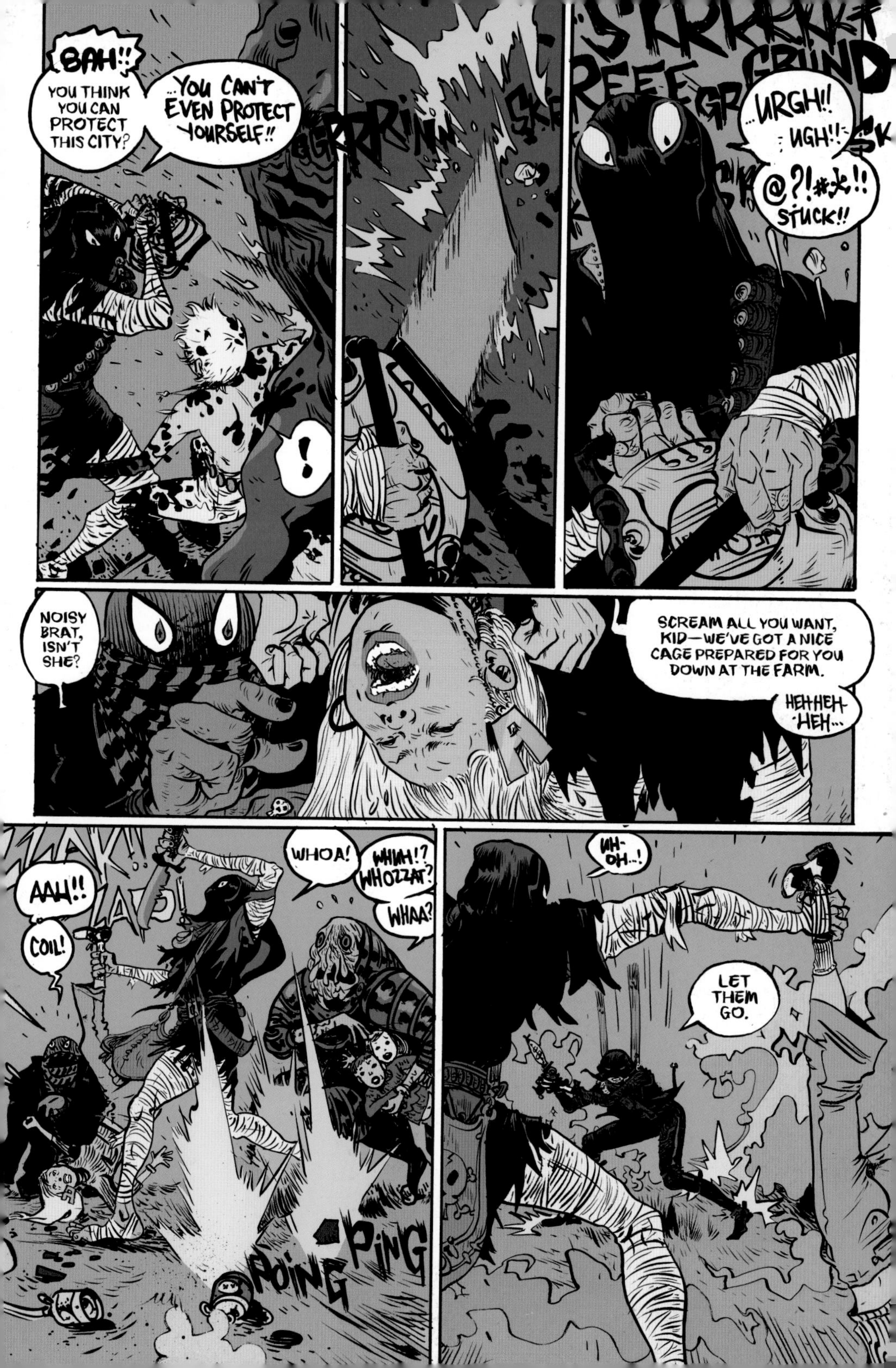

BAH!! YOU THINK YOU CAN PROTECT THIS CITY?
...YOU CAN'T EVEN PROTECT YOURSELF!!
GRRRINN
!
SKRRRRKKT
SKREEEEGRR
GRIND
...URGH!!
UGH!!
@?!#*!! STUCK!!
NOISY BRAT, ISN'T SHE?
SCREAM ALL YOU WANT, KID—WE'VE GOT A NICE CAGE PREPARED FOR YOU DOWN AT THE FARM.
HEH HEH HEH...
AAH!!
COIL!
WHOA!
WHUH!? WHOZZAT?
WHAA?
BOING
PING
UH-OH...!
LET THEM GO.

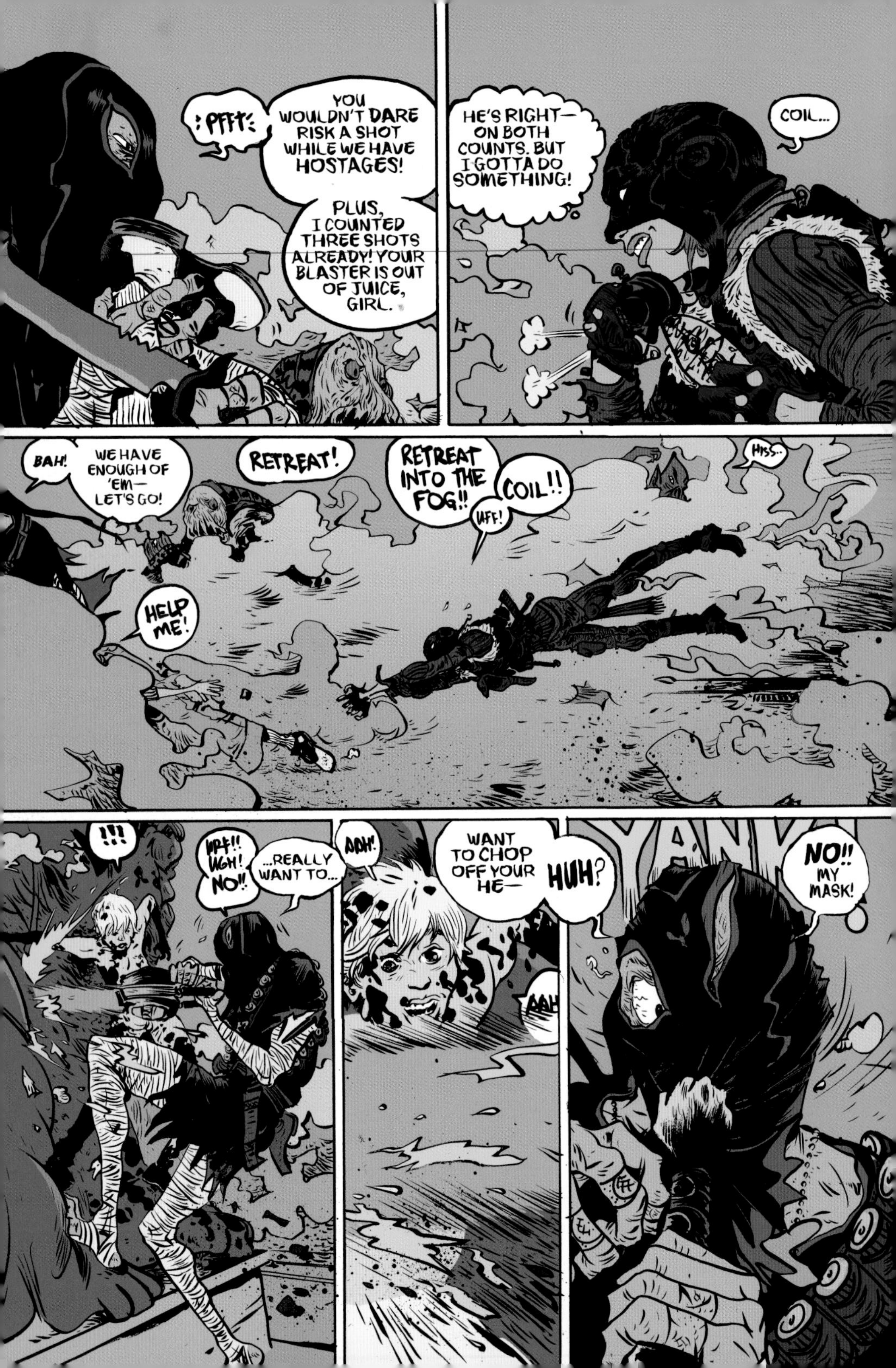
PFFT!
YOU WOULDN'T DARE RISK A SHOT WHILE WE HAVE HOSTAGES!
PLUS, I COUNTED THREE SHOTS ALREADY! YOUR BLASTER IS OUT OF JUICE, GIRL.
HE'S RIGHT— ON BOTH COUNTS. BUT I GOTTA DO SOMETHING!
COIL...
BAH!
WE HAVE ENOUGH OF 'EM— LET'S GO!
RETREAT!
RETREAT INTO THE FOG!!
COIL!!
UFF!
HISS...
HELP ME!
!!!
UFF!! UGH! NO!!
...REALLY WANT TO...
AAH!
WANT TO CHOP OFF YOUR HE—
HUH?
NO!! MY MASK!

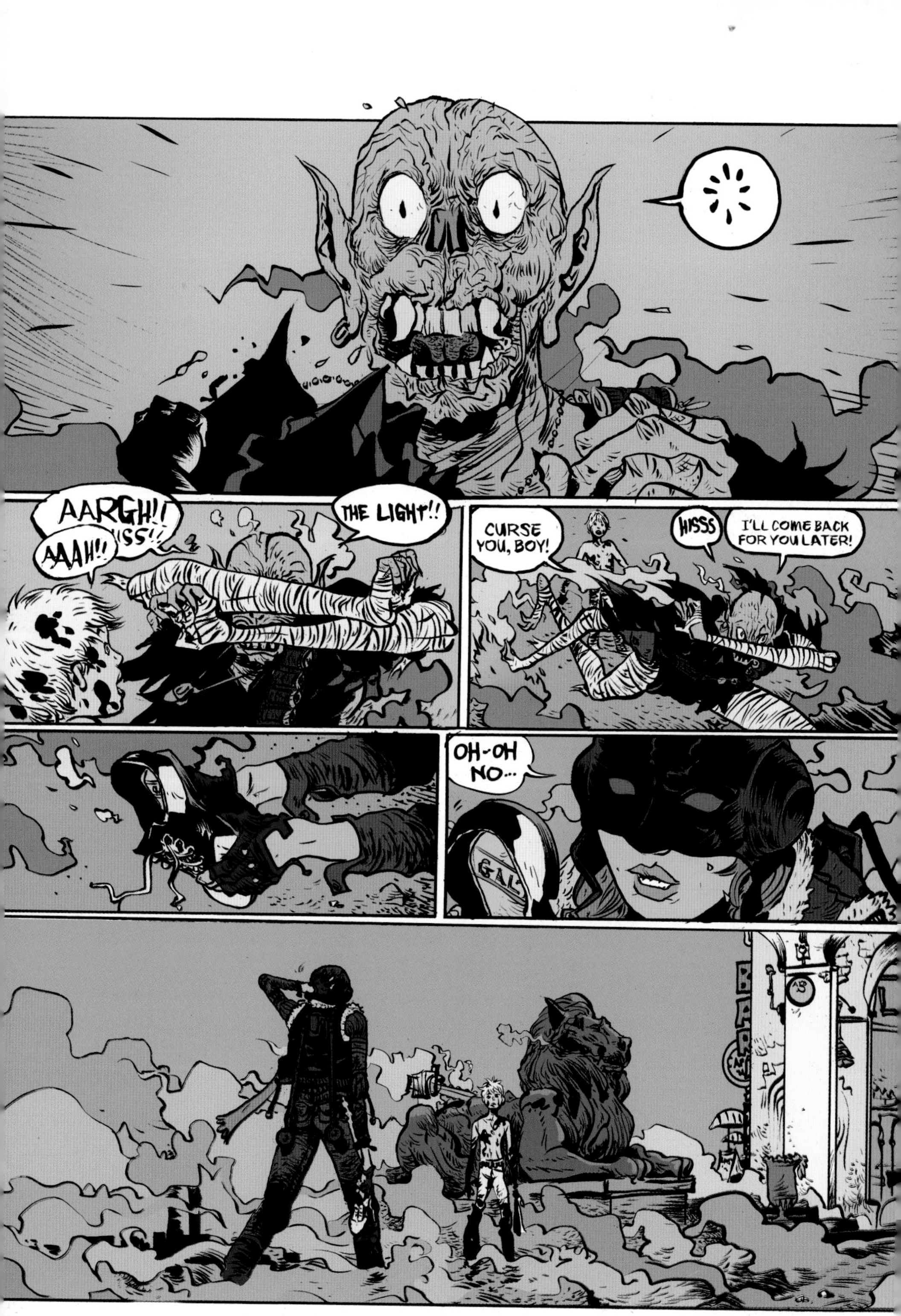
AARGH!! HISS!!
AAAH!!
THE LIGHT!!
CURSE YOU, BOY!
HISSS
I'LL COME BACK FOR YOU LATER!
OH-OH NO...
GAL

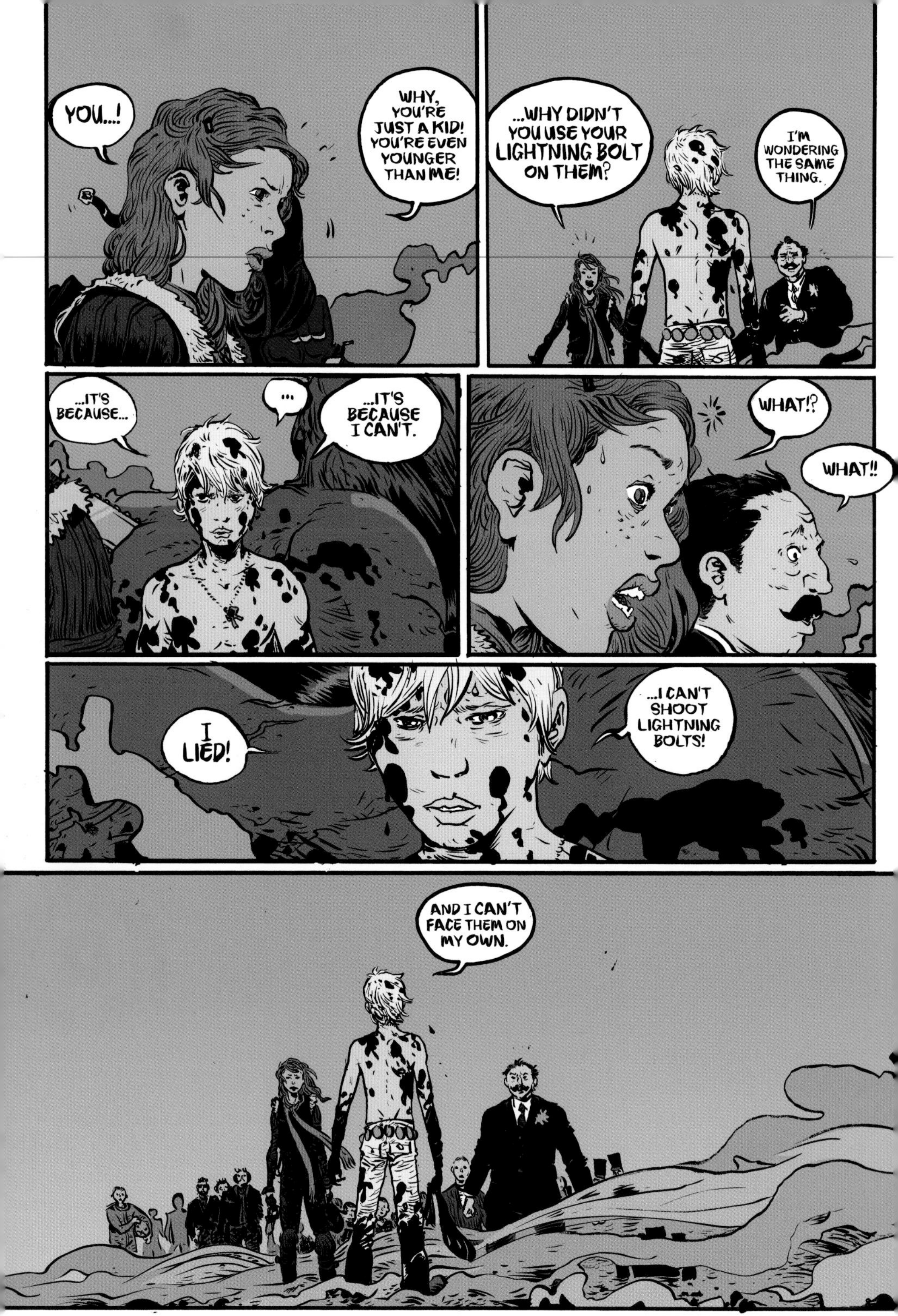
YOU...!
WHY, YOU'RE JUST A KID! YOU'RE EVEN YOUNGER THAN ME!
...WHY DIDN'T YOU USE YOUR LIGHTNING BOLT ON THEM?
I'M WONDERING THE SAME THING.
...IT'S BECAUSE...
...
...IT'S BECAUSE I CAN'T.
WHAT!?
WHAT!!
I LIED!
...I CAN'T SHOOT LIGHTNING BOLTS!
AND I CAN'T FACE THEM ON MY OWN.

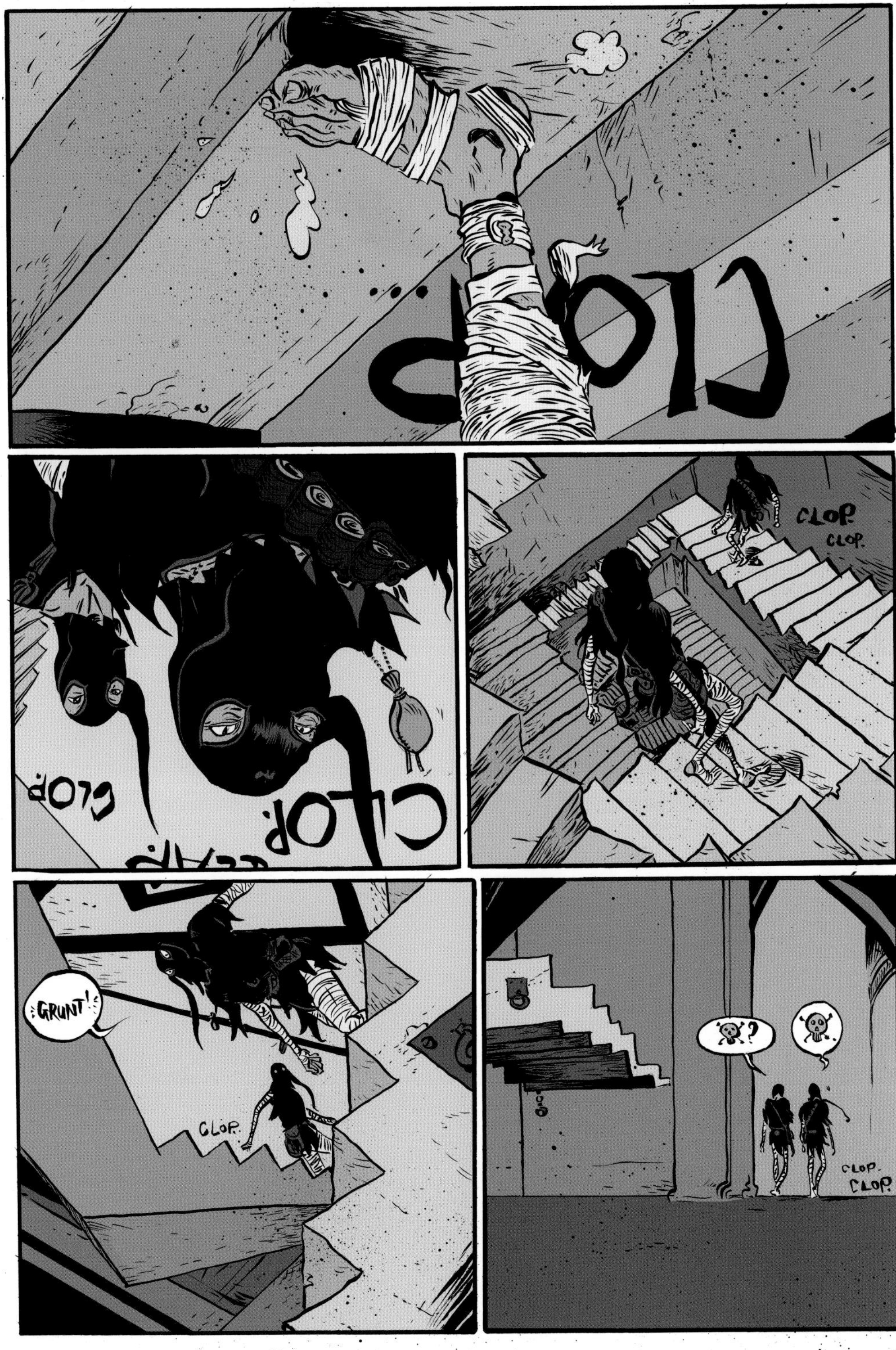
CLOP
CLOP.
CLOP
CLOP.
CLOP.
GRUNT!
CLOP.
?
CLOP.
CLOP.

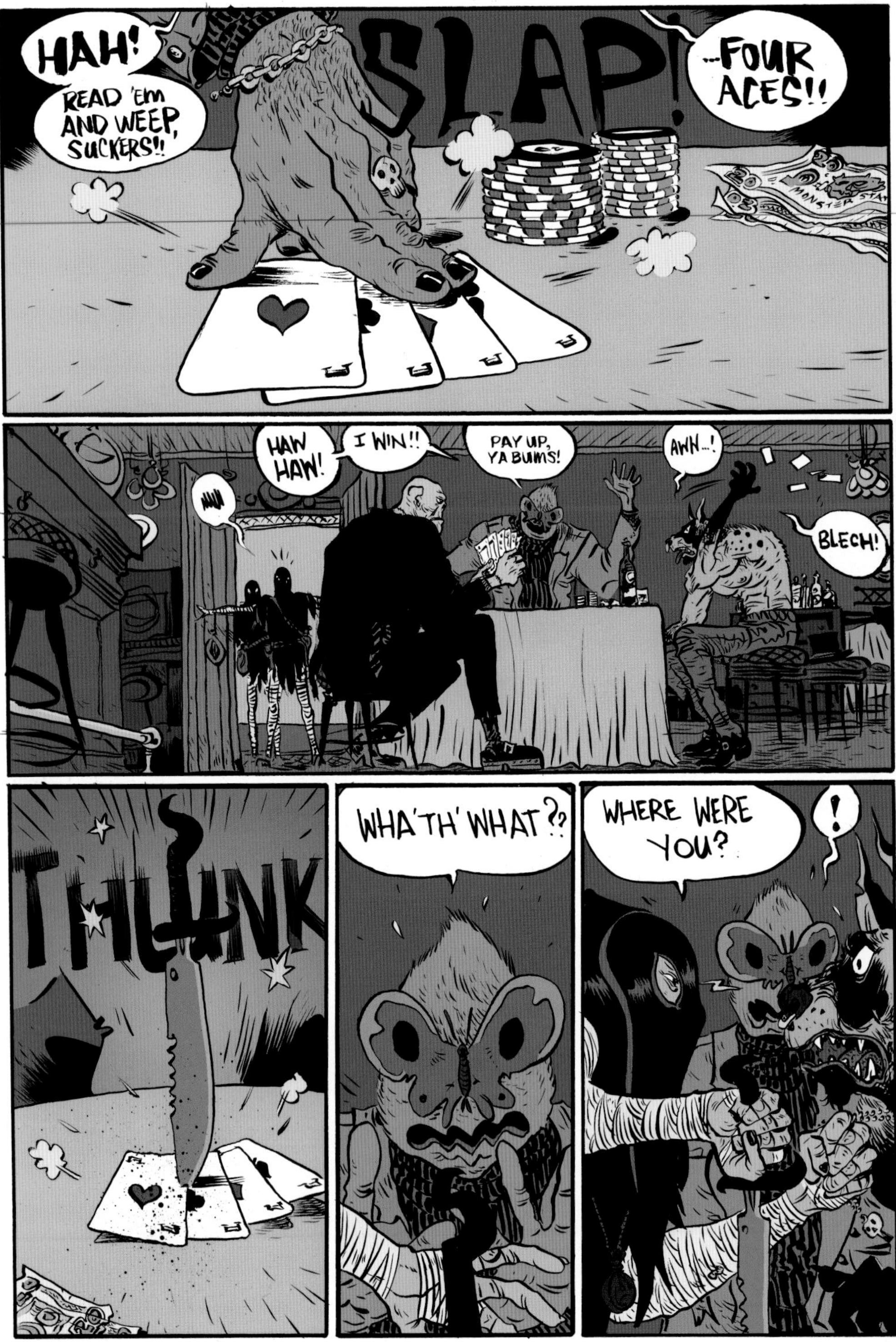

HAH!
READ 'EM AND WEEP, SUCKERS!!
SLAP!
--FOUR ACES!!
HAW HAW!
I WIN!!
PAY UP, YA BUMS!
AWN...!
BLECH!
THUNK
WHA'TH' WHAT??
WHERE WERE YOU?
!

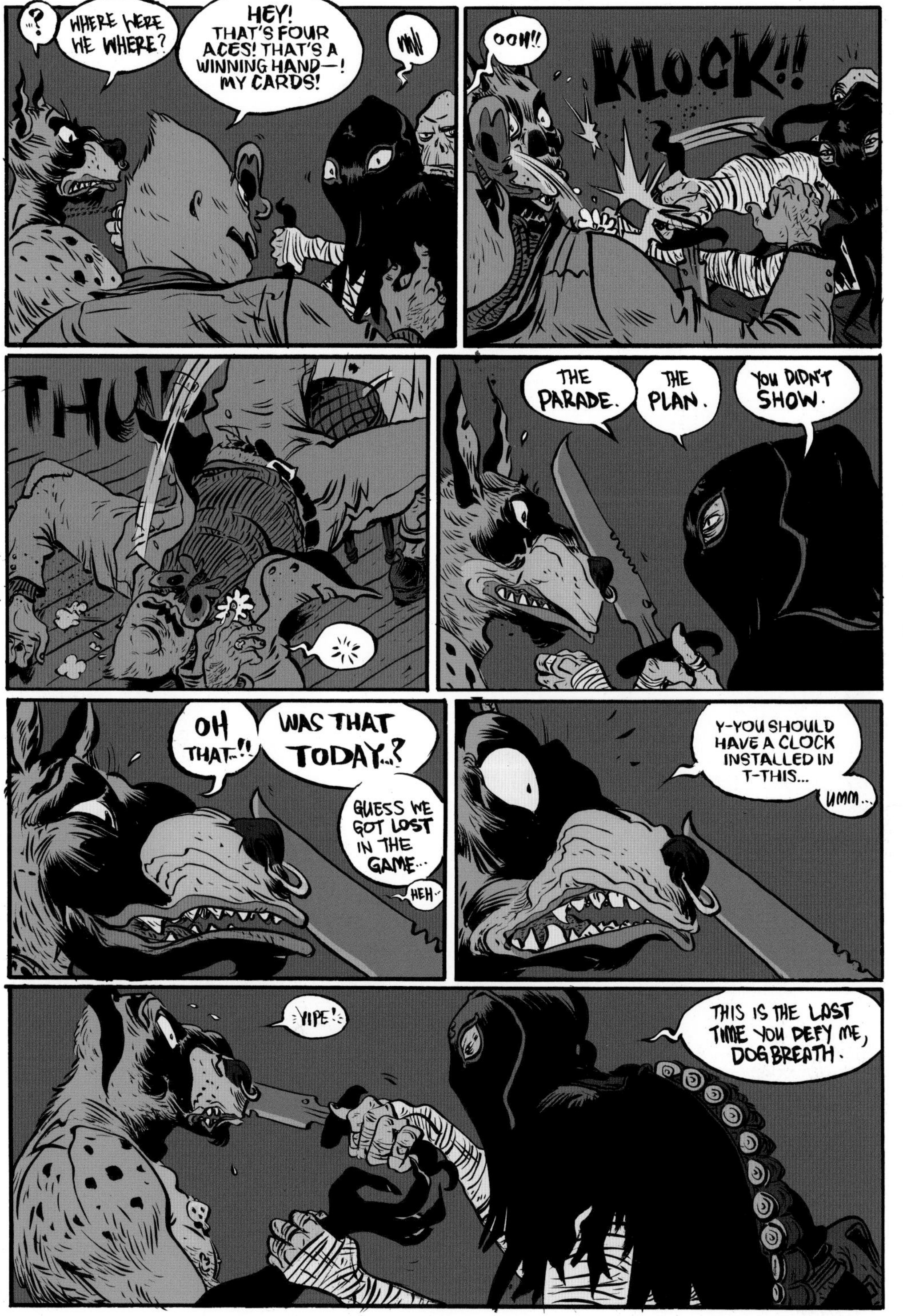
?
WHERE WERE WE WHERE?
HEY! THAT'S FOUR ACES! THAT'S A WINNING HAND—! MY CARDS!
OOH!!
KLOCK!!
THE PARADE.
THE PLAN.
YOU DIDN'T SHOW.
OH THAT..!!
WAS THAT TODAY...?
GUESS WE GOT LOST IN THE GAME...
HEH..
Y-YOU SHOULD HAVE A CLOCK INSTALLED IN T-THIS...
UMM...
YIPE!
THIS IS THE LAST TIME YOU DEFY ME, DOGBREATH.

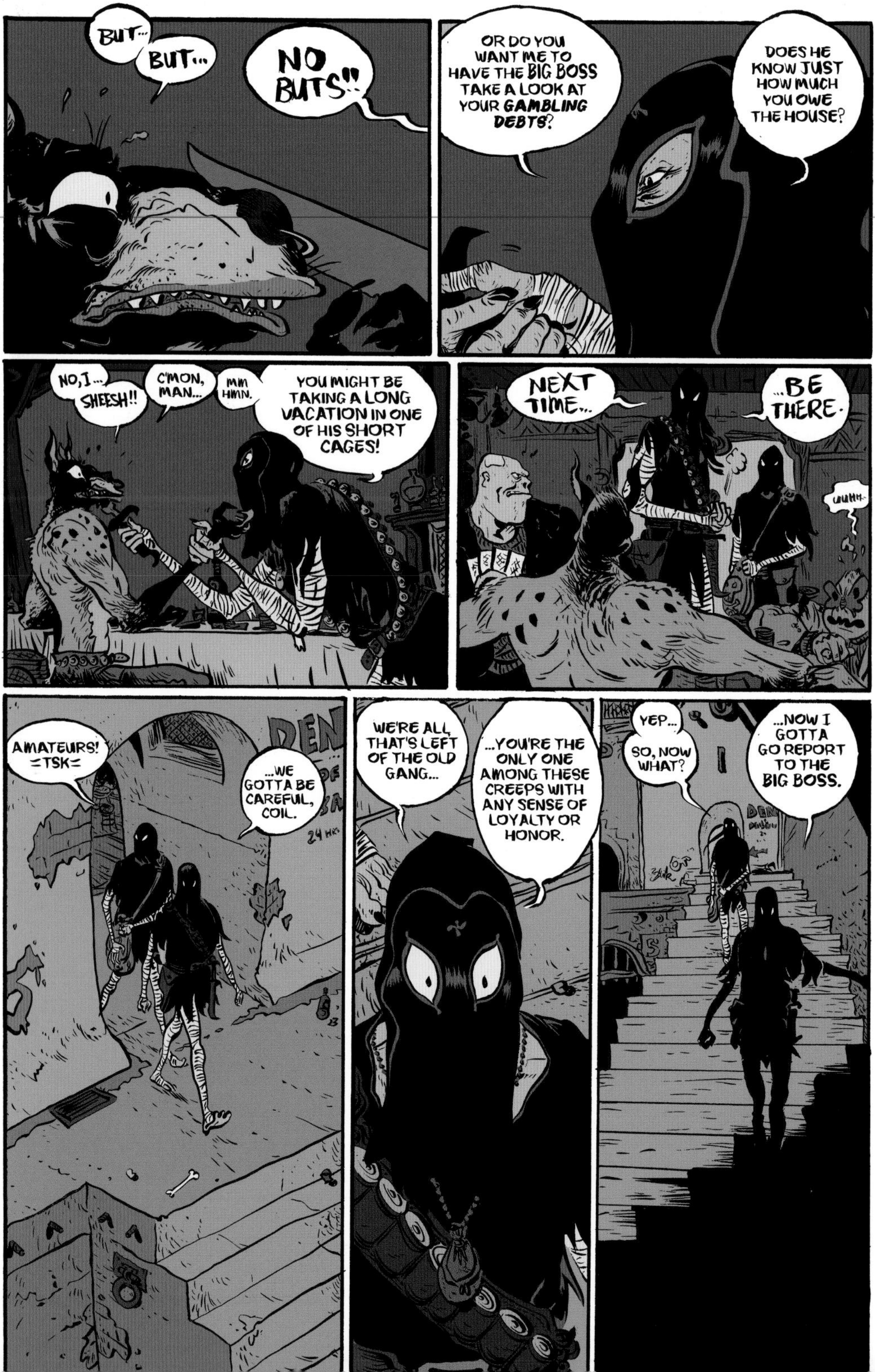
BUT...
BUT...
NO BUTS!!
OR DO YOU WANT ME TO HAVE THE BIG BOSS TAKE A LOOK AT YOUR GAMBLING DEBTS?
DOES HE KNOW JUST HOW MUCH YOU OWE THE HOUSE?
NO, I... SHEESH!!
C'MON, MAN...
MM HMN.
YOU MIGHT BE TAKING A LONG VACATION IN ONE OF HIS SHORT CAGES!
NEXT TIME...
...BE THERE.
UUHH...
AMATEURS! =TSK=
DEN
24 HRS
...WE GOTTA BE CAREFUL, COIL.
WE'RE ALL THAT'S LEFT OF THE OLD GANG...
...YOU'RE THE ONLY ONE AMONG THESE CREEPS WITH ANY SENSE OF LOYALTY OR HONOR.
YEP...
SO, NOW WHAT?
...NOW I GOTTA GO REPORT TO THE BIG BOSS.

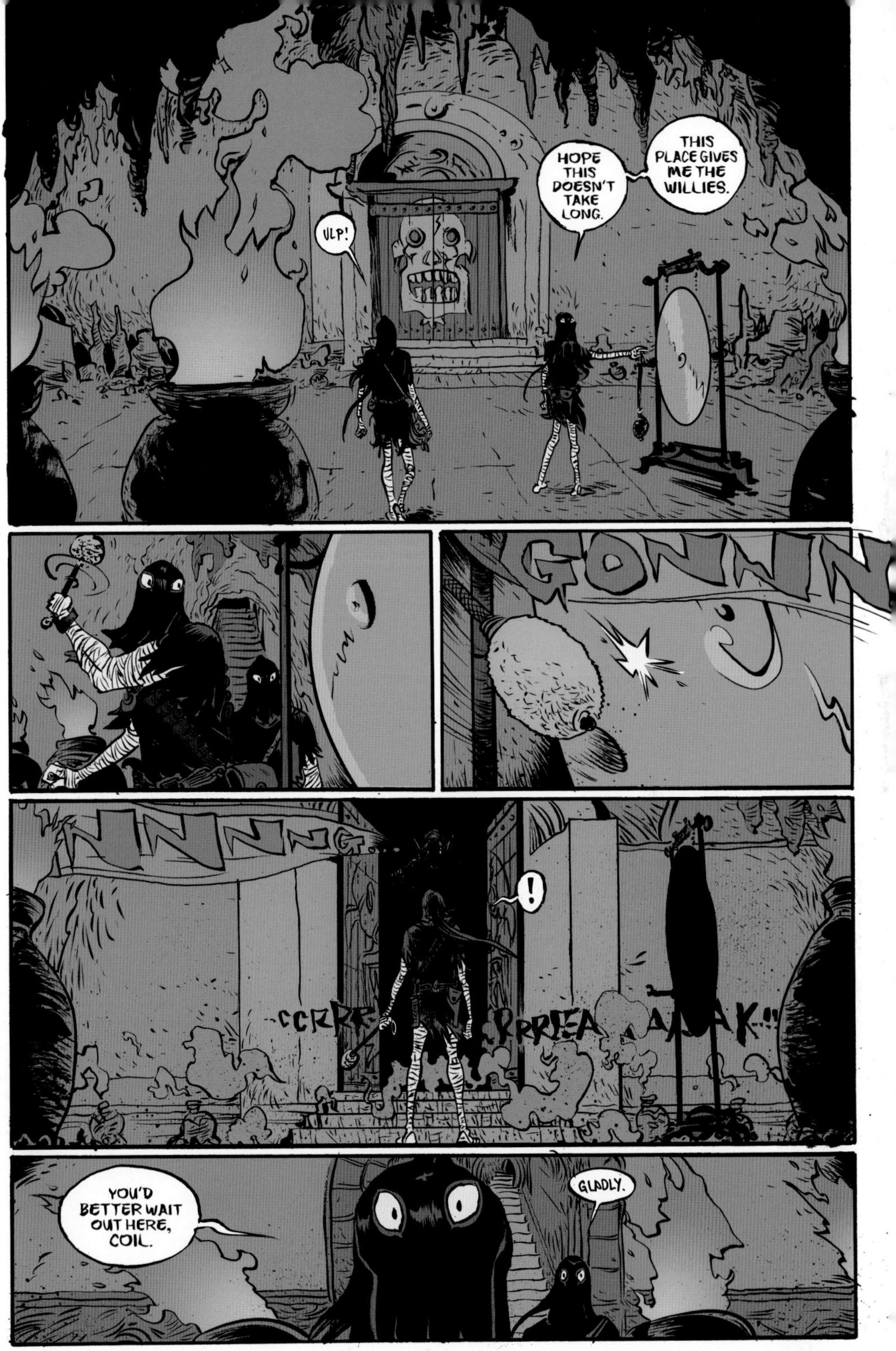
ULP!
HOPE THIS DOESN'T TAKE LONG.
THIS PLACE GIVES ME THE WILLIES.
GONNN
NNNNG...
!
CCRRR
RRREA
K!!
YOU'D BETTER WAIT OUT HERE, COIL.
GLADLY.

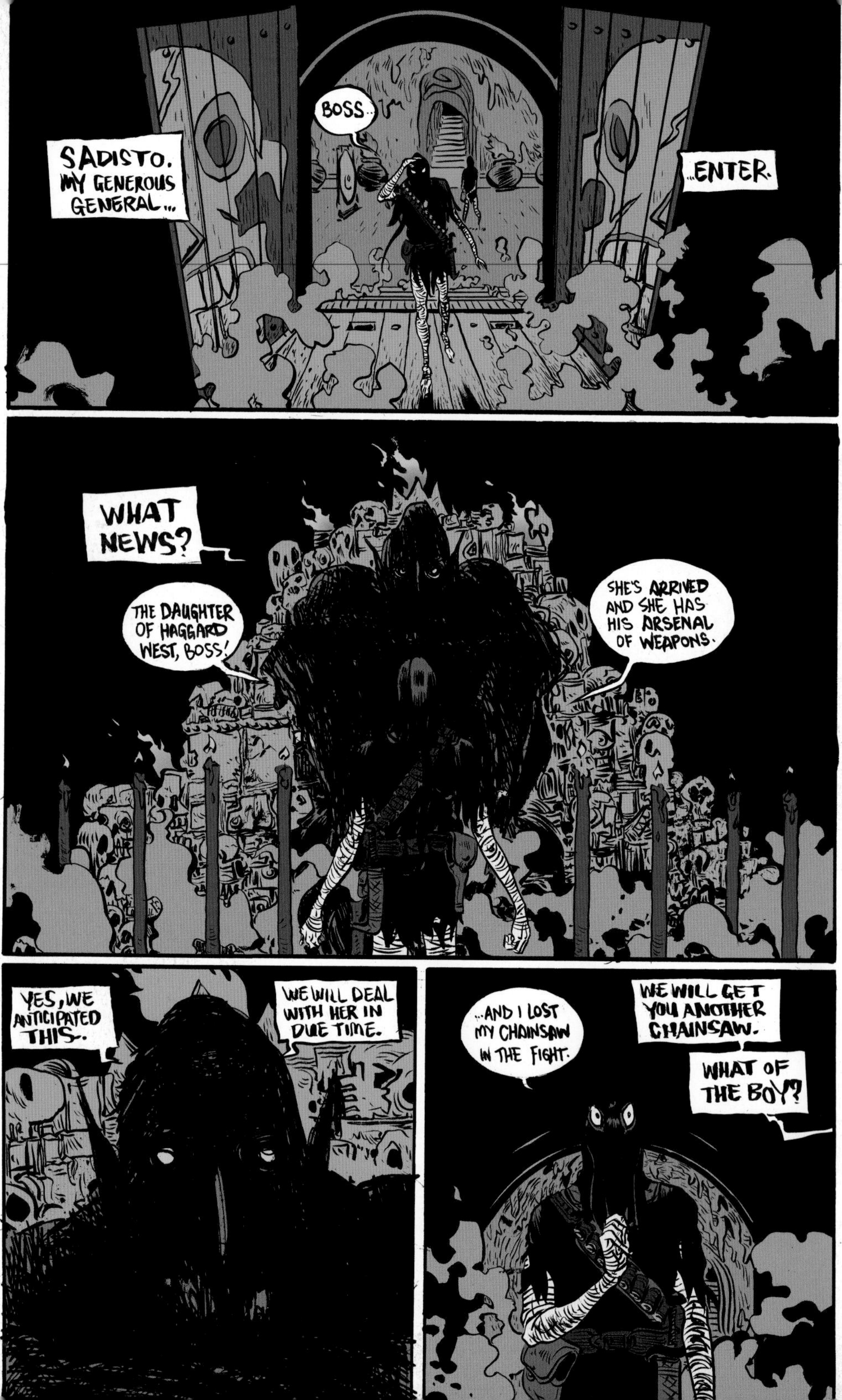
SADISTO. MY GENEROUS GENERAL...
BOSS...
...ENTER.
WHAT NEWS?
THE DAUGHTER OF HAGGARD WEST, BOSS!
SHE'S ARRIVED AND SHE HAS HIS ARSENAL OF WEAPONS.
YES, WE ANTICIPATED THIS.
WE WILL DEAL WITH HER IN DUE TIME.
...AND I LOST MY CHAINSAW IN THE FIGHT.
WE WILL GET YOU ANOTHER CHAINSAW.
WHAT OF THE BOY?

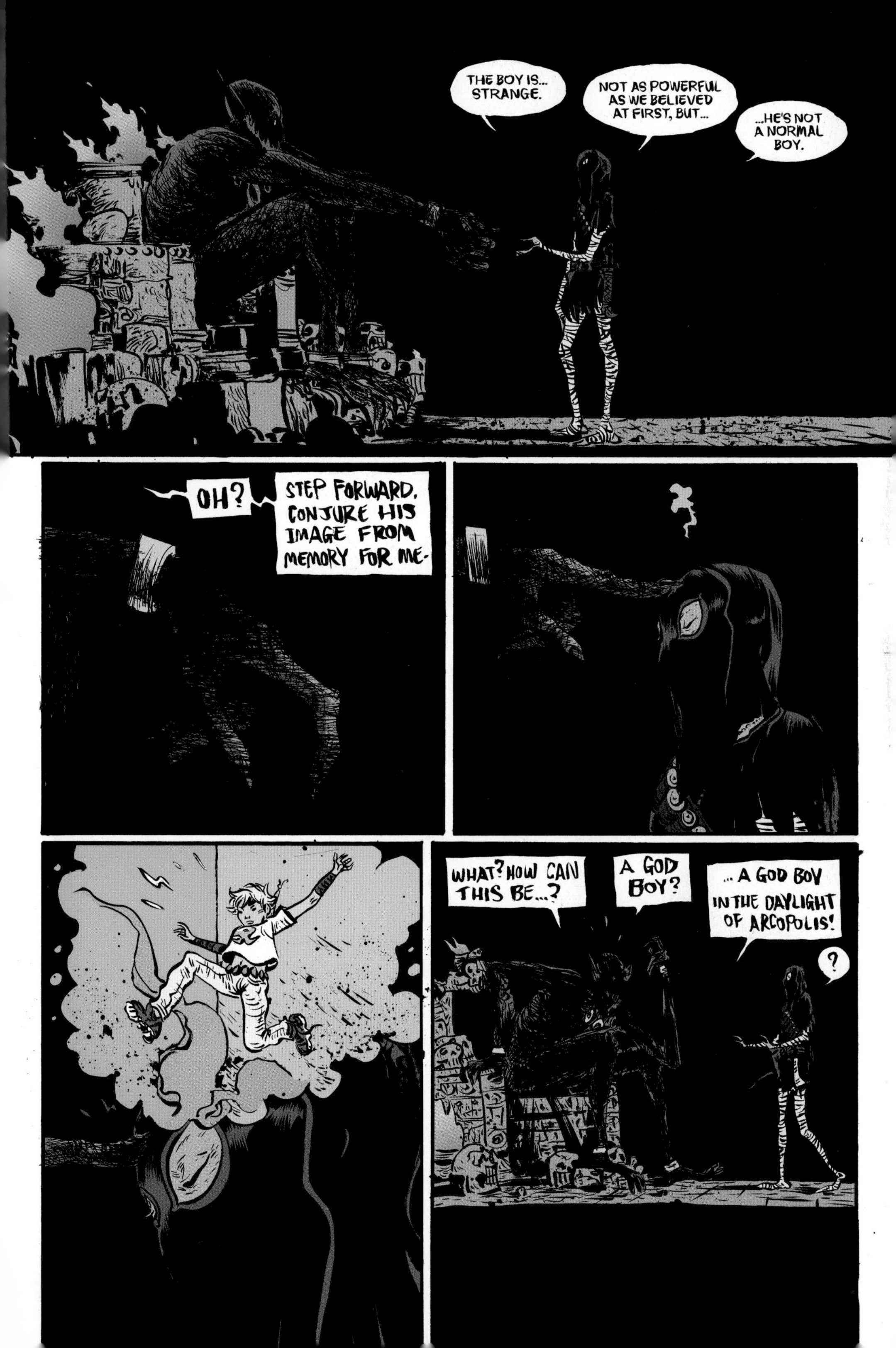
THE BOY IS... STRANGE.
NOT AS POWERFUL AS WE BELIEVED AT FIRST, BUT...
...HE'S NOT A NORMAL BOY.
OH?
STEP FORWARD. CONJURE HIS IMAGE FROM MEMORY FOR ME.
WHAT? HOW CAN THIS BE...?
A GOD BOY?
... A GOD BOY IN THE DAYLIGHT OF ARCOPOLIS!
?

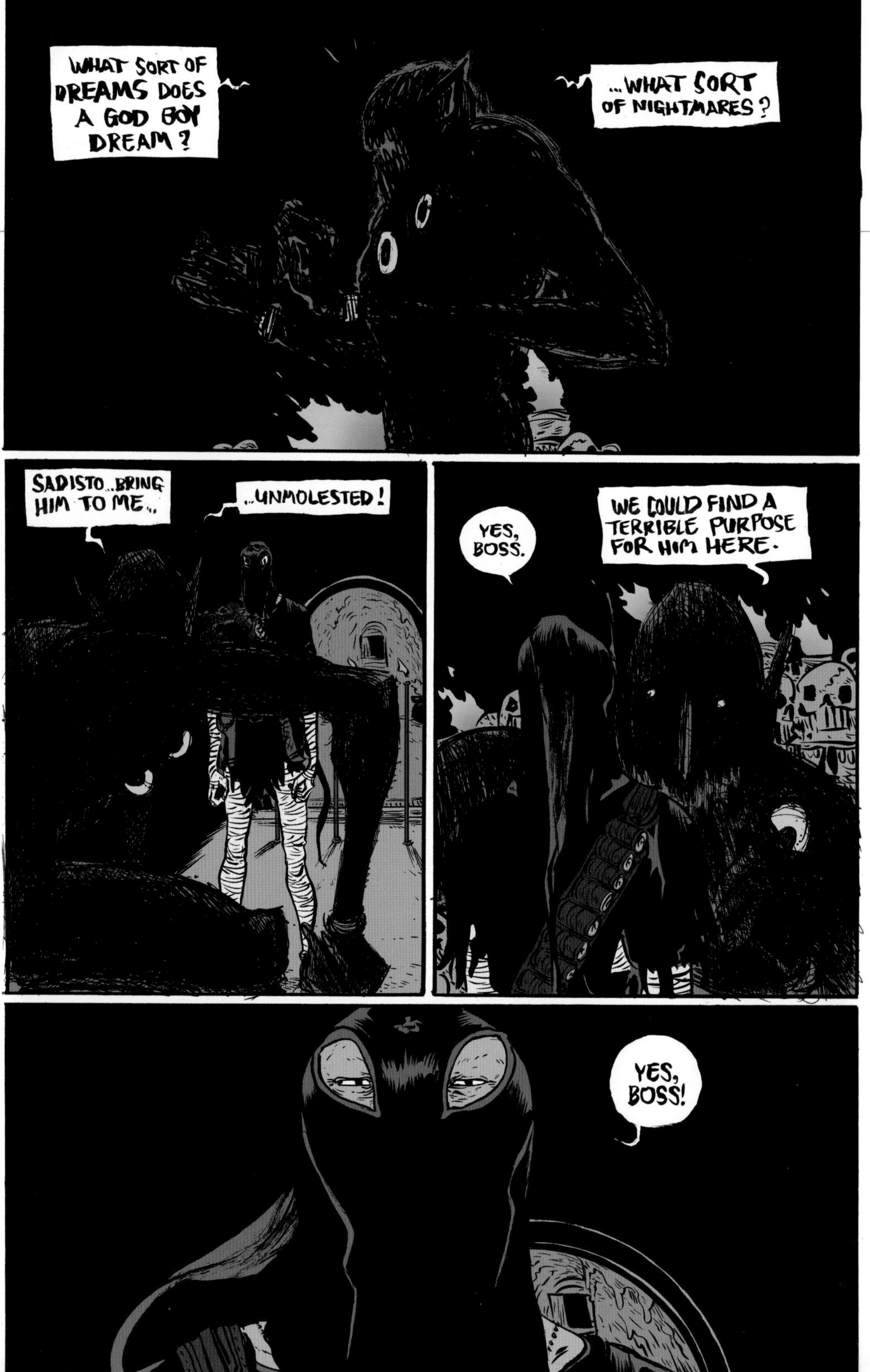
WHAT SORT OF DREAMS DOES A GOD BOY DREAM?
...WHAT SORT OF NIGHTMARES?
SADISTO...BRING HIM TO ME...
...UNMOLESTED!
YES, BOSS.
WE COULD FIND A TERRIBLE PURPOSE FOR HIM HERE.
YES, BOSS!

# For Benjamin and Alexander

First Second
Copyright © 2013 by Paul Pope

Type set in "PPope," designed by John Martz
Assistance, scanning, and art cleanup by Casey Gonzalez
Colored by Hilary Sycamore and Sky Blue Ink.

Published by First Second
First Second is an imprint of Roaring Brook Press, a division of Holtzbrinck Publishing
Holdings Limited Partnership
175 Fifth Avenue, New York, New York 10010
All rights reserved

Cataloging-in-Publication Data is on file at the Library of Congress.

Paperback ISBN: 978-1-59643-145-4
Hardcover ISBN: 978-1-59643-805-7

First Second books may be purchased for business or personal use. For information on
bulk purchases please contact Macmillan Corporate and Premium Sales Department
at (800) 221-7945 x5442 or by email at specialmarkets@macmillan.com.

First edition 2013
Book design by Casey Gonzalez, with Colleen AF Venable and John Green
Printed in China by Toppan Leefung Printing Ltd., Kwun Tong, Kowloon, Hong Kong

Paperback: 10 9 8 7 6 5 4 3 2 1
Hardcover: 10 9 8 7 6 5 4 3 2 1